David Roberts was educated at Eton and McGill University, Montreal. He was a publisher for thirty years including editorial director of Weidenfeld & Nicolson and a partner in O'Mara Books. He has published a series of ten detective novels set in the 1930s featuring Lord Edward Corinth and Verity Browne. He is married and lives in London and Wiltshire.

Praise for David Roberts

'Intricate and enthralling'
Michael Dobbs

'Lovers of golden-age crime fiction need mourn no longer. Roberts takes us back to the world of the aristocratic sleuth'
Natasha Cooper

'Roberts pays meticulous attention to period detail and the result is a really well-crafted and charming mystery story'
Daily Mail

Also by David Roberts

Lord Edward Corinth & Verity Browne Series

HOLLOW CROWN

A murder mystery featuring
Lord Edward Corinth & Verity Browne

DAVID ROBERTS

CONSTABLE • LONDON

CONSTABLE

First published in Great Britain in 2002 by Constable,
an imprint of Constable & Robinson Ltd

This paperback edition published in 2003 by Robinson,
an imprint of Constable & Robinson Ltd

Reissued in 2017 by Constable

1 3 5 7 9 10 8 6 4 2

A CIP catalogue record for this book
is available from the British Library.

ISBN 978-1-4721-2812-6

Printed and bound by CPI Group (UK) Ltd, Croydon, CR0 4YY

Papers used by Constable are from well-managed forests
and other responsible sources

Constable
An imprint of
Little, Brown Book Group
Carmelite House
50 Victoria Embankment
London EC4Y 0DZ

An Hachette UK Company
www.hachette.co.uk

www.littlebrown.co.uk

For within the hollow crown
That rounds the mortal temples of a king
Keeps death his court . . .

What must the king do now? Must he submit?
The king shall do it: must he be depos'd?
The king shall be contented: must he lose
The name of king? O' God's name, let it go.

Shakespeare, *Richard II*

How now! a rat? Dead, for a ducat, dead!

Shakespeare, *Hamlet*

October to December
1936

1

Almost against his will, Lord Edward Corinth gazed up at the sleek, glassy building he was about to enter. It brought to mind, as no doubt the architect intended, one of the new ocean liners – the *Queen Mary*, say, or the *Normandie* – and it seemed to make every other building in Fleet Street appear dowdy and old-fashioned. It was the headquarters of Joe Weaver's *New Gazette* and it stood for everything he had achieved. Lord Weaver, as he now was, had come to England from Canada during the war. With skilful use of his large fortune, he had made powerful friends in the world of politics and it is not too much to say that he was now in a position to make or break prime ministers. His great building, completed in 1931, and in front of which Edward now stood, was brash, brutal and several storeys higher than any of its neighbours.

After dark – it was now nine o'clock – from where he was standing, it looked like a shining curtain, each pane of glass illuminated brilliantly from within. One might be forgiven, he thought wryly, for imagining that its transparency was a symbol of the veracity with which the *New Gazette* reported the news in its august columns, but, as he was well aware, for Lord Weaver truth was what he wanted it to be. The press lord, for all his bonhomie, was a man of secrets. If he wished to spare one of his friends or dependants the pain of reading in his newspaper the sordid details of their divorce

1

proceedings, he would order his editor to deny his readers the pleasure of *schadenfreude*. If he wished to puff the prospects of some bright young man he had taken under his wing, he would paint such a portrait that even the man himself might have difficulty recognizing. For every favour there was, of course, a price to be paid. No money would change hands – Lord Weaver had money to spare – but from the men he would elicit information and through them exercise influence. The women were also a source of information and their influence extended beyond their husbands to their friends and lovers – and it was said that, despite having a face like a wicked monkey, Weaver was himself to be found amongst the latter category more often than a casual observer would have thought likely.

And yet Lord Weaver was by no means a bad man. He loved his wife, considered himself a patriot and used what power he had in what he considered to be the best interests of his adopted country. He was a loyal friend, as Edward had reason to know, and he was generous – when the whim took him – absurdly, extravagantly, generous. But still, Edward bore in mind that, even when the tiger smiled, he was still a tiger.

As he stepped into the entrance hall Edward again hesitated. Its art deco opulence was almost oppressive. The designer – a man called Robert Atkinson – had intended to overwhelm the visitor with the power and energy of the *New Gazette* and its proprietor, and he had succeeded. It was no mere newspaper, Atkinson seemed to be saying, but a Great Enterprise, a Modern Miracle, a temple to the *Zeitgeist*. The floor was of inky marble veined with red and blue waves of colour which glowed and shimmered in the light of a huge chandelier. The ceiling was silver leaf, fan vaulted to summon up an image of the heavens, but the massive clock above the marble staircase reminded the visitor that time was money. Two shining bronze snakes, acting as banisters, hinted that there might be evil even in this paradise and Edward wondered if it really could be the designer's sly joke. Weaver was clever enough not to have

2

any statue or bust of himself in the entrance hall. No doubt after he was dead, that omission would be rectified, but for now he was content to *be* the newspaper.

Edward went over to a horseshoe desk – rosewood and silver gilt – and was greeted respectfully by a liveried flunkey and taken over to the gilded cage which would raise him by magic to the great man's private floor on the top of the building. Edward smiled to himself – it really was too much. The porters' frog-footman uniforms were certainly a mistake. He greeted by name the wizened little man who operated the lift. He at least was real – an old soldier who had lost an arm on the Somme. He seemed to read Edward's thoughts for he winked at him as if they shared a private joke before whisking him heavenward.

Edward was in a foul mood. He had dined at his club and had by chance overheard some remarks which, because they were so apt, hurt him to the core. He had finished his cigar in the smoking room and was making his way towards the door when he saw the candidates' book on a desk behind a screen and remembered he had promised to add his signature in support of a friend's son who was up for election. As he turned over the pages, he heard the voice of the man with whom he had been chatting a few moments before. He must have believed Edward had left the smoking room and not realized he was still in earshot.

'Do you know that fellow?' the man was saying. 'We were at Cambridge together – a typical victim of the System. At Cambridge he was considered the cleverest of us all. He had brains, romantic looks, £12,000 a year. A duke's son with every advantage – we thought he would go far. But what has he done or accomplished? Nothing except to be bored and miserable.'

Edward, not waiting to hear the response, slipped out of the room, his face burning. This was what men thought of him, damn it! And what was worse, this was what he thought of himself. It was true he had told no one of his adventures in Spain a few months previously when he had uncovered the identity of a spy and a murderer, but what did that amount to in the scheme of things? He wanted a job and that was why he had decided he might as well go and see what Lord Weaver had to say. He was damned if he was going to hang about London going to dinners and balls, and make small talk with girls in search of a husband and their monstrous mothers. For one thing, he was too old for that – he was thirty-six. The world was going to the devil and he wanted to play some part in preparing Britain for the war which he now believed was inevitable. But how? What part? He was too old for the army. He had offered his services to the Foreign Office and been rejected. Was it possible Joe Weaver could help him? He would soon know.

'May 12th, isn't it?'

'The coronation? Yes – that is, if it ever happens.' Weaver had almost entirely lost his Canadian accent, Edward noted, and affected a bear-like growl.

'What on earth do you mean, Joe?' Edward, his cigarette lighter in his hand, paused and looked at Weaver in surprise.

'You remember what they were saying about Mrs Simpson when you were in New York . . . she's not pure as the driven snow, you know. For one thing she's still got a husband.'

'I see but . . . ' Edward hesitated. He didn't like to speak ill of his king. '. . . does he really intend to marry the woman? I mean, he's had these . . . infatuations before.'

'This is different, Edward, I can assure you. I've seen it with my own eyes.'

'Of course, that's the set you move in. Didn't I hear you had them on your yacht?'

'Yes, a cruise along the Dalmatian coast. You should have come with us.'

'I wasn't asked,' he said drily. 'The King seemed to be enjoying himself.'

Weaver glanced at him. 'You mean . . . ?'

'With Mrs Simpson. I gather there were photographs in the French papers of them strolling around Corfu almost naked.'

'Oh no, that's nonsense, but the King enjoys being . . . casual.'

'I thought you used to be a friend of Freda's?' Edward was referring to the King's mistress when he had been Prince of Wales, Mrs Dudley Ward, whom he had dropped overnight when he met Mrs Simpson.

'I used to be,' Weaver said uncomfortably. 'In fact, it was Fredie who introduced me to Blanche.'

'I remember. Well, she did you a good turn there, Joe. Blanche is the kind of 24-carat woman I would be looking for were I ever to marry, which at the time of going to press seems most unlikely.'

Weaver shifted uneasily in his chair. It happened that his wife, in most respects a sensible woman, had a grudge against Edward. Blanche held him to blame for the death of her daughter by her first husband – a ne'er-do-well who, mercifully, had been killed in the war. Edward, as Weaver knew, had done everything he could to save his stepdaughter from the drugs which had in the end killed her and Blanche had no reason to hold him responsible for her death.

Weaver said, 'I thought the Prince would have remained faithful to Fredie until hell froze. In fact, she told me once, he had sworn never to marry anyone else, but I was wrong. He dropped her just like that. I thought the less of him for it but that's not to say I don't like Wallis. Mrs Simpson may be a divorcee and not particularly careful about the men she chooses to go to bed with but she's done the Prince – the King, I should say – the world of good. She's a level-headed, clever woman and the King does exactly what she tells him. She's stopped his drinking for one thing. But of course, he can't marry the woman, we all know that. The King likes to forget she's still married to Mr Simpson.'

Edward sucked at his cigarette contemplatively. 'I heard she was divorcing him.'

'The King couldn't marry an American divorcee. The country wouldn't stand for it.'

'Wouldn't it? He's very popular. He goes out and meets the poor. When he went to that mining village – what was it called? – he made a very good impression.'

'The colonies wouldn't stand for it. I was talking to the Prime Minister about it. He says the Australians won't have it. SB was quite crude – I confess to being surprised. His precise words were: "If the King sleeps with a whore, that's his business but the Empire is concerned that he doesn't make her queen." The Australian outlook on life is distinctly middle-class and on morals distinctly Victorian. Mackenzie King says Canadian public opinion would be outraged if it leaked out the King wanted to make Wallis his queen and I gather Herzog in South Africa is categoric.'

'There's been nothing in the papers here about Mrs Simpson.'

'Nothing at all,' Weaver agreed, sounding smug. 'The Prime Minister asked me to see what I could do to keep it all hush-hush and, I flatter myself, I have been successful.'

'You mean, Baldwin asked you not to print anything about the affair?'

'Not just me. SB wanted me to persuade the other owners, Northcliffe in particular, not to print any story which featured Mrs Simpson.'

'Aren't any of the American papers seen over here?'

'The censors snip them.'

'Good heavens! He must be worried then.'

'The PM hopes the whole thing will go away. He thinks the King will get tired of her as he has of his other women but . . . '

'. . . But you don't?'

'No, I don't. As I say, I've seen nothing like it.' Weaver leaned over the desk and looked as if he feared being overheard. 'I don't know whether you have ever met her– Wallis. She's no great beauty but she has established an ascendancy over the King . . . '

His voice trailed off as though for once he was at a loss to know how to proceed. 'There's no direct evidence she's his mistress, you know.'

'Does she want to be queen?' Edward asked.

'She says she doesn't. I don't know. She's actually told me she would like to leave David – as the family calls him – and go back to the States but he begs her not to desert him.'

'You know her well?'

'As well as anybody. She doesn't invite intimacy but she finds me – perhaps because she and I are both North Americans – easier to talk to than some of the young idiots with whom the King likes to surround himself. And she knows I'm genuinely concerned for the King's welfare.'

'So what's going to happen?'

Weaver shrugged his massive shoulders; his turnip-like features wrenched into a mask of disquiet. 'I don't know what will happen. The King is as obstinate as a spoiled child.'

'But it's all got to be sorted out before May 12th.'

'Long before that. The American papers are full of it already and they'll have a feast day when it comes to the divorce proceedings. I've kept it quiet over here up to now by good luck and arm twisting but it can't last. Anyway, there are complications. In fact, that's what I wanted to talk to you about.'

'What on earth do you mean? How has it got anything to do with me? It doesn't matter to me whom he marries. The important thing is what's happening in Germany. All this talk of Mrs Simpson! We ought to be getting ourselves ready for war.'

'There won't be a war, Edward. Hitler's all wind. In any case, the King's fascination with Wallis *does* affect our relations with Germany. The King, as you know, is bitterly anti-Communist – when he talks about the Bolshies he can't help shuddering – and he admires the new Germany and Wallis is intimate with the German Ambassador.'

'That mountebank, Ribbentrop? The champagne salesman . . . isn't that what they call him?'

'Yes, Ribbentrop. And SB has to let the King see all cabinet papers – fortunately he's mostly too idle to read them. What he does read he discusses with Wallis, and in the morning she trots round to the German Embassy and tells Ribbentrop all about it. I'm not joking. If it ever got out there would be the devil to pay. The Foreign Office is having kittens . . . Vansittart has threatened to resign.'

'I had no idea,' Edward said, 'but I still don't see what this has to do with me.'

Lord Weaver got up from behind his massive desk and walked over to the window. He beckoned to Edward and together they stared silently into the darkness. Except of course that the city was not dark. A thousand lights twinkled below them, evidence that the city was still awake. Only the slow-moving river, secretive, unstoppable, indifferent, made a broad ribbon of blackness in the brilliance.

At last, Weaver said, 'To think, that if I'm wrong and there is a war, all this may be reduced to rubble.' He waved his hand and his cigar burned angrily. 'It makes me want to weep at the folly of mankind.' He turned away and said, more calmly, 'Vansittart spoke very well of your investigation in Spain.' Sir Robert Vansittart was the Permanent Head of the Foreign Office.

'I didn't know he knew anything about it,' Edward said, moving away from the window. 'In any case, I didn't investigate, I just got involved.'

'Oh yes, he knows exactly what happened there. He seems to think you handled yourself very well. Made some useful contacts too, I understand. I believe he's thinking of offering you some sort of a job but I told him to hold his horses as I needed you first.'

'Whatever do you mean, Joe?'

'I need something investigated . . . it's most delicate . . . and I thought of you.'

'I'm flattered but I'm not a private detective,' Edward said rudely, hoping to bring the conversation to an end.

Weaver turned and looked at him shrewdly. 'I know that and I wouldn't ask for your help if it weren't a matter of . . . '

'Life and death?'

'A matter of state, if that doesn't sound too portentous.'

'It does but I confess I'm intrigued.'

'The fact of the matter is that Wallis . . . Mrs Simpson . . . has lost some papers . . . letters. They were stolen from her and if they ever came into . . . into the wrong hands . . . they would blast her reputation to the skies.'

'I'm sorry to hear that,' Edward said coolly, 'but from what you say that might not be such a bad thing. If she is revealed as . . . as something she pretends not to be, the King will have no alternative but to give her up.'

'It's not as simple as that. You don't . . . you can't fully realize what the King feels for her. Anyway, it's much better you hear it from her own lips. I want you to dine with me in Eaton Place on Saturday. It'll be just two or three old friends and Wallis. I've told her all about you. She wants to meet you.'

Edward took a deep breath. Did he really want to get involved in the private affairs of an unscrupulous woman apparently determined to involve the monarchy in scandal?

Weaver must have seen his lip curl. 'Before you make judgements, you should hear what she has to say. It's not like you to condemn a person on the basis of rumour. In any case, it's your duty.' He almost stood to attention and Edward repressed a desire to laugh. 'Your king asks for your assistance. I don't think you have any option but to listen.'

'Oh, don't be absurd, Joe! If the King wants something investigated he can call on the whole of Scotland Yard.'

'This is not a police matter but none the less important for that. Edward, I'm surprised at you. What do you English say? *Noblesse oblige?*'

'The English don't understand French . . . ' he began but then, seeing his friend was serious, relented. Weaver had resisted the temptation to point out how much Edward owed him – not least flying him around Europe in his private aeroplane. 'I'll come, of course, as you wish it, but I can promise nothing more. I don't like the sound of this and . . . '

'Say no more. Eight on Saturday then – dinner jackets, no need to dress up. This is more a council of war than a dinner party.'

Edward took this as a dismissal and, as he got up to go, asked casually, 'Has anyone any idea who stole these papers?'

'Yes indeed. They were stolen by Mrs Raymond Harkness . . . Molly Harkness. She was at one time the King's intimate friend, and yours too, I gather.'

Blanche, Lady Weaver, raised her head for him to kiss her cheek but retreated before he had time to do more than lean towards her. She was cool to the point of *froideur*. Obviously, she had been instructed by her husband to greet him civilly and was obeying . . . just. Edward had been asked to arrive early so he could meet Weaver's other guests before he had to give his undivided attention to the *femme fatale*. His host was still changing, having been kept late at the paper, so it was left to Blanche to introduce him. He had been rather surprised that there were to be other guests, given the need for secrecy, but Weaver had explained that Wallis had particularly asked that the evening should be as normal as possible and he had agreed with her that it might cause comment if it became known that she had dined alone with Edward and himself.

'You must know Leo,' Blanche said, waving dismissively at a dapper little man with a pencil-thin moustache and a smile which revealed the yellow teeth of the chain smoker.

Edward had met Leo Scannon once or twice at Mersham and had not liked him. Scannon was a Conservative Member of Parliament, very much on the right of the party. Too idle to want a ministerial post, he nevertheless exercised considerable influence on the back benches. He was all surface charm – one of the King's intimates – an atrocious snob feared for his caustic wit and his encyclopedic knowledge of aristocratic scandals. He 'knew everybody' and dined out at least three times a week. Edward, as the younger son of a duke, was not entirely to be despised but, until now, had not been considered worthy of his serious attention. This did not prevent Scannon shaking him warmly by the hand, and greeting him as though he were an old friend.

'Good to see you again, Corinth. How's Gerald?'

Scannon had bad breath and Edward backed off like a skittish horse. He made a mental note to ask his brother whether he had ever encouraged Scannon to call him by his Christian name. The Duke was very choosy about the men he permitted to be so familiar and he doubted whether Scannon was one of them. He wore too much hair oil, for one thing, which the Duke abhorred and, for another, Scannon was an open admirer of the Nazi Party and its leader. A few weeks earlier he had been in Berlin for the Olympic Games and met the Reichsführer and had apparently been bowled over by him. He had attended a Nazi Party rally and thrilled to the sound of marching jackboots. It mystified Edward what people saw in the man but he smiled bravely and muttered inanities.

Scannon was unmarried and, when Edward caught sight of a tall woman of exotic appearance standing by the fireplace smoking a cigarette from the longest cigarette holder he had ever seen, he thought at first she must be attached in some way to him. Edward was impatient to be introduced to her but, whether to tease him or through an oversight, Blanche made no effort to do so. Instead, he had to listen to Scannon going on and on about the Duke of Mersham and others of his relations until he felt he might have to wring his neck.

At last, Lord Weaver entered the drawing-room apologizing for not having been there when his guests arrived. 'News just in from Spain, Edward,' he said. 'Government troops have recaptured Maqueda, south of Madrid.'

'Never mind that,' Scannon said scornfully. 'It's only a matter of time before Madrid falls to General Franco.'

'You hope so, Leo, do you?'

'I do, Joe,' Scannon said firmly. 'It's time this terrible civil war ended and order was restored – for the sake of the

Spanish people as much as for the world at large. I hear they have taken anarchists into the government. Anarchists! I ask you – how can one take seriously a government of anarchists! It's a contradiction in terms.'

Edward bit back the retort which sprang to his lips and said urgently to Weaver, 'Any news of Verity Browne?'

Verity Browne, the *New Gazette*'s correspondent in Spain, was an avowed Communist and, if Edward knew anything about it, she would be in the thick of the fighting. Edward had an odd relationship with Verity. He had met her quite by chance when she had given him a lift to Mersham Castle after he had driven his car into a ditch. This was a year ago and their acquaintance had ripened into a friendship that occasionally threatened to become something more than that. But Verity's political beliefs made it almost impossible for her to 'love a lord' as she had once put it. However, her principles did not prevent her from calling on Edward for help in an emergency and a few months back, just before the outbreak of the war in Spain, he had helped obtain the release from a Spanish gaol of her lover – in Edward's eyes an odious communist ideologue – by the name of David Griffiths-Jones.

Edward was not a Communist. In fact he hated everything about Communism but he hated Fascism more. He held the unfashionable belief that it was possible to oppose the Nazis without becoming a member of the Communist Party. It was certainly a stand which infuriated Verity.

'Haven't you heard?' Weaver was saying in amazement. 'She was in Toledo.'

'Good heavens!' said Edward in alarm. 'Is she all right?'

'Just about. She's back in England now, recuperating. I'm surprised she hasn't been in touch.'

'What happened?' Blanche asked.

'At Toledo? About a thousand army cadets seized the Alcázar and held it against besieging government troops for weeks. Just when it looked as though the fortress must fall, and the government had invited foreign correspondents to watch the surrender, it was relieved. On 27th September the militia were routed by Franco's Moorish troops. It was a disaster which ought not to have happened. Someone had blundered. There was savage hand-to-hand fighting . . . '

'And I suppose Verity was in the thick of it?' Edward broke in.

'I'll show you the account she filed for the paper. It's one of her most powerful pieces. You really ought to read the *New Gazette* more carefully, Edward.'

Scannon said, 'Verity Browne? She's your pet "pinko", isn't she Joe? I can't think why you employ her.'

'Because she's a damn good journalist, that's why,' said Weaver firmly.

Edward was about to say something more in her defence – not that she would have been in the least put out to be excoriated by a man like Scannon, indeed she would most likely have taken it as a compliment – when the woman by the fireplace spoke.

'She is a friend of yours – Miss Browne?' Edward was never to forget that first moment he heard her talk. She spoke excellent English but had a distinct accent which he could not place immediately. He was later to learn that she was Javanese-Dutch. Her voice was husky and low but could never have been mistaken for a man's.

'Yes, she is,' Edward said. 'I do apologize but we haven't been properly introduced. My name is Corinth – Edward Corinth.'

'I know who you are, Lord Edward.'

Weaver interjected: 'Blanche, my dear, what have you been thinking of? Edward, may I introduce Catherine Dannhorn – "Dannie" to everyone. Dannie, this is Lord Edward Corinth.'

'Lord Edward, I am so pleased to meet you. Joe has been singing your praises. I hope you will call me Dannie.' She transferred her cigarette holder to her left hand and gave Edward her right. 'I am such an admirer of Miss Browne. She has done what so few of us have dared to do: leave the comfort of our homes and families and find out what is really happening. Is she a great friend?'

'Yes, she is indeed . . . Dannie. She doesn't approve of me, of course. She thinks I waste my time and no doubt she's right. She thinks we are dangerously indifferent to what is happening in Spain. She sees it as the first great battle in the war against Fascism.'

'What nonsense!' Scannon expostulated. 'Girls belong in the home. Don't you agree, Blanche? I don't know what her father is thinking of allowing her to racket around Europe meddling in things she knows nothing about. She ought to leave journalism to men. Surely, you must agree with me, Joe? Admit it, it's just a stunt having this girl writing for you.'

Edward was almost unaware of what Scannon was saying. His eyes were fixed on Dannie's face. Her almond eyes, high cheekbones and dark, silky skin captivated him. She was like nothing he had ever seen before and Blanche looked pale and insipid in comparison. Before Weaver could answer Scannon, the butler announced that Mrs Simpson's car was drawing up in front of the house and he bustled out to greet her. The others were silent, expectant, as though the King himself was about to join the company.

'We don't have to curtsy, do we?' Blanche inquired nervously. 'I've only met her with the King before.'

'Certainly not!' said Scannon. 'Though we might have to in a few months' time.'

Edward pulled himself together and tried to think what he was going to say to the lady. It was, he thought, deuced awkward. He understood why he had been selected to retrieve her letters from Molly. He was an old friend of hers and, just as important, he would not be associated in her eyes with the King or, indeed, Mrs Simpson. He had met Molly Harkness when he had been in Kenya. She had at that time still been married to a young lawyer but Happy Valley had been anything but happy for the young couple. There had been so little to do and many of the English there were not of the best sort – rakes, remittance men, divorcees. A fair sprinkling had, as the saying went, 'left the country for their country's good'. Molly had had a string of affairs while her husband, Raymond, had become a gambler and a drunkard. It was said he had come home from Muthaiga Club late one night, found his wife in the arms of her lover and tried to shoot her. He had failed – as he had failed at everything – and had turned the gun on himself. It had been a horrible scandal and public opinion had put the blame for her husband's suicide on the widow.

Edward had offered to take her away from Nairobi – he had some business to do in Johannesburg – and she had gratefully accepted. By this time Molly's lover had been disposed of and it was widely assumed – by Lord Weaver for one – that Edward had replaced him in her bed. She was a very beautiful woman – fair hair, tanned face, lean and clean-looking, almost boyish – but, as it happened, Edward had not seduced or been seduced and he and Molly had remained good friends. It bothered neither of them that the world thought otherwise. Molly had proved to be an instinctive aviatrix and together they had flown all over the country and had several narrow escapes. On one occasion they had had to make a forced landing on the high veldt and had almost perished with cold during the night, despite being wrapped in each other's arms, and on another, had woken in a makeshift camp on the Masai Mara to find themselves an object of curiosity to a pride of lions. All in all, it had been a good, strong friendship and perhaps neither of them could have explained why it had never become a love affair.

Edward had returned to England but Molly had stayed at the Cape a few months longer. He had not seen her when finally she had come home but he had read in the social columns of *The Times* and the *Morning Post* that she had become one of the Prince of Wales's intimate friends. He guessed that she must have been 'seen off' by Mrs Simpson and was now taking revenge. Whatever Molly's failings – and, as Edward knew, they were legion – he would not have put her down as a thief and a blackmailer but he also knew from bitter experience that disappointed love could sour a man's – or a woman's – character.

Mrs Simpson entered the room without any hint of swagger but emanating an aura of 'being special' – a personage. She was quite alone, which was unusual. She normally liked to have around her a small group of trusted friends. Joe and Leo Scannon both greeted her with a kiss, which she accepted passively. Despite what Scannon had said, Blanche made her a little curtsy which seemed to please her. When it was Edward's turn to be introduced, she said politely, 'I don't think we've ever met before,' and made a little joke about a friend they had in common. It was absurd, Edward told himself later, but he had expected Wallis Simpson would be beautiful, in the way Catherine Dannhorn was beautiful but, of course, she was not. Nor was she the vulgar American adventurer her enemies labelled her. She was a demure, plain woman with large startled eyes, plucked eyebrows and a mole on her cheek. She was simply but smartly dressed in white and wore a magnificent parure of rubies.

At dinner, Edward was placed on her right and for a moment he wondered if he were going to be bored but quickly discovered she was much more intelligent than she appeared at first and exhibited a dry wit which charmed him. They discussed flying – she hated flying as so many of the friends of her youth had been killed in flying accidents. They discussed golf which she loved and Edward abominated, gardening – she was very interested in his description of the Elizabethan knot garden at Mersham which she said sounded 'divine', a favourite word of hers – the Far East, which she had visited as a girl, and jewellery about which she spoke with passion. She said she hated public events and being photographed because 'I know I'm not beautiful' but she said not a word about the King. By the end of dinner, Edward had got to like her and felt genuinely sorry for the predicament in which she found herself.

Weaver, too, was in good spirits, quite unabashed at having the King's paramour in his house, and he spoke knowledgeably, if at rather too great length, of John Knox, Wolfe taking Quebec and eighteenth-century politics in general.

Edward hoped he would not raise the subject of George IV and his unhappy queen and, to his relief, he did not. Mrs Simpson ate very little and drank less. Wallis, as she asked Edward to call her, told him she never had cocktails, preferring whisky and soda and, at dinner, she drank just one glass of claret but several tumblers of Vichy water. Blanche had obviously taken particular care with the dinner and Wallis was complimentary. They began with blinis and caviar, then *Sole Muscat* followed by *Boeuf* à la *Provençale*. The service was brisk and efficient so they were finished by eleven. Blanche and Dannie then left to drink coffee in the drawing-room but Wallis made no move to join them so Edward assumed they must be about to discuss the missing documents.

When the servants had departed, the port was circulated and Wallis had a small cup of black coffee. The men lit cigars, after first gaining the lady's permission, and Edward lit a cigarette for her. Weaver blew smoke and said, 'Wallis, I mentioned to Edward that we might need his help recovering those papers taken from you. I have only told him the bare bones of the problem. Would you like me to . . . or would you prefer to . . . ?'

There was a moment's awkward silence and then Wallis spoke in her curiously high-pitched but pleasant voice with its American lilt. 'Joe has told you what happened?'

Edward shook his head. 'I'm afraid I am completely in the dark.'

'It was two weeks ago. We . . . ' She glanced at Edward to see if he understood that she included the King in that 'we'. 'We were staying with the Brownlows – you know Perry and Kitty, don't you?' Edward said that he did. 'I guess, when I went down to dinner, I must have left my jewel box on my dressing table. Then, when I went up to bed, I found my maid in tears in my room. She said, "Oh, madam, someone's broken open your box." I went to look and the lid had been prised open with a knife or something and my letters had gone.'

'I see,' Edward said. 'How many were there?'

'Seven but some were several pages.'

'What else had gone? Were there any jewels missing?'

'None.'

'Presumably you told Lord Brownlow what had happened?'

'I didn't want to make a fuss but of course I had to. You understand why?'

Edward had to admire the woman. She spoke in her clear, even voice of having lost love letters from the King which, were they to be published, would embarrass not only herself but the King and the rest of the royal family. As a divorcee, she was already unwelcome in the homes of many 'respectable' people but this might make her untouchable. As Edward knew well, the morality of the British upper classes was built on an agreed hypocrisy. Once a girl was married and had produced 'an heir and a spare', as the saying went, she could enter into affairs with married men provided nothing leaked out to the press. It was a small world in which everyone knew everyone and was probably related in some way. Only divorce ruined a woman's reputation. Now, here was the King considering marrying an American woman of no family, without money, who had divorced one husband and was in the process of divorcing a second. Whatever her faults, Edward admired her courage in facing a world which would rejoice at her downfall.

'So whoever it was who took these letters knew what they were looking for. What about your maid?'

'Maddox is utterly trustworthy.'

'Did Perry suggest calling the police?'

'Yes, but we agreed that had to be a last resort as the news of the theft would be reported in the newspapers. In any case, we both felt that whoever stole the letters would want to return them – for a price.' There was contempt in her voice.

'And that's what happened?'

'Yes. Perry's party broke up the next day and, the morning after, I received a hand-delivered note from Mrs Harkness, one of the house party, saying that she would return the letters if I promised to leave the country and never see . . . never see him again.'

'When was that?'

'That was Wednesday, ten days ago.'

'What did you do?'

'I consulted Perry. He suggested either I go to the police or go see Joe. Joe's a true friend,' she said, giving him a look of genuine warmth. 'He said he could discover, without arousing suspicion, if anyone had offered my letters to a newspaper and they hadn't. He then remembered you were a friend of Mrs Harkness and said he would talk to you. Of course, if you can't do anything, there will be no alternative to asking the police to get them back but I'm afraid to do that, as I told you.'

Edward pulled on his cigar and said, 'Of course, I will do what you ask but you must not assume I will be successful. Molly's a determined woman. Might I ask – and you must forgive me if I am being impertinent but it is necessary for me to know what I'm up against – the letters, are they from the King – intimate letters?'

'Yes. He writes me every day we are parted and some-times – you'll think it absurd – even when we're staying in the same house. But they . . . they're not just what the press would call love letters. They are almost diaries. He writes me exactly what he's thinking, what he is doing, who he saw in the day, his opinions . . . '

'Good heavens! Why did you not keep them in a safe? Did it not occur to you that you might lose them if you took them with you on weekend visits?'

Edward wondered if he had been too harsh but Wallis, with a quiet dignity, said, 'I took them with me because I liked to read them.'

After a long pause, Edward turned to Weaver. 'Joe, would any English newspaper print these letters? Surely, stolen property . . . the lawyers could stop . . . '

'No reputable newspaper would publish stolen letters but of course the American newspapers would make hay with them. That would leak back into the English press – not the *New Gazette*, but scandal sheets like *Cavalcade* or political papers with an axe to grind such as the *Daily Worker*.' Weaver looked meaningfully at Edward. He was indirectly warning him not to say anything to Verity Browne about Wallis Simpson's loss. As a card-carrying Communist, she might feel the *Daily Worker*, the Party's official mouthpiece, ought to report the failings of the King.

Edward made one final effort to avoid having to undertake a task which gave him a sick feeling in his stomach. 'Ought it not to be someone Molly knows to have the King's ear, like Perry or even Leo? By the way, I assume the King does know about the theft . . . ?'

'Not yet,' Weaver said. 'He's got enough to worry about at the moment. We'll have to tell him if this doesn't work but . . . '

Scannon said, 'The idea is you join a house party at Haling . . . ' Haling was Scannon's country house in Wiltshire. 'I've got a dozen or so people coming so Molly won't feel I've set anything up. She'll assume I don't know anything about what she's been up to if no one else . . . I mean like Wally or Perry or even Joe . . . are part of the party . . . ' Edward was momentarily nonplussed to hear Wallis referred to as Wally. It sounded so absurd a name for her. 'She'll be thrilled to know you're coming, Edward. She was talking about you only the other night and wondering why she never saw you.'

Wallis looked far from pleased. Scannon was talking about her enemy as if she were still a friend.

Edward said, 'Well, I'll do my best. Have you got Molly's letter here?'

'Yes,' Weaver said. 'I'm keeping it in my safe but I assumed you would want to read it.'

He passed Edward a blue envelope which smelled faintly of violets. Apart from the words 'Mrs Simpson', heavily underlined, there was no address. He took out a single sheet of blue paper. It had no address or telephone number on it and it began abruptly, without a 'Dear Mrs Simpson': 'If you want your letters back give up David and go home to America. If not . . . I mean it . . . I will take them to the newspapers. Go away!'

It was signed with the initial H.

'We're sure H is Molly Harkness? I haven't seen her handwriting for some time.'

'Yes,' Scannon said, 'I have compared it with letters from her I have received . . . I keep every letter anyone ever sends me . . . ' he said with a wolfish grin. 'Not only is it in her hand but the scent is unmistakable – *Après l'Ondée*. It's Molly all right.'

Edward sighed. 'Right then, but ought I not to go and see her privately . . . ? Where is she living?'

'Knightsbridge . . . Trevor Square,' Weaver said. 'But we mustn't make too much of it. Best you tackle her on neutral ground, I think.'

Edward sighed again and Mrs Simpson looked at him with clear black eyes showing no emotion. 'It would be a great service to me and to the King, Lord Edward, if you would do this. I know it is distasteful to you but . . . '

'Please say no more. I will do my best. Which weekend are we talking about, Scannon?'

'Next weekend. The sooner the better.'

'Short notice! Will everyone be able to come?'

'They have already been invited.'

'I see,' Edward said. He did not like the idea that his willingness to drop everything and come down to Wiltshire had been taken for granted.

'If you had refused to come, I would have tackled Molly myself, but I know she would have taken no notice of anything I had to say,' Scannon said, as if he could read his mind.

'Don't look so gloomy,' Weaver said jovially. 'Dannie's going to be one of the party, isn't she, Leo? You'll like that, won't you, Edward?'

The tiger smiled.

2

Edward was still feeling bad-tempered when, the following Tuesday, on the way to his bank, he saw a girl he knew coming out of Galeries Lafayette struggling with an unruly gaggle of carrier bags and beribboned boxes.

'I say, driver, stop the cab, will you. I've got to rescue a damsel in distress.'

The taxi screeched to a halt causing the driver of an omnibus to swerve and curse. Edward opened the door and called, 'Verity! Let me give you a hand with those.'

'Oh, Edward, is that you! I can't see anything through these parcels. I was just wondering how I was going to get home without coming an almighty cropper.'

The girl who dropped with relief into the back of the taxi was a none-too-tall, black-eyed, merry-looking child of about twenty-five. When she had struggled out from under her parcels, she kissed her rescuer and then began rearranging her hat which had been knocked askew in her efforts to negotiate a particularly large hatbox on to the folding seat. She was very fond of hats.

'Golly,' said Edward, regarding her with frank admiration. 'What on earth has happened to your hair, Verity?'

'Oh, do you like it? Mr Cizec has "bingled" me. I'm short-haired for life.'

'It *is* short but I like it. I think it makes you look *gamine*.'

'*Gamine*? Is that good? Anyway, where are we off to?'

'Wherever you want. I was on my way to Coutts but that can be postponed. If I can take you home . . . By the way, where is home?'

Verity Browne had given up her Knightsbridge flat when she had gone to Spain for the *New Gazette* twelve months before and on her brief visits to London since then she had stayed with friends. 'I'm staying with Adrian Hassel. You remember him?'

'The artist? Does he still paint green stick men and orange suns?'

Edward had met Hassel soon after he had first met Verity and to his surprise – because he disliked 'aesthetes' on principle – liked the man. He had a house and studio in the King's Road. Edward gave the address to the cab driver.

'He's very successful, I'll have you know,' Verity said as the cab cut in front of a brewer's dray, occasioning a cascade of parcels on to Edward's lap. 'The nibs think he's the goods. His last exhibition was at one of those swanky galleries in Albemarle Street and everything sold, so don't sound so superior. You should have bought one of his pictures when you had the chance. You won't be able to afford them now.'

'But surely you're not staying with Hassel unchaperoned?'

'Oh, don't be so old-fashioned, Edward. I'm not a blushing virgin, you know.'

'Verity!' Edward expostulated.

'If you must know, Adrian's married now so it's all quite respectable.'

'Married! I didn't think he was the marrying kind.' A vision of the elegant young man, dressed in green, his favourite colour, gesturing with his cigarette holder, sprang unbidden into his mind.

'Well, you'd be wrong then. Adrian is a red-blooded Tarzan, so there, and Charlotte is a dear.'

'Charlotte?'

'You won't know her. She was Charlotte Bracey. We were at school together – though I went to so many, I really can't remember which one.'

'But I do know her. She writes books, doesn't she?'

Verity looked at him in surprise. 'I didn't know you had arty friends!' She was a little bit annoyed to find he knew any of her circle. It wasn't that she was ashamed of Edward but her friends liked to tease her for having as a beau a member of the class which she, as a Communist, absolutely deplored so, as far as possible, she kept him out of sight.

'Oh yes, I know Charley,' said Edward thoughtfully.

'What does that mean? I don't like your tone of voice.'

'Sorry, V. It wasn't a tone of voice at all. Her parents lived near Mersham. We knew each other as children. Went to the same parties – that sort of thing. I once dropped ice-cream down the back of her neck. She played a good game of tennis,' he mused. 'I'd love to see Charley again. We rather lost touch when she went to London after her parents died. I didn't even know she was married.'

'She's married,' said Verity crossly. She hated talking at length about other women when she was with Edward. She might not want him for herself but she disliked the idea of his being some other woman's friend. She glanced across at him. She had to admit it: he was attractive. He was slim but broad in the shoulders. He had all his hair. He looked – she thought appraisingly – rather less than his thirty-six years but his brown eyes were those of a man who had seen some of the world's less comfortable corners. He had a good chin, always so important. She could never find any man attractive with a weak chin. Round his mouth two or three creases furrowed his face when he smiled, which he did frequently, but his rather thin lips and beakish nose suggested that, beneath the veneer of the perfectly dressed 'man about town', a more formidable figure lay dormant.

'I saw Joe on Saturday, Verity,' he said seriously. 'He said you had a narrow escape at Toledo. I'm afraid I missed seeing your report in the paper. You won't get yourself killed, will you?'

Verity turned her head away and looked out at the Ritz which they happened to be passing. 'We were defeated. We

24

have to face facts. Those Arab troops of Franco's . . . they behaved like . . . '

Edward saw from the back of her head that she was upset. He said gently, 'Might I be allowed to take you out to dinner? I would like to hear all about it.'

Verity looked at him and seemed to be satisfied with what she saw. His was not idle curiosity. He would understand, she thought. After all, he had seen the first few days of the war. So many of her London friends said they wanted to hear what it was like in Spain but, when she began to tell them, she saw their attention wander. She sometimes wondered if she alone saw the importance of this fight with Fascism. But, of course, the Party understood what it was they were fighting for.

As if he had read her thoughts – it was odd how different they were and yet how often they found themselves thinking the same things – he said, 'I really do want to hear what's been going on in Spain. I've been worried sick about you.'

He hadn't meant to sound so intense but it was good to put the feeling he had suppressed into words. With an effort, he tried to lighten the atmosphere. 'Am I allowed to ask how a Communist Party member squares her conscience with these?' He poked with his foot at one of the Galeries Lafayette bags.

'The comrades are so serious it sometimes gets in the way of their dress sense,' she giggled. 'I really refuse to look dowdy just because the cause is good. You do agree?'

'Not being a comrade I really can't comment, V, but I do like seeing a pretty girl dressed . . . ' He was going to say 'dressed to kill' but stopped himself. '. . . . to brighten up our sad old world. In fact, you look so good I have half a mind to . . . '

'Ah, here we are!' Verity said suddenly as the cab pulled up outside the house of her friends. 'I would ask you in but I happen to know Adrian and Charlotte are out so it wouldn't be proper, would it? Now help me out with these.'

When Verity, after a struggle with the door key, had let herself in and Edward had dropped her parcels in a pile in the narrow entrance hall, she said, 'Well, goodbye then. You rescued me once again so I suppose I ought to collapse in your arms. I tell you what, come to lunch on Sunday.'

''Fraid not. I'm spending the weekend in Wiltshire.'

'Oh, I see. Going to murder a few peasants? Please God defend me from the upper classes at play.'

'Ha! ha!' Edward said ironically. 'Anyway, it's pheasants, not peasants. What about dinner at Gennaro's on Tuesday?'

'Mmm, maybe. I've got a meeting in the afternoon.'

'A Party meeting?' he inquired ingenuously.

'Sort of,' she admitted. 'They're sending some of us on the Jarrow march.'

'Jarrow? Bede's home?'

'It will be known for something other than the Venerable Bede in a day or two, I can tell you,' she said grimly. 'I sometimes think we really are two nations – the privileged and the people.'

'Disraeli.'

'He wasn't CP, was he?'

'Yes he was – if you mean Conservative Party.'

'Idiot! It may have escaped your notice that Jarrow's shipping industry has been destroyed and the poverty of the people there is heartbreaking.'

'I suppose I did know.'

'No you didn't. No one could if they hadn't seen it with their own eyes. That's the point of the march: to bring the reality of what has happened to the town, and other towns like it, to London so that people like you can begin to understand what is happening to our country.'

'So when's it to happen?'

'It's happening already. They've started marching and should reach London before the King opens the new parliament. They think he will do something for them, poor dears.'

'They're marching three hundred miles to see the King? It sounds like a nursery rhyme.'

'It isn't a nursery rhyme for them. More like the Peasants' Revolt. Anyway, it's just the sort of thing the King might do to annoy Baldwin. He's very good with people, you know.'

'I know, I'm sorry. I didn't mean . . . Hey! I thought you didn't approve of kings?'

'Not in principle but this one – whatever his politics – has a feeling for ordinary people in distress. Perhaps he knows what it's like to be bullied.'

'Please, Verity, you're going to give me palpitations! If you start defending the monarchy I'll start believing Colonel Lindbergh is Little Bo-Peep.'

'Now that's interesting. Why should such a brave man be a Fascist? Anyway, the point is the Jarrow marchers hope to shame all you lot who don't give a tinker's cuss how the other half of the country lives or dies into some sort of action.'

'You're not marching?'

'The last bit. A party of us is going to meet them at St Albans – or somewhere just outside London. But it's going to take them three weeks to get here. Tommie's coming, and some of the others.' Tommie Fox had been at Cambridge with Edward and was now vicar of a parish in Kilburn. He was one of the only truly *good* men Edward knew. 'Why don't you join us?'

'I don't think I would be welcome. It's not my fight and they would have every right to resent me pretending it was. Tell you what, when you all arrive in London and have presented your petition . . . I suppose there is a petition?'

'Darn right there is!'

'I'll give you and Tommie, and anyone else you want to ask, a slap-up meal – a celebration.'

'Mmm,' said Verity doubtfully. 'I suppose that will be all right. We'll have to see.'

'Ungrateful little beast!'

'Oh, do shut up, Edward. You think it's all a game, but it isn't. It's deadly serious.'

'But that doesn't stop you shopping your way through the West End?'

'I'm allowed recreation but you're on a permanent holiday.'

'*Touché*,' he said wryly.

'Sorry, I didn't mean to be schoolmistressy but what are you doing now? Going to hobnob with a load of silly asses with more money than sense to kill a few innocent animals.'

'Hey, steady on! I say, when do you go back to Spain, or don't you?'

'Soon,' she said shortly.

'It was bad out there?' he asked, almost shyly.

'Yep, bad.' She shut her lips like a trap closing and the blood left her face. It was obviously too recent and too painful to talk about casually with a taxi waiting at the door. 'Go on! You have to get to Coutts before they shut, you capitalist exploiter of the down-trodden masses. Do they still wear frock coats, by the way? I suppose it helps them kowtow to the bourgeoisie. Thanks for the rescue.'

Edward grinned. 'I'll telephone . . . '

When the taxi had disappeared, Verity took off her hat and then stood in front of the little mirror in the hall and stared at herself. Suddenly, despite her friends, despite the Party, she felt very lonely. All the girls she knew were getting married and having babies. What was she doing playing at politics, dabbling in what most people considered to be men's work? She would admit it to nobody but in Toledo she had been very frightened. Alongside her, men she knew well – comrades in arms – had died and died ignominiously. She knew they had been betrayed by their leaders, and the Republicans had been made to look fools in front of the world's press. When the city fell, Franco's men had been allowed to rape and murder the townspeople unchecked. It was deliberate policy – to terrorize the people into submission.

She leant forward and pressed her forehead against the cool of the glass and closed her eyes. How long could she go on? Was her idealism crumbling in the face of the brutal reality? All she wanted now was to rest and it occurred to her that the place she most wanted to rest was in the arms of the man whom she had so firmly dispatched in a taxi a few moments before.

'Sometimes I think I'm the biggest fool on earth, Fenton.'

'My lord?'

'Stop pretending you don't know why we're bowling down the Great West Road when we might be enjoying the fleshpots of the metropolis.'

Edward put his foot down on the accelerator pedal and the Lagonda responded like the thoroughbred she was. Despite everything he had said, it was a joy to feel the wind in his face and know that he had a job to do at journey's end, however distasteful. He had been idle too long and had been seriously considering leaving for America and getting a job on a ranch in Texas or wherever was furthest from decadent, demoralized Europe.

'I did happen to overhear your lordship on the telephone to Lord Weaver. Without wishing to eavesdrop, I understood that your visit to Haling Castle is not entirely a matter of pleasure.'

Edward snorted and, to Fenton's alarm, took both hands off the wheel to make a gesture of protest. 'Pleasure! I might as well tell you all, Fenton, in order to avoid any misunderstandings. Before you entered my employment, when I was in Africa, I became a close friend of Mrs Raymond Harkness – Molly Harkness. She had a brute of a husband and, to cut a long story short, he did away with himself. Though I don't like speaking ill of a woman, I have to say Molly had not proved to be the most loyal of wives. I took her away from Nairobi and the scandal surrounding her husband's death and we were together for some months while she . . . recuperated.'

'My lord?'

'I know what you're thinking, Fenton, but in this instance you would be wrong.'

'My lord!' said Fenton, shocked.

'She's a very beautiful woman – or she was then – but we stayed just good friends. It's against my principles to take advantage of a woman when she's at a low ebb and Molly was pretty down in the mouth I can tell you.'

'Would that be the Mrs Harkness who is a close friend of the King, my lord? I have often seen her name in the society columns.'

'No longer. Lord Weaver informs me she has been dropped like the proverbial hot potato. Between ourselves, I don't think Mrs Simpson appreciated her.'

'I understand, my lord. And when you dined with his lordship the other evening ... ?'

'I was informed that Molly, in what I can only assume was a fit of pique, had removed certain letters from Mrs Simpson's room when both ladies were staying with Lord Brownlow and naturally she wants them back. I have been selected for that duty. As you can imagine, I do not relish the thought of trying to persuade Molly that it would be in her best interests to hand over the purloined letters.'

'I quite understand, my lord. Might I inquire whether I can be of any assistance?'

'Maybe, Fenton, maybe. I hope it won't come to searching her room or anything so unpleasant but ... well, I shall want to consult you, I am sure, and, if you can do so without embarrassment, it occurred to me that you might be able to elicit information from Mrs Harkness's maid – I assume she will have her own maid with her – which might be of use. I trust I am not putting you in an awkward position? You can always say no. A word from you will be taken as a *nolle prosequi* and nothing more will be said on the subject.'

'My lord, I will do whatever can be done.'

'I'm most grateful. I need hardly say absolute discretion is called for. Our host, Mr Scannon, knows what we are about and,' he added casually, 'a Catherine Dannhorn, who is also staying at Haling and is a close friend of Lord Weaver, may also know something of what's afoot, but no one else.'

30

'I appreciate being taken into your confidence, my lord, and you can depend on me to be as silent as the grave.'

'Very good! Ah, take a squint at that finger post will you? We can't be far now.'

Haling Castle proved to be not a castle but a large grey stone house covered in Virginia creeper – handsome but by no means beautiful. It was surrounded by a stone wall in bad repair, the gaps in it roughly filled with loose stone and barbed wire. A short gravel drive debouched on to the road through great stone pillars upon which hung two ornate iron gates. Scannon told Edward later that the house had been built by his father, a wealthy Birmingham industrialist, at the end of the last century. It had been fitted with every modern convenience including electric light and a primitive central heating system which banged and gurgled, only slightly warming massive brown-painted radiators. It now needed complete renovation but Scannon said he hadn't the money to do it.

Scannon himself came to the door to welcome Edward and tell him in a conspiratorial whisper that Molly had arrived the previous day.

'I've said nothing, of course, but she seems nervy and unhappy. Anyway, come in and meet her. She's very eager to see you. I don't know what you did to her but she certainly thinks the sun shines out of . . . ah, there you are Pickering. Take Lord Edward's bags to his room, will you.'

Fenton went off with the butler and Scannon led Edward across a gloomy-looking hall through a gothic-style door into what was obviously the drawing-room. At the far end of this barn of a room several people were huddled round a huge open fire. Laid across great fire dogs, logs the size of small trees burned fiercely but the architect had so arranged it that most of the heat generated went straight up the chimney. Only if one were standing very close to it could one be toasted and even charred.

Edward was offered a cup of tea by a bespectacled female to whom he was not introduced. He sipped at the liquid gratefully and then turned to greet his fellow guests.

'You know Boy, I gather,' Scannon said, indicating a man of about forty with the lean, tanned look of someone who spent most of their life in hot climates.

'Boy, yes of course,' Edward said, trying to sound enthusiastic.

'Hello, old sport,' Carstairs said, shaking his hand.

Sir Richard Carstairs – always known as Boy for reasons lost in the mists of time – had been in Nairobi when Edward was there and they had been on safari together a couple of times. He was not exactly a popular figure in the colony but everyone knew him and he was thought to be in some unspecified way 'useful'. He had no money himself but managed to live in the houses of the rich without their seeming to mind. In short, he was a sponger but he paid his way by being an amusing raconteur and a knowledgeable guide to what passed for fleshpots in Nairobi. He took English and American visitors on safari – he was a crack shot – and showed them the country in perfect safety while letting them feel they were being adventurous. Women liked him, and it was said he had serviced many bored wives, but there had never been any scandal and in Happy Valley that was what mattered. Boy was a bounder but he was discreet.

A soon as he decently could, Edward turned to greet Molly and they kissed with genuine warmth.

'Molly, my dear, I had heard you were in England and I kept on meaning to telephone you but I didn't know where you were living.'

'I know, Edward darling. It's my fault. Why is it one never sees one's real friends and spends all one's time with bores.'

'Tut-tut,' Scannon said, 'I think you're being hard on me.'

'Oh Leo, I don't mean you of course, but . . . '

Fortunately, perhaps, Edward's attention was drawn by Scannon to the other couple standing beside the fire.

'Edward, let me introduce you to Lord and Lady Benyon. I don't believe you have ever met, have you?'

'I'm delighted to meet you, sir, at last. When I was in Madrid a few months back they said you had been there giving a lecture. I was very sorry to have missed it.'

Edward was immensely pleased to meet the distinguished economist and his Russian wife. He had long thought Benyon was one of the few economists who made sense and moreover was, at least in his private life, an outsider and a rebel. His interests were not the usual pursuits of the English upper class – hunting, shooting and fishing – but books, theatre, painting and ballet. Inna – Lady Benyon – had been a dancer with the Russian Ballet and Diaghilev had been almost a father to her. Benyon had seen her perform at Covent Garden just before the war and had fallen passionately in love with her. He had bombarded her with flowers and, as they say, swept her off her feet. Despite being told by all their friends that the affair would be short-lived and 'end in tears' they had married and lived – as far as anyone knew – happily ever after. Inna was still very lovely – petite, very slim, with the kind of heart-shaped face rare in Englishwomen. Edward guessed she must have been exquisite when she had danced with Nijinsky before the war and he could quite understand why Benyon had fallen in love with her.

Edward had read several of Benyon's books and, though he knew very little of economics, thought he knew good sense when he came across it. Now in his mid-fifties, Benyon – unlike his books which were lean and muscular – was physically unprepossessing. He was thin, round-shouldered and had a limp, the result of a childhood illness. His skin was bad, he was almost bald and his moustache was wispy and illnourished but his eyes glittered with intelligence and he had a smile which illuminated his face. Apart from being an academic and a member of several influential commissions, he was also a patron of the arts and he had even managed to squeeze out of the government a little money for the Opera House.

Edward was about to ask Benyon for his views on the depression which still gripped towns like Jarrow when the drawing-room door opened and Dannie entered. Though he knew she was to be a guest of Scannon's, her loveliness again took him by surprise. Benyon was amused to see Edward so obviously *bouleversé*, and even Molly, who was nervous and impatient to get Edward on his own, had to smile despite being rather jealous. Dannie kissed Edward and then threw herself into a large, battered armchair and demanded tea and muffins.

'You English . . . ' she said in her dark, husky voice with its trace of an accent, 'you English cannot cook – you do not know the meaning of good food! I'm sorry, Leo, but it is only the simple truth. But your afternoon tea – that is a good thing you have invented.'

'Dannie treats this place as though she owned it,' Scannon said in mock exasperation. 'I'll have you know, my dear child, that chair you threw yourself in is Louis Quinze and valuable.'

'Don't be so silly, Leo. There's nothing worth anything in this house. You're too mean to put in proper heating even. I'm freezing.' She wrapped herself in her arms dramatically.

'Well, you should wear more clothes. Our fathers and grandfathers dressed in several layers of good English worsted before they ventured out so they did not need mollycoddling with heated pipes and radiators.'

Edward thought the conversation was getting a little too acerbic for comfort – no one likes being called mean – so he hurriedly broke in with a story of how as a child his father had allowed them all to freeze in sympathy with the troops at the front. It was ridiculous, Edward knew, but all the time he was talking he was imagining what it would be like to take Dannie in his arms and make violent, passionate love to her. This woman had only to utter a few banalities and it made the blood pump through his veins and all powers of intelligent conversation left him. There was something pagan . . . elemental about her which intrigued

34

and baffled him. He thought of Rider Haggard's *She*, a favourite book of his when he had been a child.

Lord Benyon, half annoyed and half amused, saw what was happening and relinquished Edward to the siren with some degree of disappointment. He hoped the young man, whom he had liked on sight, was not going to be led astray by this strange-looking woman. He would ask Inna what she thought. He usually found his wife percipient about the love lives of their friends. Molly too watched Edward intently. Her face was drawn and her brow furrowed. She was clearly unhappy. Edward caught her eye and his heart almost failed him as he remembered why he was here at Haling. He shivered. How pale and wan Englishwomen, even Molly Harkness, seemed in Dannie's presence.

Before long, Scannon dismissed the party to rest and change for dinner. 'Pickering will show you your room, Corinth,' he said, escorting him to the foot of the stairs where a grave, bespectacled man awaited him. 'The gong goes at seven and we foregather here for cocktails. It's my custom to take anyone who wishes it on a guided tour of the house after dinner. In spite of what Dannie says, I do at least have a picture or two which might interest you. Oh, by the way, the party's not yet complete. We're being joined by Sir Geoffrey and Lady Hepple-Keen and Mr Larry Harbin, the American millionaire. Harbin's a most interesting man. I met him in New York last year and we found we had much in common. He's a close friend of President Roosevelt. I shall be interested to hear what you make of him.'

'And Hepple-Keen? He's one of your lot, isn't he, Leo?' Edward said.

'My lot? Oh, yes. He's MP for Leicester North and a coming man. The PM thinks well of him.'

'No, I mean he's an admirer of the Führer, isn't he?'

'Yes, he was one of our little party in Berlin for the Games. Does that bother you? I know you do not share our admiration for what the Reich Chancellor has achieved. Hepple-Keen had a very good war, you know, Corinth. He knows what it is to have Germany as an enemy but, like me, he now thinks we ought to make it our friend and ally.'

'I understand the Führer also had "a good war", as you put it. So good he wishes to repeat it.'

Scannon looked at Edward with distaste. He hoped his guest was not going to be a bore about politics. He said, 'That's nonsense. The Führer wants to be our friend if only warmongers like you would let him. He admires the British Empire. His enemies should be ours.'

Realizing he was becoming shrill, Scannon said more quietly, 'By the way, I make it a rule in this house to keep off politics when the ladies are present. Perhaps over a cigar and a brandy we might try and convert you, Corinth, but ... ' he lowered his voice so only Edward could hear, 'we mustn't let anything distract you from ... from your real reason for being here.'

Pickering escorted him to his bedroom on the front of the house. Fenton had unpacked and laid out his clothes for the evening. 'Arctic, eh, Fenton?' he said, rubbing his hands.

'My lord?' Fenton inquired.

'This room ... it's icy. Is that all the heating there is?' He pointed to a single bar electric fire which glowed feebly in the fireplace.

'Yes, my lord. I inquired whether it might not be possible to light a fire in the grate ... '

'It's big enough.' The electric fire was lost in a gaping aperture in which a huge metal grid, resembling some instrument of medieval torture, stood gleaming with lack of use.

'Yes, my lord. Unfortunately, Mr Pickering informed me the bedroom fires are never lit for fear of causing a conflagration which might endanger the house.'

'Well, we don't want that, I suppose. Throw me my dressing gown, will you,' he said, taking off his jacket. 'I suppose one can have a bath?'

'Yes, my lord. There is a bathroom at the end of the passage. I deferred drawing a bath for you, my lord, until you came up as I understand it is shared with two other guests on this corridor, Mrs Harkness and Mr Harbin. If I may say so, I would advocate having your bath in good time, my lord. Mr Pickering indicated to me that the plumbing is . . . antiquated and the hot water is not to be relied upon.'

'I see. Well, yes, poor Mr Harbin. After Mrs Harkness and I have bathed I doubt there will be anything for him. As I remember it, she was quite happy to rough it for days at a time but when she is in civilization, so to speak, she likes to indulge herself. By the way, Fenton, where is her room? I would like to have a chat with her . . . a private chat.'

Fenton raised an eyebrow – a liberty permitted by his long and intimate connection with his master which, on occasion, went beyond that of master and servant to trusted aide and partner in the detection of crime.

'Don't try my patience,' Edward said irritably. 'My interest in Mrs Harkness is purely business.'

'Indeed, my lord,' Fenton said hastily. 'Her room is next to yours. Indeed, there is a connecting door behind the screen but the door is locked so it is necessary to go out into the passage.'

Edward went over to the corner where a chinoiserie screen of surpassing ugliness made an unavailing attempt to suppress a draught or two. He peered behind it and saw a stout door which looked as if it had not been opened in years. He did not try it because if Fenton said it was locked, then it was. It was typical of the man's efficiency that he had surveyed his master's sleeping quarters so carefully. Edward noticed that, rather unusually in a country house, his bedroom door had a key in it.

'What's your room like?' Edward asked.

'Modest, my lord, but, if I may say so, more comfortable than this one. It is on the top floor where the other servants sleep.'

'Well, you'd better go and draw my bath then. Though wait a moment, perhaps it would be polite if I first discovered whether Mrs Harkness wanted to bathe now or later. I'll just knock on her door.'

Molly answered his knock after a moment's struggle with the doorknob. She was still fully clothed and said she was going to rest on her bed before having her bath so Edward put his head back round his own door and told Fenton to go ahead.

'Come and sit down over here, Edward dear,' she said when he had returned. 'Would you like a snifter?' She waved a silver flask at him.

'Where did that come from?' Edward asked admiringly.

'Oh, I have stayed with Leo before and, knowing how cold this house is, I took the precaution of bringing my own supplies of warmth. I can't rely on you providing bodily warmth, can I?'

Edward knew she was alluding to their nights on the veldt when they had clung together against the wind that chilled the marrow in their bones, and he smiled.

'What is it? Brandy? Yes please, Molly, just a drop. Is Leo really hard up or just a skinflint?'

'The latter. He's rolling in it. Come and make yourself comfy on the bed, darling.'

'Do we use these?' Edward brought over two water glasses that stood beside a carafe on the bedside table. In companionable silence he watched her pour two inches from her flask in each glass.

'Chin-chin,' she said, and they touched glasses.

Edward drank, spluttered but felt with gratitude a warm tingle spread through his stomach. 'More please! Have you got enough?'

'Yes, here.' She passed him the flask. 'Hey, not too much. I must keep some for later. You know Pickering can't bring us booze without his master's express permission. Leo keeps the keys to the tantalus himself. Isn't that the limit? By the way, you *are* coming to see me later?'

'Well, yes, I do want to talk to you. Perhaps just before we turn in?'

'Talk? I never understand why we only talked when we were in Africa. I suppose it was my fault. I was still feeling ghastly over that business with Raymond. You were so sweet to me.' She came up close to him and Edward knew she wanted him to kiss her.

'Hey, steady on, old girl,' he said, choosing his words to sound as unenthusiastic as possible. 'I thought we agreed we would just be good pals?'

'Oh, that was in Africa. It's different now.'

'But surely, I mean, a beautiful woman like you . . . '

'You think I must have lovers?' she said bitterly. 'I could have. I did have. Don't you read the papers? But at the moment I'm – what do they say? – fancy-free.'

'Well, yes. That's what I need to talk to you about . . . later.'

'What?' she said, suddenly suspicious.

'Lovers, ex-lovers.'

'You don't have a message for me from *him*, do you?'

She was suddenly breathless and her pupils dilated.

'Not exactly,' he said awkwardly. 'Tell me something, Molly. How was it you met the Prince of Wales? I mean, to put it crudely, you weren't moving in those sort of circles in Kenya. That man you were consorting with – what was his name, Davenant? He wasn't exactly out of the top drawer if you'll forgive me for saying so.'

'Douglas? Yes, he was rather awful, wasn't he? He couldn't stay in the colony after Raymond shot himself – not without marrying me and neither of us wanted that. I don't hold it against him. We never pretended we loved each other or anything like that. We were lovers, yes, but only because we were so bored. Raymond was such a swine . . . '

'You loved him once,' Edward said reprovingly.

'I know I did,' she said sombrely, 'but he was so weak. Drunkards are such bores, aren't they, darling? I thought I could make him something important in the colony – top dog – but he was too idle, too bloody weak.'

She spoke with a contempt which chilled Edward. He now remembered why they had never become lovers. He had been sorry for her, he had admired her spirit – she was as brave as a lion and flew totally without fear – but she was cold. She had never spoken of her own childhood but it cannot have been happy. She had never managed to learn how to love. That was Edward's diagnosis. Freud might have been interested in her, he thought. She was seductive, she could pretend to love but poor Raymond had not lived up to her expectations and had been humiliated by her. He must have known long before he found her in bed with the odious Douglas Davenant – a remittance man of the worst kind who had never done a day's work in his life – that she was cuckolding him. She had driven the man to drink and suicide. It was as simple as that and yet, as soon as she got back to England, she had been taken up by the Prince and his circle. Edward knew he had some pretty raffish friends but it needed some explaining.

'Raymond left me quite well off, you know,' she said, looking at him speculatively.

'Yes, but how did you meet the King – or rather the Prince as he was then?'

'I met this very sweet man in Cape Town. Lewis Van Buren. I don't know whether your paths have ever crossed?' He shook his head. 'Well, he was an absolute dear. He took charge of me and took me back home and introduced me to David.'

'Were you and this man lovers?' he inquired brutally.

She blushed and Edward felt he had been a cad.

'Sorry, my dear, but you do attract men, don't you?'

'Well, if you want to know, we were lovers, very briefly. He's a diamond merchant – very rich.' She opened her eyes wide. 'I mean *very* rich. A Jew but a nice Jew. I liked him. I felt . . . I felt safe with him.'

'And he introduced you into royal circles?' Edward said ironically.

'Yes, I think he had lent the Prince money . . . anyway, he knew him very well. He said the Prince would love me . . . and he did,' she said simply.

Edward understood that Van Buren was one of those useful men who hang about the rich and famous – lend them money, find them women and do their dirty work. He wondered if Verity might find out something about him through the paper.

'I see. Look, Molly, there are things we have to talk about. I know it's not my business but, as a friend, I hate to see you get into trouble . . . '

'Oh God, Edward, you're not going to lecture me, are you? Anyway, I'm not the one who's going to get into trouble. I've seen a lot of things and I could tell a lot of tales . . . but I don't want to. I just want to be treated . . . fairly. I'm not just a whore to be chucked out with the garbage . . . '

At that moment, to Edward's relief, there was a light knock on the door and Fenton informed him his bath was ready for him.

'Molly, I'd better go and do my ablutions, don't y'know,' he said awkwardly. 'Let's talk after dinner. There are things I want to say to you – not a lecture, I promise, but not just now . . . Fenton, my man, tells me the hot water system in this place is suspect so I ought to go. See you later, eh?'

The bath was a huge ornate affair and the taps were in the shape of dolphins and difficult to manoeuvre but the water was warm enough – just. As he lay looking at the peeling paint on the ceiling, he wished he was in his rooms in Albany. But then his heart beat a little faster. Despite the horror of having to break bread with men like Scannon and his cronies, despite having to extract a lover's letters from a woman betrayed, there was the sheer excitement of being in the same house as Dannie.

3

Larry Harbin was by no means a typical American tourist. At first glance he might have been taken for an academic or a lawyer, and indeed he had a law degree from Harvard, but he was in fact a businessman and financier. He had been born in Baltimore of a wealthy family and was now in his mid-fifties. He had made his own fortune investing in China and Japan but he had travelled the length and breadth of Europe – he could speak French and German fluently. His wealth and influence with President Roosevelt – they had met and become friends at Harvard – had given him access to most of Europe's political leaders and he despised them all, with the possible exception of the German Chancellor. He was not himself a politician and had no wish to be one. He liked to say back home he owned half a dozen senators and as many congressmen and that was enough politics for him. However, Roosevelt trusted his judgement particularly when it came to European politics on which the President was not well informed.

Harbin was impressed with the way Hitler had transformed Germany's economy and given its people self-respect even if it had been at the expense of the Jews and the Communists. He was by instinct and nurture anti-Semitic and his hatred of the trade unions in the United States had made him virulently anti-Communist. He despised French politicians whom he had found to be more corrupt even than the Chinese and he had no faith in England – which was how he always spoke of Britain – being able to win a war against Germany – a war which he considered inevitable. He strongly believed that the United States should keep out of European affairs and had persuaded the President to his view of the hopelessness of Europe.

In his personal habits he was an ascetic. He neither smoked nor drank alcohol. He wore wire-rimmed spectacles which he had a habit of pushing up the bridge of his nose, which was thin and beak-like, whenever he gave an opinion. His suits were made in Savile Row, his only extravagance, and his American accent was so slight as to be hardly noticeable. He was unmarried and had absolutely no sense of humour.

He let slip he owned an oil well in Texas, not in any attempt to impress but to make a point. 'In my view, Leo,' Harbin said in his rather prissy voice, 'your great empire is defenceless unless you guys can assert control over your source of oil – Persia, Iraq. If those places prove indefensible, as I guess they will, then you're lost.'

'So you think there will be war in Europe?' Scannon asked.

'I most surely do. In the next few months your friend Mr Hitler will declare a glorious union between the Reich and Austria – *Zusammenschluss*, – they call it. You've read *Mein Kampf*, haven't you, Leo?'

'I confess I haven't yet, though the Führer signed a copy for me in Berlin.'

'Well, read it. It's all there. On the very first page he declares German-Austria must return to the great German motherland and, as I hear it, the British have said they won't interfere. Lord Halifax told me himself he sees it as a legitimate aspiration of the German people to be at one again.'

Edward was shocked. 'Is that really true, Leo? We would do nothing to prevent Germany swallowing up Austria?'

Scannon nodded. 'In practical terms, what *could* we do?'

'It's natural justice,' Hepple-Keen said. 'We won't go to war about the union of two peoples who share a language and a culture – a voluntary union. If the union happens, in my view it will be an expression of true democracy.'

'Maybe you won't go to war when Herr Hitler walks into Austria, sir, nor when he walks into Czechoslovakia or Poland, but there will be time a when the Reichsführer will walk into France and then you will have to fight and, without wishing to give offence, gentlemen, you're going to lose.'

There was a stunned silence after Harbin had finished speaking. A cold shiver ran down Edward's spine. He didn't like Harbin. There was something bloodless about him but he could not deny the man saw clearly and his vision was by no means comfortable. Edward remembered how his mother had called these shivers 'someone walking over my grave'. The American had expressed Edward's own views on what would happen if Britain did not stand up to Hitler, but hearing Harbin spell out the future in so menacing a way was like finding death itself at the dinner table. And Harbin hadn't quite finished. He was determined they should hear the truth even if they did not like it. 'Where I come from,' he went on, 'we have enough oil to mobilize an army or two but, I have to tell you, there is no way the American people would do that except to defend their own frontiers.'

Scannon said, 'That's what President Wilson said in the last war but in the end you had to come and help sort out the mess.'

'And we learned our lesson,' Harbin said flatly.

Edward noted with interest that the American was hardly eating anything but merely messing his sole about with his fork. On what oil did this man run, he wondered. If Harbin was voicing the President's own views, it was a bleak lookout for England.

The Hepple-Keens were, in their way, just as curious as Mr Larry Harbin. Lady Hepple-Keen – Daphne – was placed next to Edward and sat almost silent during the first two courses. He tried valiantly to find a subject on which she

44

felt strongly enough to express a view but to no effect. She seemed not to like her husband, which Edward thought perfectly reasonable as he put the man down for a bullying cad after being in his presence less than five minutes. She was uninterested in her husband's career and, to judge from her monosyllabic replies to his questions, thoroughly disliked his politics. She was scared of him, Edward decided, and he felt a surge of sympathy for her. She had just lapsed into what he thought might be terminal silence when she suddenly mentioned a child and, to Edward's relief, she now became almost voluble. She had three children, she told him. Little James was only eight and her 'precious little angel', a boy of ten and a girl of eleven who worried her mother sick by refusing to talk. Edward hardly dared guess what the child might be trying to deny by remaining silent. He saw Hepple-Keen looking at him strangely. He was clearly far from pleased to see his wife spilling out family secrets to a complete stranger.

Dinner drew painfully to a close. It had been a dreary affair and Edward was heartily glad when Scannon declared it at an end. Instead of the ladies withdrawing to leave their menfolk to talk politics and smut over the port, Scannon suggested a tour of the house and Edward for one was happy to accede. Molly, too, seemed enthusiastic though she had stayed in the house several times before and knew it well. She grasped Edward by the arm and the rest followed more or less reluctantly. Scannon said, 'We'll go first to the long gallery. My father bought a lot of pictures when the house was being planned and he wanted to show them off. The architect suggested a long room like those you see sometimes in Elizabethan houses. They were used by the ladies as places in which to exercise in bad weather. My father thought it was a good idea to provide exercise for the mind and the body in one room so he hung the pictures on the wall and had some weights, a vaulting horse and a climbing frame fitted. As far as I know, he never used any of them and he certainly never looked at his pictures.'

They climbed the heavy, ugly staircase stopping now and again to look at a claymore or crossed swords attached to the wall. 'Family heirlooms?' Edward queried.

'Not at all,' Scannon said breezily. 'My father was the first of his line to make any money and he didn't see why he had to wait several generations to have a family history. It was much easier to buy it ready made, so to speak.'

'I see. So these portraits . . . ' he was referring to paintings of colourfully dressed gentlemen and ladies of bygone ages on the staircase, 'aren't anything to do with you?'

'Only in so far as my father adopted them. I believe most of them came from a house or castle in Fife that was being broken up at the time my father was building this place.'

The long gallery, when they reached it, proved gloomy and ill lit. There were wall brackets but the electric light was feeble and it was almost impossible to make out the pictures despite their huge size. It was apparent that Scannon's father wanted value for money when he was buying paintings and purchased art by the square yard. Relinquishing Molly's arm, Edward peered at one particular picture which seemed to show several semi-naked ladies around a pool or lake. A strangely muscled man was watching them from behind a bush. Edward wanted to laugh.

'The Judgement of Paris, I believe,' Scannon said, 'by Rossetti or one of those Pre-Raphaelites. My father held the view that art had to do with the classical world. I remember once admiring a picture of card players by Caravaggio and he was indignant. How could card players, however well depicted, be art, he said to me.' He hesitated and then said a little guiltily, 'I hope you don't think I am making fun of my pater. In fact, I admired him greatly. He was one of a family of thirteen and grew up in poverty in Birmingham. By sheer grit and hard work he became rich and, by the time he was twenty, he was supporting the rest of his family. He had no education but was determined I would have what he had not. He wanted me to be an English gentleman so he sent me to Harrow. He refused to let me anywhere near the family business, so I grew up utterly useless.

I had no option but to enter the House of Commons. I was not fit for anything else, and,' he added, 'it made my father happy.'

'He must have been very proud,' Hepple-Keen said.

'I think he was,' Scannon said meditatively.

'When did he die?' Molly asked.

'Ten years ago, but my mother is still alive. I thought we might visit her if that wouldn't be a bore.'

Everyone indicated that they would be only too delighted and Edward was curious. Somehow, Scannon was one of those men you did not think of as having a mother. They stopped on the floor below the gallery and Scannon knocked on a huge mock-gothic door. A voice – quite a young-sounding voice – called on them to come in. They entered – not a room – but a suite of rooms and were greeted by a plain woman – in her mid-thirties, Edward guessed – with heavy spectacles and her hair in a bun on the back of her head. The word spinster might have been coined for her.

'This is Miss Ruth Conway who is good enough to look after my mother for me. Since her stroke she has had to have someone with her all the time.'

'You were there at tea-time when I arrived,' Edward said, recognizing her as the rather severe-looking woman presiding over the teapot to whom he had not been introduced.

'I was, Lord Edward,' she agreed. 'I help out when I can. But come and see Mrs Scannon. I'm afraid it's not one of her good days.'

Rather reluctantly, the party trooped past Miss Conway and entered a bedroom the size of a ballroom. A massive four-poster bed dominated the room and the heavy brocaded canopy, no doubt extracted from some ancient house fallen upon hard times, was moth-eaten and dirty-looking. An old lady lay in the bed supported by pillows. A Pekinese dog was curled up beside her. 'Mother,' Scannon said gently, 'I have brought some people to see you.'

With a gesture Edward was always to remember and which did much to mitigate his dislike of the man, Scannon took out his silk handkerchief and wiped away the spittle from her mouth. Then he sat on the edge of the bed and lifted her papery hand in his, as gently as if he were holding a moth, and kissed it.

There was no response from the recumbent figure and after a minute Scannon stood aside and ushered his guests nearer her bed as though to receive the old woman's blessing. There was something absurd and yet touching in this display of his mother for inspection by strangers. Edward was sure Scannon meant it for the best. Perhaps what he saw was not this wreck of a human being but a woman he had loved and could remember in her prime. None of the visitors were able to think of anything to say. It was clear the old woman was unable to speak or even move her head and it was profoundly embarrassing for those grouped around her bed. She looked straight ahead of her, a thin dribble of spittle leaking down her chin despite her son's mopping. It was with considerable relief that they left the room to Ruth Conway and her charge.

'She's tired today,' Scannon remarked, as if it explained everything.

'It must be difficult for Miss Conway,' Edward ventured.

'In what way?'

'I mean being alone with your mother all day,' he stammered, not wishing to sound unsympathetic.

'She likes it,' Scannon said firmly. 'She has a day off in the week when a girl comes in from the village, but she has nowhere to go.'

How unutterably sad, Edward thought. He found himself thinking of Verity Browne, the absolute opposite of poor Miss Conway, and he suddenly wished he was with her now instead of in this gloomy house with all these people in whom he had no interest whatsoever and whose politics he detested. He caught Dannie's eye at that moment and a slight shiver of guilt or of anticipation – he hardly knew which – ran up his spine.

Gratefully, the little party found themselves once again in the hall but they were not yet to be released. 'We have dungeons here,' Scannon said. 'Not really dungeons,' he added seeing Daphne Hepple-Keen go white. 'There's a games room – a billiard table, ping-pong, that sort of thing.'

'Do you know, I think I'll turn in,' Lord Benyon said, and Inna looked at him gratefully.

'I'm rather tired, too,' Lady Hepple-Keen began timidly.

'Nonsense, my dear. Do buck up, Daphne. You can watch me beat Lord Edward at billiards before going to bed. What about you, Carstairs?'

'I'm game. A hundred up, Corinth?'

Daphne looked beseechingly at Edward who said, 'It *is* rather late – how about tomorrow?'

Dannie said, 'I'm going to bed but you boys do what you want.'

Harbin said, rather unexpectedly, 'Sure, count me in, though I warn you, Leo, I haven't played in years.'

'Right then,' Scannon said. 'Pickering, bring us brandy and cigars, will you?'

They went through a green baize door, down a flight of stairs into a cavernous games room. Scannon switched on two chandeliers but their feeble light left a black pool over the billiard table.

'Turn the table light on, will you, Harbin, there's a good fellow,' Scannon said, making for a rack of cues underneath a score board. Harbin went over to the billiard table and switched on the light which hung low over the green felt, soft as new-mown grass. In a moment, the huge expanse of dark green was transformed into a swathe of emerald, lush as swamp grass. Harbin let out an oath and fell back a pace. The others turned in surprise. To their amazement they saw, sitting plumb in the middle of the billiard table, a huge rat. The animal, half the size of Mrs Scannon's Pekinese, stared back at them, his eyes gleaming yellow in the light. At last, as though reluctant to give way, he lolloped off the table and disappeared into a dark corner of the room. Daphne Hepple-Keen gave a shriek of horror and Hepple-Keen's cigar dropped from his mouth. 'Damn my eyes!' he exclaimed and then apologized. Edward said, vacuously, 'I say, Leo, you'll have to do something about your friend in the morning.'

Carstairs suggested an immediate rat hunt but found no takers. Harbin said sharply, 'Sir Geoffrey, might I suggest you take your wife upstairs and give her a drop of brandy. She's very shaken.'

Edward saw the American was right. Daphne was fighting back tears and, since her husband seemed unable or unwilling to do anything to calm her, he took her gently by the arm and led her up the stairs into the drawing-room. They were soon joined by the others, Scannon apologizing and saying he would get 'the damn thing seen to first thing'. They met Pickering bearing glasses and a decanter.

'Brandy for Lady Hepple-Keen, Pickering, quick as you like. We've all had a bit of a shock. Did you know there were rats in the billiard room?'

Pickering put on an expression of concern. 'I feared there were rats downstairs, sir. I have spoken to Williams about it but he looked and said I was imagining things.'

'Williams is my head gardener,' Scannon explained. 'Well, send him to me after breakfast, will you, Pickering.'

Scannon seemed unmoved by having rats in his cellars. Perhaps it was inevitable in this huge, run-down pile of a house. Edward hoped the bedrooms at least were vermin-free. When he had said his goodnights – Carstairs still protesting at missing a sporting opportunity – he went to his own room and found Fenton turning down the bed. 'There is a hot-water bottle in the bed, my lord,' he said.

'Glad you warned me,' Edward replied. 'I have had enough surprises for the time being,' and he told Fenton about the rat incident.

'Most unpleasant, my lord. I confess to having an antipathy towards the animals, amounting to a phobia.'

'Well, you go to bed, my lad. I expect we gave the rat as much of a shock as he gave us so he won't be exploring.'

'I very much hope not, my lord.'

When he had undressed and donned his pyjamas, Edward wrapped himself in his dressing gown and, rather reluctantly, went out into the corridor and knocked on Molly's door. There was a good deal of scuffling on the other side of the door and he wondered what was up. It was odd how embarrassing it was to be doing this when, after all, he had spent so many nights alone with her in Africa – chastely enough, but intimate nevertheless. But this was England and he determined he was going to tell her he would postpone their talk to the morning. He could not understand what had made him suggest talking this evening except that he wanted to get the whole thing over and done with. It wasn't late but he would have some explaining to do if he were caught corridor–creeping.

Molly opened her door clad in a diaphanous dressing gown which barely covered her pyjamas. 'Oh, it's you,' she said, as though she had been expecting someone else. She looked – as no doubt she knew – alluring. He noticed she was still wearing her make-up. 'Sorry to take so long opening the door but it's rather stiff.'

'I say,' he said, 'I thought maybe it would be better if we had our chat tomorrow. I've got a bit of a head, made none the better for meeting a rat on Leo's billiard table.'

'Oh, how priceless! Do tell. Come in for a moment. It would be much safer than talking out here. People will get quite the wrong impression. It would be the wrong impression, wouldn't it, Edward? I find I've been regretting all those missed opportunities in Africa. It was bliss, wasn't it, darling?'

Edward did not like the 'darling'. He had not come to Haling to have an affair with Molly Harkness.

'It was fun but we were all a bit younger then.'

He couldn't think why he had said that. It wasn't what he had meant to say and it sounded rude. 'I mean, you're still deliciously young, but I'm . . . '

'Oh, do shut up, Edward. You know you only feel old when you want to.' She drew him into the room, got into bed and insisted he sat on the edge of it, not in the chair he made for at first. 'I want you near me. We can't talk about . . . intimate things if you're the other side of the room.'

He was now highly embarrassed. What if he was to start accusing her of theft and blackmail and she made a scene and screamed rape? He oughtn't to be here. He got up, but she pulled him down.

'Darling Edward. You're so good-looking and you think I'm just an old witch.'

'No, no, of course not,' he said desperately.

'Well, if you haven't come to make love to me what have you come for?'

There was a hint of steel in her voice which gave him pause.

'I . . . I was dining with Joe Weaver the other night and he . . . '

'Joe! He's such a sweetie. Did he say anything about . . . ?'

'He said you had run off with some letters belonging to Wallis Simpson. Is that true?'

Molly wrapped her dressing gown round her with exaggerated care. 'I hope you haven't come to scold me, Edward. That would be so unlike you. You're my friend – my closest friend.'

'I am your friend and that's why I am trying to prevent you making the most awful fool of yourself. You did take the letters, then?'

'What! You're not some sort of policeman too, are you?'

'No. Joe thought that, as a friend, I might be the best person to sort all this out before anyone had to resort to policemen.'

Molly said nothing for a moment and Edward wondered what she had meant by asking if he was 'some sort of policeman, *too*'. He supposed there was never going to be a good time to accuse her of theft but eleven thirty in her bedroom might very well be the worst. He wondered if she would deny having taken the letters or accuse him of betraying her.

In the event she said, 'I did take the letters.' She spoke in a small, tight voice, close to a scream. He must try and calm her, he thought. It was like dealing with a wild animal, small, unpredictable and with sharp claws.

'But why? Why take them? Was it to embarrass Mrs Simpson?'

'That woman!' Molly spoke in a vehement hiss. 'She's evil. David loved me. He really loved me and she came and took him from me and now she's going to ruin him.'

'From what I've heard,' he said sourly, 'I begin to wonder if he can love. He seems infatuated with Wallis but I'm not sure it's love.'

'He *did* love me. He's a dear man. He wrote to me – lots and lots and I've got those letters. He's never even asked for them back.' She sounded puzzled, insulted. 'It was awful, Edward. I used to speak to him on the telephone several times a day and then one day they said he wasn't at home, only I knew he was. And I never spoke to him again.'

'You mean, he never tried to explain or anything?'

'No, he just wasn't there. I couldn't get near him. His secretary . . . his friends like Fruity Metcalfe just wouldn't let me see him. It was her. I know it was her. She told him to forget me and he did.'

'Oh Molly,' he said, getting up from the bed, 'I'm so sorry. You must be very hurt but there's nothing you can do. You've just got to accept that royals do things differently.'

It was lame. He knew it was lame but what could he say? She had been turned off without a word like a pregnant lady's maid. Her lover's conduct had been shameful but there was no way back. He must try and make her see that.

'But there is something I can do about it. I know I can't get him back. I wouldn't want him back – not if he came crawling . . . ' Edward did not believe that for an instant. He had seen her face when she had imagined he had come with a message from him. '. . . but, I *can* stop him having Wallis Simpson. I can do that . . . for the good of the country,' she added piously.

'You mean you can blackmail her . . . ?'

Molly looked at him suspiciously. 'They've told you about my letter, then?'

'Yes.'

'That wasn't blackmail. I didn't ask for money. I didn't ask for anything for myself. I just asked that she should go away.' She spat out the words. 'And, if it came to a court of law, no one could say . . . '

Edward shuddered. He had a vision of Mrs Simpson standing at the witness box discussing her private affairs in front of the gawping crowd. That at least could not be allowed to happen. 'But Molly, your bitterness I can understand. You have been treated shabbily.'

'Shabbily! I *have* been treated shabbily, as you so quaintly put it, but you don't seem to understand. That woman is a monster.'

Edward thought about the woman with whom he had sat at dinner: calm, reasonable, intelligent. She might be – what did they say? – 'on the make'. She might be a little too avid for precious stones; she might have an unhealthy influence over the King. But to call her a monster – that was patently ridiculous.

'Surely not,' he said gently.

Molly made as if she were going to embrace him. He could smell the wine on her breath and see the crow's-feet under her eyes. She was still a beautiful woman but in a few more years she would – if she did not find a good man – descend into that circle of hell reserved for 'women with a past', women who had been dealt a good hand but had been destroyed by kings and knaves.

'Did they say I had taken anything else from Mrs Simpson?' She demanded. 'I'm not a thief.'

'No, they just said you'd taken letters.'

'Letters, yes. Letters from the King revealing the power that woman has over him. He tells her everything, Edward, not just love talk. He says in one letter how the Prime Minister feels about the possibility of Germany uniting itself with Austria. He quotes Lord Halifax . . . and so on,' she ended, seeing that Edward's eyes had opened wide.

'He oughtn't to have discussed government policy with her . . . '

'And he says "ask Ribbentrop what I should do".'

'I don't believe it,' Edward said after a moment to take in the folly of the man who was his king. 'But you cannot possibly think of giving these letters to the newspapers. They wouldn't print them, of course, but if any of it leaked out . . . '

'I know and of course I wouldn't. Did you know, they've already tried to take them back?'

'Who?'

'I don't know – the police, I suppose,' she said vaguely.

'You think it wasn't burglars?'

'What burglars don't steal jewellery lying on a dressing table, or money in a wallet?'

'I see. Presumably they didn't find what they were looking for?'

'No,' she said, smiling like a naughty child. 'They did not. You see, I never leave them anywhere I am not. Even when I go down to dinner I carry them on me.'

'You've got them on you now?'

'I might have. Are you going to find out?' she said archly.

Edward withdrew his hand which was resting on her arm. 'No, of course not. But don't you realize you are in danger? Aren't you afraid that if it gets around you have these . . . these documents, someone – maybe someone you know nothing about, an enemy agent, a newspaperman – might try and take them from you? You're in deep water, Molly. Hand them over to me and then you will be able to sleep in peace.'

'No!' she said defiantly. 'Why should I? Anyway, there's more to it than that. In one of the letters the King refers to a report he has seen – a government report about her.'

'About Wallis?'

'I think so. There's not much about it but I get the feeling it's a report about her background. You know there are some quite unpleasant stories about her first marriage?'

'She was in the Far East?'

55

'Yes, but I heard her husband was a drunkard and a crook – I know about those,' she said bitterly. 'I've heard it said he humiliated her – took her to houses of . . . well, they say he did horrible things to her, made her whore for him.'

Edward thought for a moment. It was more than likely that the intelligence services would have looked into Mrs Simpson's background and, if they had found out she was . . . unsuitable to be a decent man's wife, let alone a king's . . . It hardly bore thinking about. He said at last, 'Molly, it frightens me, all this. I thought you were just indulging in . . . I don't know . . . understandable pique, but what you are telling me is very serious. I beg you to hand over to me what you have – for your own safety.'

'No!' she said firmly. 'If the King invites me to Fort Belvedere and asks me nicely . . . '

'Oh God . . . Molly, he won't do that.'

'Well then . . . '

'Look, I'm going to go off to bed. I won't be such a *connard* as to offer you money for returning the letters but just think about what I've said. I do care about you, Molly, and I would hate to see you hurt – I mean hurt more than you have been. I suppose you won't show me them – the letters?'

'Sorry, Edward dear – nothing doing. I'm not that much of a fool!'

He was shocked. 'You don't think I would grab them out of your hand and make a run for it, do you?'

'Better not put temptation in your way. I know I couldn't resist it.'

'Let's talk again in the morning. You have had bad luck, my dear, and I'm truly sorry for you but this is . . . you must see, this is different. You are meddling in affairs of state.'

'Don't patronize me, Edward, and don't be pompous. You're just a messenger . . . a carrier pigeon,' she said contemptuously. 'Go back and tell the people who sent you, I want the King to ask me . . . ask me nicely to hand back his letters. I don't think it's so very much to ask.'

'I'm sorry. I don't mean to be a bore but . . . ' He almost saw her hackles rise and decided not to say what he had been going to say: that what she wanted was out of the question. Instead he said, 'Will you be able to sleep?'

He had noticed a bottle of Maalox tablets beside her bed.

'Oh those,' she said, following his eyes. 'I don't find those are strong enough on their own. I've got veronal in the cupboard. I couldn't live without it.'

'You will be careful, won't you, Molly? You shouldn't mix Maalox and veronal.'

'Dear Edward! You're so sweet. Of course I'm careful. Look, I'll think about what you have said, I promise.'

'Right then. Good night.' He went to kiss her on the cheek but at the last moment she turned her head and kissed him on the mouth. He hesitated for a second and then, rather guiltily, returned her kiss.

'Go now,' she said. 'We'll talk some more in the morning. In the daylight things can look . . . different . . . clearer.'

Edward opened the bedroom door a crack and, seeing the corridor empty, slipped out of Molly's bedroom and into his own. He had achieved precisely nothing – made things worse if anything, but at least he now knew the scale of the problem. Weaver had been less than frank with him, unless he did not know himself the full explosive power of what Molly had got hold of.

It was almost midnight. His room was in darkness but there was a moon and a little light shone through a gap in the curtains and illuminated the bed. There was no way of switching off the light from the bed so he decided not to switch it on. As he walked towards the bed he was startled to hear a voice from among the bedclothes – a deep, husky voice he recognized instantly. 'You've been gone a long time. I hope Molly hasn't exhausted you.'

'Dannie!' he whispered fiercely. 'Is that you? What are you doing in my bed?'

'What do you think I'm doing in your bed? I admit I had no idea there was a queue and that I would have to wait so long but now I'm here . . . '

'But Dannie, I . . . '

'You do want me, don't you? You've making eyes at me ever since we met.'

'Of course I want you but . . . '

'Not now? I hope you're not one of those Englishmen who can't deliver what they promise. Have you been making love to Molly?'

'No! It was business.'

'In the middle of the night. How very mysterious! Is it what Joe was talking to you about? Mrs Simpson . . . ?'

'I'm not at liberty to . . . '

'Don't be pompous. Everyone says you can be terribly pompous. I hope you weren't pompous with Molly. Perhaps you *ought* to have made love to her. She'll not sleep, you know, if you've left her . . . upset.'

'Yes she will. She's taken something to make her sleep,' he said weakly.

It was an odd thing, but having his fantasy become reality so unexpectedly, so easily, almost unmanned him. He was old-fashioned enough to believe that it was the man who should make the first move and the lady – if she were a lady – ought to put up a show of resistance . . . at least at first. Anyway, there had to be some sort of verbal lovemaking . . . some sort of declaration, however insincere, before the act of love. But, of course, this woman wasn't English. She probably didn't even understand what it meant to be an English lady . . . But she was so beautiful: a sleek, potentially lethal animal and she was offering herself to him as casually as Pickering had offered him dessert at dinner. If he didn't take what was offered him, he would insult her and he had a feeling that insulting Dannie would be a dangerous thing to do. He stood there in his dressing gown, silk pyjamas, and bedroom slippers almost paralysed by indecision.

'Well, my sweet,' the voice from the bed was impatient, caustic, '*I* haven't taken anything to make me sleep . . . yet.'

The moon, which had passed behind a cloud, reappeared and its silvery light came to rest upon a brown silky arm.

Her eyes, the eyes of a wild cat caught in the headlights of a car, gleamed brightly as she threw back the sheet which covered her. He groaned aloud and the woman on the bed laughed – a low, throaty laugh which mocked his weakness. He wanted this woman worse than any woman he had ever seen and the stirring in his loins suggested that he wasn't as tired as he had thought. He sighed, slipped off his dressing gown and pyjamas and slid under the bedclothes.

'That was a big sigh for a little boy,' she whispered into his ear. 'I hope it doesn't mean you're not up to . . .' A warm hand travelled down his stomach making him arch away from her. 'Ah! That's all right then,' she said.

The feel of her arms about him, her warm, silky flesh pressed against his, the smell of her – a bitter scent of sexual excitement – the way her tongue found its way into his mouth . . . kindled in him a raw lust he thought he had left behind with boyhood. He knew he was weak, and possibly wicked, but somehow it didn't seem to matter.

'Dannie!' he cried as he entered her, but she placed her hand over his mouth to silence him.

4

Fenton woke his master with a knock on the door at eight o'clock and, as was his custom, placed a cup of tea on the bedside table and then went over to the window to draw the curtains. Before he did so, he picked up the discarded dressing gown from the floor and hung it on the back of the door and folded the pyjamas on a chair. He looked meditatively at the bed where Edward lay comatose, only the top of his head visible from within a tangle of sheets and blankets. With a dramatic flourish which signalled disapproval, he opened the curtains letting the sun pour into the room. Edward groaned, opened one eye and said reproachfully, 'I say, Fenton ...' Then, as he recalled the events of the night before, he fell silent. He had no secrets from Fenton but there were proprieties to be observed. Furtively, he stretched out an arm and, to his surprise and relief, did not come across warm flesh. Had it been his imagination? Had his night with Dannie been a dream of love-making? But no! A dry, very slightly bitter scent flooded his nostrils as he turned in the bed. The musk of her body was evidence enough that he had not been dreaming.

'I trust you slept well, my lord,' Fenton said with studied indifference.

'Oh, very well ... that is, I was a little restless,' he said, noticing the state his bed was in. 'Too hot ... I was too hot . . . had to get up in the middle of the night and take off my . . . you know, my togs.'

'Indeed, my lord?' Fenton said, making no effort to disguise his scepticism. 'Breakfast in thirty minutes, my lord, unless it is your desire that I bring you a tray from the kitchen.'

'No thank you, Fenton. I will dress and descend. Is everyone else up, do you know?'

'I saw Mr Scannon as I was coming up the stairs, my lord. I have not seen any other of the guests though I did hear Mr Harbin in the bathroom. He was singing.'

'Damn! Does that mean I can't have a shave?'

'No, my lord. I have ascertained he has vacated the bathroom.'

'What about Mrs Harkness?'

'I have not heard anything from her room, my lord. She has no maid here, I understand. Would you want me to knock on her door?'

'Righty ho! Pass me my dressing gown, there's a good fellow, and stop looking as if you've just been notified of a death in the family.'

He was suddenly overcome by the langour of a night spent in love-making and sank back on his pillows with a smile on his face. Fenton knew that smile and, though not a muscle in his face twitched, he smiled too. He could not long be disapproving of his master's 'little adventures', as he labelled them, but he was curious as to whether the lady who had spent the night in his master's bed had been Mrs Harkness or the woman they called 'Dannie'. He didn't approve of her at all. She was not a lady in his view. The opinion of the servants' hall was that she was 'no better than she should be'. Though Fenton did not gossip, he had heard Cook say 'the foreign girl was nothing but a trollop' and that 'Lord Weaver had the keeping of her and ought to be ashamed, him being a lord and all'. Why, he even preferred Verity Browne to that 'baggage'. But a lady's name was not to be bandied about between servant and master so nothing would be said, though in time all would be revealed.

Edward must have dozed off because he was suddenly aware that Fenton was shaking his arm.

'My lord, I have knocked on Mrs Harkness's door but there is no answer.'

'Oh well,' Edward said yawning, 'I expect she has already gone downstairs.'

'No, my lord, she has not gone down yet. I have spoken to Mr Pickering whom I happened to see on the stairs.'

'Is her door locked?'

'Yes, my lord.'

'She must have taken too strong a sleeping draught.' Sighing, he got out of bed and put on the dressing gown Fenton handed him. He went out into the passage and knocked loudly on Molly's door but there was no response.

'I say, Fenton. I'm probably going to make a fool of myself but can you ask Pickering if he has a duplicate key to the door? I'd feel easier in my mind if I could just see she's all right. She was in a bit of a state last night and I suppose it's possible she might have taken a little too much of whatever it was she was taking to help her sleep.'

'Yes, my lord.'

While Fenton went to find the butler, Edward contemplated doing battle with the primitive-looking shower he had noticed above the bath. He wanted only a burst of cold water over his head, and then to be fed scrambled eggs and bacon, to feel ready and able to cope with anything the new day might throw at him. Harbin, whose room was on the other side of Molly's, appeared, pulling his braces over his shoulders. 'Something the matter?' he said, seeing Edward.

'I hope not. I've been trying to rouse Molly – Mrs Harkness – but she isn't answering.'

'She's probably gone downstairs.'

'Fenton, my man, says not and the door seems to be locked.'

Harbin came and twisted the door handle. 'Mmm, I told our host she would cause trouble.'

'You told Leo that Molly would cause trouble? Why?'

'She didn't tell you? I met her with the Prince a few months back. I told him then he ought to get rid of her. I don't know why it took him so long.'

'I'm sorry, you must think me obtuse – why do you have it in for Molly?'

'The usual thing – sex. When she saw how Wallis was prospering, she started rumours about her – about how she had had affairs – gossip and scandal-mongering. Your young friend was making trouble for a lady – a lady from my home town. I said to Leo, if I'd known she was going to be one of the guests here, I would not have come.'

Edward was disapproving. In his book, one did not make those kind of remarks without very good reason and certainly not when one was outside the bedroom door of the lady in question. He temporized: 'She's not very sensible about men, I grant you, but I think you're being a bit hard on her. Ah! Here they are!'

Fenton rounded the corner of the corridor with Pickering and Scannon in hot pursuit.

'Oh, Scannon, I didn't mean them to disturb you. It's just I wanted to be sure Molly hadn't taken too much of her sleeping draught. It's easily done.'

Before Scannon could reply, Pickering had opened the door and Edward went straight over to the bed. Molly lay on her back covered by a sheet up to her neck. The blankets were on the floor as if they had been thrown off by a restless sleeper. Molly's eyes were wide open but unseeing, blinded by death. Even before he felt for a pulse, Edward knew she would never again sleep with a man or feel the wind in her face as she flew her aeroplane across the African Karoo.

'Oh Molly! Molly!' he murmured to himself in extreme agitation. 'It can't be. How could it have happened? Oh God! Molly, my lovely, foolish Molly!'

As he rose to his feet, his face ashen, he almost stumbled. Was it his fate always to bring death to the people he knew and valued? Did he contaminate every house he entered? It seemed so. Here was an old friend with whom he had shared danger and discomfort and now she was dead. How had it happened? By what route had death entered the room? Was it an accident? Is death *ever* an accident? His eyes fell on the flask, from which he and Molly had drunk the previous evening, lying on the floor beside the bed. He stooped to pick it up and then checked himself. He had better leave everything as he had found it. He turned to the little group of silent men in the doorway – Fenton, Pickering, Harbin and his host, Leo Scannon. This was going to cause trouble for Scannon . . . for all of them, he thought. Poor Molly! She would cause trouble in death as she had in life – it was not much of an epitaph and he grew suddenly angry.

'I'm very sorry, Leo, but Molly's dead,' he said flatly. 'It looks as though she must have taken too much of whatever it was she was using to help her sleep – veronal, I think she said. There was brandy in her flask. She gave me a nip last night. If it *was* veronal she was taking, she must have forgotten that mixed with alcohol it can be . . . well, you know . . . it might have made it . . . lethal.'

Still Scannon said nothing, too shocked to speak, so Edward addressed the butler: 'Pickering, will you ring for a doctor and for the police. I expect it was just a tragic accident. Molly was rather overwrought but we have to face the fact that her death might be . . . '

'Murder?' Scannon squawked, his agitation almost preventing him from speaking.

'I was going to say suicide but, yes, of course it might be murder. The last thing she said to me was that we would talk some more tomorrow. She wasn't suicidal.'

'Her door was locked,' Fenton pointed out, 'and there is no key in it.'

'But where is the key if it's not in the door?' Scannon demanded, grasping at this simple puzzle as though it were the answer to everything.

'I suppose Molly must have put it somewhere when she went to bed,' said Edward, 'but I admit I can't see it anywhere.'

Harbin came into the room and stared impassively at the dead woman. 'I guess I shouldn't have said what I did a moment ago,' he said to Edward.

Edward ignored him and went over to the window, which was open. The Virginia creeper was strong and had entwined itself round a drainpipe to make an easy climb for a fit man – or woman. There was no obvious sign of it having been used as a ladder, however. He checked himself. That was something for the police to consider, not him. 'Leo, I think the best thing we can do is to leave the room as we found it until the police have a chance of examining it.'

Harbin said, 'You say Mrs Harkness did not seem suicidal to you, Lord Edward, when you last spoke with her. When did you have this conversation?'

'Just before I turned in – about midnight. I suppose I was the last person to see her alive.'

'And you heard nothing during the night?' Harbin persisted.

'No,' Edward said shortly, 'did you?'

'Nothing.'

It was suddenly borne in on him that the police would expect some straight answers from him to some fairly obvious questions and he did not know how far he could go in answering them truthfully. They would want to know what he had been talking to Molly about so late at night, for one thing. The police would assume he had slept with her unless he told them about Dannie and he couldn't do that. They would soon hear the stories that he had been Molly's lover in Kenya. Untrue they might be, but he could never disprove them. Damn and blast! He was now going to pay for taking his pleasure so unwisely last night. He had heard nothing in the night. Why? Probably because there was nothing to hear but perhaps because, after making love to Dannie, he had fallen into a deep post-coital sleep. Had *she* heard anything? He must talk to her as soon as possible to 'get their story straight'. He grimaced. He hated the idea of lying to the police but, unless she gave him permission, he couldn't drag Dannie into it. Could he tell the police why

65

he was in the house in the first place? Not without Mrs Simpson's permission. Oh God! What a mess!

Pickering returned from telephoning. 'The police and Dr Fisher will be with us shortly, sir,' he said to Scannon.

'Very good,' Scannon said abruptly. 'Who did you speak to?'

'Inspector Lampfrey, sir.'

'Lampfrey? Oh yes, I remember him. Didn't he come here when Lady Biggar lost her diamonds?'

'Yes, sir.'

'I ought to ring the Chief Constable though. Dear me! Dear me!'

Scannon made a visible effort to pull himself together and, as far as Edward could tell, his agitation was unfeigned.

'Did Mrs Harkness have a maid with her, Pickering?' he barked.

'No, sir, she did not. I offered her Betsy – one of the housemaids – to help her dress, but she said she had no need of anyone.'

'I see. Dear me! What a . . . Look, I think the best thing is if we all go down and wait in the drawing-room for the police to arrive. There's nothing else we can do here. Pickering, lock the door and keep hold of the key until the police arrive.'

'Yes, sir.'

'Lord Edward, may I have a brief word with you?'

Scannon led Edward into a small room he used as a study, closed the door and began immediately to abuse him. 'For God's sake, what the devil did you do to the poor girl last night to make her take her own life? Or did you put something in her drink and do it for her? And what about the letters? Did she give them to you?'

'No, I . . .'

'I told Weaver I thought you'd make a mess of things but, by God, I never imagined it would come to this! To have one of my guests die and the police crawling all over the house. And what do we say about why you were interrogating the woman in the middle of the night, eh, Corinth? What do you say to that? My God . . .'

'Steady on, Scannon, this is nothing to do with me . . . '

'Nothing to do with you that the moment you start talking to this bloody woman she dies!'

'I had a perfectly reasonable conversation with her about the letters – a conversation we were going to continue today. There was no hint that she would take her own life and I certainly don't believe she did. Either she took an overdose of her sleeping draught by mistake or someone murdered her and probably took the letters.'

'You don't mean the stuff she had stolen was actually in her bedroom and you didn't get hold of it?'

'How could I? I wasn't going to knock her about until she parted with them, was I?'

'Well, for God's sake, we ought to search her room before the police arrive.'

'That's not a good idea, Scannon,' Edward said evenly.

'Why not? Are you yellow?'

'No, Scannon, but . . . ' they heard the front door bell pealing, 'it's too late and in any case it would have been totally irresponsible.'

'But what do we tell the police?'

'I have been thinking about that. I believe you ought to telephone Joe Weaver and get him to speak to Mrs Simpson. She must be told what has happened straight away and that we have no alternative but to tell the police the truth and trust to their discretion. We don't need to give them any details about what the letters were – just that Molly had stolen them and I was trying to get them back without causing a scandal.'

'Without causing a scandal . . . pfff! I suppose this isn't a scandal?'

'If we don't tell them what I was doing here, they'll think of all sorts of motives for her killing herself – if that's what they decide happened – and when, as is inevitable, they find we have been concealing the obvious motive, it will all get horribly messy. What sort of man will they send us?'

'Inspector Lampfrey. He's all right,' Scannon said, calming himself with an effort. 'I'll go and ring the Chief

Constable as soon as I've spoken to Lampfrey and impress on him how important it is to keep all this as quiet as possible . . . So, we'll just say Molly was an old friend of both of us and we were trying to persuade her not to be a damn fool. But heavens!' Scannon was looking aghast. 'It's just struck me. If she was murdered, someone here – someone in this house did it. And the letters . . . where are they? They may be half-way to Fleet Street or even America by now.' He buried his face in his hands. 'Oh Christ! The King will blame me for this and . . . '

At that moment, there was a knock on the door and Pickering entered. 'Inspector Lampfrey has arrived, sir, and he would be grateful for a word with you.'

'Yes, of course,' Scannon said and, throwing one further look of disgust at Edward, went out of the room. Edward sighed and then rubbed his forehead with his hand as if to wipe away sweat. It was a gesture he often made at moments of extreme pressure and he had no idea he made it. Then, pulling himself together, he followed his host out of the room.

He hesitated in the corridor and then, instead of going downstairs, he made his way back to his room. He didn't know if it was callous of him but he felt he could not meet the policeman until he had shaved and dressed. Fenton was not in the bedroom but he had laid out his clothes on the bed. Edward was about to go to the bathroom at the end of the passage when he saw that the screen in the corner of his room had been moved to reveal the door which it normally concealed – the door which connected his room with Molly's. On an impulse, he went over to it and tried the handle. It was unlocked. He knew he ought to have been surprised but he was not. There was no key on his side of the door. He hesitated and then turned the doorknob and entered Molly's room. He noticed that there was no key on Molly's side of the door either. A screen, similar to the one in his room, blocked his view. He peered round it and was once again shocked to see the body on the bed. The foolish but so very much alive woman, whom he had threatened and cajoled the night before, was now so very dead.

A tide of sadness swept over him. He knew it would be only a matter of seconds before the police were in the room so he looked about him for some obvious hiding place in which Molly might have secreted Mrs Simpson's love letters. He opened the cupboard. One thing struck him immediately. The bottle of veronal she said she had kept in it was not there now. He glanced round the room but there was no sign of it. He saw a small brown leather attaché case – hardly bigger than a lady's handbag – in the corner of the room. He went over and tried to open it but it was locked. He thought for about half a second and then, hearing the sound of approaching feet, took up the case and returned with it to his own room, closing the door behind him. He thrust it under the bed as if the very sight of it made him feel as guilty as an Egyptian tomb robber. It was odd that robbing a dead person seemed so much worse than stealing from a live one. He replaced the screen and then sat on the bed and thought. Someone had opened the door connecting his room and Molly's between the time Fenton had tried it – say six o'clock the previous evening – and when he woke up. That person could only be Dannie. He supposed it was just possible someone had opened the door from Molly's side but for what possible reason? No, it had to be Dannie.

He grimaced. It occurred to him that he had probably left fingerprints on the door handle in Molly's room but there was going to be so much to explain anyway he really couldn't worry about it. He heard the door to Molly's room open and the sound of feet as one or possibly two police officers went over to examine the body. He cursed. They would soon notice that the door connecting her room to his was unlocked. What if they searched his room before he could remove the attaché case? He was beginning to wish he had left it where it was. Was it safe under his bed? He looked around the room but, big though it was, there weren't many obvious places in which to hide an object as

69

bulky as a handbag. He went over to the fireplace and peered under the chimney piece. He thought he could see a ledge there. Yes! He could feel there was. Without further ado, he removed the case from under his bed and stuck it up on the ledge, managing to get some soot on his hands and dressing gown as he did so.

Then he marched out of his room, past a police constable on guard outside Molly's room, who looked at him with some surprise, and into the bathroom where he shaved and washed himself and his dressing gown sleeve as thoroughly as he could. Twenty minutes later, bathed – the water had been almost cold but nonetheless welcome – shaved and dressed in a suit of heather mixture, he walked downstairs with as much of an air of innocence as he could muster.

Inspector Lampfrey was cool but not hostile. In fact, his courtesy was rather alarming. Only a fool would have heard his slow Wiltshire burr and put him down for a country bumpkin. The silence with which he listened to Edward's account of his conversations with Molly suggested not disbelief but ironic detachment, as if he had heard every story ever told but was quite prepared to hear them again. As Edward completed his account of what had happened the previous night, there was silence. Lampfrey regarded him with clear grey eyes which seemed to weigh him up and judge him. He was glad that, on reflection, he had decided to tell the truth – though not quite the whole truth. He doubted whether he could have withstood for long the disconcerting habit the Inspector had of leaving long silences after a question had been very fully answered. It encouraged the witness to tell more than was wise or reveal himself through some inappropriate joke or comment about someone else.

While he was waiting to be interviewed by the Inspector, Edward had had another word with Scannon. The latter had spoken to Joe Weaver and then to the Chief Constable who had been told why it was necessary the press should be kept in ignorance of Molly's death for as long as possible. They were bound to find out sooner or later – there would have to be an inquest for one thing – but, if the coroner was able to find that she had died of an accidental overdose of veronal, there wouldn't be much of a story. In the meantime, it was agreed that every assistance was to be given to Inspector Lampfrey short of telling him in detail the contents of the stolen letters. Edward would never have agreed to anything less. He was in an awkward enough position as it was, without putting himself absolutely in the wrong by withholding information from the police. There was one thing he held back from the Inspector and that was finding Catherine Dannhorn in his bed when he had got back from his late-night interview with Molly.

He had not had a chance of talking to Dannie. Rather annoyingly, he had discovered, when he had gone down to breakfast, that she had ridden out early with Boy Carstairs and had not yet returned and, it was to be supposed, remained in ignorance of Molly's death. However, he assumed she would not volunteer that she had been in his bed instead of her own. In fact, there were several reasons for his deciding to be silent on this one point – perhaps too many reasons to be entirely convincing. He had been told as a child that if one decided to make an excuse for behaving badly, then one should limit it to one. The more excuses one made, the less weight they carried. But, of course, he wasn't actually lying; merely being gentlemanly. Gentlemen do not talk about their sexual adventures. But this wasn't it exactly. He also did not wish to seem promiscuous, unscrupulous or unprincipled. He might not have much respect for middle-class morality but he fancied the Inspector would look at him with those cool eyes of his and find him wanting. What this all boiled down to was that he was embarrassed. It was not like him to jump into bed with a woman he had only known a few days and whom he had never spoken to at any length, let alone kissed. His escapade, as he termed it in his own mind, was lust pure and simple. Could lust be pure, he wondered? He wasn't certain it was even simple now he came to think about it.

71

His feelings for Dannie were surely more complex than lust, weren't they? He had been hit by a thunderbolt; he was obsessed, he was captivated – all these; but he was not 'in love'. He was almost sure he was not in love.

'I see,' Lampfrey said after a pause which seemed to stretch out until kingdom come. 'So when you left Mrs Harkness at . . . ' he consulted his notes, 'twelve fifteen, she did not seem to you suicidal?'

'No, she was upset – no, not upset exactly but nervous, strung up. But she specifically said to me that we would continue our conversation in the morning.'

'That certainly doesn't sound like a suicide but I suppose she might have lain awake worrying, or slept but woken in the middle of the night and decided to end it all.'

'It's more likely she woke and mixed herself another sleeping draught and overdid it. I knew her quite well in Africa, as I told you, and she wasn't the suicide type. She had great guts and, even after her husband's death, she never gave way to depression. By the way, here's one odd thing. Mrs Harkness said she had a bottle of veronal in the cupboard – I had asked her if she would manage to sleep. In my brief inspection of the room, I didn't see it. It certainly wasn't in the cupboard. I looked.'

The Inspector grunted. 'We found nothing – no bottle – just the flask.'

'When will we know for sure what killed her?'

'Dr Fisher says we will have his report by tomorrow evening at the latest. Speaking of her husband – you said she had a lover? Was it certain – what was his name . . . ?'

'Douglas Davenant.'

'No, I mean the husband.'

'Oh, Raymond Harkness.'

'Yes. Do we assume it really was suicide?'

'What do you mean?'

'She and the lover didn't "bump him off"?' The Inspector seemed pleased with his attempt at American slang. He enjoyed going to the pictures and the films of Edward G. Robinson were favourites of his.

'No, certainly not. Her grief – or rather her shock – was very deep. That was why I wanted to take her away.'

'Very commendable.'

'And don't forget, she finished with Davenant.'

'Mmm. Well, I'm sure you're right, Lord Edward. You knew her well.'

'I did but, as I said to you, we were never lovers. I just felt sorry for her. She was a fool with men. Some women seem to have a talent for picking rotters and there were plenty to choose from in Kenya. I think her affairs were a sort of despair. Happy Valley! What a misnomer. That place destroyed many a happy marriage.'

'Very public-spirited of you,' the Inspector said and then added, in case Edward thought he was being sarcastic, 'I mean it.' He paused again. 'So you haven't found these letters then?'

'No.'

'But she said she had them with her?'

'That's what I understood her to say.'

'My men have been through the room with a fine-tooth comb and they aren't there so we must assume they were either stolen or she left them elsewhere – hid them.'

'I suppose so.'

'Mr Scannon says she gave him nothing to put in the safe. They had a burglary here last year – some diamonds were stolen from a guest – and since then, Mr Scannon tells me, he has insisted house guests give him anything of value to be locked in the safe.'

'She would not have trusted Mr Scannon – or anyone else – with the letters. She told me her flat in London had been ransacked quite recently and, since nothing had been stolen, she believed whoever had done it had been looking for the letters.'

'But they didn't find them?'

'No.'

'Did she have any idea who might have searched her flat?'

'She thought it might have been someone acting for the letters' owner.'

'Hmm. I suppose that is the obvious conclusion. So these papers are a motive for murder?'

'Yes.'

'Right, thank you, Lord Edward. You have been very helpful. Oh, by the way. I suppose you won't have any objection to one of my men searching your room?'

'Whatever for?'

'Well, I believe your story but you can understand that I would be failing in my duty if I did not establish that you had not taken the opportunity of removing the letters at some time during the night. Please don't think, Lord Edward, that I am picking on you, so to speak. We will search the whole house. We must be thorough.'

Edward tried not to gulp but he saw the Inspector look at him speculatively.

'Yes, I understand. Um, Inspector, I'm now going to seem to you to be very foolish.'

'My lord?'

'Just before you arrived I did remove a handbag, or small attaché case, from beside her bed. It was wrong of me, I know, but I thought, if it did contain the papers we were talking about, I could return them to their rightful owner without a fuss.' He was sweating and he felt like a murderer under the Inspector's gaze. 'It was idiotic of me. I see that now,' he babbled.

'And did the handbag or small attaché case contain the letters?'

'It was locked. I hid it . . . I hid it in the chimney meaning to examine it later.'

'Well, I think the best thing we can do is to retrieve it and open it, don't you, Lord Edward?'

The Inspector examined the rather sooty bag which now lay on the table at the foot of Edward's bed. 'I really don't see much point in testing this for fingerprints after being covered in soot,' the policeman said, examining the case closely. 'Presumably there must be a key to the case?'

'I haven't seen it,' Edward said, still feeling like a school-boy found out in some prank, 'else I would have used it.'

'It's just a toy lock. Sergeant, pass me your penknife, will you?'

'Sir,' said the Sergeant, who was even more taciturn than the Inspector, handing over a stout penknife.

The Inspector selected the spike designed – but, as far as Edward knew, never used – for taking stones from horses' hooves and wiggled it in the tiny lock. After a few moments it sprung open and the Inspector opened the bag. It was quite empty. Lampfrey looked at it in silence for a minute and then felt in the lining and passed his hand along the bottom of the bag.

'Nothing here,' the Inspector said with some disappoint-ment. 'Do I have your word of honour that you have not opened this bag, Lord Edward?'

'You have my word, Inspector.'

'Hmm, ah well. Someone was there before you.'

'Or perhaps Mrs Harkness had hidden whatever was in the bag somewhere safer, before she went to bed.'

'You didn't notice the bag when you had your late-night interview with Mrs Harkness?'

'No. I'm sure I would have done had it been where I found it this morning, on the floor beside her bed. It must have been in a cupboard or somewhere.'

Edward was now uneasy again. He thought he knew what had happened. Dannie must somehow have entered Molly's room during the night – he had told her himself she had taken something to make her sleep – searched her room, found the bag and removed the papers. He did not dare think that she might have harmed the sleeping woman. It was bad enough to think that she had used him to gain entrance to Molly's room. And what did she plan to do with the letters? Return them to Mrs Simpson? He hoped so. After all, as far as he knew, if she owed anyone loyalty it was Lord Weaver. Hadn't he heard she had been his mistress? God, what a mess. He must speak to Dannie before she was interviewed by the police.

As the Inspector departed – taking the bag with him – he said, 'Oh, one thing more, Mr Scannon does not seem to know if Mrs Harkness had any living relatives.'

'I never heard her speak of any. She must have a lawyer who could tell us.'

'I suppose so. I'm going to London tomorrow to go through her flat. There may be official letters there with a lawyer's adddress.'

'The owner of the flats will have dealt with her solicitors presumably.'

'Yes, and if the letters Mrs Harkness stole are not here, then the next place to look is in the poor woman's flat even though she told you she always took them with her. She just might have thought Haling Castle was not a good place to take such dangerous documents.'

The Inspector hesitated and then said, surprisingly, 'I was wondering if you would like to accompany me. You seem to be the nearest to a close friend she had – unless we look toward royalty – and no doubt you would like to find these letters, or whatever they are, before they get into the wrong hands.'

'Thank you, Inspector, that is very thoughtful of you. I would certainly like to come with you.'

'I've got some work to finish off here. If I were to pick you up tomorrow morning we could catch the nine o'clock.'

'I've got a better idea, Inspector. Why don't I run you up to town in the Lagonda? She needs a spin and that way we'll be independent of the railway timetable.'

'Well,' said Inspector Lampfrey, considering the offer and finding it good, 'if you're sure you don't mind . . . '

'It would be a pleasure,' Edward said.

Dannie and Boy Carstairs did not return from their ride until eleven fifteen, muddied and windblown. Edward and Scannon had been in the drawing-room, the latter making a series of telephone calls, when they heard the sound of the horses in the drive. They followed them to the stables,

Edward hoping for a quiet word with Dannie before Inspector Lampfrey got to her. Watching the two of them dismount, he was struck by what a good-looking pair they made. For the first time he found he could appreciate what it was women saw in Carstairs. It wasn't just that he was tall and muscular with a fine head topped by a leonine mane of hair, it was more his air of physical command which was not quite English. It was not just his haircut – most Englishmen had their hair cut short and then smothered it in oil – it was his air of being at home in his body. Englishmen, even if they had not been in the war, carried themselves like soldiers, erect in bearing and marching rather than walking. Carstairs loped rather than walked and on horseback slouched in the saddle as any Boer would who spent whole days on his horse. Edward, trying to put into words what made Carstairs different, could only come up with the word simian and, while he found the man faintly repulsive, he understood Dannie might find him attractive.

Carstairs slipped out of the saddle with grace and economy of movement and then went over to Dannie and helped her dismount. She had no need of help but she permitted what was almost an embrace as she slid between his arms. Edward thought he saw him whisper a word in her ear as she did so.

'Whatever's the matter,' Dannie began. 'I'm sorry we're late but we haven't missed anything, have we?'

Edward thought it was a rather odd thing to say but perhaps it was clear from Scannon's excited manner that something was amiss. Their host poured out the news to them and though they made all the right noises, expressing shock and dismay, Edward was convinced they already knew Molly was dead. There was something in Carstairs' tone of voice – Dannie, as was her custom, said very little – which gave him the strong impression that he was acting.

Unfortunately, before Edward could have his private talk with Dannie, the Inspector materialized and she and Carstairs were whisked away to be interviewed. He paced around the garden smoking furiously until Dannie reappeared looking a little shaken.

'Oh, there you are, Dannie,' he said. 'Could I have a word with you?'

'Not now, Edward, I must shower and change before lunch.'

'Please, this won't take long.'

With evident reluctance, Dannie allowed herself to be drawn into the garden. It was raining very slightly and her hair glinted with a fine mist.

'Cigarette?' he said.

'No. If it's about last night, I'm sorry. It was a mistake.'

Edward grimaced. He wasn't sure he liked being 'a mistake'.

'Did you go into Molly's bedroom last night while I was asleep?'

'Why should I do that?' she prevaricated.

'You know very well why. Don't pretend you don't know why I am in this ghastly house.'

'To make love to me, or at least that was what I hoped.'

She spoke with the cool lack of emotion which made him think of an actress in rehearsal, not bothering to do more than walk through her part.

'And you were happy to make yourself available to me? Is that right?'

His voice was scathing and she glanced at him with something approaching interest. 'I don't know what you mean,' she said evenly.

'I think Joe Weaver is your lover and he . . . gave you permission to let me make love to you.'

'That's not very flattering. You seem to be accusing me of whoring. Is that how you normally speak to the women you have slept with? Perhaps you don't have much experience of making love to any other kind of woman.'

Edward, attempting to hide his anger, said, 'That's not what I meant. Do you have any feeling for me?'

She turned her lovely head and looked at him. 'We are two grown-up people without wives and husbands to betray. Is it not possible to go to bed with each other for the simple physical pleasure of it? If you are asking "do I love you?", the answer is no and nor, I hope, do you love me. But if you mean did I enjoy myself last night, then the answer is "yes". Does that satisfy your male vanity?'

Once again Edward had to restrain himself from doing or saying something he would later regret. 'It's not a question of male vanity, Dannie. I just wanted to know if . . . if you felt anything for me. I think you are the most beautiful woman I have ever met.'

She let the ghost of a smile curl her lips. 'Oh Edward, I thought you were more intelligent than the others. Do you think I want to hear you tell me I'm beautiful? Is that what you tell Verity Browne? I think not.'

Edward felt as if he had been slapped in the face. 'What I say to Miss Browne,' he said as pompously as he could manage, 'is nothing to do with you. Did you take anything from Molly Harkness's room last night?'

Dannie stopped walking and Edward also halted. The rain had begun to fall more heavily now and beat on the rhododendrons like the pulse which beat in Edward's head. 'I did not,' she said at last.

They heard the sound of the gong from inside the house summoning them to luncheon. With scarcely another word they returned to the house. Just before they went in the front door, Edward grabbed Dannie by the arm: 'Can I see you again? I don't even know where you live.'

'Let go my arm,' she said icily and stepped into the hall to be greeted by Leo Scannon.

'There you are,' he said. 'Dannie, you're soaking. Edward, how could you let Dannie get so wet?'

The next day Edward picked up the Inspector from Marlborough police station. Lampfrey seemed a little embarrassed as he stowed himself in the passenger seat and no doubt, Edward imagined, he had had to endure some ribbing from his colleagues. When Edward asked him if he were comfortable he just grunted but as soon as they were on the main road, he began to cheer up. The rain had ceased so they had the hood down which made conversation difficult.

'Grand car, this, my lord. I've never been in a Lagonda before.'

'It's a beauty, isn't it,' Edward said, overtaking a farm wagon at speed and narrowly missing a dog which chose that precise moment to chase a rabbit into the road. 'It has a 4467cc six-cylinder Meadows engine and is said to do a hundred, not that I've ever tried to do anything like that. However, I'm thinking of taking her over to Germany to try her on one of the new autobahns. I suppose one has to give Herr Hitler credit for building some real roads. Even our *main* roads are quite inadequate for the modern automobile. But I'm sorry, I'm being a bore. Are you interested in motor cars, Inspector?'

'In theory, my lord. On my salary I can't afford one but the missis is wanting me to get one of those Austin Sevens. Nothing like this, of course.'

'No, but it's a sturdy little car. You could do worse.'

'We've got four Wolseleys in the force,' Lampfrey added as an afterthought, 'but we need more. The criminals all seem to have cars nowadays. Careful, my lord!'

'I say, I hope I ain't scaring you, Inspector,' Edward said as he wrestled the car back on to an even keel. 'That damn fellow oughtn't to be allowed a bike. Do you think we should arrest him for riding without due care and attention, or something? No? Oh well, you're probably right.'

They stopped at the Fox and Goose in Reading for refreshment. As they swung by the Huntley and Palmers biscuit factory, well over the speed limit, the Inspector was compelled to remonstrate with his chauffeur. 'My lord, I must beg you to slow down and observe the speed limit. It would be highly embarrassing if we were stopped by an officer of a neighbouring force.'

'Of course! How insensitive of me, but was I really going so fast? It's the only problem with a car like this. It just refuses to travel at twenty miles an hour.'

Over a pint and a plate of ham and eggs the Inspector looked less formidable than he had done at Haling. Edward liked the look of him and decided on the spur of the moment to trust him. 'I have a confession to make, Inspector.' The policeman looked up from his food. 'No, I don't mean that sort of a confession but I have been less than candid with you.'

'Indeed, my lord,' said the policeman equably, resuming his attack on the ham.

'I was not alone in my room last night. I can't mention the lady's name but . . . '

'Not to worry, sir,' said the Inspector comfortably, 'Miss Dannhorn informed me that she had spent the night in your bed and that during the night she had entered Mrs Harkness's room with a view to finding the letters we've just been talking about. She said she didn't find them.'

Edward was taken aback. Here he was indulging in a bit of conscience clearing and he'd been made to look a fool. 'I . . . I didn't know she had told you . . . ' he said weakly.

'You were trying to protect the lady's honour?' the policeman suggested helpfully.

'Yes, I mean . . . well dash it! I suppose I must now be your main suspect. I had a motive for wanting Mrs Harkness out of the way. I have lied and obstructed you. Why don't you arrest me now?'

'So you think there has to be a suspect, do you?'

'You mean, do I think her death was a tragic accident? No, of course I don't. Nor do you, I imagine, unless you are stupider than you look and that's meant to be a compliment.'

'Thank you, my lord – taken as a compliment I'm sure. I want to wait for the medical evidence but, yes, it's too convenient for too many people that the poor lady should have died when she did.'

'And I'm the chief suspect?'

'Have one for the road?' the Inspector said, getting up to go to the bar.

They reached Molly's flat in Trevor Square just after one and Inspector Lampfrey got out of the Lagonda with relief. He was exhilarated, never having travelled so fast before, but a little giddy as if he had just alighted from a carousel. Edward drove with élan and at a speed which, despite the Lagonda's excellent suspension, had rattled every bone in his body. He wondered if he could survive a return journey, possibly in the dark, and began contemplating excuses for taking the train.

The flat was on the first floor in one of the larger build-ings on the north side of the square. Most of the houses in the square were still family houses but a few – like this one – had been converted into flats. Lampfrey rang the electric bell and then knocked but there was no answer. There was either no one in the building or there was no one prepared to answer his stentorian summons so the Inspector let himself in with the dead woman's keys. The flat was pleasant and airy. The drawing-room looked over the quiet square and there was a balcony upon which sev-eral flower pots stood containing nothing but some leggy geraniums. Everything was neat and tidy as though it was regularly cleaned. The other big room in the flat was the dining-room and that too was almost sterile in its cleanli-ness. There was a tiny kitchen, a bathroom and lavatory and, at the back, a bedroom.

There was a bureau in the drawing-room and it was to this that the Inspector went first. It was unlocked and seemed to invite inspection. Lampfrey went through it with great care but found little of interest. There were no letters, diaries – just a few bills including several from a local chemist which he pocketed. Edward had better luck. He had wandered into Molly's bedroom. He had a pet the-ory that when women wished to conceal something they found a hiding place in their bedroom and, whatever its general validity, on this occasion he was proved right. Under the bed he discovered a small, black tin box. It was padlocked. He asked Lampfrey whether he should open it and, after thinking about it, the Inspector shrugged his shoulders and said he might as well. Edward found a screwdriver in a cupboard in the kitchen and with its help levered off the lock. Grunting with pleasure, Edward removed half a dozen letters tied in pink ribbon. They had to be love letters and he untied the knot in the ribbon with trembling hands. The first letter began 'Dearest Molly' and was signed 'your loving David'.

'Here,' he said passing it to the Inspector, 'it's from the King.'

Rather guiltily he looked at the other letters. They were all from the King and made it absolutely clear that, for at least three or four months the previous winter, he and Molly had been lovers. Edward and the Inspector looked at each other.

'I can hardly believe he could have been so unwise as to have written letters like these,' the Inspector said slowly.

A decent man and a loyal subject, he was profoundly shocked to discover his sovereign was, if not an adulterer, then a fornicator. He told himself he was being foolish, expecting his king to behave better than his subjects, but he *was* shocked. He shook his head. He was aware the rich lived by different rules from 'normal' people but he had been particularly put out to discover Lord Edward had slept with that strange-looking but undeniably handsome woman – Miss Dannhorn – though he had tried to conceal it. His first impression of Edward was that here was a thoroughly decent man. He knew he was old-fashioned but he did not hold with what Betty – his wife – called 'loose living' and it upset him that Edward was an immoralist. In his thirty years in the police he had seen depravity and corruption enough but – and he knew he was naive – he expected the upper classes and the aristocracy in particular to set a good example. He supposed he would be labelled a Victorian by his younger colleagues but this woman they called Dannie was, in his eyes, little better than a whore. He snorted. A mannequin! Wasn't that what she called herself? As for his king, well, Inspector Lampfrey read biographies and enjoyed history. Intellectually, he appreciated that

83

throughout history kings had had their mistresses. Why, he had only just finished Hume's *History of Great Britain* but this was the twentieth century. What might have been acceptable behaviour for a king in the seventeenth century was surely not acceptable today.

Edward had confined his speculation to the practical and would have been amazed if he had been able to read the Inspector's mind. 'And having been so foolish as to have taken Mrs Harkness to bed,' he said, meaning the King, 'imagine treating her the way he did. He not only gave her the dynamite, he provided the fuse and the match to go with it.'

'Well, I suppose these ought to be handed back to . . . to the Palace. Would you like to attend to that? I think it's better that there should be no official record of them being found here.'

Edward nodded. 'I'll see to it, Inspector. There's nothing else?'

'Nothing as far as I can see, except this blotting paper.' He held it out to Edward, who looked at it closely. 'Can you make this out, my lord?'

'Um, let me see. What's this? "Dear . . . " Is it "Dear G" or is it a C?' He went over to the mirror in the hall and held the blotting paper up to it. 'Yes, I think it's "Dear G". Then what's this further down? " . . . blame me". Probably, "don't blame me". Hmm, interesting but damnably little to go on. Inspector, you're absolutely sure there's no drawer or anything you've overlooked?'

'Look for yourself.'

Edward did so but the bureau contained no secret drawers. Edward went back to the bedroom. He looked round, scratching his head. He had an instinct that Molly was the kind of woman for whom her bedroom was her holy of holies and that it had not yet given up all its secrets. Whereas the drawing-room and dining-room were so neutral as to be featureless, the bedroom did have personality. There were some photographs on the chest of drawers: one of them of an army officer. Edward remembered that Molly had said her father had been killed in France in 1918. There was another photograph of the man he supposed to be her father taken on his wedding day. Molly's mother was something of a beauty and it was obviously from her that Molly had got her looks. There was no photograph of her husband, hardly surprising perhaps, but there was one of a group of young people in tennis clothes. Edward could not be sure but it looked as though the picture had been taken at Muthaiga Club and he recognized one or two faces from when he had been in Kenya. When he looked closer, he thought he recognized Boy Carstairs in the back row just behind Molly.

He looked round the room again. There was a little horse-shoe-shaped dressing table with a mirror above it. On the table there were the cosmetics which Molly had not needed to take with her to Haling. There was a bottle marked Milk of Gardenias, lipsticks and a powder puff in a china dish. Around the kneehole were little curtains and, when he drew them back, he saw several small drawers. It was distasteful to pry into so intimate a place but he reminded himself that, if it turned out Molly had been murdered, he owed it to their friendship to discover why and, most importantly, who had taken her life. The top two drawers held costume jewellery – nothing of any value. If Molly had any valuable jewels, they were either at Haling or in the bank. The bottom drawer contained knick-knacks and mementoes – a sea shell, a paperknife with a curiously decorated bone handle, several beads and a brooch. He took out the brooch and looked at it closely. Then, glancing towards the door to check that he was unobserved, he slipped it in his pocket.

Leaving the Inspector to make his telephone calls, Edward went out into Trevor Square to smoke a cigarette and think things through. He had found letters – letters which the King would hardly want to fall into unfriendly hands – but they were not the letters for which he was looking. And what of Molly? She had thought she had met her Prince Charming when, instead, she had been a few weeks' entertainment, nothing more, for a bored and foolish man who, like himself, he told himself ruefully, ought to have known better. Molly had been dispatched as casually as one might put down a troublesome dog and it made him angry. She wasn't the most admirable of human beings but she was more a victim than a villain. The men in her life had used her even when she imagined she was using them. Her only power – her only way of making a space for herself – was through sex and it was sex which had led to her murder, Edward was sure of it. Her theft of Mrs Simpson's letters was an absurd and futile attempt to win back the King's affections. Politically, she was an innocent but there were people in her circle who were highly political. One of these had killed her to get them off her. But to do what with them? Did the man – or woman – want to destroy them or use them for blackmail or did they have some other use for them?

It all came back to Dannie. Edward sighed and rubbed his forehead. What a fool he had been! It was easy to see now, after the event, that he should never have slept with her. He had desired her so much and he had been scared of losing her. He had thought she would think him a dull beast, a stick-in-the-mud, a prude, if he had said, 'Not yet, we must get to know each other better before we go to bed together.' He had had affairs before now with women he had liked but not loved and never regretted them but this was different. He had been a rabbit and the snake had swallowed him whole. It was humiliating. Whether she had found what she was looking for – whether she had murdered Molly – he could not say for certain but he was determined to find out. A phrase he had once heard his father use of a woman he despised came back to him – 'a brazen hussy'. Dannie was a brazen hussy or, if she were something more complicated, then he needed to know what.

As he meditated, he strolled across the square enjoying the sunshine. This was the Indian summer that in England so often came like a blessing before the winter rains. Feeling a sharp breath of wind cool his cheek as the sun went behind a cloud, he looked up and saw that he was in Knightsbridge, almost opposite Harrods. A small figure was tottering towards him laden with carrier bags and hat-boxes and, though he could hardly see her face, he immediately recognized Verity.

5

'And may a gentleman rescue a lady for the second time in a week or would that expose her to unwelcome gossip?' he inquired, tossing his cigarette into the gutter and catching a particularly awkward hatbox as it slipped out of her fingers.

'Edward! Is that really you? Are you haunting me or is it pure coincidence you're here? Yes, thanks,' she added, letting him take some other of her parcels. 'I was looking for a taxi but, just when I thought I had one, a brute of a man leapt in from the other side and made off with it. Where is chivalry? Has this blighted age done away with gentlemen?'

'Please, miss,' Edward said, 'they likes to call me a gent.'

'If that's supposed to be cockney, forget it!' Verity exclaimed. 'Anyway, I'm glad it's you. I wanted you to do something for me.'

'Yes, ma'am. No problem, my lady. I'd touch my hat if I had one.'

'Why haven't you got a hat?' she demanded. 'You always wear a hat. You'll catch your death – a man of your age and thin on top too. Have you been visiting a friend in the locality?'

'Well, yes and no. Why not come and have a cup of tea at Gunter's and I'll tell all. Cakes, éclairs, meringues, scandal – irresistible surely?'

'Éclairs, meringues! Pah, too bourgeois. You'll have to try harder than that. You're to come to dinner tonight. Adrian said if I bumped into you to invite you and there – I have bumped into you.'

'I don't know if I can. I need permission from a policeman.'

'Good heavens, Edward, don't tell me you've been arrested.'

'No, but . . . look, come with me into the square and you can rest for a moment and I can get the Inspector's view on whether I'm allowed parole.'

They were only a few hundred yards from Molly's house and, when Edward knocked, Lampfrey answered the door.

'Inspector, may I introduce you to Verity Browne? Verity, this is Inspector Lampfrey. Inspector, despite the Harrods bags with which Miss Browne is decorated, I have to warn you that she is in fact a well-known political extremist and a paid-up member of the Communist Party of Great Britain.'

'Miss Browne,' said the Inspector smiling. 'I so much admire your reports in the *New Gazette*. I am correct in thinking you are *the* Verity Browne?'

'I don't know about *the* but, yes, I do work for the *New Gazette*. Of course, I'm flattered that you know my name but perhaps that's because you've been investigating Lord Edward's shady friends?'

There was just a slight flicker in the Inspector's gaze which suggested her retort had been a little too accurate for comfort but he was able to say without any other sign of being disconcerted, 'In a manner of speaking, Miss Browne. I am afraid I am investigating the sudden death of Mrs Harkness. This is – or I should say was – her house.'

'Oh, how perfectly dreadful. I had no idea. Edward, why didn't you tell me? Mrs Harkness? When . . . how did it happen?'

Edward said soberly, 'I didn't have time to tell you, V. Molly was at Haling. I told you I was going down to Wiltshire. She was one of the guests.'

'Haling? What's that?'

'It's Leo Scannon's house. You know, the Conservative MP.'

'And what happened?'

'Molly died of an overdose – veronal or barbitone, we think. It's the same thing – a sleeping draught.'

'Oh, I'm so sorry. Was it an accident?'

'We don't know yet,' the Inspector said. 'Did you know Mrs Harkness, Miss Browne?'

'No, but I'm sure I've heard Lord Edward mention her. You knew her in Africa, didn't you?'

'Yes.'

'Didn't you . . . know her rather well?'

'V! Wash your mouth out with soap. I did not have an affair with Molly if that's what you are implying. I do wish someone would believe me,' he said plaintively. 'I merely rescued her, as is my custom,' he said, looking at Verity meaningfully, 'from scandal and contumely.'

'Contumely?'

'I'm sure I told you: Molly's husband shot himself in front of her and, although the marriage was . . . unhappy, it was a dreadful shock as you can imagine. In fact, she was in such a bad way I took her off to the Cape to recover.'

'I remember. She'd been having a string of affairs and her poor husband couldn't stand any more of it.'

'You're too hard on her. She was as much a victim as she was to blame,' Edward said, feeling a pang of guilt at the mention of affairs. 'The husband was a drunkard and beat her.'

'Anyway,' the Inspector broke in hurriedly, 'the poor lady died of an overdose.'

'I see,' Verity said. 'I'm sorry. I shouldn't have spoken ill of her. I'm the last person to throw stones. Inspector, can you give this man parole for a day or possibly two? I need him . . . as a chauffeur,' she added hastily, in case he got the wrong idea.

'I don't see why not,' the Inspector said, silently breathing a sigh of relief that he would not after all have to suffer another hair-raising journey in the Lagonda.

'Oh, I don't know,' Edward said, looking troubled. 'I can't just desert the Inspector like that. Anyway, if it turns out Molly was killed, then I'm a prime suspect and he won't want to risk me absconding.'

'Killed? Whatever do you mean, Edward? You're not going to tell me it was murder? I assumed it was an accident or . . . or suicide.'

'It probably was an accident,' Edward said hurriedly, seeing her evident distress and wishing he hadn't been flippant. 'You want me back at Haling, don't you, Inspector?'

'Not for a day or two, until I get the post-mortem report. If you give me your telephone number . . . '

'I don't know . . . ' Edward repeated. 'How would you get back to Marlborough?'

'Don't worry about me,' the Inspector implored him. 'There's a train at eight o'clock from Paddington. That'll get me back almost as fast as the Lagonda.'

'I hope you haven't been scaring the Inspector,' Verity said reprovingly. 'Did he drive you as though he thought he were Malcolm Campbell, Inspector?'

'No, I assure you. Lord Edward . . . I am very grateful but I really can manage. I'm sure Miss Browne will answer for you not jumping police bail. That was a joke,' he added, seeing Edward's face cloud over.

'I'll deliver him back to Haling in one piece, Mr Lampfrey, I promise.'

'That's all right then. You two run along and leave me to do a bit of work. Oh, Miss Browne, I am quite sincere in saying I admire your work. Your account of the siege of Toledo was . . . very vivid. You really ought to write a book.'

'As it happens, I am, Inspector. Mr Gollancz, the publisher you know, has asked me to collect up my *New Gazette* articles for the Left Book Club.'

Edward said indignantly, 'You didn't tell me.'

'It's only just happened. I was going to tell you.'

'I am sure it will be a bestseller,' the Inspector said. 'When is it to be published?'

'If I can do the work in a month, then in January or February.'

Edward was still in a state of shock. Verity – an author! But why not? Now he thought about it, it was her obvious next step. Why did one always think one's friends could never be famous? He was impressed.

'I say, Verity, jolly good show. Congrats and all that. What's the book to be called?'

'*Searchlight on Spain*, I think, but that may change. Anyway,' she said, wanting to change the subject, 'I must gather up my parcels. Edward, would you be a dear and get me a taxi?'

'Nonsense, I'll take you in the Lagonda.'

The Inspector coughed. 'Forgive me for saying so, Miss Browne, but do Communist Party members usually shop at Harrods?'

'Precisely!' Edward said. 'Just what I said the other day with reference to Galeries Lafayette.'

Verity blushed. 'Oh, do stop ragging, Edward, and you too, Inspector. Why shouldn't I shop where I want? This is a free country, or so I've heard.'

'Not if you Reds had anything to do with it,' Edward said nastily.

'Do put a sock in it, won't you. But please, Inspector, if it turns out Mrs Harkness was murdered, you will tell me, won't you?'

The policeman and Edward looked at each other interrogatively. Edward said, 'If we do say anything, V, you'll have to promise not to write about it, cross your heart and hope to die. This is all highly confidential and not for reporting in any of the rags you work for.'

'I'm a journalist . . . '

'Well then, nothing. See no evil, hear no evil, speak no evil.'

'Dash it, I really can't . . . '

'No!' the Inspector and Edward said in unison.

'Not until I give you my permission, at any rate,' Lampfrey relented.

'Oh, all right then. I promise.' She raised her hand and made the scout's salute.

When the Inspector had seen them out and the door had shut behind them, Edward said, 'Before I take you back to the King's Road, why don't you come and have a cup of tea with me at Albany. It's hardly out of the way.'

'It is but . . . will Fenton be there to chaperone me?' she asked mischievously.

'No, but I promise you I'm a perfect gentleman, at least where women are concerned.' Then he remembered Dannie and looked guilty but Verity didn't seem to notice.

'That's what I was afraid of,' she said naughtily. Edward glanced at her to see if she were joking but was unable to decide.

'Gosh! I didn't know you were a cook!' Verity said admiringly.

'I can boil a kettle and toast a muffin.'

'That's more than I can do.'

'But you must have cooked when you had that flat in Hans Crescent.'

'I didn't need to. There was a delightful little Italian restaurant just across the road. Giuseppe did all the cooking. You see, I never had a mother so there was never anyone to teach me the basics of living. That's why I turned out to be such a frightful rapscallion.' Verity looked thoroughly pleased with herself and then disappointed that Edward did not tell her how sorry he was she was a motherless child, but he was thinking of his own mother.

'My mother – I did have a mother and a very good sort of mother – but she never cooked so much as an egg in her life. If you had shown her a kettle she would hardly have recognized it.'

'Precisely!' Verity said, this sort of remark being the proverbial and, in her case, almost literal, red rag. 'The working classes exploited by the idle aristocracy. No offence to your mother. It's the system which is to blame. I have no doubt there are hundreds of women out there who would like nothing better than to run their own lives and not be "at the mercy" of servants, as I have heard some of them say. To have a room of their own, as Mrs Woolf puts it. Do you know why I could never bear ever again to go to one of those dinner parties my father used to take me to?'

'Because they bore you, I suppose.'

'Yes, they do or would if I let them. You've never had to sit with the women after dinner leaving the men to talk politics and smut. The women have nothing to talk about but children, the servant problem and their hairdressers or couturiers. I mean, if they could only be shown the way two-thirds of the population have to live – in squalid slums, surrounded by hungry children . . . Don't smile, Edward, I'm serious.'

'I'm not smiling. I mean I'm not smiling at the plight of the women, but I like it when you get indignant.'

'Now you're being patronizing. I've had to talk to you about that before.'

'I don't mean to be. I just like remembering the plucky little fighting cat I met on the road to Mersham a year ago. In fact, I would go further and make a profound point about the way our world is changing. You are living a man's life – economically, I mean. You're earning your living doing a tough job instead of behaving as our mothers might have expected. And what's more,' he said, following up his argument, 'until it becomes possible for a girl to have a job *and* a husband and children, then you're in the rotten position of having to choose which life you want to lead. And because you're the brave, spunky girl you are, you choose the difficult way.'

'Hmm,' Verity said, rather taken aback. 'There may be something in what you say but it doesn't mean I won't ever marry and do . . . do normal things,' she ended almost grudgingly.

'Kick me if I'm speaking out of turn,' he said, avoiding her eye, 'but I get the feeling . . . I expect I'm talking nonsense . . . that Spain was much worse than you expected and it knocked the stuffing out of you. Tell me I'm a fool and talking rot.'

Verity hesitated. 'I don't know. I wouldn't say it knocked the stuffing out of me. I hope not anyway, but I have seen things which make it difficult to live in England now. I mean it's so parochial, so smug. Talk about burying the collective head in the sand! And yet, can one blame people? Perhaps they sense that before long "the piping days of peace" are going to give way to blood and guns. Perhaps they feel they should be allowed to enjoy their families and their humdrum jobs while they can.'

'But if they – or at least the government – weren't so complacent it might not need to come to blood and guns. Leaders have a duty to lead and we've been let down.'

'Yes, but politicians can't make the people who elected them stand up and fight unless they can be persuaded they are fighting to protect their own families, their own back gardens. I used to think people would fight for right but I don't think that any more.'

They were silent, wondering perhaps how similar their views were despite their different perspectives. Eventually, Edward said carefully, 'Toledo was bad?'

'Yes, bad,' she said through gritted teeth.

'Do you want to talk about it?'

'Sometime.' She put out her hand for tea and the cup rattled on the saucer. 'I saw some bad things in Spain, after you left. Convents and monasteries razed to the ground, priests and nuns being torn apart – by our side I mean. We had justification – God knows we had justification – but I did see . . . ' She halted again as though on the verge of breaking down. Edward neither spoke nor tried to touch her. He knew he had to let her get out her grief and disillusionment, like drawing pus out of a wound.

'I don't feel now that . . . that it's good against bad. It's not so simple. Franco's men . . . they are barbarians but our side . . . not so much better.' She drew a deep breath. 'At Toledo we were winning but for some reason we could not get the rebels – officer cadets they were – to lay down their arms. They fought like . . . like they believed in their cause . . . but how could they?'

'And they were relieved?'

'Our leaders were overconfident. They wanted to show off before the world's press. They thought they had time. They thought they could starve them into submission and that their ammunition would soon be exhausted but . . . but there wasn't time. We were surprised . . . betrayed I shouldn't wonder. It was rumoured some of our top people were in Franco's pay. We were defeated. No, not defeated, routed.'

'But there is something else?'

She looked directly at Edward for the first time and said, 'You swear you won't say "I told you so" or "What did you expect?" or sneer?'

Edward was hurt. 'Do I need to swear, Verity?'

'The politicians, the apparatchiks, the party bureaucrats . . . they were . . . they wanted something different from simple victory but I never could quite understand what it was. People like David, their first loyalty – I see that now – is to Stalin, not the Spanish Republic. They obey Stalin's orders but they never tell us what those are. We just had to obey orders from our superiors in the Party and I . . . I wouldn't. They threatened me, Edward, they threatened me . . . they said if I didn't do what I was told I would . . . I would be shot.'

'David said that?' Edward asked, horrified.

Verity nodded her head. David Griffiths-Jones had been Verity's lover, her hero, the epitome of what was good about being a member of the Party and now she was learning that he was not the idealist she thought him. Edward suppressed a feeling of utter delight that she should at last have seen through this man and recognized him for what he was. He had always hated and despised him, not just because he had Verity's love and loyalty but because he was a ruthless ideologue who used people without scruple. For Griffiths-Jones, the Party was the alpha and omega of his life and it could do no wrong. Edward's heart went out to the girl sitting opposite him. It must have been so painful to have had to recognize the truth and it was a tribute to her innate honesty that, in the end, she had made herself face it. She was too brave and too intelligent to live a lie but she had obviously been wounded to the core. He wanted to hold her in his arms and comfort her. He thought she would let him but he decided that it might be too easy. She must come to him as an equal and there must be no taste of defeat in her decision – if she ever made it – to love him. He dared hope now that it might happen but it must happen in a different way.

To ease the tension he said, 'There was a philosopher at Cambridge when I was up called Wittgenstein. I went to a lecture he gave once – just out of interest, don't y'know. I hardly understood a word he said, and not only because he muttered and mumbled, but he did end with one phrase which has stayed with me and which makes me feel, against all my instincts, that he must have been a wise man. He said, "Whereof one cannot speak, thereof one must be silent." I think that's what I feel about what you have been through. Your wounds are still open and you must give them time to heal. Don't torture yourself with imagining things could have been different.'

He looked at her now and was troubled to see that her lower lip was trembling and her eyes were wet with tears. Hurriedly, he tried to avoid the embarrassment which he, like most Englishmen, suffered in the face of raw emotion.

'Let me tell you what I have been up to. I promised Joe Weaver not to tell you. He thought you might feel you had to put it in the *Daily Worker* but this is one time I don't have any compunction in breaking my promise. I told you Molly died . . . was killed, but I didn't tell you why.'

She raised her head and looked at him with interest, and he was glad to see that he had distracted her from her troubles.

'The silly girl had stolen some love letters from Mrs Simpson.' Edward went on to tell Verity everything and his story acted on her like a tonic. She was angry, too, at the way Molly had been let down.

'It confirms all my prejudices against royalty,' she said. 'I was talking to Charlotte – your childhood friend – and, do you know, she had to curtsy to a cake!'

'A cake?'

'She was a deb – got presented at Court and all that tosh – and she had to go to Queen Charlotte's Ball with all the other debs and parade around in pearls and curtsy to a cake! Can you credit it?'

'Oh, *that* cake! Yes I can, actually. I did the season, you know.'

'You poor fish!' Verity looked at Edward with contempt. 'What on earth made you go through such an idiotic charade?'

'Oh, I don't know. I suppose my mother expected it and I didn't want to hurt her. Anyway, I enjoyed it – sort of.'

'You couldn't have.'

'The dances – some of them were fun. I remember one – I expect Charlotte was there, the Prince certainly was – at Melton Mowbray . . . Craven Lodge. Michael Wardell had a grand party there. The Prince had taken to riding with the Quorn and the Belvoir . . . '

Edward was well away remembering his foolish youth and Verity looked at him with amazement.

'Freda was the belle of the ball in Lanvin – I'm sure it was Lanvin – anyway, she looked exquisite and there were fireworks and I . . . I thought I was in love . . . ' He suddenly caught sight of Verity's face. 'Yes, well, I got bored with it all. I think the girls did too. I remember Connie telling me she had an alphabet.'

'An alphabet?'

'When she had to dance with these boys they were mostly tongue-tied and she struggled to find some topic on which they could exchange a few words without stammering to a halt. She would start with apples and go through the alphabet until she reached – I don't know – zebras, I suppose. I know she said she got to rabbits before Gerald found anything to say for himself.'

Gerald was the Duke of Mersham, his elder brother, and Connie was the Duchess, a woman of whom he was extremely fond and whom he admired for making his brother happy without going mad with boredom.

'Well, I think it's all bosh and, come the revolution, it will all be swept away and a good thing too.'

'I expect you're right,' Edward said mildly, still feeling nostalgic for times past. 'To be honest, I never thought it would survive the war but class seems to survive the worst that democracy can throw at it.'

Verity was now throroughly disgruntled and insisted on going home. When she had gone, Edward lit a cigarette and sat in his armchair still in a dream. There was however something in his smile which hinted that, in annoying Verity out of her self-pity, he felt he had done a good day's work.

He had not had lunch so, when he turned up at the Hassels' house in the King's Road that evening, he was hungry. He had taken the precaution of telephoning Charlotte to confirm that he really was expected – Verity might easily have forgotten to tell her hosts that she had invited him to dinner – but she had been gratifyingly enthusiastic about his coming. He was curious to see how the years had changed her. He reckoned it must be at least twenty years since Charlotte's family had moved away from Mersham. She had not been a particularly pretty child but he remembered her delightful fits of giggles, her tomboy pleasure in the life they led roaming the countryside from dawn to dusk without much in the way of adult supervision. Looking back on it, he thought their childhood had been close to perfect but at the time he took it for granted as perfectly natural. Now he could see how privileged he had been.

'Edward darling!' Charlotte opened her arms and planted a kiss on his cheek. She ushered him into the house, talking all the time so that he was not called on to say anything himself. The tomboy child had turned into a plump, comfortable-looking woman whose high spirits manifested themselves in chatter punctuated by loud guffaws. She made a comic companion for her husband who was thin, etiolated, and never without a cigarette which he smoked from an absurdly long, green, onyx holder. Adrian's paintings covered every spare wall and were packed like playing cards in neat piles wherever there was space. If Verity was right and he was beginning to sell his work it looked as though he could sit back and do nothing for several years and still have paintings to sell.

'Lord Edward,' Adrian said, taking the cigarette holder from his mouth and putting out his hand, 'how good to see you again. And before you ask, yes, I'm still painting thin green men and orange suns and you will still hate them.'

'What on earth do you mean?' Charlotte expostulated. 'Why should Edward dislike your work?'

'Oh, it's just a joke,' Verity chipped in. 'Tommie invited him to one of Adrian's parties last year to meet me. Adrian asked him how he liked the paintings – not, of course, letting on that he was their creator – and Edward said he hated them.'

'It wasn't quite like that,' Edward said faintly.

'Tommie's coming tonight. He said he hadn't seen you in ages.'

'Oh, that's excellent,' Edward said, genuinely delighted.

Edward liked and admired Tommie and, although they didn't see very much of each other, they had kept in touch, particularly as Tommie was one of Verity's few close friends. Tommie was not a Communist – he called himself a Christian Socialist – but he and Verity went on marches together, protested in front of the same embassies and generally pursued the same left-wing causes.

Tommie was late and, when he did arrive, he was sporting a black eye.

'I say,' Verity exclaimed, 'have you been punching your parishoners? The bish won't like that, you know.'

Tommie laughed weakly. ''Ah, Edward, good to see you. I could have done with your support a couple of hours ago.'

'Good heavens, why?'

'You know I run this boys' club near my church? Well, just recently, Mosley's people have been recruiting in places like mine. The fact is, there are plums ripe for picking – for the most part, my lads are unemployed, tough, bored . . . it's the boredom mostly, and the feeling of not being part of respectable society. Mosley makes them feel important and valued. They get some sort of uniform, they march up and down a lot and they gain some sort of self-respect. I try and tell them they're being used but they don't listen.'

'So what happened today?' Verity inquired sharply.

'Oh, one of Mosley's toughs came to the club and started haranguing the lads. I told him the club was not to be used for political purposes and . . . and we got into a scrap.'

'I bet the Mosleyite thug got the worst of it,' Charlotte said with a laugh.

Tommie had played rugger for Cambridge and might have been an international if he hadn't had 'the call'.

'Oh, I don't know. I'm afraid I did lose my temper and then I repented.'

'But not before you had laid him out?'

'Well, yes, V. I think he'll complain to the police.'

'Don't worry about it,' she said. 'The police are soon going to have much more to worry about than a punch in the eye.'

Edward looked puzzled. Tommie explained: 'Mosley's planning to march through the East End on Sunday and we're going to stop him.'

'Mosley?'

'And his bully boys,' Verity confirmed. 'That's the party I've invited you to, Edward. Didn't I say? Educational for you and convenient for me. It will be useful to have a chauffeur and if the worst comes to the worst – which it probably will – the Lagonda can pretend it's an ambulance.'

'Hey, I say. I can't risk the Lagonda.'

'I see. Eye of the needle stuff, is it? Tommie, what does the Bible say about that rich man who couldn't give up all his possessions to follow Christ?'

'Hang on a moment, V. Tommie may be more up-to-date than I, but since when has Christ been a member of the Communist Party?'

'Stuff! He'd have much more likely joined the Party than the C of E. Can you imagine him sitting through matins at Tommie's barn in Kilburn – the church empty except for three old ladies and that girl who's in love with . . . ?'

'I say,' Tommie broke in. 'Verity, you know how I hate it when you talk like that.'

Verity was immediately contrite. 'Sorry, Tommie, but Edward has that effect on me. He's so . . . so . . . uninvolved.'

It wasn't quite what she had meant to say and it surprised Edward too. He supposed she meant he wasn't passionate and she needed passion like adrenalin.

Adrian said mildly, 'They're planning to march through the Jewish quarter, Lord Edward, and that can't be allowed. It's deliberate provocation.'

'Just call me Edward, won't you, Adrian, or I won't feel able to be rude about your painting. All right, Verity, I'll be your chauffeur but . . . '

'Good. You're a brave little boy and Mummy's proud of you.'

Charlotte was not a good cook but, as Verity remarked afterwards, at least she did most of it herself with only a maid to help and a half-witted boy to wait at table and wash up. The soup was frankly watery but the poached salmon, though a little overcooked, was good and Adrian produced some perfectly acceptable Muscadet.

Edward was persuaded to give a censored account of Molly's death at Haling – he did not, of course, mention finding Dannie in his bed. Rather surprisingly, Charlotte said, 'We know the Benyons quite well. In fact, Inna bought one of Adrian's pictures. They're really super people. We also know something of Leo Scannon, don't we, Popsie?' Popsie was her pet name for her husband.

'We do. I'm afraid he's not quite so nice. He made a friend of a boy we know – an artist. Well, he was trying to paint pictures but he wasn't very good and I'm afraid he knew it. Anyway, I'm not sure where – at a party, I think – he met Scannon who took him up in a big way. He introduced him to a lot of people; sponsored a show at the Albemarle which was a bit of a disaster. Made Matt look rather ridiculous, you know, like putting costume jewellery in a Cartier case. For about six or seven months they were inseparable and then, as suddenly as he had taken him up, Scannon dropped him. To cut a long story short, the poor boy got more and more depressed and, despite everything his friends could do or say, he cut his wrists.'

'Good God!' Edward exclaimed. 'Is Scannon a . . . you know, a pansy then?'

'So I believe though, of course, I never discussed it with Matt.'

Nothing more was said and Edward got the impression Charlotte was unhappy that Adrian had told the story of their friend's suicide. However, the dinner was a success. He talked to Charlotte about childhood adventures and caught up with her career. It appeared she had gone to New Zealand, married and divorced a sheep farmer, returned to London and gone rather wild. 'As anyone would,' Adrian said loyally, 'after New Zealand.' Then she had met Adrian and they had – as he put it – 'done what neither of us had thought we would ever do: fall in love. The old cliché but somehow, when it happens to oneself, it don't seem a cliché but just as though one had invented it.'

Edward was touched and liked Adrian even more.

As Edward was leaving, Charlotte said, 'I'll do a bit of sleuthing about friend Scannon. You never know, I might find something interesting.'

'Well do,' he said, 'but be careful not to seem you're accusing him of anything. There is such a thing as the law of slander and no reason to believe he has anything to do with Molly's death, even if it does prove to be murder.'

'Don't worry, "I will roar you as gently as any sucking dove", as Shakespeare puts it. See, Verity, even as a child he was timid and a bit of a prig. No wonder I had to put an ice-cream down the back of his neck.'

'Half a jiff, he told me *he* put ice-cream down *your* back!'

For the next few days Edward rattled around London talking to people in Molly's 'set', friends of the King such as Fruity Metcalfe and Dickie Mountbatten. He had dinner one evening with Perry Brownlow at his club and questioned him about the weekend Molly had robbed Mrs Simpson. Perry, indiscreet to the point of idiocy, told him stories of what went on at Fort Belvedere which made him furious. To think that a man who behaved in that way and surrounded himself with such worthless people was now his king! However, he could discover nothing which shed further light on what he was still convinced was murder. He also investigated, as far as he dared, Leo Scannon's friends and associates. He didn't want it to get back to Scannon, or indeed to Joe Weaver, that he had been asking questions about him and his set so he was careful merely to sound curious rather than suspicious. The man knew 'everyone' and, from behind their hands, 'everyone' seemed pleased to gossip about his 'underground life'. There was no question he had some undesirable acquaintances. A 'grisly crew' as he termed them when Fenton brought him his whisky on Friday night. He valued Fenton's intelligence and had no hesitation in going over with him what he had found out but he had to confess that, when all was noted and accounted for, there was nothing tangible to add to what he had known or at least suspected when he began his inquiries.

Fenton had made a few inquiries himself. He had talked the murder over with Pickering but the butler had been unable or unwilling to tell him anything of interest. 'He hinted, my lord, that there was some mystery about old Mrs Scannon's companion, Miss Conway, but, when I tried to make him talk about it, he clammed up on me.'

'Hmm, interesting, but I don't see how anything to do with Ruth Conway could relate to Mrs Harkness.'

It was a frustrating business and Edward found that when Sunday dawned he was glad to have something else to think about.

It was a perfect day. The sun shone and London looked almost foreign – as though a respectable married lady was displaying herself like a street walker. As the Lagonda weaved through the crowds near the Tower, Edward remarked that it might be a public holiday – Derby Day for instance – but he was wrong. The mood of the crowd, though outwardly good-natured, was purposeful and even stern. The Lagonda attracted curious and sometimes hostile stares and Verity, unusually quiet, said suddenly, 'I'm beginning to wish we had walked or gone on a tram like everyone else. I'm not sure this car makes quite the right impression.'

'You mean, they'll think we're going to support Mosley?'

'Well, we don't look "working class".'

'But I thought you said Communism was for *all* the people.'

'Not class enemies, you ass. People still remember the General Strike, you know.'

Edward narrowly missed running over a child which had rolled out of its mother's arms into the road. He raised his hat and apologized to the woman, who swore at him.

'Mmm, maybe you're right but, damn it, I don't like to be intimidated.'

Obstructed by the ever-increasing crowds which overflowed the pavements and colonized the roads, they slowed to walking pace and even Edward began to feel uncomfortable. This was not the good-humoured crowd of the Peace Pledge marches of the previous year. These people were earnest and determined. They came level with a policeman who held out his hand to halt them. 'You can't take this motor car any further, sir. It wouldn't be safe. I suggest you leave it round the back of Goodman's Yard. It ought to be safe there.'

It was with some relief that Edward obeyed, feeling that the officer had enabled him to surrender his car without loss of face. Even on foot, Edward and Verity stood out from the rest. Fenton had recommended an old suit, sensibly fearing the violence which might be offered it by the mob, but it was perfectly cut and his tie was perfectly knotted. His hat, one of Lock's best grey homburgs, was perfectly placed on his head which Lionel, his barber at Trumpers, had only recently shorn. He wore no spats but he might as well have done. He was immediately recognizable as a man about town who ought not to have ventured into this other world of cloth caps and threadbare jackets.

Verity had her own ideas about what to wear on marches. Long experience had taught her that comfortable shoes were the first priority and that the hats she liked – wide of brim and often heaped with fruit or feathers – attracted derision and usually ended up in the gutter. Instead, she wore a tight little brown felt hat. Her faintly military coat had heavily padded shoulders but again, her whole outfit suggested money. It was too bad, she thought, that comrades had to look so dreary. She wanted to show solidarity with the less well-off but considered it would be hypocritical to 'dress down'. Like it or leave it, she was who she was. She held her chin a little bit higher and clung on to Edward's arm a little bit tighter.

It was a considerable relief to both of them when they heard a yell and caught sight of Tommie signalling to them. The man of God pushed his way through the mob with the practised ease of a fly half and greeted them with slaps on the back. Edward winced. 'Sorry, old boy. Didn't mean to hurt you but isn't this glorious?'

He was excited and, when Tommie got excited, he tended to get physical.

'Yes,' Verity said, the sparkle in his eyes energizing her. 'We haven't missed the fun, have we?'

'No, no! But there are hundreds of police. They have orders to keep us well away from the BUF but they won't succeed. We're all just a bit fed up with Mosley's posturing.'

106

'So what's going to happen?' Edward felt nervous. He wasn't a natural political agitator. He certainly wasn't a Communist and he felt Verity had put him in a false position but, on the other hand, it was right he should stand up against the National Socialists as Mosley now called his party – that or the British Union. He had dropped the word Fascist, not wanting to be too closely associated with the Nazis. He had even changed the Party's emblem from the Roman 'fasces' to a lightning flash in a circle, which the Communists had labelled the flash-in-the-pan.

The sound of bells from half a hundred City churches, summoning Londoners to worship another god than mammon, rebuked them for what they were about to do. 'Oughtn't you to be in church?' Edward asked Tommie – Verity thought rather meanly. 'It is Sunday.'

Tommie looked momentarily downcast and Edward immediately regretted his jibe.

'I think the Lord would want me to stand up for the just against the unjust,' he said. 'He didn't himself spend many hours in the Temple, you know. He liked to be among the people,' he added stiffly and Edward was silenced for a moment.

'Where are we going exactly?' he inquired at last.

Verity said, 'Jack Spot – you know who I mean?'

'He's one of your Party's organizers, isn't he?'

'Yes, we're meeting him and other Party workers in Cable Street. I think the idea is to build a barricade to stop the Mosleyites marching through the East End.'

'I see,' Edward said, wondering if he could make an excuse and leave before the bricks started flying. 'I thought this was just going to be a peaceful demonstration, not a revolution.'

'Don't be so wet, Edward,' Verity said crossly. 'Tommie and I will look after you if you're scared.'

'It's not that, it's just that . . . '

They had turned down Chamber Street and a dull roar, like the sea breaking on a distant shore, came on their ears. It thrilled and excited Verity and she wondered if Edward might be right: perhaps this was the revolution. They increased their pace, as did those around them, suddenly fearful they might be missing something. When they turned into Cable Street, an amazing sight greeted them. A wall of furniture, corrugated iron and scrap metal had been thrown up across the street and a man whom Verity identified as Jack Spot, the Communist agitator, was standing on it shouting and waving what looked like a chair leg. He was conducting the crowd in the chant which Marshal Pétain had coined in 1916 at Verdun but which Verity had first heard in Spain: 'They shall not pass!'

'*No pasaran!*' A shiver of recognition ran down her spine and, letting go of Edward's arm, she thrust herself forward towards the barricade, carried along by others equally caught up in the moment as herself. Edward looked round and, finding he had lost her, turned to speak to Tommie but he too had disappeared. He sighed but was not unduly alarmed. He took it that, given Verity had survived the siege of Toledo, she would not come to much harm in this crowd of like-minded thinkers. He made his way into Dock Street to get out of the worst of the crowd. When he had been walking for five minutes, he saw that he had come out, as it were 'behind the lines', at the Royal Mint. There were crowds here too but of a very different kind to the mob of chanting anti-Fascists he had left in Cable Street. He was faced with rank upon rank of Mosley youths and, Edward noted with some surprise and not a little disgust, several hundred young women, all dressed in uniform – black shirts, broad belts, breeches and boots. He guessed there might have been as many as three thousand.

As he watched, there was a roar of engines and Mosley himself appeared, standing upright in an open Bentley with a police motor-cycle escort. The Bentley came to a halt and Mosley solemnly got out with two or three men who were not in uniform and began to inspect his troops. Edward recognized William Joyce, chief propaganda officer of the BUF, among them. Mosley was wearing the uniform he had designed himself – a black military-style jacket with an armband of red and white, which he said signified 'action within the circle of unity' whatever that meant. His breeches were grey and, inevitably, he wore jackboots. Edward thought he looked rather absurd and – his greatest criticism – un-English. The would-be dictator solemnly walked up and down the ranks of blackshirts inspecting them as though they were a regiment of soldiers rather than a private army of thugs.

Edward said out loud, 'That has to be the rummest thing!'

'It is a bit odd, isn't it?'

He looked round in surprise. He was hardly aware he had spoken aloud but obviously he had and now he saw who had answered him. It was none other than Sir Geoffrey Hepple-Keen.

'For goodness sake – what are you doing here?' he exclaimed.

'I might say the same of you,' Hepple-Keen replied mildly. 'I'm here on official business.'

Edward looked at him searchingly. 'You're not a policeman. You're an MP.'

'I'm a politician and this is politics.'

Just as Edward was going to press him to be more explicit, a man appeared on a rooftop brandishing a red flag. As Edward watched, he gave the clenched fist salute of the Communists and then bent over to pick up either a stone or a roof tile, which he threw as cleanly as though he were aiming a cricket ball at the stumps. By some amazing fluke, the missile hit Mosley on the shoulder. He had just returned to his car and was standing in the front ready to take the salute. He staggered and then righted himself. As if it had been a signal, from behind the barricade came a shower of stones which rattled against the Bentley, one smashing the windscreen. Mosley looked round in bewilderment, as if he could hardly credit what was happening. His chauffeur rapidly backed the car out of range and, as he did so, Mosley lost his balance and fell back on the seat. Edward laughed and turned to Hepple-Keen to see his reaction, but he had disappeared.

The situation was now getting out of hand. Missiles were pouring over the barricade and the sound of shouting seemed to suggest that the artillery attack presaged an all-out charge. To do the blackshirts justice, they remained in ranks and had not yet retaliated but their leaders were looking towards Mosley for instructions. More police arrived and a senior police officer who, Edward learned later, was Sir Philip Game, Chief Police Commissioner, went over to talk to him. Edward could not hear what was said but Mosley was gesticulating violently towards the barricade so it was not difficult to guess what he was demanding. He had permission to march down Cable Street and he was now prevented from doing so by a rabble of Communists and anti-Fascists. The Commissioner scratched his head but at last gave an order. From out of nowhere, it seemed to Edward, the street was full of mounted policemen and, at a word from their commander, they charged the barricade. It was an awesome sight and Edward wondered if London had seen anything like it since the Gordon riots a hundred and fifty years earlier.

He decided he ought to try and find Verity and warn her that she and her friends were in serious danger but, of course, they must have realized that. In any case, there wasn't time. Many of the horses had not been able to break through the barricade but one particularly determined group, supported by officers on foot brandishing batons, had made a gap at the far end, furthest away from where Edward was standing. By the time he had doubled back the way he had come and made his way round the barricade, the fight had degenerated into chaos. The rioters were throwing marbles and broken glass under the horses' hooves and women appeared at an upstairs window and began pelting the police with stones. One horse stumbled and fell. Edward could not see its rider as the fallen horse was quickly surrounded by rioters, but he feared the worst. Several policemen had been hit by missiles and were lying in the road being tended to by their colleagues. Dodging stones and bottles, Edward made his way to an upturned lorry where Jack Spot was rallying his troops.

He thought it most likely that Verity would be as near the centre of the storm as possible. Oddly enough, as though this was at the very eye of the storm, there was relative quiet here and he was able to shout to Spot: 'The police are never going to let you anywhere near the blackshirts. Oughtn't you to retreat and fight another day?'

'Never!' gasped the little man, still clutching his chair leg. 'They shall not pass. London will not allow Jew baiters through and . . . '

At that moment a police horse jumped right over the barricade and one of its hooves caught Edward on the forehead and knocked him to the ground. He could only have been unconscious for a few seconds but, when he came to, he found he was being dragged unceremoniously into Grace's Alley. 'The Old Mahogany Bar', in what had once been Wilton's Music Hall but was now a Methodist Mission, was serving as the protesters' headquarters. The 'barley-sugar' pillars were draped in red banners and the mahogany bar – which gave the place its name and which the Methodists had been canny enough to retain from its less respectable days – served as a huge desk from which the leaders dispensed badges and instructions. Absurdly, Edward thought for a moment of what Fenton would say when he saw the state of his suit and he tried to laugh.

'Oh, so you're awake,' a voice said briskly. It was Verity and she was not pleased. 'I've had to desert my post to look after you.'

'Sorry,' he said meekly.

'Thanks, boys,' she said to the two lads who had been manhandling him. 'He's all right. You can leave him to me.'

Edward noticed that, in a quaint gesture totally inappropriate to the situation, they touched their caps to her before running off. Verity might be a paid-up, card-carrying member of the Communist Party but she was always going to be a lady to men like these and the thought amused him.

'I was trying to find you,' he said plaintively.

'Oh, you were attempting to rescue me, were you?' she said callously. 'Quite the little hero. Oh well,' she relented,

'I suppose you meant well. Anyway, you've been wounded in the war against Fascism and you'll probably have a scar to prove it. Do you know, I saw something very strange on the barricades,' she said, mopping his head with something soft. 'Ugh. You've ruined my best silk handkerchief. Here, give me yours. You really are the limit, Edward.'

'What did you see that was strange?' he said, feeling rather sick and giddy.

'You remember when I went to that horrible dinner party at the German Embassy when we were investigating General Craig's murder?'

'Yes,' he said, hardly able to concentrate.

'Do you remember I said I was sitting next to a really awful man called Stille – Major Stille?'

'I think so.'

'I'm sure he was a major in the SS or something. Anyway, he was the most frightening man I've ever met.'

'And you saw him here, with Mosley?'

'No, that's the queer thing. He was *this* side of the barricade. We can't even see the blackshirts from here. But what was so queer was he was tossing bricks and urging us to do the same.'

'Golly, that's odd. Do you think he's changed sides?'

'Has that horse addled your brains? Of course he's not changed sides. He's an *agent provocateur*. We had them in Spain.'

'Is he still there?' Edward tried to raise himself to take a look.

'No, lie still. He caught my eye just as I saw him and smiled and then, as I started to shout for someone to get hold of him, he made himself scarce.'

'He smiled at you?'

'Sort of like a challenge – as though he was taunting me.'

'What was he wearing?'

'Nazi uniform. What do you think he was wearing? He was dressed like anyone else, of course.'

'Perhaps you were mistaken. Maybe it wasn't Stille.'

'It was Stille all right,' she said grimly.

'Well, do you know who I saw the other side of the barricade?'

'Who?'

'Sir Geoffrey Hepple-Keen, that's who.'

'Who's he?'

'Of course, I didn't tell you. He is a very right-wing Conservative MP – a friend of Scannon. He was at Haling when I was there. That's where I met him.'

'Was he with Mosley?'

'I don't know,' Edward said, feeling distinctly woozy, 'I don't think so. He was standing beside me, at least for a moment.'

He sat on the ground and felt very sick. Verity looked at him anxiously. 'Oh God. Are you all right? I suppose I had better get you home.' She looked round wildly and to her amazement saw Fenton.

'Can I help, miss?' he inquired.

'Yes you can. Lord Edward's taken a bit of a knock from a horse's hoof and he's feeling a bit sick. Gosh, am I glad to see you. Where have you sprung from?'

'Mr Fox telephoned me this morning after you had departed and suggested you might be glad of – as he put it – "back-up". So I thought I would make my way here by public transport and see if I could locate you.'

'Gosh! Who needs guardian angels when they've got you?'

'Very kind of you to say so, miss.'

'The car's about half a mile away, in Goodman's Yard. Do you think you can find it?'

'Without any difficulty, miss.'

6

'You don't want all this toast, do you, Edward? . . . Thanks.'

It was the next morning and Verity was sitting on Edward's bed eating his breakfast. They were discussing the riot.

'It's an odd thing,' he said, 'but you're the only girl I know who perches herself on a fellow's bed at breakfast for reasons of greed and not for the immoral purposes which modern literature prescribes.'

'Fenton doesn't approve.'

'Of you visiting me while I'm still in my pyjamas or for eating my toast and marmalade?'

'Both, I should think but mainly the former. He doesn't say anything but he looks. Am I the only lady who is to be seen on your bed before luncheon?'

He felt a twinge of guilt recalling that someone had actually been in his bed only a few nights before, though why he should feel guilty, when he was perfectly aware that Verity too had had lovers, he really couldn't say. He prevaricated. 'Now you're being impertinent. Ouch!' he added, as she cuffed him.

'Oh sorry, I forgot. How is your poor head?'

'As well as one might expect after being trampled on by a two-ton police horse.'

'Don't exaggerate. You suffered what the medical men call a "glancing blow" from the animal's hoof and, quite honestly, I think you deserved it.'

As soon as they had reached Albany the previous day, Fenton had insisted on calling the doctor. He had seemed to think Verity was personally responsible for his master being wounded and would hardly let her in his rooms. Once the doctor had arrived and checked that he had only suffered bruising and would recover after a good night's sleep, Fenton had sent her packing, politely but firmly. He had not liked it when she had turned up to see the patient before nine this morning.

'Why, for goodness sake? I was coming to your rescue.'

'I didn't want to be rescued. As it happened I was enjoying myself.'

'Tossing broken glass to maim those poor brutes you were commending a moment ago for knocking me flat?'

'No, not that but I knocked off a policeman's helmet.'

'And you lost your hat,' he said nastily. 'Fancy going to a riot in a hat. Fffou!'

'If you knew anything about protest marches, you'd know women always wear hats so the police can't grab you by the hair. As it happens, it was the hat I always wear for marches and I was very attached to it.'

'Obviously, not attached firmly enough.'

'Ha, ha. Anyway, what do you mean, "fffou!"?'

'I mean fffou,' he said haughtily, grabbing a piece of toast and honey before she could devour it.

They munched in companionable silence. 'Have you seen the papers?' she asked at last.

'Yes, Fenton gave me *The Times* and the *New Gazette*.'

'Did you like my report?' she asked defensively.

'Mmm,' he said, gulping down the last of the coffee. 'A little over the top perhaps but,' he added hurriedly, seeing the look in her eye, 'indubitably vivid. Why, you might have been there yourself.'

'Chump,' she said affectionately. 'Apparently we missed another two hours of rioting so you probably ruined my dispatch from the front. There were two police baton charges after we left and the police used water hoses. Dash it! In Spain we learnt never to tend the wounded until after the battle was over.'

'By which time it was too late, I suppose?'

'Very often it was,' she said soberly.

'See here,' she continued, opening *The Times*. 'It says "The Chief Police Commissioner asked the Home Secretary if he should tell Sir Oswald Mosley his march was cancelled and he said he should." The interesting thing is that apparently Mosley was rather relieved and dismissed his band of thugs without making a fuss. Here, he is quoted as saying "The Government surrenders to Red violence and Jewish corruption but we shall triumph because our faith is greater than their faith, and within us is a flame that shall light up this country and the world." What nonsense!'

'Yes, but it may just be nonsense which *will* light up the world,' Edward said seriously. 'Light it with the light of bombs and cannon fire. When I was with Joe in his office the other evening, he showed me the view – the Thames like black velvet, the streets streaked with orange and yellow, St Paul's glowering at us like some holy mountain – and I felt a bit like Faust. Joe said he didn't believe there would be war but that, if there was, he foresaw this peaceful scene transformed into a hellish bonfire. I tell you, Verity, I felt as if someone had walked over my grave. I imagined old Sam Pepys watching the great fire destroying the city he knew and I wondered if he had felt fear or excitement, or dread.'

'I watched towns burn in Spain and that was awful – it was like being a tourist in hell but I would be lying if I didn't say there was an excitement about it.'

'That reminds me. I've been summoned to the *New Gazette*. I expect Joe wants to talk to me about Molly's death and what happens now.'

At that moment the telephone rang and they listened while Fenton answered it. Then there was a tap on the door and Fenton said, 'My lord, Inspector Lampfrey is on the line and would like a word with you if it is convenient.'

'Of course, tell him I'll be right with him. Verity, pass me my dressing gown and then turn your head away or, better still, remove yourself to the drawing-room.'

Verity tossed him his red and blue-striped silk gown and flounced out of the room. She hated to admit it but, deep down, she too felt that 'nice' girls did not make themselves at home in a man's bedroom if they were not married to them and it annoyed her to find herself still so conventional. In any case, she had no wish to scandalize Fenton so she threw herself into an armchair and picked up the *New Gazette* and prepared to reread her account of what was being called the Cable Street Riot. Her report was on the front page which was pleasing. After all, she was the paper's only female news reporter. *The Times* had no female correspondents except writers on fashion, food and other domestic matters, so perhaps she had a right to be a little pleased with herself. But that raised the whole matter of what she did next. It was part of her nature never to be satisfied with what she had achieved. There was the book, of course, and then back to Spain, she supposed.

The fact of the matter was she did not particularly want to go back. She knew the Republicans were losing the civil war but it wasn't just that. When she had first gone to Spain, the issues had seemed to her to be clear. Spain's legitimate government was being challenged by the army and the Catholic Church in unholy alliance. The Republic had been corrupt, chaotic and ineffectual but its government had been freely elected and was trying to bring some hope to the vast, voiceless, impoverished peasant class. In her heart she doubted the new Republican leaders had the same priorities. Her commission to write a book on her experiences in Spain had been a godsend. It gave her an alibi for staying in England for a month or two. After Christmas, the whole situation in Spain would have changed and it might be easier to see her way forward.

Edward stuck his head round the door. 'It was as I thought. Poor Molly *was* murdered. She had taken ten grams of veronal – about twenty times what she might have been prescribed. It's conceivable she committed suicide but I don't think she did. She certainly didn't give me any hint that she was thinking of doing away with herself. Quite the contrary. She wasn't depressed. She was angry. Angry people don't kill themselves. If anything, they kill the person they're angry with. I say, Fenton, is my bath ready?'

'Yes, my lord.'

'Very good. Will you bring the car round in about ten minutes? The Inspector wants us back at Haling as soon as possible.'

'Very well, my lord. Might I be forgiven for reminding you of your appointment with Lord Weaver?'

'Dash it. Yes, thank you, Fenton. I had better go to the *New Gazette* first. I say, V, if you're not doing anything urgent, why not come down to Haling with me. When I've had my meeting with Joe, I can pick you up from the Hassels' and tell you all about it on the way.'

'Oh, I don't know. What business have I got at Haling? Anyway, I've got to be here when the Jarrow marchers arrive.'

'But that won't be for another few days, will it?'

'No, but . . . '

'But what?'

'I've got my book to do.'

'Surely a couple of days won't make a difference?'

'Leo Scannon, he's frightfully anti-us. He won't want a CP member like me cluttering up his hallway.'

Edward hesitated. 'Yes, I see your point. Half a minute. I'll telephone him and see what he says. Fenton, would you be good enough to get Mr Scannon on the line?'

Left to herself again, Verity fell into what her father called 'a brown study'. It was not usual for her to be uncertain where she was going and what she wanted out of life. Just a year ago it had all seemed so obvious. She was to be a famous foreign correspondent and help alert the world to the perils it faced from Fascism. Now . . . now it all seemed more ambiguous; the rights and wrongs less clear cut. Just at this particular moment she wanted to relax into the care and unqualified love which she knew – without any words having passed between them – the man in whose rooms she now sat was prepared to offer her. When he came back from telephoning she would hint at it.

However, when he did return he had something to tell her which put all thoughts of offering herself to him out of her mind.

'It's all fixed,' he said with a geniality she found unconvincing. 'I spoke to Dannie who said you must come. Dannie's a great admirer of yours and longing to meet you.'

'Dannie? Who's he? A friend of yours? I don't remember you mentioning him before.'

'She, not he. Dannie's Catherine Dannhorn. She's a famous mannequin. A friend of Joe Weaver's. I met her at Joe's, you know – when he had me to dine with Mrs Simpson. To tell you the truth, I think she might be Joe's mistress.'

Edward was trying to sound breezy but failing. He saw Verity hesitate. 'Please do say you'll come. Molly was my friend and she's been murdered. I can't sleuth properly without you.'

He wisely stopped himself saying, 'After all, you've nothing better to do,' and instead added, 'There may be a scoop there – "Conservative MP involved in society girl's death".'

Despite herself Verity's ears pricked. It was perfectly true that, if Molly Harkness had been murdered, it was news. Her friendship with the Prince of Wales had been chronicled in all the illustrated papers and the association was enough to make her death of considerable interest to the 'yellow press'.

'But you'll say I can't report anything we discover.'

'Perhaps not everything but I'm sure, if we can find out what happened to the poor girl, there'll be enough for a good story. Come on, V, I'm serious. I need you. We'll pop Fenton in the dickey and have a good old chin-wag in the car.'

He wasn't sure himself if he was just being kind – trying to cheer her up and distract her – or if he really did need her. If the latter, he really ought to do something about it.

'Ass,' Verity said automatically and gathered up her things. 'I suppose I'll have to brave your Fascist friends being boorish to help you but I warn you, if I get tried too much I do tend to bite.'

'Don't I know it,' Edward said with a theatrical shudder.

'I can't believe it!' Lord Weaver was not his usual self, in control of the world. He was edgy and irritable and paced up and down on the carpet flicking ash from his cigar all over the place. 'I can't believe it. I really don't think you understand how serious the situation is. Mrs Simpson relied on you and you've let her down. God knows where her letters are now. We'll probably be reading them in the *Daily Mail* tomorrow.'

'Hey, I say,' Edward interjected. 'Don't blame me. I had a perfectly reasonable conversation with her and, if I had been able to continue it, I think I might have persuaded her to give them up. Instead of which she was killed. I don't know who by but I intend to find out and, if I do, I will probably find the wretched letters.'

'And if not?'

'Then whatever happens, happens.'

''You realize it may mean the King having to abdicate?'

'Would that be altogether a bad thing? I mean, he seems to be hand in glove with the Nazis.'

'That's an exaggeration. But who is there if he did have to go? His brother is a half-wit stammerer.'

'Wait a bit, Joe. All I've heard of him makes me think he's a sound man. Not a Hollywood film star like the present one but do we really want glamour? With a war coming we want steady leadership – nothing flashy. Anyway, it may not come to that. Have you told Baldwin what's happened?'

'I have and he accused me of – how did he put it? – "having fumbled the catch". He wasn't pleased. Not pleased at all. He always seems to think I have some scheme on to do him down. I don't know why.'

'Does the King know about the theft yet?'

'Wally was going to tell him today but I told her to hold off for a few days. I said you were going to Haling and that Inspector Lampfrey was a good man – discreet. too. You've got a week,' he said, stabbing his cigar in Edward's direction. 'A week and then it all blows up in our faces.'

On the way down to Haling, Edward told Verity everything . . . or almost everything. He had already given her the bare outline but now he told her in detail while trying to make sense of it himself. She whistled.

'Heavens, I can see why the poor woman was killed. She threatened the whole rotten structure. It confirms my opinion that the monarchy ought to be done away with.'

'I say, V, steady on,' Edward said in alarm, swerving to avoid a tree which seemed to jump out of the side of the road at him. 'You really will get us thrown out of Haling if you say things like that!'

'I'll be good, don't worry. I'll save all my spleen until I can get you alone.'

'You never know, I might like that,' he said offensively and she poked him in the ribs, causing him to swerve again.

'But I haven't told you the final bit of news the Inspector gave me on the telephone – by the way, Lampfrey's a good egg. We won't have the sort of problems we had with what's his name? Chief Inspector Pride.'

The latter was the Scotland Yard man who had investigated General Craig's murder and who had taken an instant dislike to both Edward and Verity.

'Anyway, what was I saying? Oh yes, Lampfrey says Molly was pregnant.' As he half turned to see how Verity took the news, she screamed. The scream was not, however, a reaction to this piece of news but to the dog which dashed straight under the Lagonda's wheels. As they sped on, she turned to see the bewildered-looking canine brush itself down and continue its dangerous journey.

'Edward,' she said. 'You will kill us both if you don't concentrate on your driving.'

'You sound like my late-lamented mother,' he said crossly. He prided himself – like most men – on being a skilled driver and the reprimand annoyed him.

'So?' he said. 'If anyone knew she was pregnant, it might have given any friend of you-know-who an added motive to get rid of her. I mean, can you imagine it! Coronation Day and the papers are full of the King's love child by a discarded mistress. The mind boggles.'

'No question. It oughtn't to be too difficult to find out which of the King's friends decided to do away with her – like Henry the whatever and Becket. I suppose you are the prime suspect,' she said consideringly. 'After all, you had been officially commissioned to deal with Molly.'

'Hey, I'm getting fed up with people blaming me! Joe was most offensive. According to him, I will be responsible for the fall of the Empire if the letters get into the wrong hands. You know he calls her Wally?'

'No, really? Wally?' Verity giggled.

'Yes, and Joe says she grew up as Bessiewallis Warfield. Not surprising she wanted to change things.'

'No! Don't forget, I'm dedicated to seeing the end of the British Empire, so Joe can't threaten me with that eventuality. Did you tell him I was going with you to Haling?'

'Yes.'

'And what did he say?'

'He groaned.'

Edward had a sudden urge to tell Verity about Dannie. She was bound to find out sooner or later and it was better she heard it from his own lips.

He gripped the steering wheel tightly and said, as casually as he could, 'The Inspector knows I couldn't have killed Molly. I've got an alibi – Dannie – Catherine Dannhorn, the girl who wants to meets you.'

'I don't understand,' Verity said slowly. 'How can she give you an alibi?'

'Well, you see, she spent the night with me – or part of it. I don't know when she left. In fact, that's the problem,' he went on, speaking quickly and hoping that Verity would make no comment. 'I mean, she might have – I think she somehow probably did – unlock the door between my room and Molly's and take Mrs Simpson's letters and . . . '

'But I thought you said you'd only known the woman – Dannie or whatever you call her – just a few days.'

'That's right. That's what makes me think she was using me. I found her in my bed when I came back from talking to Molly.'

'And instead of turfing her out of your bed you . . . you . . . '

'She is very beautiful,' he said, making a bad situation worse.

'And it never struck you that the only reason a beautiful woman would throw herself at you was if she wanted something from you. I'm . . . I'm shocked and disgusted.'

'Well, damn it,' Edward said, stung by the tone of her voice, 'you have not been exactly celibate. What about that novelist fellow – Belasco – you had an . . . ?'

'That was quite different,' she said hurriedly. 'We were in love.'

'Hmm!' Edward responded through tightened lips. Then, feeling he was behaving badly, he said with an effort, 'I'm sorry, V, forgive me. You're right – it was shabby and – well, sordid. I've been playing the fool. I don't know why but I can't seem to . . . All I know is everything is going to the devil and I along with it.'

Verity was not mollified. She turned her head to stare out of the window as they sped past puzzled cows and apprehensive sheep.

They both felt in the wrong and that made each of them angry. It surprised Verity how greatly she felt betrayed. She had no rights over him, she knew that. She had deliberately refused to commit herself to him or, for that matter, to any man. She liked sex but it was easier to have it with a man like Ben Belasco whom she did not love and who she knew did not love her. It made no sense to feel dirtied by Edward's confession. Perhaps it was that she had – quite unconsciously – raised him above other men. She had turned him into a 'parfait gentil knight' and attributed to him virtues he did not possess and had never pretended to possess. She knew he had had affairs but this was different. Wasn't it rather squalid – this one passionless night with a high-class whore?

Edward too was unhappy. He blamed himself for not having had the moral courage to reject Dannie and, now he was sure she had used him, he felt even more disgusted with himself. He had let himself down in front of Verity and his own conscience and that made him angry with Verity, Dannie and, most of all, himself. He wondered now what had possessed him to get Verity invited to Haling. He had premonitions of disaster.

They had arranged to call in on Inspector Lampfrey at Marlborough police station and, in the forty minutes it took to get there, they hardly exchanged a dozen words. Edward halted the Lagonda outside the disarmingly attractive building, redolent of a country-house hotel. Only the blue lamp and the noticeboard, with its stern warnings and appeals for information, made its true purpose apparent to the casual passer-by. He jumped out and went round to open the passenger door but Verity had already opened it and studiously ignored him.

Lampfrey was his usual courteous self and, if his eyes showed surprise at seeing Verity, he disguised it with a smile and a firm handshake.

'You're sure it's murder?' Edward demanded when they were seated in the Inspector's office. 'I feel so much to blame if it was.'

'Why is that, Lord Edward?' asked Lampfrey mildly.

'I may have drawn attention to her in some way. I may have made the murderer frightened I was going to discover something from her which would endanger him or his friends.'

'I think, if I may say so, you're being fanciful. Mrs Harkness had made no secret of her relationship with . . . with royalty.'

124

'But did someone murder her because she was pregnant or to recover the stolen letters? If it was the latter, possibly it was I who let it be known she had them.'

Lampfrey shrugged his shoulders. 'Well, that is what we will have to find out, but I think it's best if you stop worrying about "ifs" and "maybes". You were asked to retrieve stolen property by its owner and you cannot be blamed for failing in the attempt.'

Edward shifted uncomfortably in his seat. It was all very well the Inspector telling him not to flagellate himself but Molly had been a friend and he had failed her as much as he had failed Mrs Simpson and Joe Weaver.

'I've asked Mr Scannon if he would mind playing host for another couple of days to everyone who was in the house when Mrs Harkness died. He is a very busy man but has kindly agreed.'

'Ah yes, I happened to see Sir Geoffrey at the Cable Street riot.'

'That was where you sustained your injury, was it, Lord Edward?'

'What? Oh that,' he said, touching his forehead which was still red and sore. 'It's nothing. I was clipped on the head by a horse's hoof. Totally my fault.'

Verity, who had up to now been silent, said, 'Inspector, forgive me for asking, but isn't it possible Mrs Harkness took the overdose of veronal herself, either by accident or on purpose? Maybe she didn't like being pregnant?'

'It is just possible, Miss Browne, but unlikely. If she had wanted to, I'm sure one of her friends would have arranged for her to have had an abortion. Yes, I know it's illegal but you know and I know it happens every day in some back room in the East End of London. I have talked to everyone who was at Haling the night she died and everyone, not least Lord Edward,' he said, nodding in the latter's direction, 'has convinced me she was not suicidal. Angry, perhaps, but not in a mood to do away with herself.'

'But could she not have taken too much by mistake?' Verity persisted. 'Perhaps she woke in the night and reached for the bottle forgetting she had already dosed herself and then . . . '

'It might be just possible but the overdose was very substantial. If she had taken a normal dose, she would have been most unlikely to wake or, if she had, would have had difficulty taking so large a second dose. But there's another point we should consider, there's no sign of the bottle of veronal. Veronal wasn't in her flask when Lord Edward drank from it, so she must have added it some time after he left – she or someone else. Then that someone removed the bottle.'

'You've searched the ground outside her window, of course,' Edward broke in, 'but are you sure the bottle's not lodged in the Virginia creeper? It might have been thrown out . . . I don't believe it, mind you, but . . . '

'We have searched but, you're right, it might be a good idea to have it looked at again. We interviewed the chemist round the corner from where she lived who supplied her sleeping draughts. He is adamant she did not have as much as ten grams. We are making inquiries of other chemists in the neighbourhood but . . . '

'We found some invoices in her house,' Edward explained to Verity, 'so we knew who was her chemist and her doctor. Her doctor didn't know she was pregnant?'

'No, and he also said he did not consider her suicidal.'

'So she was killed by someone staying in the house?' Verity said flatly.

'Maybe,' Lampfrey said, 'but the situation is complicated by the existence of the Virginia creeper just outside her bedroom window. Someone might have used it to gain entrance to her room.'

'No footprints?'

'No, Lord Edward, nothing. The ground was quite hard at the foot of the creeper and there were no obvious signs of someone climbing up it, but that doesn't mean they didn't.'

'So what now, Inspector?' Verity asked. 'Lord Edward said you hadn't been able to trace any family?'

'No, the poor lady seems to have been quite alone in the world. She had a solicitor – to buy the flat and so on – but he hardly seemed to know her. He had no knowledge of any will.'

'That's why I want so much to see her killer caught,' Edward said fiercely. 'Someone thought no one would care if she lived or died, but I care.'

The Inspector looked at him gravely. 'And I care,' he said. 'I have arranged to come up to the house after breakfast tomorrow and I'm going to go through the statements everyone made to me.'

'You think someone will remember something, or are you hoping one of us will contradict ourselves?' Edward asked ironically.

The Inspector shrugged his shoulders. 'I know a good deal more than I did about what happened that night but there's plenty I don't know.'

'Do you think Mrs Harkness was killed to keep her quiet – to keep her from embarrassing the monarchy?' Verity asked in her straightforward way.

'It looks like that, but she may have had other enemies with quite different motives for wanting her dead. That's what I intend to find out.'

Leo Scannon met them at the front door. 'Miss Browne, how very nice to meet you,' he said blandly.

Verity looked at him suspiciously but managed a smile. 'It's very good of you to have me. I hope you won't blame Lord Edward for inflicting me on you.'

'Please Verity – may I call you Verity? Although we see things from a different political perspective, I hope you will feel welcome here. Lord Weaver speaks so highly of you and any friend of Lord Edward's is a friend of mine.'

It all sounded gracious enough and given that Verity had all but invited herself – or at least that was what Scannon had every right to believe – she could do little but smile and thank him and admire the house.

It occurred to Verity as she was dressing for dinner that, though the aristocracy – men like Edward and his brother, the Duke of Mersham – were opposed to Communism and everything it stood for, the Party's most diehard enemies were people like Scannon whose social position was less assured; men who had, as it were, 'risen through the ranks' or their fathers had. It was, after all, perfectly natural that, having fought to 'better himself', a man might resent any movement which seemed to threaten his achievement. It was sad, though, that what she and the Party saw as social justice, so many saw as institutionalized burglary.

Verity was, of course, particularly curious to meet Catherine Dannhorn and, though she did not admit it to herself, she was also a little frightened of her. She dressed with particular care and wore a Schiaparelli dress her father had insisted on buying her during one of his fits of guilt at not providing her with a settled home life. Verity's father was the well-known barrister, D. F. Browne, who had devoted his life to defending left-wing causes. When trade union leaders made legal challenges against employers or radical newspapers were sued for libel, they turned first to Verity's father. He was a fine advocate and well enough off to run a green Rolls-Royce of which he was very proud. He was on a host of committees and the boards of several socialist organizations and businesses such as the *Manchester Guardian* as well as more or less bankrolling the *Daily Worker*, the official organ of the Communist Party, though he was not a CP member himself. Had he been, he would effectively have been prevented from practising law. His responsibilities and stern sense of duty meant he had very little time for his daughter, left motherless while still a child. So on her birthday and at Christmas he tended to try to compensate for his absence in her life by embarrassingly lavish gifts.

She had only worn the dress once before at a dinner at the German Embassy in Carlton House Terrace where she had been – dangerously – spying on the enemy. She knew she looked stunning in it and, without admitting as much, was determined that Edward's 'Dannie' was not going to have a walkover that evening. For over a year now, she had been so sure of Edward's – well, why not say it? – love, she was inclined to take it for granted. It had scared her a little and she had deliberately resisted it but now, when she seemed on the point of losing it, she discovered she would mind that very much indeed.

It was a disaster. As Verity was shown by the butler into the drawing-room, she was met by stares of frank amazement. She had thought that everyone would dress for dinner – wasn't it that sort of house? – but the men were in dinner jackets and the women in short dresses.

'Oh, I'm sorry,' she gasped. 'Edward, you didn't tell me.'

'My dear, you look absolutely divine,' Scannon said, coming to take her by the hand and lead her into the group round the fire. 'We've got so lazy but you are quite right to show us up for it. Dannie, doesn't Verity look simply charming?'

'Charming,' Dannie said, taking the cigarette holder out of her mouth and offering Verity her hand. 'I have so much wanted to meet you, Miss Browne. I do admire your writing.'

'Oh, thank you, but Edward, you've made me feel a fool. Why didn't you tell me not to dress up?'

'Verity, I do apologize. Leo asked me to tell you not to be smart but it quite went out of my head.'

She gave him a look which made him blench, before she turned once more to Dannie. 'He talks so much about you, Miss Dannhorn.'

'Please do call me Dannie, everyone does. I hope he *doesn't* talk about me. It's not likely to be complimentary.'

'He said you were beautiful and you are,' Verity said simply.

Dannie looked a little taken aback. She was indeed looking beautiful and sophisticated, as though she had stepped out of a play by Noel Coward. Her black lace dress worn

129

over peach silk-crepe was set off with a pearl choker and pearl earrings. She wore very little make-up and her hair, though not as short as Verity's, gave her a clean-cut, almost boyish look. Verity loathed her on sight. She couldn't bring herself to call her Dannie so called her nothing at all but she found it difficult to take her eyes off her.

'Where's Miss Conway, Leo?' Edward asked.

'My mother's not well and she is looking after her,' Scannon replied rather tersely.

'I'm sorry to hear that,' Edward said, wondering how it was possible to know when the comatose old woman they had viewed on their previous visit was having a worse day than usual.

When they went into dinner, Verity found herself sitting between Lord Benyon and Sir Geoffrey Hepple-Keen. Benyon she liked immediately and, since he began by praising her father, whom he knew quite well, she soon forgot her embarrassment and began to enjoy herself. When, out of politeness, she turned to her other neighbour, things did not go so smoothly. Edward had, of course, told her he had seen Hepple-Keen at the barricades in Cable Street, on Mosley's side, but she hardly thought it was the time or place to bring this up. She had no wish to get embroiled that night in a political confrontation with anybody – that would have been too easy and quite disastrous – so she looked for something else to talk about. She tried a variety of subjects from the weather to London restaurants but Hepple-Keen either did not reply or answered in monosyllables. Feeling that she had done what she could and as Benyon was deep in conversation with the American, Larry Harbin, she relapsed into silence and drank her wine.

Scannon, at the head of the table, saw her plight and leant across to ask her about Spain. 'We were so interested to read your account of the raising of the siege of Toledo,' he began. 'Do you really think anyone can stop Generalissimo Franco from entering Madrid?'

To do Scannon justice, he had not meant to needle her and was merely trying to make conversation but Verity thought she was being taunted and, her tongue loosened by the wine and her bad temper, she embarked on an impassioned defence of the Republic. Gradually, conversation round the table faded and then stopped altogether as everyone turned to listen to Verity. Benyon looked at her with sympathy, enjoying this passionate outburst which brought the blood into the girl's cheeks and made her eyes sparkle. He liked young people and found this child a delightful antidote to reptilian politicians such as Scannon and Hepple-Keen. Harbin, too, was much taken with Verity but he shook his head in mournful disagreement when she insisted the Republic could still win the war against Fascism. Dannie's smile was that of a leopard who sees its prey become entangled in the undergrowth and her beautiful eyes became almost feline.

Edward, consumed with embarrassment, was wondering what on earth had made him invite Verity to Haling but, in the end, his embarrassment faded and he watched her with all the tenderness of a father. She was, he thought, the most adorable girl and grinned to himself as he considered how much she would resent being so described. Dannie was more beautiful. He flashed a glance at her and met her eye. She raised a glass to her lips and made a little *moue* – a moment of conspiracy which made him feel he was betraying Verity.

Benyon diplomatically guided Verity out of the hole she had dug for herself and talked of a new exhibition of Italian art, of his battle with the Chancellor over finding money for the Opera House and of a recent visit to New York. During dinner, no one mentioned Molly but her presence hung over the table like an aura. Edward was probably the only person present who had liked her and even he had to admit she had been tiresome and foolish, like a spoiled child. Someone, he thought, had wanted her out of the way and had dispatched her with the callous competence of a technician. It was possible – it was likely – that one of the people round this table had been responsible for Molly's murder. He brooded on what possible motive any of them might

131

have had and came to the uncomfortable conclusion that, to an objective investigator such as Inspector Lampfrey, he had the most obvious reason for wanting Molly dead and he certainly had the opportunity. He had been commissioned by Mrs Simpson to retrieve her letters. It now appeared Molly had been pregnant with what was almost certainly a royal by-blow. Wasn't the unspoken command: silence the wretched woman?

He knew, and Lord Weaver must have known, that he would never have harmed her. He wondered if it were too cynical to believe that another person in the house party had been there to make sure he did not fail and, if he did, to tidy up the mess. But he had not been given time to succeed or fail, so why had the murderer struck that first night? Why not wait until Edward had got back the letters?

Two reasons presented themselves. First, the murderer might have had no knowledge of Edward's mission and acted independently. Second, Edward might have been marked out as what Americans called the 'fall guy'. He had been instructed not to approach Molly in private. He was told he had to make his attempt to talk her out of her foolishness at Haling, and for no very good reason as far as he could see. The police would have been bound to discover why he was in the house, even if he had not admitted it to Lampfrey immediately. He had been given the room next to Molly's and the communicating door had been unlocked. Two people were obvious candidates for the role of murderer in this case: Dannie and his host, Leo Scannon. Scannon was a much more ruthless man than his rather foppish exterior might lead one to believe. Edward knew about his vicious tongue from personal experience but Weaver had told him how he liked to conspire and manipulate. He was never happier than when playing *éminence grise*.

But did that make him a murderer? Would he have chosen to murder a guest in his own house? Even Lady Macbeth had fainted at the idea. For what it was worth, Edward was convinced that Scannon's shock, when they found Molly dead, had been genuine. Dannie, on the other hand, was tough enough, he guessed, to use him to gain entrance to Molly's bedroom. If she had been frightened of Molly waking while she was searching her things, might she not have made her drink the veronal? Perhaps Scannon or Weaver had asked *her* to retrieve Mrs Simpson's letters. Edward strongly suspected she was, or had been, the newspaper proprietor's mistress. Lady Weaver's attitude to her had more or less confirmed that. The hostility had been so marked, she had not even been able to introduce her to him. He pursed his lips. It was possible but, if seducing him had provided her with access to Molly's bedroom, it was not something she could hide. If she had a key to Molly's room, wouldn't it have been easier to have gone in through the passage door?

What about the others? Lord and Lady Benyon? He could hardly imagine they had anything to do with the business. They were innocent bystanders, surely. The American? Harbin was a physically unprepossessing man but he had a brain and he had fought his way to the top in business and politics. Edward guessed that you didn't get where he was without standing on a few faces on the way. He had the opportunity – his bedroom was next to Molly's on the other side – and he had a shadow of a motive. Mrs Simpson was from Baltimore – Harbin's home town. Might he not wish to preserve her reputation? He had been quite frank with Edward about his dislike of Molly just before they had found her dead – unnecessarily frank, one might think, if he had murdered her. It was a long shot but Edward decided he would see if there was a communicating door between the senator's bedroom and Molly's – not that it really mattered. Harbin – like any of the others – could easily have obtained a key and entered from the passage. He must ask the butler – Pickering – where duplicate keys to the rooms were kept and how many there were. Most country houses he had stayed in didn't have keys to the bedrooms so the key was probably just a red herring.

He looked round the table. The fellow Carstairs – Boy Carstairs – he had known Molly in Africa – might have been her lover at one time or another. He must be investigated.

If there were reasons for Molly being murdered, which had nothing to do with Mrs Simpson and her carelessness with royal love letters, then Carstairs might know them. There was the husband who had killed himself and the lover who had been discarded, or who had discarded her, after the scandal of the suicide. Edward tried to recall what Molly had said to him as they had lain chastely in each other's arms on the veldt. When he came to think about it, considering how reckless she was and how she had loved gossip, she had been surprisingly reticent about her own affairs and Edward had not questioned her closely. He had been trying to cheer her up – not encourage her to wallow in the miserable mess she had made for herself.

He finished his fish and caught the eye of Sir Geoffrey Hepple-Keen. He couldn't make much of him. Was he an out and out rogue – a supporter of Mosley and the Fascists? He made his wife miserable, that was certain. He must try to get to know him but he had the feeling it might be difficult.

Inevitably, the topic of Spain was raised once again – this time by Lady Hepple-Keen who was apparently involved in the efforts of the Red Cross to bring succour to victims on both sides of the divide. She asked timidly if Verity had seen 'horrors' and Edward was relieved when she was able to speak calmly, but with feeling, of what she had seen. She dwelt on the human tragedy of the civil war, the ruin of the countryside, and described as neutrally as she could the siege of Toledo, praising the courage of the young officers who had held out in the fortress long after they must have given up hope of being relieved, and the incompetence of the Republicans – her own friends – who had allowed precisely this to happen. She told of how, in the savage hand-to-hand fighting, she had found a baby underneath the body of its mother who had been killed by a stray shot. She had taken the baby with her as she fled the Moorish troops swarming across the city.

'What happened to it?' Lady Hepple-Keen asked, fearing to hear it had suffered some terrible fate. 'Was it a boy or a girl?'

'A girl. I took her back with me to Madrid. What else could I do?'

'And?'

'And I handed her over to the Red Cross. They have set up orphanages but I don't know . . . ' Verity looked distressed.

'The Red Cross is doing wonderful work in Spain,' Lady Hepple-Keen said, looking at Verity nervously. 'I expect you know that there's a man called Dr Aurelio Romeo who is organizing relief work there.'

'I met him,' Verity said. 'If I believed in saints, I would appoint him my patron saint. The trouble is, there is so little difference between civilian and soldier in Spain and there's no question of exchanging prisoners or anything like that. The bitterness is too great.'

'We're trying to arrange for some of the children to be brought to England,' Lady Hepple-Keen said.

Verity was impressed. Perhaps this timid, put-upon woman had more to her than she had supposed. 'If I can help in any way . . . '

'Oh, could you? Perhaps in the *New Gazette* . . . ?'

'I'll talk to Lord Weaver about it,' Verity promised. 'It's just the sort of thing he might like to put his weight behind.'

Harbin said, 'You had a near miss at Toledo, I understand, Miss Browne?'

'Oh, I was in very little danger.'

'I don't believe that, young lady. You were a woman among savages . . . ' He looked ferocious, as if Verity had put herself in a position to be raped and killed deliberately to annoy him, but in fact he was jealous of her war. She had tested her courage and found it true. Like so many men who have never been in battle, Harbin had a sneaking fear that, were he put to the test, he might find himself a coward.

'I don't think anyone knew I was a woman,' Verity said with a smile. 'I wore the same clothes the men wore – baggy trousers, a shirt and a sort of military jacket I picked up somewhere. I've got a photograph a friend took of me beside my motor bike. I look rather absurd but no temptation to any self-respecting rapist.'

Edward wanted to ask who the friend was who had taken the photograph but he did not dare. Instead he said, 'I didn't know you rode a motor bike.'

'Oh yes,' she said breezily. 'It was the only way to get about. The roads hardly exist and I needed to see what was happening and then get somewhere I could file my report. The motor bike was essential.'

'What did you see of that novelist fellow – what's his name – Belasco? Was he in the front line? You were pretty thick with him, weren't you?' Hepple-Keen asked.

'How did you know that?' she said, surprised.

'I don't know,' he said, rather uncomfortably Edward thought. 'Didn't you say something about him in one of your articles?'

'Actually, I rather got one over on him,' Verity said, grinning. 'Press weren't allowed on the front line and women weren't allowed within miles of it in theory. That's one of the reasons why, as I told you, I disguised myself in men's clothes.'

'You fought as a soldier?' Scannon asked, scandalized.

'I did have a pistol for self-defence but I never used it. I was a journalist . . . an observer . . . '

'Doesn't sound that way,' Scannon said drily.

Harbin said, 'Gee, I envy you that, Miss Browne, being at "the hot gates". I guess I'm not made to be a military man – ain't got the physique for it, as you can see, but before I close my eyes and enter Elysium – or maybe the other place, who knows? – I would dearly like to be involved in battle.'

Verity looked at him speculatively. 'I have to tell you, Mr Harbin, that battle's not what it's cracked up to be. I found it more like your Hart Crane described it in *The Red Badge of Courage* – much waiting around for something to happen followed by a confusing mêlée and, in my case, ignominious flight.'

'Still,' Harbin said reflectively, 'I guess a man who has never fought is not quite a man.'

Rather unexpectedly Benyon broke in to say, 'I can't agree with that. In fact, it's just the kind of nonsense that made all those poor boys join Kitchener's army in 1914. They thought it would be a great adventure and they would come back to their girls as heroes but, of course, for the most part they didn't come back.'

Edward thought the conversation might have got interesting if they had gone on to discuss the nature of courage. He would have particularly liked to have Carstairs' notion of it. The hunter had been in many tight corners in his life but now he seemed oddly reluctant to join in the conversation and Scannon had something else on his mind. 'The Inspector wants to talk to us tomorrow at about eleven in the drawing-room. After that, I gather, we are all free to go. He apologizes for the inconvenience, knowing that most of us . . . all of us have other things to do, but I thought we owed it to him, and of course to Molly, to do what we can to sort this out. So far, we have managed to avoid anything appearing in the press and I would be grateful if we could keep it all quiet a little longer. Of course, there will have to be an inquest.'

'Why is Miss Browne here then?' Carstairs asked in his lazy drawl. 'Isn't she a journalist? I don't see what she has to do with all this anyway.'

'Verity's a friend of mine and she's not wearing her journalist's hat, Carstairs,' Edward said hurriedly.

'And I wanted to meet her,' Dannie chimed in.

Carstairs grunted, clearly unsatisfied, and Verity found herself trying not to blush.

All through dinner Edward was nervous that Verity would make a fuss when the ladies had to leave the table to let the gentlemen smoke their cigars and drink their port but, to his surprise and relief, she rose meekly from the table and went off with Dannie. As Edward chewed on his cigar and half listened to Boy Carstairs telling big-game stories, a new worry surfaced in his mind: how were Dannie and Verity getting along? He half expected to hear screams and to have to break up fisticuffs but no such refereeing exercise was called for. He was not vain enough to think he would be their sole topic of conversation but he had an idea that at this moment his reputation might be being savaged by two extremely strong-minded women and it made the hairs on the back of his neck prickle.

The men did not linger long at table but Edward stirred himself to say in a low voice to Hepple-Keen, 'I still don't understand what you were doing at the Mosley march.'

Hepple-Keen shrugged his shoulders. 'I was a friend of Mosley in his younger and wiser days and I'm still curious as to what sent him off the rails. Call it "human interest".' And with that Edward had to pretend to be satisfied.

When they joined the ladies in the drawing-room, there was no sign that Dannie and Verity had been doing more than chatting on neutral subjects but Verity avoided him when he crossed the room to talk to her. The fire was lit but it was still too cold for comfort. It wasn't long before the Benyons announced that they were going to bed and this broke up the party. Verity was sleeping in Molly Harkness's room and it occurred to Edward she might be nervous. When he walked over to say goodnight and, if necessary, reassure her, she again avoided him and he was left looking rather foolish as she swept past him. He saw Scannon wink at Carstairs which annoyed him. However, no sooner was he in his own room with Fenton taking charge of his dinner jacket than he heard a scream. He looked at Fenton and Fenton looked at him. Without a word, they made for the door which linked his room with Verity's. It was locked. They both went into the passage, Edward grabbing his dressing gown as he stumbled past the bed. Harbin arrived at the same moment and Edward had a horrible sense of *déjà vu*. Could it be that he was going to find Verity dead as they had found Molly?

He knocked noisily on the door and with relief heard Verity turning the key and trying to open it. When at last she succeeded, he was confronted by a red-faced, irate young woman dressed in a fetching silk kimono holding in her left hand, by the tail, a very dead rat.

'What took you so long and what on earth are you doing with that, V?' he inquired vacuously. 'It's a rat, isn't it?'

Verity stared at him and said through pursed lips, 'Yes, Edward, as you say, it is a rat. I discovered it when I got into bed.'

'Good lord, I say, what a stunt!' Carstairs said, arriving just at this moment with Pickering. 'I mean, how revolting!' he corrected himself. 'I say, Leo,' Scannon had appeared clad in a green dressing gown and slippers, 'is it your custom to put dead rats in your guests' beds? It beats me, doesn't it you, Harbin? Have you looked in your bed? I expect there's something exciting there for you as well.'

Scannon looked at Carstairs with disgust. 'I need hardly say, Verity, that it's nothing to do with me. Someone has played a nasty trick on you and I do apologize. Here, Pickering, Miss Browne has found a dead rat in her bed. Do you know anything about it?'

'Nothing at all, sir.' He took the rat from Verity. 'I shall dispose of this, madam, and if you can wait for a few minutes I will have your bed made up with clean sheets.'

'Pickering, presumably Gladys turned down the beds while we were in the dining-room?' Scannon said. 'Send for her, if you please, so we may question her.'

'Yes, sir, but I don't think . . . '

'Nor do I, man,' Scannon said irritably. He turned to Verity. 'Gladys has been with us for fifteen years at least and I have no doubt that, whoever played this trick on you, it wasn't her.'

'Please, it's late. Don't send for Gladys. We can ask her in the morning if she noticed anything. If I could just have some clean sheets, let's all go back to bed. It was silly of me to scream like that. As you say, it was no more than a silly joke. Nothing to be alarmed about.'

7

'We have completed our investigations and we have found no evidence of foul play.'

A shocked silence followed Inspector Lampfrey's words. They had all gathered in the drawing-room expecting the Inspector to tell them they were all suspects in a murder investigation but here he was telling them that Molly Harkness had not been murdered. Edward said at last, 'Might I ask in that case, Inspector, if you have come to a conclusion as to *how* Mrs Harkness died?'

'That will be for the inquest jury and the coroner to decide. All I can say is there is no evidence of anyone else being involved in her death. Whether she died accidentally or took an overdose deliberately it is in my view impossible to say.'

Carstairs said, 'So we will not have to give evidence at the inquest?'

'Mr Scannon and Lord Edward will be called to give evidence of Mrs Harkness's state of mind the evening before she died but, at this stage, there appears to be no necessity for inconveniencing anyone else.'

The faint West Country burr in the Inspector's voice was rather more pronounced than usual and Edward guessed that, despite his cool exterior, the Inspector was under considerable strain.

Verity had not been invited to hear the Inspector address the household and she had not been at breakfast – Scannon said she had 'gone out walking' – and Edward had to assume he was still *persona non grata*. However, the Inspector's announcement was so unexpected he decided he had to talk it over with her. Pickering said she was in the garden and he found her examining the rhododendrons with exaggerated interest.

'Oh, it's you,' she said as he came up to her.

'Were you expecting someone else?' he inquired. 'Perhaps *anyone* else?'

'Look, Edward, you made an utter fool of me last night and, I am tempted to think, deliberately.'

'Verity, really! I just forgot to pass on the message. Anyway, you looked . . . spiffing.'

'Spiffing!' she sneered. 'Do grow up. You're not at your preparatory school now.'

'You looked stunning,' he amended. 'Don't you want to hear what Inspector Lampfrey said?'

'I suppose he accused you of murder. It would be perfectly reasonable.'

'No, he said she had died by accident. I ask you! The man's been got at. That's the only possible explanation.'

'What on earth do you mean?'

'Lampfrey knows Molly wasn't in any mood to kill herself so he says it was an accidental overdose.'

'It could have been, and we both know there's not an atom of evidence to show she was murdered.'

Edward refused to be deflated. 'I had a few words with him after his announcement and he more or less admitted he had had orders from the Chief Constable to give up the case.'

'What did he say exactly?'

'There was a lot going on and he was needed to investigate an attempted rape and the Chief Constable had told him he could not afford to let him spend more time on this.'

'It may all be true.'

'Yes, but I'm sure the Inspector knows he hasn't got to the bottom of the case. No, Verity, he's been shut up. Someone's afraid the inquiry might throw something up – bad publicity for the King. We've seen it all before. The powers-that-be don't like anyone rocking the boat. The public must not see their rulers with their trousers down.'

'So there's nothing much left to do? We can all go back to London? I must do some work on my book, in any case.'

Verity sounded cold, unsympathetic, and Edward wondered what, if anything, Dannie had said to her.

'Yes, you go back and get on with your book,' he said nastily. 'I'm going to find out why Molly was killed. I know she was. She was pregnant, she had stolen incriminating letters which could only make a delicate situation more delicate. Molly was a nuisance. Of course she was killed.'

'You're just going to make a fool of yourself. Talk to Joe. See what he says, though I can tell you what he will say: "Shut up and take your nose out of other people's business."'

'Well,' said Edward haughtily, 'I'm disappointed in you. You do what you like. Molly was my friend . . . '

'She was your lover; Dannie was telling me – one of your other lovers.'

'Molly was my friend,' he repeated, 'and I'm not going to be shut up.'

'I thought you said you were hoping to get some sort of job with the Foreign Office. I can't think you'll improve your chances of employment by making a stink about this.'

'Verity! I'm ashamed of you. Have you no principles?'

'Damn you!' She turned on him fiercely and Edward, angry as he was, recoiled at her fury. 'Don't you dare say anything to me about principles. You're a rat and I never want to see you again.'

Verity stormed off towards the house and Edward strode in the other direction, furious with her, with the Inspector and, most of all, with himself. He walked off his irritation in half an hour but when he got back to the house – as the gong was going for luncheon – his host informed him that

142

Verity had asked Carstairs to take her to the station as she had remembered an important engagement in London, 'which she was anxious to miss'.

Edward looked at Scannon, for a moment not understanding.

'I was joking. I suppose you two had a row?'

'Not at all. By the way, Leo, now that we have the Inspector's leave to depart I think I, too, ought to get back to town.'

'As you wish,' Scannon said airily. 'Perhaps you can give Harbin a lift. He is also anxious to be in town tonight. I feel rather insulted. It seems none of you can wait to leave Haling – I can't think why.'

The Lagonda cut through the gathering dusk, the throb of its six-cylinder engine discouraging conversation. Savernake Forest encroached on the road and roe deer peered at them from behind the trees, their eyes yellow in the headlights. Edward liked this sort of driving. The roads were almost empty and he sped through Newbury and reached Reading in record time. His passenger was almost invisible under a heap of travelling rugs and a heavy ulster he had borrowed off his host. Edward had left Fenton at Haling to take the luggage on the train.

He glanced at Harbin and said conversationally, 'Looks like rain. I think I'll stop and put up the hood. No sense in getting soaked.'

Harbin grunted, which Edward took for assent. When they started again, Harbin suddenly said, 'You'll forgive me for speaking my mind, Lord Edward, but when I first met you last week, I didn't rate you.'

It was odd, Edward thought, how the man suddenly sounded more American than he had at Haling. Here, he thought, was the true Harbin, the self-made millionaire, tough as they come but veneered, as it were, with the manners of an English gentleman. Physically desiccated he might be, but there was a toughness of spirit which made him formidable.

'I have seen a little of your aristocracy,' he went on, 'and while there are men I admire, such as Lord Halifax whom I am proud to call a friend, for the most part the English aristocrat does not impress me as a type. He appears to me, as an American, to presume on his position in society. In short, the English aristocrat seems to believe the system owes him a living. It's not the way it works in Baltimore. But I pride myself on being a judge of character and I'm not afraid to admit a mistake. I'm inclined to think I misjudged you. I think you are a lot smarter than you look. Would I be right in thinking, for instance, that you smell a stinking fish in this business of Mrs Harkness's death?'

Edward grinned to himself. He liked bluntness and he realized the American was paying him an honest compliment.

'I do indeed, Mr Harbin,' he said. 'I can't prove anything but I am pretty sure Molly was murdered and I believe Inspector Lampfrey thinks so too.'

'So why has he said the investigation is closed? He struck me as an honest man.'

'I agree, Lampfrey is honest – I'm sure of it – but I'm equally certain he has had instructions to drop the case.'

'Instructions from whom?'

'Well, that's the question. It could be any number of people who don't want to see anything in the press which might reflect badly on the King and Mrs Simpson.'

'You've met Mrs Simpson, I believe, Lord Edward. Tell me frankly. What did you make of her?'

'I liked her. She's on the make but so are most of us. She's certainly not the monster some people would have you believe. She's intelligent, genuinely concerned for the King's welfare but – and who could blame her – she would enjoy being queen.'

'And will she be?'

'Your guess is as good as mine but I don't think the people – the ordinary English – would stand for it. Did you see in *The Times* today the Bishop of Bradford sounding off against divorce? He said remarrying after divorce is bigamy. Of course, he did not mention Mrs Simpson and most of the people reading his views will never have heard of her but if – or rather when – they do, they will be shocked. The middle class here in England, Mr Harbin, is very "moral". "Moral" may be a synonym for "hypocritical" but they expect and demand that their betters set them a good example.'

'Mmm. In Baltimore, too, I guess. The President, for many ordinary Americans, is above criticism. He personifies America so to talk ill of him is unpatriotic – and yet we know that Warren Harding, for one, was more corrupt than the sachems of Tammany Hall. We all want our leaders to be above reproach but know them to be mortal men like ourselves. I guess that's the way you think of your king.'

'Yes, Queen Victoria set us an example of probity and rectitude and our middle-class Englishman – and his wife – are Victorian. But you come from Mrs Simpson's part of the world – what do you think of her?'

'My feelings for Mrs Simpson are ambiguous, Lord Edward. I know a great deal about her past life and it don't make pretty reading but, on the other hand, she is, as you say, from my home town and I would hate to see her humiliated.'

'You said you don't think much of our aristocracy, Mr Harbin. If I may say so, I think you ought to understand the effect the war had on my generation. Those of us who were too young to fight – some of us at any rate – felt almost unmanned by the sacrifice our elders made for us. My eldest brother was one of the first officers to be killed in France in 1914. That was over twenty years ago but I confess I am still wrestling with the idea of how I can live up to that example. And, what's more, we feel – I feel – the sacrifice may have been futile. They promised us that it was to be the war to end all wars but another even more beastly one looms. We've had economic depression – my friend Miss Browne is joining the march from Jarrow protesting at the poverty and unemployment which has sucked the life out of the place – and the politicians are powerless, or too inept, to do anything about it. Can you wonder that our young men feel their lives to be futile? I feel it myself – what can I do to serve my country? I'm still trying to find out. A friend of mine who was in the war and came out physically unscathed said to me: "I have a coffin in the back of my head." It may sound melodramatic but I know what he meant.'

The American was silent for a minute or two, hunched down in his seat. At last he said, 'I stand rebuked, Lord Edward. I have seen this sense of futility you speak about in France and in Germany and it is just what Herr Hitler has used to gain power. America came out of the war economically stronger. We had flexed our muscles and found them stronger than we thought but, more significantly, we gained a new confidence in ourselves. Then came the Wall Street Crash and the Depression but we do not have a coffin at the back of our heads. Some of our confidence comes from having a great man at the helm – I mean President Roosevelt whom I am proud to call my friend. He took us off the gold standard against the advice of all the economists and now they claim it was their idea. He introduced fifteen major pieces of legislation in just three months and his New Deal has given hope to the unemployed and the dispossessed.'

Edward was impressed that a man as cool as Harbin could be inspired to such devotion. Clearly, Roosevelt was no ordinary man. 'You like him as a man – the President?'

'I most certainly do, Lord Edward. He is serene when all about him are reduced to inaction by anxiety. He's a cripple but you forget about it when you're in his presence. He's confident when there's nothing to be confident about. Sure I like him. He smokes two packets of Camels a day in an ivory cigarette holder he waves in front of him like a conductor's baton; that I don't like but hell, if it's all there is to dislike about him, I ain't complaining. He's a new broom – and I mean almost literally. I was in his office on the first day of his presidency. He opened a drawer in his desk and a huge cockroach jumped out. Turned out the whole place was infested. He had the White House cleaned right through. No more cockroaches, no more crooks, no more corruption.'

'But he doesn't want anything to do with us on this side of the Atlantic?'

'We feel – the President feels . . . and call it arrogance if you want to – that Europe is finished and that the new century will be ours. It may not be altogether healthy but that's the way it is with us and it's why we are so determined to keep out of the next European war.'

'But what about Hitler? Surely you can't stand back and let him turn Europe into one of the prison camps we read about in the press.'

'That ain't nothing to do with us. He can do what he wants in his own back yard, I guess. If a skunk is loose in Europe, why should we be expected to clear up the mess? Or, to put it another way, if you see a car wreck is inevitable you make damn sure you're not in either automobile.'

Edward dropped his passenger at the Connaught Hotel in Mayfair and, when Harbin had struggled out of the car and the porter had taken his bags, he shook Edward warmly by the hand. 'Let's keep in touch, young man. Maybe I can help find you the work you say you are looking for. And if you felt like taking the investigation into Mrs Harkness's death any further – on an informal basis, of course – I will do what I can to help. I don't like to see the truth muzzled. You might begin with our host. I don't say for one moment he's a murderer – but he has got something to hide. When we went into Mrs Harkness's bedroom and you went to see if she were ill, or dead as it turned out, I saw him pick something up from the lady's dressing table and slip it in his pocket.'

'Did you see what it was?' Edward asked sharply.

'No, but it might have been an envelope – something white anyway. And there's another thing: Leo was wearing a dressing gown but underneath he still had on the trousers and the shoes he had been wearing at dinner.'

'You mean he hadn't been to bed?'

'Maybe, maybe not, but it might be worth you asking him. Goodbye, Lord Edward. Thank you for the lift and for the instructive conversation. I look forward to meeting you again. Here is my card. If I am not there, they will always know where you can get in touch with me.'

Edward lay fully clothed on his bed and stared at the ceiling. He had told Scannon he needed to be in London urgently but, now he was here, he couldn't think what it was he wanted to do. His heart was racing and there was sweat on his brow. He wondered if he was going to be ill but decided it was anxiety. He put it into words and felt better: 'I'm having a nervous attack.' It was odd the way labelling something made it easier to cope with. So how was Molly's death to be labelled? Accident, suicide or murder?

One of the causes of his anxiety was Inspector Lampfrey. He would lay odds the man was honest and yet he had changed his mind about investigating Molly's death without reason. Except there must be a reason – pressure from someone in authority. Then he was anxious about Dannie. It looked as though she had used him and, what was more humiliating, she didn't seem to have any compunction about it. She had something to do with Molly's death but was she merely a liar and a thief or was she a murderer? This brought him to his main anxiety: why had Verity run off like that? He knew why, damn it! He had put her in an impossible position by taking her to Haling, where she had no business to be, and surrounding her with people for whom she had – to put it mildly – an antipathy. But this wasn't it either! She had trusted him in some unspecified way and he had let her down. He felt diminished in her eyes and that wasn't pleasant.

He got up from the bed and paced about the room. What ought he to do? Go and see Joe Weaver and tell him he wanted nothing more to do with Mrs Simpson and her friends and the monarchy could go to blazes. He gave a bark of laughter. He was being absurd. The monarchy was going to blazes whether he minded or not. If he went to see Weaver, he probably wouldn't even see him. Hadn't he more or less told him he was a failure last time they had met? In fact, that was odd: Weaver had been nervous and preoccupied – most unlike him. He was normally so confident and overbearing.

Just at that moment the telephone rang. Edward went out into the hall and picked up the receiver. 'Lord Edward

Corinth's residence,' he said on an impulse. If it was some-one he didn't want to speak to, he could pretend he was Fenton and say his master was not at home.

'Edward, you idiot, what are you playing at?'

'Verity, is that you?' he said stupidly.

'Of course it's me. Why are you pretending not to be you?'

'Oh, I . . .'

'Anyway, no time for that. I've got some news. Edward? Are you there?'

'Yes, I'm here. I say, you aren't too . . . disgusted with me?'

There was a silence and then Verity said, 'It's me who should apologize – if that's what you were trying to do. I had no right to mind who you . . . get friendly with.'

'You've every right. You're my conscience and anyway I . . .'

'Tommy rot,' she broke in hurriedly. 'Don't start getting maudlin.'

'But you rushed off . . . I thought . . .'

'For God's sake, Edward,' Verity said sharply. 'You sound quite unlike yourself. I hope you're not suffering from what the papers call "moral degeneration". I believe it is painful and incurable.'

'Verity, be serious, I . . .'

'I rushed up to London because I suddenly remembered I've got to give a lecture tonight and I hadn't prepared for it and all my notes and diaries and so on are here.'

'A lecture?'

'Didn't I tell you? The Party has arranged a series of lec-tures for me all over the country to try and drum up sup-port for the Republic and tell the story . . .'

'From the Communist point of view.'

'That's more like it! I detect a sting in the tail?'

'I was just jealous – no one has ever asked me to lecture.'

'Well, that's hardly surprising. What could you lecture on? The decline of the aristocracy? The inequality of British society in the twentieth century?'

'Don't be sarcastic. I know, I know.'

'Sorry.'

The clear, bright voice which came squeaking down the telephone line was bracing him as nothing else could. He knew the one thing she hated about him was his tendency to give way to self-pity when, as she never tired of pointing out, he was one of a privileged elite with nothing to be self-pitying about. She was twittering again.

'Edward, are you still there? I said sorry. By the way, talking of lectures, Frank has asked me down to Eton to lecture to the Political Society.'

'Frank?'

'Yes, your nephew, remember him?'

'He's invited you down to Eton?'

'Why ever not? Don't you remember how well we got on? He's more to the left than Comrade Stalin, you know. He makes me sound like Stanley Baldwin.'

Edward certainly did remember how, when he had taken Verity to meet his nephew at Eton a few months back, they had got on like . . . he wanted to say like young love, but that was patently ridiculous: a seventeen-year-old boy and a twenty-six-year-old . . . girl with ambitions to destroy public schools and everything they represented. The more he thought about it, the less ridiculous it seemed. Then he pulled himself together. Was he going mad to be jealous of his nephew? And there was nothing to be jealous of . . . there was the rub. Was there anything between him and the maddening girl on the other end of the telephone?

'Sorry,' he said, 'I was just remembering. When's the lecture – Frank's, I mean?'

'Next week – Wednesday. Will you come?'

'Would you mind?'

'I'm asking you to come, ass. I wouldn't ask you if I didn't want you. To be honest, I'm pretty nervous about it and would welcome some support.'

'Well then, of course. I say, V, didn't you say you had some news?'

'Yes. You almost made me forget with all your idle chat. I was talking to our man here – I'm at the *New Gazette* – and he was telling me that Molly was dropped by the King not just because of Mrs S but because she had been carrying on with someone else.'

'You mean she had been having an affair with another man?'

'For goodness sake, Edward. Isn't that what I've just said. You've got to wake up a bit if we are to be partners.'

'Partners, yes.' He felt a flood of energy surge through him. 'So who was she seeing?'

'I haven't been able to find out who she was "seeing" – as you so euphemistically put it – but I intend to ask around.'

'Be careful. We don't want the whole world to know what we're up to. And it might be dangerous.'

'Hmm. You think we might flush the murderer out? We'll talk about it when we meet.'

'When's that?'

'I thought you might like to take me to dinner after the lecture tonight – that is unless . . . '

'No, that would be . . . Where's tonight's entertainment taking place?'

'At a church hall in the East End – I'll give you the address. Six o'clock sharp – don't be late. Come to think of it, you don't have to attend the lecture as you'll be hearing the same thing at Eton.'

'No, I'd like to, then I can prompt you when I hear it again, if you get nervous.'

'Good. I must go now and polish the finer points – or rather think what the hell to say. Till tonight then?'

'Mmm, I'll be there. V . . . '

'Yes?'

'Pals?'

'Yes, pals – you dope.'

Edward thought it prudent to arrive late for Verity's lecture fearing that, if he were placed in the front row, he might put off the speaker and, more importantly, be in the thick of it when the soft fruit began to fly. The taxi got lost so he was very late when he arrived at the Church Hall, Pitt Street. It might be that the street was named after the celebrated Prime Minister but it might equally have hinted at the black grime which seemed to coat every building. A smell, which might have been boiling glue, hung over the neighbourhood and, as he fished in his trouser pocket for a half-crown, the cabbie looked Edward up and down: 'Sure you don't want me to take you back to Mayfair, guv?'

'Oh no, thanks all the same. I'll be all right.'

The cabbie shrugged, gave him one more pitying look and accelerated down Kingsland Road, obviously relieved to be leaving the neighbourhood.

Edward had dressed down for the occasion but, seeing a group of ragged children eyeing him speculatively, he had to admit he might not have dressed down far enough. It occurred to him, looking around, that what Verity said was perfectly true: there was a whole world which people like him knew nothing about. Pitt Street might be only a few miles from Piccadilly as the crow flies but the reality was that the crow never did fly in that direction. His world was delimited by Regent's Park in the north and Chelsea Bridge in the south. He seldom went west of Kensington Gardens and apart from the occasional lunch with his broker in the City he never went east of St Paul's, unless he was attending a riot with Verity.

The area in which he now found himself was as foreign to him as if he had been in Calcutta. The slums all about him were home to many thousands of people – it was one of the most heavily populated parts of the city – and the centre of the furniture and clothing trades. He suddenly felt the force of the cabbie's remarks. He might like to believe that there was no part of London to which he could not go if he so wished, but he realized that his presence here might easily be construed as an insult and a provocation to those who sweated all hours, destroying their eyesight over sewing machines, and returned with the merest pittance to insanitary, disease-ridden rookeries.

Attempting to ignore the jeers of the urchins at his back, he stepped smartly into the church hall and was met by a stink of humanity and a noise which deafened him. It was a few moments before he could see Verity. She was not actually speaking but was sitting beside a large woman in twinset and pearls, a fur tippet and a remarkable hat laden with highly coloured fruit. A small man in black with a Charlie Chaplin moustache was muttering to the front row. Even if the audience had been quite silent he would have been inaudible at the back of the hall but, in the circumstances, Edward doubted whether even the front row heard what he was saying. The large lady was restless, clearly appreciating that a riot was imminent if the little man did not give way to someone more popular. At last, unable to bear it any longer, she got to her feet and in stentorian tones called the meeting to order and proceeded to introduce Verity.

Edward's emotions on seeing Verity – looking very small and vulnerable – stand up and take two or three steps towards the lectern were similar to those of a father watching his child being taken away by a teacher into the school playground for the first time. She was so close yet quite beyond his reach and at the mercy of a hostile mob. Verity would, of course, have resented any such feeling on his part as patronizing. She would have pointed out that 'the mob' was just a few hundred people, the majority of whom were sympathetic to Communism if not actually Party members. In addition, she was by now reasonably used to public speaking and, being naturally confident that her views on any matter, political or personal, were the right ones, she was not diffident. She had witnessed so much suffering and horror in Spain – suffering of which most middle-class English girls were blessedly ignorant – that addressing a meeting in an East End hall could hardly be considered intimidating. The odd thing was that, despite all this, Verity was nervous. It was partly that her nerves had not recovered from the battle for Toledo and, more immediately, that she had been warned by the lady who was to introduce her – in a hurried, whispered colloquy while the little man was failing to make himself heard – that the meeting had been infiltrated by a group of blackshirts who were planning trouble.

She stood for a moment, her rather absurd hat quivering like a black halo over her head, waiting for the crowd to be silent. Edward had never heard her speak in public before and was frightened for her. What if they laughed at her? What if they threw things at her? He need not have worried. Her voice was light but audible even at the back of the hall where he was standing sandwiched behind a costermonger smelling of fruit and sweat and a navvy, to judge from his calloused hands, who kept on looking at him as if he were from another planet. Verity spoke of 'the war against war, against want, against poverty and against exploitation'. There was nothing new in what she had to say but she said it with such evident sincerity, blazing with anger when she mentioned 'the employers' and the 'exploiting classes', that no one could remain indifferent. Some in the audience were soon shouting their support, cheering and clapping, and Edward joined in the applause until he saw the expressions on the faces of those near him. It was borne in on him that he was being identified as the nearest representative of the 'exploiting classes' and that his approval of the speaker was seen as ironic. He tried to melt into the background but was unable to do so. He looked what he was: an English gentleman who had 'never done a day's work in his life', as Verity had labelled him during one of their rows.

He was just wondering if he was going to be able to edge out of the hall without being pulled limb from limb when he was saved by the blackshirts. An organized barracking began from a group of them in the middle of the hall which drowned out Verity. Enraged supporters of the speaker started their own noisy protest and, inevitably, scuffles broke out, fists flew and noses were bloodied. The large lady on the platform rose to her feet appealing for order and received a vegetable – Edward thought a turnip but Verity identified it later as a tomato – on her majestic bosom. There was a moment's pause as this affront to the lady's dignity was digested – not, of course, literally – and then chaos. By sticking together, the blackshirts, who probably only numbered about thirty, were able to do considerable damage before being ejected into the road just as a group of burly policemen arrived in a Black Maria. Edward was ejected at the same time – his shirt torn where his neighbour had grabbed it and the jacket of his suit covered in muck from the floor on which he had briefly been rolled. Reluctantly, because, as he tried in vain to explain to his assailants, he was not himself a blackshirt, he had begun to return punch for punch and was soon laying about him with some effect. By the time he had been thrown out of the hall by the coster-monger and three of his friends, he had gained their respect as a fighter if not as a political theoretician.

He panted to one of the policemen, 'I say, I think . . . ' and was knocked unconscious by the constable's truncheon.

Edward woke with a blinding headache. He was in an ambulance and the clanging of its bell made his head hurt worse than ever.

'Don't move,' a voice said. He looked up at the speaker expecting to see the calm, beautiful face of a nurse com-plete with starched uniform and wimple but instead he found himself gazing into the distinctly cross face of Verity Browne. He closed his eyes and groaned.

'I can't understand why it is, whenever you are any-where near a political rally, you get yourself knocked out by one of our brave policemen. First it was the horse in Cable Street and now . . . a policeman said you assaulted him. You really mustn't assault policemen. They're sup-posed to be on your side – you are a member of the ruling classes, aren't you?'

Edward did not feel in the mood for irony and said, 'I say, what happened back there?'

'Loyal supporters of the cause took you for a blackshirt – that's what happened. You hurt one poor fellow quite badly. Oh well, I suppose I must forgive you. Were you try-ing to protect me from the nasty men, diddums?'

'No, I was not! I just . . . ouch, you're supposed to soothe me not bang my head.'

'Sorry, it's not easy being soothing in a moving vehicle.'

'Where are we going anyway?'

'They thought you ought to go to hospital. I said you had a thick skull and would soon come round but I was overruled. Sorry.'

'No, I probably need hospital treatment.'

'Anyway, the interesting news is that guess who I saw in the middle of the rioting?'

'Major Stille?'

'How did you guess?' Verity said, annoyed. 'The point is that, once again he wasn't with the blackshirts, as you might suppose, but close to them pretending to be one of us.'

'One of us?'

'A Party worker – a member of the proletariat. He swung a punch at one of Mosley's thugs and I think it must have been some kind of signal because that was when the riot started.'

'Give me some water and an aspirin, will you,' Edward said, struggling into a sitting position.

'I don't think you ought to get up,' Verity said doubtfully. 'Concussion is a very tricky thing, you know. Even with a bean as thick as yours, you've got to be careful. I remember Tommie saying – when he was knocked out in some rugger match – that he had revelations of angels and whatnot for two weeks afterwards. In any case, it's very discouraging for the ambulance people if their patients heal themselves. Hey, hold on! You're pushing me over.'

'No, I'm not,' he said. 'I'm kissing you. Patients always fall in love with their nurses. It's the done thing.'

Whether it was the knock on the head or the scent of the girl so close to him but Edward was at last able to do what he had wanted to do for eighteen months and take her in his arms and kiss her. She struggled at first but then seemed to accept the inevitability of it and even began to return his kisses. Fortunately, or unfortunately, at that moment they arrived at St George's and stumbled out into the hospital, all linoleum and white paint. Edward tried to say he did not need treatment but was bundled into the emergency room by an unsympathetic nurse as starched as her white cap. A young doctor cleaned his wound and asked if he had been in a fight. Verity said they had been at a political meeting which made the doctor purse his lips and slap iodine on Edward's head as if he enjoyed seeing his patient wince. When he had finished, he put a bandage on it and told the nurse to give Edward a cup of tea and discharge him. The general feeling seemed to be that he had only got what he deserved and was wasting the time of busy people with more pressing cases to deal with. It was no good his trying to say he thoroughly agreed with them. He was in the wrong and that was that.

They were oddly subdued in the cab on their way to Albany. Edward was now feeling faint and rather sick. He was not up to renewing his lovemaking. Verity, too, seemed unenthusiastic but, when he gripped her hand, she did not try and remove it. At Albany they were met by Fenton who was predictably disapproving. His look said more plainly than words: 'Why is it, Miss Browne, that whenever my master is in your company he comes home wounded?'

Gently but firmly, he took charge of Edward and when he had put him to bed he encouraged Verity to leave by not offering her refreshment of any kind and saying sternly, 'Lord Edward needs rest and if you would care to telephone tomorrow morning, miss, he may . . . ' or may not, was the implication, 'be able to talk to you.'

Verity went back to the Hassels' house contemplating the day's events. She had a feeling she was reluctant to analyze that something significant had occurred and, despite everything, she felt happier than she had for some time.

8

Two days later an excited Verity overcame Fenton's studied hostility and Edward, still feeling headachy and sick, was summoned to the telephone.

'It's just come through – the news. I think we should go down straight away. Do you think it's worth ringing Inspector Lampfrey?'

'What news, Verity? Stop burbling and tell me what's happened. I thought reporters were supposed to be lucid in an emergency.'

'It's your pal Leo Scannon. He's dead . . . . murdered. Apparently he ate rat poison yesterday. It's on our front page. I was trying to get to see Joe to ask if he can put me on the case but apparently he's closeted with the PM. The whole Mrs Simpson business is coming to a head.'

'Steady on, old thing. My head's still hurting. You say Scannon's dead – that he's been murdered? I can't believe it. Who on earth would want to do such a thing?'

'Well, I can think of some people I know who will be happy to hear he's dead,' Verity said grimly. 'Perhaps the person who put the rat in my bed put the poison in Scannon's porridge.'

'In his porridge! How disgusting. Do we know who was at Haling when he died?'

'No. Look, telephone Inspector Lampfrey. See whether he will talk to us. Remind him you will see him at Molly's inquest tomorrow, in any case.'

'Oh, gosh, the inquest. I had almost forgotten.'

'Well, don't. You're a star witness. If you forget to turn up, they'll probably send you to prison for contempt of court or something. Anyway, I've got to go. I'm still hoping to have a word with the boss when he gets back from Downing Street. Can't spend all day chatting with the idle rich. I'll come round about lunch-time.'

'But what can I say to Lampfrey? What's it to do with us?'

'It's all tied up with Molly's death and probably with your friend Dannie as well,' she added unwisely.

'I don't see what it has to do with Dannie . . . ' Edward shook the receiver but the line was dead. Verity had a habit of not waiting to hear his excuses for inaction. He sighed and guiltily went back to bed to think. Scannon dead! What did it all mean? He certainly had not liked the man but this . . . If it were rat poison surely it had to have been administered by someone in the house or nearby so there couldn't be any connection with Molly's death because all Scannon's guests had dispersed. He had begun to wonder if it hadn't been Scannon himself who had killed Molly but now it seemed impossible unless, of course, someone was taking revenge for her death. Damn. He just didn't have enough facts. He realized, suddenly, that he hadn't even started investigating Molly's murder; he had just let himself react to events. He got out of bed and began pacing up and down, galvanized by this new, quite unexpected death. One thing was certain: Haling Castle was certainly not a place to recommend for a rest cure, unless it was that one last rest you were talking about. Damn and blast! He should be up and doing.

He went to the door and called to Fenton. 'Run me a bath, will you, while I make a telephone call.'

Fenton, who had anticipated his master's command and was already in the process of drawing a bath, raised his eyebrows.

The Inspector was not a happy man. His voice crackled noisily down the wire.

'The Chief has got someone down from the Yard to look into Mr Scannon's death. They don't think we local yokels are up to a murder investigation – at least not when it concerns the death of a Member of Parliament and friend of the Prime Minister.'

'Might I come and talk to you, Inspector? As you know, Mrs Harkness's inquest is tomorrow so I have to be in your neck of the woods anyway. I know you will think I'm an interferin' busybody but Mr Scannon was a . . . ' he was going to say 'friend' but decided on 'an acquaintance of mine.' 'And what's more,' he went on, 'I have a hunch his death may be tied up in some way with Mrs Harkness's.'

'Ah,' the Inspector gave an embarrassed cough, 'I think I owe you some sort of explanation about that. Come and see me by all means. You'll be staying at Mersham, I suppose?'

'Yes, that's right, Inspector. My brother's place is only forty minutes from Marlborough – less if I break a few speed limits.'

'Ah, now, please don't be doing that, my lord. When shall you be here, then? I should say there isn't a great deal I *can* tell you but you're very welcome to what information I've got.'

Edward fancied the Inspector would have been less accommodating if his nose had not been put out. It must be galling to have had the chance to shine taken from him and handed to a Scotland Yard man.

'Oh, by the way, my lord, I'd appreciate it if you would come on your own. Miss Browne's a charming young lady but she's a journalist for all that and, if it came out I had been playing favourites with members of the press, they'd have my guts for garters.'

'Of course, Inspector. I quite understand,' Edward said and rang off.

Damn it! He would have to explain to Verity that her presence was not required. On the other hand, as an accredited member of the press, there was nothing he could do if she decided she wanted to attend the inquest. That was a public inquiry. He rang the *New Gazette* but she was not at her desk so he left a message that he would ring again about four.

Verity was not at her desk because she was hunting big game: her boss, Lord Weaver. The editor of the paper, Mr Godber, hated Verity and resented her position as Weaver's pet but there was nothing he could do about it except undermine her as much as he dared. Unfortunately for him, Weaver insisted on vetting the newspaper every day before it went to press, unless he was out of London, and had no hesitation in overruling the editor if he wanted greater prominence given to an article by one of his favourite journalists. It was unfair but there it was. Verity had long ago given up trying to sweet-talk the paper's editor and now just ignored him.

Somewhat unexpectedly, she had made a friend of Lord Weaver's formidable secretary, Miss Barnstable, and had even been invited to call her by her Christian name, a privilege not extended to Lord Weaver who probably had no idea she even had a first name. Miss Barnstable had been highly suspicious of her at first but, quite fortuitously, Verity had been in a position to do her a favour. Miss Barnstable lived with her aged mother in a small house in Acton. The mother was a semi-invalid, with nothing to do all day but look out from behind the net curtains at her neighbours and devour romances penned by Ethel M. Dell, Marie Corelli and Florence Barclay, obtained for her by her daughter from Boots' library. She also adored periodicals such as *Modern Woman* and film magazines such as *Screen Romances* and *Picturegoer*. Every Saturday the two women would sally forth to the pictures and, for a couple of hours, Miss Barnstable would forget how lonely her life was, despite her busy and important position at the *New Gazette*, while her mother would imagine what it would be like to be abducted by an Arab sheikh and carried away on a camel or wooed by the oh-so-dashing Thin Man, William Powell.

One evening, Miss Barnstable had casually mentioned to her mother that Lord Edward Corinth had been in the office to see her employer. Her mother, much to the daughter's alarm, had reacted with delight verging on hysteria. She had read about Lord Edward and seen his photograph in the 'society pages' of the *Sunday Pictorial*. For a fortnight, Miss Barnstable was asked if 'Lord Edward had been in today?' until she got quite cross, reducing her mother to tears. She felt guilty at making her mother cry and, greatly daring, had asked Verity if Lord Edward would ever sign a photograph for her mother.

'As though he were a film star?' inquired Verity mirthfully but then, seeing how much it meant to Miss Barnstable and how difficult it had been for her to ask the favour, she said, 'He can do better than that. If your mother would like it, I will bring him along to tea one day.'

Edward was reluctant but, the promise having been made on his behalf, he felt he could not disappoint the old lady. One Saturday, the Lagonda drew up outside the little house – Verity had said there was no point being a lord if he did not bring his 'flash car'. The tea was a great success. Edward was charming and Mrs Barnstable ecstatic. All her neighbours would know about her distinguished visitor and her pleasure made the whole effort worthwhile. Even Verity was forced to admit that, if having a lord to tea could bring an old lady so much simple pleasure, perhaps the class system had something to be said for it. The result was that Verity called Miss Barnstable 'Val' and she called Verity 'Verity' and if she wanted information on the activities or whereabouts of Lord Weaver, she had only to ask.

'He's back in his office, if you want to come up. He said no visitors but I'm sure he doesn't mean you.'

Verity wasn't so sure but jutting out her chin, as she always did when she was preparing herself for a difficult meeting, she went down to the ground floor to take the lift up to the tenth. It was one of the peculiarities of Lord Weaver's personal elevator that it didn't stop at the intervening floors. Miss Barnstable motioned to her to knock on the great man's door, which she did with some trepidation.

'Who is it? I said no visitors.'

'It's just me, Joe. Can I come in for a few moments? I know you're having a bad time and I wondered if I could help in any way.'

'Oh, it's you, is it? Well, as you're here, I suppose you can come in. What do you want to badger me about this time?'

'I don't want to badger you about anything, honestly. I just wondered if I or Edward could . . . '

'Don't mention his name. He's caused me enough trouble already.'

'I don't see how you can say that,' she said loyally. 'You asked him to get back those letters and he was on the point of doing so when Mrs Harkness was killed and the letters were stolen again.'

'She wasn't killed. She took an overdose.'

'The police know that's not true. They just can't prove anything. And now there's Mr Scannon. Inspector Lampfrey . . . '

'That man's a liability . . . '

'Inspector Lampfrey?'

'Corinth!' the big man growled. 'Anyway, how do you know all this? I especially asked your friend not to tell you. Typical he couldn't keep his mouth shut.'

'Oh, you did, did you? And why didn't you trust me?'

'Damn it, Verity – you're a Communist, dedicated to destroying the royal family, that's why.'

'Not destroying, exactly. More like reforming – modernizing.'

'Destroying – don't prevaricate. You used to be honest, at least.'

Verity very nearly lost her temper but then, with a flash of intuition, it occurred to her that Lord Weaver was taking his bad temper out on her because he couldn't be rude to the Prime Minister.

'I'm sorry Joe,' she said in a softer voice. 'Don't be cross. You know when you asked me to work for you and I accepted, you had my loyalty. I would never do anything to damage you or the paper.'

He looked at her strangely. 'I hope I can believe that. They say your first loyalty is to the Party and that, if they wanted you to . . . use your position here, you wouldn't have any alternative.'

'Who says?' Verity asked defiantly, wondering what indeed she would do if the Party required her to do something which conflicted with her loyalty to her employer.

'People,' was all he would say.

'Please Joe, tell me what is happening.'

He looked at her again – a shade more his usual self. 'On whatever you hold most dear, promise me you won't tell anyone, not even Edward?'

'I promise.'

'Well then,' he said, mollified. 'Mrs Simpson is about to get her divorce. She's staying in a house near Felixstowe.'

'Felixstowe?' Verity exclaimed in bewilderment.

'Yes, the lawyers think she can get her decree at Ipswich Assizes without too much attention from the press.'

'Will we report it?'

'Just the fact of it – on an inside page – but God knows what the others will do. It's all going to get out soon.'

'And then?'

'The King says he'll marry her. I was with him yesterday at Fort Belvedere. Couldn't make him see sense. Mind you, he'll have to wait six months for the decree nisi to be made absolute. A lot can happen in six months. He says he is going to marry her before the coronation and the PM is saying if he does marry her he will have to abdicate.'

'Abdicate! Golly!' She hesitated before then unwittingly repeating what Edward had said to Weaver on another occasion. 'But would that be altogether a bad thing? I mean,' she added hurriedly, 'even if you wanted the monarchy to . . . ?'

'His brother's not up to the job. Not just his stammer but he's not a fit man and his wife says the strain would kill him – particularly if there is a war.'

'I see,' Verity said slowly, 'but Edward says the King is hand in glove with the Nazis. If there is a war . . . '

'Damn it . . . I just can't believe the King . . . ' Weaver got up from his chair and paced the room, seeming almost to forget to whom he was talking. He needed to spill out his thoughts to someone and Verity happened to be there.

'Mrs Simpson's an intelligent woman but she can't see Ribbentrop is the very devil. She hates Jews and Communists and she thinks Hitler is a god. Damn and blast the woman. At first, I thought she could be trained to be a queen but I was mistaken. Maybe, in her past, things happened to her – bad things. Anyway, now the only English people she trusts are men like Dickie Mountbatten who egg her on.'

'What about Mr Scannon? What's behind his murder?'

'I really don't know but I do feel a responsibility. I feel responsible for both deaths, I suppose. By sending Edward to Haling to retrieve Wally's letters, I stirred up someone to get there before him, and Leo was involved in the same business.'

'You mean, he was trying to retrieve the same stuff?'

'No, it was too late for that but he had been . . . I can't tell you it all but he had been acting as an intermediary between . . . certain parties.'

'The King and . . . ?'

'I'm sorry, Verity,' Weaver said turning to look at her. 'I oughtn't to have said as much as I have but, to tell you the truth, the whole business is getting under my skin. That damn fool of a man . . . ! Ah, what's the use!'

'Could Edward be in any danger?'

'Maybe . . . I don't know. Not if he drops the whole thing.'

'But you know Edward, Joe, that's just what he won't do.'

'Well, ask him, as a special favour to me. Tell him I made a mistake. It's not worth getting killed for . . . that's for sure.'

'Joe, is Catherine Dannhorn involved?' Verity expected to get her head snapped off but the old man grunted and began to light a cigar. As he did so, he peered at Verity through the smoke.

'What did Edward tell you about Dannie?'

'Nothing,' she said, more or less truthfully – after all he had only confirmed what she had already guessed. 'Nothing, but she looks to me to be a dangerous woman.'

'I haven't seen her since she had dinner at my house when I introduced Edward to Wally.'

'You haven't answered my question, Joe. Is Dannie involved in all this?'

'I guess she must be but don't ask me how because I don't know. Now, Verity let's talk about you. How's the book going? We ought to serialize it on publication.'

'Oh, nearly finished,' she answered, trying to forget that she had done nothing whatever about it and the delivery date was fast approaching.

'Finish it,' Weaver ordered. 'Spain's still in the news but, if this blasted business of Wally's comes to abdication, no one will want to read about anything else.'

'I wondered if you would let me report on Scannon's murder.'

'Certainly not! We've got a perfectly good crime correspondent, as you very well know.'

'But I have an "in" . . . I knew the man. I stayed at Haling on Monday.'

'You did what?'

'Dannie wanted to meet me,' she equivocated, not wanting to get Edward into trouble.

'Hmm. Well, I don't know about that. You get on with your book like I tell you. You have a habit of getting into hot water and there may be more to this than you imagine.'

'But isn't that why I'm such a good journalist, Joe, because I like getting into hot water?'

'Or heat it yourself if you have to . . . ' He looked at her and then grinned. 'I can't give you authority to cover this case. Godber would resign. But if you turn up anything . . . '

'Thanks, Joe, you're a great man.' She darted round the desk and kissed him.

'Run along then,' Weaver said, knowing he had been bamboozled but enjoying the feeling, 'and, whatever you do, say nothing to Godber or Strang.' Strang was the crime correspondent.

'Of course not!' Verity said, almost running out of the door. In the adjoining room, she blew Miss Barnstable a kiss and took the stairs, two at a time, being quite unable to wait for the elevator.

'It was in the whisky.'

'The rat poison?'

'Yes.'

'I thought it was in the porridge.'

'Apparently not.' The Inspector lit his pipe and wreaths of smoke enveloped their heads in a stygian mist.

'But wouldn't it have tasted odd – the whisky?'

'They say not but I wouldn't like to experiment. The doc says a spoonful of Rodine was dissolved in the whisky decanter and one glass of the hellish brew would have been fatal.'

'It was definitely Rodine?' Edward asked.

'There doesn't seem much doubt about that. Williams, the gardener, bought a tin of it in the village on Mr Scannon's orders.'

'Rodine comes as a sort of paste, doesn't it?'

'Yes, a paste of bran and molasses – black treacle to you and me. A one ounce tin contains ten grams of phosphorus. A tenth of a gram, I'm told, can kill an adult.'

There was a silence in the little room which neither man seemed ready to break. At last, the Inspector got up from behind his desk and went over to the window. Edward hoped he was about to throw it open but instead he stared through the glass at the uninspiring view of shrubberies and sucked on his pipe until the tobacco glowed in the bowl. He was not a happy man. Inspector Lampfrey had admitted to Edward – though not in so many words – that the Chief Constable, Colonel Philips, had put extreme pressure on him to complete his investigation into Molly's death and accept that murder could never be proved. He had made it clear to the Inspector that suicide was not an acceptable verdict as it would lead to press speculation as to Molly's motives. 'The last thing anyone wants is the press having an excuse for mentioning her relationship with His Majesty,' the Chief Constable had added meaningfully. 'There must be no mention of Mrs Harkness having been pregnant, you understand, Lampfrey? It's irrelevant to the investigation into her death and we must avoid scandal at any cost.'

'And Mr Scannon, sir, can I not investigate his death?'

'Not possible, old man,' Colonel Philips said, hardly bothering to conceal his indifference to Lampfrey's feelings. 'It's too sensitive – too much politics – too many ramifications about which we know nothing and, what's more, don't want to know.'

'Surely, sir, whatever the political ramifications, it doesn't affect a murder investigation. Whatever the reasons for killing Mr Scannon, the murderer must be brought to justice.'

Colonel Philips looked at his subordinate pityingly. 'It's not that simple, Lampfrey. For one thing, there are rumours that the dead man had . . . had odd sexual habits, know what I mean? If we start digging, God knows what muck we'll find.'

The Inspector opened his mouth to remonstrate but the Chief Constable raised his hand imperiously. 'I'm sorry, Lampfrey, there's nothing to discuss. I've made my decision. I have telephoned a friend of mine at the Yard – a good man – Chief Inspector Pride. He'll be here in an hour or two. Leave it all to him. You'll be grateful, I promise you. Oh, and Lampfrey . . . '

'Sir?'

'Give him every possible assistance. I don't want to hear that you have been in any way . . . obstructive. Understand?'

'Sir!'

Edward stared at Lampfrey's back and was sorry for him. He understood without being told that the Inspector felt he had been judged and found wanting and resented it.

'You did what you could,' Edward said. 'We may think Mrs Harkness was murdered but there was no evidence.'

Still with his back to Edward, the Inspector said, 'The Chief was under pressure to tidy up the whole case.'

'Political pressure?'

'Maybe,' he turned to face Edward, 'but I would never admit I had said that to you.'

'Of course not!' Edward said, shocked.

Reassured, Lampfrey said, 'We *are* short of manpower and we had – have – a good deal else on at the moment. Mr Scannon's death changes the whole situation, of course. Now we must wait and see if this man from the Yard finds anything we have overlooked which might link Mrs Harkness's death with Mr Scannon's.'

'There was no question of you investigating the murder?' Edward probed gently.

'No, the Chief called in the Yard immediately and I was glad he did,' the Inspector said, stoutly. 'I don't have the skills for that sort of thing. The Yard has a new scientific laboratory at Hendon Police College – have you heard about it?'

Edward nodded. 'Dr Davidson's operation – I know him quite well as it happens.'

'Yes, well, the gentleman is coming down to examine the corpse. Poison's always tricky. Chief Inspector Pride will have all that sort of support.'

Edward started and changed colour.

'You know Chief Inspector Pride?' Lampfrey was surprised. 'You seem to know everyone at the Yard,' he added drily.

'Not at all, Inspector, but I have met him. He investigated a murder at my brother's place – Mersham Castle – and I'm afraid we didn't hit it off.'

'He has a good reputation.'

'Well deserved, I'm sure,' Edward said smoothly, 'but he doesn't like people like me poking their noses into his affairs so I would be grateful if you could refrain from mentioning my name unless you absolutely have to.'

'Officially, Mr Scannon's death is nothing to do with me now, my lord, so I doubt I will be seeing much of the Chief Inspector.'

'Let's go back to the whisky,' Edward said. 'What happened? How did the rat poison get into the decanter? I may be wrong but I thought I saw Mr Scannon use one of those old-fashioned things called a tantalus, designed to stop the servants getting at the drink.'

'That's correct. Mr Scannon had a reputation for being – I think we should say "careful".'

'Mean,' Edward corrected him. 'He inherited pots of money from his father but he admitted to me he had never spent much on the house and he survived on a small staff.'

'Or didn't survive,' Lampfrey corrected him.

Edward smiled wryly. 'So – let me get this straight – Williams, the gardener, bought the Rodine? We saw a rat on the billiard table the first time I stayed at Haling – and Pickering was told then to do something about it.'

'You must tell Inspector Pride about the rat,' Lampfrey said sententiously.

'Pickering will tell him,' Edward said airily. He had absolutely no wish to talk to Pride. 'Let me see, Scannon certainly served his guests whisky on Monday. I wonder when he last had a drop – before it was tampered with, I mean.'

'He went to town on Tuesday,' Lampfrey said.

'So sometime when Scannon was in London his tantalus was broken into and the whisky poisoned?'

'Yes. He returned to Haling on Wednesday by train arriving at the house about six thirty. The first thing he did was pour himself a whisky. When Pickering came into the drawing-room an hour later to tell him dinner was served, he found his master dead. I'm afraid it must have been a very painful death.'

'He was in his chair?'

'Yes, with *The Times* still in one hand. The whisky glass had rolled on to the floor.'

'I see. Presumably, there was no one in the house except the servants?'

'When the tantalus was tampered with or when he died?'

'Either . . . both.'

'There were no guests in the house. He was expecting some people on Saturday.'

'And when the whisky decanter was tampered with?'

'Well, we don't yet know exactly when the whisky was poisoned but there was no one in the house after everyone left on Tuesday except the servants and his mother and her companion. Did you meet the lady, Lord Edward . . . Miss Conway?'

'I did. She must be a suspect? She really can't say who might have entered the house and opened the tantalus?'

'You'll have to ask the Chief Inspector that.'

'I mustn't make a nuisance of myself. I presume the tantalus wasn't actually broken by whoever poisoned the whisky, otherwise Scannon would have guessed it had been tampered with?'

'That's correct, my lord. It was either opened by someone who had access to the key – though since Mr Scannon kept it on his key ring that seems unlikely – or someone managed to open it with a skeleton key or even a penknife. It's an antiquated contraption – belonged to Mr Scannon's father, I understand – and wouldn't have been hard to open.'

'Still, it seems to let the staff out of it, wouldn't you say, Inspector?'

'I would, my lord, and in any case it's hard to imagine Mr Pickering as a murderer.'

'Mmm, yes. I say, Inspector, would you mind awfully if I kept in touch?'

The Inspector stroked his chin and looked doubtful.

'Nothing underhand,' Edward said hastily, 'but, if I do come up with anything . . . interesting, I'd much rather tell you than the Chief Inspector.'

'I suppose there is nothing wrong with that,' Lampfrey said at last. He tried to resist the idea that he might enjoy passing on to the man from the Yard information he had overlooked.

'To be honest, my lord, I felt I owed you something. Mrs Harkness was a friend of yours and I felt bad at having to give up my investigation into her death without having got to the bottom of it. Oh, by the way, Miss Conway said one thing which might interest you: Mr Scannon's diary has disappeared.'

'You mean his engagement diary?'

'No, my lord. I thought you might have known – apparently it was common knowledge in Mr Scannon's circle – that he kept a diary. For posterity, he said. Every night he wrote down who he'd met, the parties he had been to, conversations – everything. He had this idea that he was living at an interesting moment in our history – or so Miss Conway says – so his diary might possibly contain the name of his killer. But that, I am happy to say, is not my problem. Scotland Yard will no doubt show us plodders how to find a murderer.'

'I am most grateful, Inspector. I'm the most infernal nuisance – a busybody stirring up trouble for people like you who have enough on their plate as it is – but I have this absurd need to find out the truth. This is not one of England's most glorious moments but I agree with the late Mr Scannon – these are interesting times.'

'What will you do now?' Lampfrey said.

'Think it through, I suppose, and see if there is anything I can do to aid the Chief Inspector in his work.' Edward smiled sweetly and the Inspector smiled back.

9

Edward got to Mersham just after four. He had telephoned his sister-in-law to let her know he was coming and demanding food and a bed for the night. The Duchess met him at the door and fussed over him.

'No lunch! My poor boy, you must be famished. We'll have tea straight away.'

'Connie, darling, it's so good to see you. How's Gerald?'

'He's staying with the Conningsbys in Norfolk – shooting. I'm afraid I begged off. I can't bear the rain and trudging after the men pretending to admire them for killing several hundred stupid birds bred for slaughter.'

'Ah well, it's a blessing to find you alone. I want your advice on one or two matters which are absorbing me at the moment and, I don't mind telling you, it's rather a relief having you to myself.'

'How long can you stay, Ned?'

'Just a couple of nights, I'm afraid, old girl.'

'Oh, must you dash off? You never can sit still for a minute.'

'Now then, Connie, don't chide me. May I make a telephone call before we have tea?'

The Duke was highly suspicious of the telephone and there were only two in the castle – one in his study and one in the hall. It was to this instrument Edward repaired. As he asked the operator for the *New Gazette* number he felt a little nervous. It occurred to him that Verity was the only person he was ever afraid of speaking to and, as he waited to be connected, he turned over in his mind whether this meant he cared for the little termagant or simply suffered her as one might a favourite terrier that had a habit of biting large chunks out of one's trousers.

It was a full five minutes before he was speaking to the newspaper's switchboard, the local exchange seeming to believe that London was as exotic a location as Istanbul. Verity was at her desk and predictably wrathful.

'I left you a message . . . ' he tried ineffectually to defend himself and then listened in silence for three minutes of sustained abuse. 'Of course we're partners, V, but as I tried to explain, the Inspector won't talk to you in case it looks as if he's favouring one journalist over another. Anyway, I've got a lot to tell you. Shall we meet at the inquest and then we can talk in the car on the way back to town?'

He removed the telephone receiver a few inches from his ear but, for all Verity's vehemence, he could sense she was cooling down. 'Till tomorrow, then,' he said at last and replaced the receiver on its rest with exaggerated care.

'Yes, what is it, Bates?' he said more sharply than he intended to the butler hovering near the drawing-room door.

'Her Grace asked me to say there was tea in the drawing-room when you were ready.'

'Thank you, Bates. Oh Bates, do we keep rat poison in the house?'

'Rat poison, my lord?' asked the bewildered butler.

'Yes, man, rat poison.'

'We do have rat poison, my lord,' he said a trifle haughtily, unaccustomed to being spoken to by Edward in this way.

'I'm sorry, Bates,' Edward said humbly. 'I didn't mean to snap. It's just been rather a long day. Now, about the poison – is it kept in the house?'

'No, my lord. It is kept in the gardener's shed, I believe. I am glad to say we very rarely have occasion to use rat poison.'

'But it's easy to obtain? There's no book you have to sign when you buy it – I mean like when you buy poison from the chemist you have to sign for it?'

'I don't believe so, my lord. Would you wish me to make inquiries?'

'Thank you, Bates, that would be helpful and could you also establish whether the rat poison in the gardener's shed is kept under lock and key . . . and what brand of rat poison it is?'

'Yes, my lord. I shall attend to the matter at once.' The butler disappeared, obviously puzzled by Edward's fascination with rats. Edward felt in a better humour for having stirred up Bates and then felt ashamed of himself.

He wiped away the jam from his mouth and said, 'Connie, blessed among women, you have saved my life. I hadn't realized how devilish hungry I was.'

'Chocolate cake?'

'Just a slither . . . ' He held out his plate and for a moment looked like a small boy back home for the holidays and making up for weeks of school rations.

Connie waited patiently for him to satisfy his hunger before subjecting him to an inquisition. She could restrain herself no longer. 'The inquest is tomorrow? I don't quite understand how you are involved, Ned.'

'I knew Molly Harkness in Kenya. Don't you remember, there was a scandal. Her husband found her in bed with her lover – tried to kill her – failed and turned the gun on himself. It was a mucky business.'

'I do remember, and somehow – from what I read in the newspapers – when she came back to England she became one of the King's circle?'

'Yes, I tried to help her in Kenya . . . ' He saw his sister-in-law's expression and said heatedly, 'Honestly, why can't people believe I acted altruistically. I promise you, Connie, we were never more than friends. I just felt sorry for her.

She was a bad girl but, as I keep on telling people, she was as much a victim as anything else.'

'I really don't want to hear the details, Ned. Everything I have heard about Happy Valley, and the life those people live there, makes me feel ill. I was very glad when you came back to England.'

'Anyway, the point is – and this really is confidential, Connie, and it won't come out at the inquest – Molly was the King's mistress. Perhaps only for a few months, I don't know.'

His sister-in-law looked shocked and distressed. 'Oh really, Ned. I'm not sure I want to hear any more.'

'It's not just gossip, Connie. There's no one else I could tell and I would welcome your advice. You've a wise as well as beautiful head on you.'

'Get away with you, Ned,' Connie said, tapping him on the wrist but pleased for all that. The Duke was a good man but not given to paying his wife compliments. 'Well, go on then, if you must.'

'Molly was, as it seems, put aside by the King without a word of apology or farewell, in favour of Mrs Simpson.'

'The American woman! But surely, he wouldn't . . . Of course, I've heard rumours but . . . . '

'I'm afraid it's more than rumours. The King's obsessed with the woman – wants to marry her.'

'Marry her! But that's impossible.'

'Nevertheless, Joe Weaver says he will.'

'But will it be allowed?'

'I rather doubt it. Anyway, the point is Molly stole some of the King's letters to the woman – broke open the box she kept them in. She said in a letter to Mrs Simpson that, if she didn't give up the King, she would use them to damage her. To cut a long story short, Joe sent me to retrieve them.'

'Good heavens, Ned. Why you?'

'They knew I knew her and, like you, they thought . . . I'd been her lover and that therefore I might have some influence over her.'

'So what happened?'

'I went down to Leo Scannon's place, Haling. It was to be just an ordinary weekend. I had a talk with her late on that first night. In the morning she was dead. The coroner is going to say she took an overdose of her sleeping draught but she wasn't suicidal. I'm convinced it was murder.'

'What about the King's letters?'

'Gone – lost – stolen again – who knows.'

'And Leo Scannon is dead too. I was just reading his obituary in *The Times*. We knew him, of course, but Gerald couldn't abide him. He was one of those men who flattered you to your face and you knew was spiteful behind your back. But, of course,' she added hastily, 'I was sorry to see he had died, and so horribly. Presumably, you think the two deaths are connected?'

'It seems more than likely.'

'Oh Ned, do you have to get involved in all this? It's so . . . tawdry.'

Edward looked seriously at her. 'I think I do. I don't care much about Scannon, to tell you the honest truth. He was not a nice man and what's more he was a Fascist, though he called himself a Conservative. But poor Molly. You would never have received her here, nor would I have wanted you to, but she was just a pawn. She was used and then, when she got troublesome, she was wiped out, like you would wipe clean a blackboard. That can't be right, can it?'

'No, of course not . . . but Ned, I can't bear you wasting your time on this sort of . . . '

Edward flushed. 'I don't consider it a waste of time. I may be able to help prevent the royal family being tainted with . . . well, with murder.'

'You surely don't believe . . . ?'

'Why not? I'm not saying the King knew about it – in fact, I'm sure Wallis didn't even tell him the letters were stolen – but . . . '

'I'm sorry, I didn't mean to criticize. I just meant you deserve so much . . . '

'You'd like to see me as an ambassador or a general . . . ?'

'No. I mean . . . yes, Bates, what is it?'

Perhaps mercifully, the butler had appeared at the door. 'I am sorry to disturb you, Your Grace, but there is a telephone call for Lord Edward.'

'Who is it, Bates?' Edward asked, rising from the armchair and almost spilling his tea.

'Inspector Lampfrey, my lord.'

'Lampfrey! I wonder what he wants. Excuse me a moment, Connie.'

'Lord Edward, is that you?'

'Yes, Inspector. What can I do for you?'

'It's about the inquest, my lord. Chief Inspector Pride has asked the coroner for a postponement pending further police inquiries.'

'Good lord. So Pride has come round to my view that Mrs Harkness may have been murdered?'

'Yes, my lord, and confidentially . . . ' Lampfrey had lowered his voice to such a level Edward could only just hear him, 'I can't say much on the telephone, you understand, but there's a bit of a fuss here. I wondered if, before you went back to town, you would care to look in at the station?'

'Yes of course, Inspector, thank you. About nine tomorrow? Good.'

He put down the receiver and rubbed his forehead thoughtfully. Here was a turn-up for the books. Colonel Philips would not like it if Pride was questioning his judgement in preventing Lampfrey from completing his investigations into Molly's death – or had he managed to put all the blame on Lampfrey? If that was the case, Lampfrey might be more than happy to help him in his own investigations. He was about to go back into the drawing-room when he remembered Verity. There was no point in her coming down if there was to be no inquest. He rang the *New Gazette* but she was not there so he left a message and telephoned Charlotte Hassel with the news.

'I don't know where Verity is at the moment but I'll give her your message when she comes in. By the way, Edward,

Adrian's got something to tell you about Mr S's personal habits – rather mucky, I'm afraid. What about a council of war tomorrow night over shepherd's pie? I think I can make it worth your while . . . '

'Who was that, Ned?' the Duchess asked on his return to the drawing-room.

'Inspector Lampfrey. Apparently, the inquest is postponed. Chief Inspector Pride, who has been brought in to investigate Leo Scannon's death, believes there may be some connection with Molly's. It's one in the eye for poor Lampfrey who, under pressure from the Chief Constable, was going to say Molly died accidentally.'

'Did you say Chief Inspector Pride is investigating Leo's death? Surely that means you can't do anything? As I remember, you fought like cat and dog when he was here investigating poor General Craig's murder.'

'Mmm. Maybe. Anyway, I said I wanted your advice. What else do you know about Scannon – I mean apart from his being a social climber? What were his roots? He was filthy rich, wasn't he?'

'Oh Ned, I don't know. It's true we have known him a long time. After all, he was practically a neighbour and Gerald and he used to go on about politics whenever they met. Gerald said he was one of Mosley's supporters, and you know what he thinks of Mosley.'

'But who was he?'

'Let me think. His father made his fortune from matches, I believe – in Birmingham. Yes, that's it – Starburst matches. You know the ones I mean?'

Edward drew a box from his waistcoat pocket. 'These?'

'That's right. I know there was a spot of bother – Gerald knows the details. Apparently matches are very dangerous things to make. Is it phosphorus? I think it's phosphorus – anyway, some of the poor girls on the factory floor got very ill and several died. The health and safety people closed him down but it all blew over and the factory reopened.'

'And Scannon senior got even richer?'

'I suppose so.'

'When was this? I thought the match girls' strike was in 1888.'

'Was it? I'm afraid I was never very good at history. I think Leo's father had his troubles in 1913 because then the war came and – yes, I remember now – Gerald said it was horrible – the factory was turned over to making poison gas. Don't they use phosphorus in gas?'

Edward was silent, his face grim. So that was why Leo had been reticent about the source of his father's wealth; it was based on poison and, of course, Leo died of poisoning. Didn't rat poison contain phosphorus? He got up and rang the bell. When the butler appeared, he said, 'Bates, any luck with the rat poison?'

Connie looked startled but the butler said, 'Yes, my lord. There is rat poison in the gardener's shed and I'm afraid to say it wasn't locked up. It was just stored with some old petrol cans. I've instructed Merry that from now on it must be kept in a locked cupboard clearly marked as poison.'

'Very good. I wonder if you would be kind enough to have Mr Merry bring me the can to look at tomorrow morning before I go back to London.' He saw the butler look disconcerted. 'Don't worry, Bates. It's nothing sinister. I just want to remind myself what the ingredients of rat poison are.'

'Very good, my lord.'

'And Bates – the inquest has been postponed so I will be going back to town immediately after breakfast tomorrow.'

At dinner that night, Connie said, 'I've been meaning to ask you about Frank, Ned. His housemaster has been worried about him. I'm not blaming Verity but . . .'

'But what?' Edward asked, prepared to spring to Verity's defence.

'Gerald thinks – and I agree – that she has encouraged him.'

'What on earth do you mean, Connie? Encouraged him in what?'

'In his silly Communism – he's joined the Young Communists, would you believe it? Gerald's very upset.

Frank says he won't be a duke and that we are "exploiters". I mean, that's too ridiculous! Can you imagine Gerald exploiting anyone? What with the depression in agriculture, the estate runs at a loss and Gerald refuses to accept rent from his tenants until things improve.'

'Oh dear,' Edward said. 'Actually, Verity is going down to Eton next week to address a school society and I've said I'll go with her. Frank invited us . . . invited Verity,' he added, defensively.

'Must you?' Connie sounded distressed. 'His housemaster says he has started this magazine called – what is it? – *Beyond Bounds*, I think he said. I haven't seen a copy but I think it's very Communist – lots about Spain.'

'It's just natural schoolboy rebellion, surely. Frank's a sensible boy with a strong sense of duty. Once he gets it out of his system, he'll be right as rain.'

'I do hope so, Ned. I do hope so.'

'Look, if I may, Connie, I'll come back here in a few days with – Verity and make our report. I'll do my best when we are at Eton to talk some sense into the boy.'

10

Rather surprisingly, Verity made only a token protest when they foregathered at the Hassels' the following evening. Edward made a full report and included Adrian and Charlotte, who were now tacitly accepted as part of the team.

'So there we are,' he finished, clutching his glass of cheap Italian wine which was already giving him a headache. 'Rodine is easily available. Most gardeners have it in their sheds and pharmacists make no difficulty about supplying it. The phosphorus, especially mixed with alcohol, kills almost immediately. Might we speculate that Scannon's murderer used rat poison not just because it was easy to get hold of but because his father had been responsible for the death of a near relative either in the war – a victim of a gas attack – or in 1913 when Scannon senior was prosecuted after several workers in his factory died of phossy jaw?'

'Phossy jaw? It sounds almost cosy,' Charlotte said.

'I don't want to spoil anyone's appetite but it's anything but cosy. The phosphorus is breathed into the lungs and so gets into the bloodstream, weakening every bone in the body, not just the jawbone. I looked it up in the London Library this afternoon. Initially, you feel as if you've got the flu – you sneeze a lot and get toothache. After some weeks, or even months, the pain spreads throughout the face –

your glands swell and your gums are inflamed. Then your teeth fall out and . . .'

'Ugh! That's enough, Edward,' Charlotte stopped him. 'It's illegal now, I suppose, to use phosphorus in matches?'

'Yes, as a result of Scannon's case and one or two others, it was made illegal to use white phosphorus in matches. In fact, its use was outlawed by the Berne Convention in 1906 but it took time for our great democracy to take the necessary action to ban it.'

'It's too horrible,' Verity said. 'I knew I hated Scannon and now I hate his father as well.'

Adrian said, 'Yes, but it's more complicated than that. There are other reasons why Scannon might have been murdered.'

'You mean because of his links with the Nazis?' Verity said.

'Not that either, or rather not only that. I mean – dash it – I don't like talking about this in front of you girls . . .'

Charlotte said, 'Don't be silly, Adrian. This is a murder investigation and we're not blushing virgins.'

Edward sighed as he recalled being admonished by Verity on another occasion in almost the same words. He wondered what his brother would say if he could hear their conversation. Well, he knew what he would say; he would be outraged.

Adrian shrugged and went on, 'Well, you've been warned. Scannon wasn't just a pansy – he liked . . . he liked being treated roughly.'

'What do you mean?' Verity asked, intrigued.

'Well, I've got a few friends who . . . it's illegal but you can't legislate away human feelings.'

'Oh for God's sake, Adrian, spit it out. We do know about Oscar Wilde and they say Noel Coward is . . . that way.'

'You know I said Matt had committed suicide when Scannon and he fell out? Well, I talked to some of his friends and they said it wasn't just about his art being a failure. They said Scannon liked to . . . to tie him up and do horrible things to him and when he couldn't, or wouldn't, take it any more Scannon went off and found other young men who would . . . oblige. And these were often violent, ill people – the dregs. I don't know, perhaps it's all lies. I hope it is. I'm just repeating what I was told but when news got out about Scannon's murder, people who knew about his sexual habits assumed he'd been killed by one of his . . . his boys.'

There was silence after this. Both the girls prided themselves on being unshockable and Verity had seen terrible acts of violence in Spain but this seemed so disgusting. She said viciously, 'He deserved to die. Why don't we leave it at that?' The idea that violence could be *desired* . . . could be *domesticated* made her feel physically ill.

'Yes, I agree. Leave that for Pride to deal with. I want to know about Molly's death,' Edward said stubbornly. 'From what we've discovered, it makes it less likely than we first thought that the two killings are related and that makes things easier. Molly's death must be because of her relationship with the King – the baby and or the letters she stole.'

'Maybe,' Verity said slowly, 'but not certainly. I've been doing some digging, too. You probably already know this, Edward, but by coincidence a friend of mine has just got back from Kenya and he says you haven't been as frank with us as you might have been about Molly's . . . trouble.'

'What do you mean? I've told you the facts.'

'No you haven't – at least, not all the facts. I don't mean to speak ill of the dead,' Verity went on, sententiously, 'but you didn't tell me how much she was disliked – perhaps hated is not too strong a word. Respectable people, my friend says, would have nothing to do with her. Not to put too fine a point on it, they called her a whore. He says she broke up two marriages and apparently Douglas Davenant – the man her husband found her in bed with – was destroyed by the scandal. Molly dumped him, society ostracized him and he went off to Lake Rudolph and got speared by a native or eaten by a lion or something. My friend couldn't remember the details. I'm sorry, Edward, it's no good looking like that at me. It may be beastly but, if we are to find who killed Molly, we have to face facts, however unpleasant.'

Edward hesitated and then said, 'Molly wasn't a whore but she was promiscuous. As for the rest, don't forget I took her out of Nairobi so I never heard what happened to Davenant. I really don't think you can blame Molly if he went off the rails. Perhaps he just wanted a bit of adventure and it was just bad luck he was killed.'

'Well,' Charlotte said, 'Verity's right. We can't assume Molly was killed for political reasons. We have to look at who was at Haling when she died and see if anyone had a link with her. Didn't you say Boy Carstairs knew her in Kenya? Could he have had it in for her?'

'I think he might have been her lover at some point,' Edward said slowly. 'I must talk to him. We've hardly exchanged a dozen words. In fact, I got the impression he was trying to keep out of my way at Haling. However, I don't think he's a murderer. Molly was murdered for politics, by which I mean her relationship with the King. That has to be the most likely explanation. There is one thing I haven't told you – I didn't even tell Lampfrey – but it was when we were going through her flat – you remember, Verity, when I met you coming back from Harrods?'

'Yes.'

'I found a brooch or badge by her bed. It was a swastika set with diamonds and rubies. Look . . . ' He put his hand in his pocket and passed the object to Verity.

'It's horrible,' she said, almost dropping it. 'Why didn't you give it to Lampfrey?'

'I don't know. I should have done but, to tell the truth, I don't believe she was a Nazi and I didn't want her name besmirched.'

'Besmirched!' Verity said scathingly. 'I don't believe this, Edward. You've got to face up to the real Molly Harkness. You say yourself she wasn't perfect. If, after she's dead, you start trying to "save her face", or whatever it is you're doing, we'll never get to the truth.' Edward looked down at his shoes.

Adrian said gently, 'She's right, you know. Mrs Harkness, from what you tell us, was a gutsy woman and she wouldn't thank you for trying to protect her reputation if it meant not finding her killer.'

'Anyway, there's another explanation for the swastika being in her bedroom – two others, actually,' Charlotte broke in. 'She might have been given it – maybe even by the King himself. It's not impossible.'

'And the other explanation?' Edward queried.

'You said she told you her flat had been searched by someone looking for the letters. Maybe whoever that was dropped it.'

'Sounds unlikely. If her flat was being searched by someone who knew their business, they'd hardly be carrying a piece of Nazi jewellery, let alone dropping it.'

'They missed the King's letters to Molly which you found under the bed, Edward,' Charlotte responded tartly.

'Perhaps they weren't under her bed when the flat was searched. We just don't know,' he pointed out.

There was a moment's silence before Verity said, 'There's another thing I've found out, Edward – about Dannie. I know you'll think I'm just being . . . . spiteful or something but I was talking to a Party worker about Stille – you know how he keeps popping up and pretending to be one of us . . . stirring up trouble? I had to report what I knew to the Party. Well, I was told something I didn't really want to know.' Verity took a deep breath: 'They say she works for Stille – Dannie, I mean. It may be she was at Haling as Stille's agent.'

Verity knew she did not need to spell it out to Edward that she was suggesting Dannie might have slept with him on Stille's orders just so she could be near Molly's room, steal the letters and murder her to stop her talking.

What Verity had said did not greatly surprise Edward. He had resigned himself to the knowledge that Dannie had used him and, though he was inclined to think she had not killed Molly, he did believe her to be capable of it. She was a ruthless woman, of that he had no doubt.

'I didn't know she was a Nazi but what you say doesn't altogether surprise me. But what you don't explain, Verity, is why she should kill Molly. Look at it logically. The Nazis are hand in glove with the King and Mrs Simpson – we can't doubt that – so surely it's in their interests to protect his reputation?'

'No, it's you who aren't thinking clearly, Edward,' Verity said vehemently, determined to have the whole thing out, however painful it might be. 'I'm not saying they would use the letters to discredit the King. Just the opposite, as you say. They would want to take them to *protect* him from Molly's trouble-making. They'll be destroyed by now or lodged somewhere safe in Berlin.'

'And if they thought Molly might kick up a stink – even say she was pregnant with the King's child – to protect him they might very well have decided to kill her,' Charlotte said excitedly.

Glumly, Edward studied his boots again. 'Well, this is just speculation. We must get some hard facts, as you say, Verity,' he said at last.

'When you had your talk with Molly on the night she died, did she tell you anything that might give us a clue to her murderer? Didn't you say she gave you the impression she was waiting for someone?'

'I've thought about that a lot. She definitely hinted that she half expected me to be someone else when she opened her bedroom door.'

'A lover?'

'I don't know. I thought so at first but now I'm not so sure. She said she was – how did she put it? – "fancy-free". She said, rather bitterly I thought, that there had been lovers but she hadn't got one at the moment. Those weren't her exact words but that was what she wanted me to understand. Oh, that reminds me. She told me she had been introduced to the Prince of Wales, as he then was, by a man called Lewis Van Buren. I think he must have been South African. She admitted to me he had briefly been her lover. I got the impression he lent money and supplied women, and no doubt other things, to the Prince's set.'

'A Jew?' Charlotte inquired.

'Yes, I think so. Molly genuinely liked him. I wondered, V, if you could find anything about him in the *Gazette* files?'

'I'll look him up but I can't see what he would have to do with her death.'

'Nor can I, but she might have told him more than she told me about what happened in Kenya. They either met in Cape Town or on the boat – he might have seen someone or know something.'

'It's worth looking into, I suppose,' Verity said doubtfully. 'Anything else, Edward?'

'Only that Mr Harbin told me he saw Leo Scannon remove something from Molly's room while I was examining her body.'

'Golly! Did he say what?'

'He wasn't sure but he thought it might have been an envelope – something white, anyway. He also noticed that, under his dressing gown, Scannon was still dressed in the clothes he had worn at dinner. He hadn't been to bed.'

'A cool customer, Scannon,' Adrian commented.

'No, he didn't seem cool. He was genuinely shocked when we found Molly dead – in fact he was almost "struck dumb" as they say in romances. It was left to me to tell Pickering to call the police and the doctor. Then, when he had recovered himself a little, he suggested searching Molly's room before the police came, but I refused. Anyway, it was too late by then. Lampfrey arrived very quickly.'

Edward thought about telling them of his botched attempt to tamper with the evidence and how he had hidden Molly's bag in the chimney but it was so absurd and, having made such a fool of himself with Dannie, he did not want to heap more ridicule on himself. He wondered if Verity had told Adrian and Charlotte that he had slept with Dannie, and how she had tricked him. He thought she probably had and he certainly wasn't going to broadcast his idiocy.

'Well,' Verity said, 'let's assume for the moment Molly was killed by someone at Haling. I know . . . I know . . . ' she said, raising her hand as Edward opened his mouth. 'Someone from outside could have shinned up the creeper and got into her room through the window . . . '

'This really is the opposite of a "locked-room" mystery,' Adrian said. 'I have just read *The Hollow Man*, you know, by John Dickson Carr. It's brilliant. You see, no one could have got into the room where the murder happened . . . '

'Yes, all right, Adrian, but can we keep to the business in hand,' Verity reprimanded him.

'Sorry,' Adrian said, humbly.

'There weren't so many people staying at Haling. Why don't I write them down like they do in books.' Verity took a piece of paper and a pencil from Adrian's desk and licked the lead in a businesslike manner. 'We all know about Edward,' she said brightly. 'He's the prime suspect. He had opportunity and motive. His job was to shut Molly up and she was shut up.'

'I say, V,' Edward said plaintively, 'don't rag. I'm not in the mood.'

'We have to face facts,' she said, and then relented. 'Anyway, to continue. There were the Benyons. You know them, don't you, Charlotte?'

'Yes, we know them and they are the nicest couple. I could never believe either of them could . . . '

'You mean just because they were fool enough to buy one of Adrian's pictures . . . '

'Verity!' Edward and Charlotte exclaimed in unison.

'It's no use you all being so lily-livered. We must be objective if we're to get anywhere. I think you, Edward, and Adrian ought to go and see them and see what they remember.'

'Right,' Adrian said. 'The Hepple-Keens sound an odd duo from what you say, Edward.'

'They are. There's something sinister about him. I have a suspicion he might be a sort of policeman, unless he's a dyed in the wool Mosleyite. I think I'll have a word with my pal Basil Thoroughgood at the FO. He might be able to tell me which or know who to ask. Hepple-Keen's certainly a ruthless man and it's possible he is working for someone who wanted Mrs Simpson's letters back badly enough to kill for them.'

'And Lady Hepple-Keen?' Charlotte asked.

'A mystery, that one,' Edward said, scratching his chin. 'I thought at first she was a dull, put-upon little woman, scared of her husband and with no other interests than her children but now . . . '

'"Now" what?' Verity asked sharply.

'Now I'm not so sure. Do you remember, V, she got quite excited when we were talking about the child victims of the fighting in Spain. I wouldn't be surprised if she didn't turn out to be a fierce fighter for them.'

'Yes, well, I'm taking her to see Joe at the *New Gazette* tomorrow so perhaps I'll get to know her better but, on the face of it, she had no motive for killing Molly. Dannie – well, we know about her, don't we, Edward,' she said meaningfully. 'I don't think we'll get much out of her if either of us were to try and talk to her but I've put the Party hounds on to her, so they might turn up something interesting, and I'm going to harry Joe. He knows a lot about her he hasn't told yet.'

'Oh V,' Edward said weakly, 'don't let your prejudices get in the way of . . . I mean, I know you don't like her but you said we have to be objective . . . put our feelings to one side and all that.'

'I have no feelings for her either way,' Verity said coldly, 'but the facts are she is an associate of a known Nazi, one Major Stille, and we know she had the best opportunity of killing Molly of anyone at Haling with the exception of you, Edward. She had, in a word, motive and opportunity.'

'Two words,' Edward said, unwisely, and Verity threw a glance at him which chilled him. 'Larry Harbin,' he said to prevent either of the Hassels asking Verity what she was going on about. 'I took him back to London in the Lagonda and I liked him. He's on his way back to America now so we can't interview him. Anyway what motive could he have?'

As he said the words, Edward remembered what Harbin had said outside Molly's bedroom door as they were trying to open it. 'There is something though. He told me he didn't approve of Molly; had warned the King about her in fact. You see, Harbin comes from Baltimore, Mrs Simpson's home town, and though I got the feeling he didn't approve of her much either, he didn't want Molly bringing down scandal on Wallis's head.'

'Hardly a motive for murder,' Charlotte said.

'No, I don't think for a moment he killed Molly but we agreed we had to put all the facts on the table.'

'Who else is there?' Verity said, finishing her notes on Harbin.

'Scannon himself. He knew all about Molly and, if I hadn't agreed to approach her about returning the letters, he said he was going to do it but he didn't think she would take much notice of him.'

'He obviously had a motive then,' Verity said, 'and he would have had less trouble getting a key to her room than anyone else.'

'Yes,' Edward agreed, 'but, as I told you, his reaction when we found Molly dead did not seem to me to be that of a man who knew what he was going to find. He would have been much calmer, unless he was an accomplished actor. And don't forget Carstairs,' Edward continued. 'I need to talk to him. When he came back from riding with Dannie, he didn't seem awfully surprised when we told him about Molly.'

'I think you're right, Edward, you ought to tackle him,' Verity said. 'Man to man stuff.'

'The servants are in the clear?' Adrian asked.

'I think so. Pickering has been with Scannon for years. Still, I would like to have an opportunity of talking to him,' Edward said. 'And we haven't mentioned Ruth Conway.'

'Who's she?' Charlotte asked.

'She's the woman Scannon hired to look after his bedridden old mother. If I know Pride, he'll be trying to pin Scannon's murder on her.'

'Why?' Charlotte asked.

'She's there the whole time and knows exactly how the house is run and has access to the keys, but the main thing from Pride's point of view will be that socially she is of no account. His one idea is to protect his political masters from scandal.'

'Edward!' Charlotte protested. 'That's so unfair. What evidence do you have for saying that?'

'Oh, sorry, Charlotte. I know, Pride's a clever man but I've had experience of his investigations on two occasions and he seemed less interested in getting to the truth and more in avoiding a bad press . . . '

'He's doesn't like us,' Verity explained. 'He thinks I'm the worst sort of political extremist and he considers Edward to be . . . well, someone who interferes where he should leave well alone.'

'He thinks I'm an ass,' Edward said bluntly.

'And you're not an ass, are you?' Verity said as if she were comforting a three-year-old.

Adrian said hurriedly, 'Right, let's get down to some sleuthing. It's all very good fun.'

'It's not just self-indulgence,' Edward said soberly. 'I have no faith at all that Pride or anyone else will find out who killed Molly. I don't care very much who killed Scannon but Molly was my friend and I refuse to let her death go unavenged just because that would be more convenient.'

Verity looked at Edward with interest. There was a vein of bitterness in what he said and the way he said it that surprised her. He was no longer the light-hearted young aristocrat with the time and money to harry the police. He was, she thought, disillusioned, disillusioned with the police, with men of power like Joe Weaver and with society as a whole. Was it just that, as one got older, one had the experience to see things as they really were or was it something more profound? Even she had been forced to recognize there was no 'good' side to be on. Everyone – even the Party itself – had objectives of which she was largely ignorant but of which she instinctively disapproved. Surely Edward was right: where there was justice to be done one should not avoid doing it. One could argue that finding Molly's murderer wasn't their business and there was so much evil in the world and so many victims of oppression that one more case was neither here nor there. That wasn't her attitude and she was glad it wasn't his. She wanted to get up, put her arms around him and kiss him but she caught Adrian's eye. He was smiling at her as though he knew exactly what she was thinking and, to her considerable annoyance, she blushed as though she were a child and not the hardened journalist she liked to imagine she was.

11

Verity worked on her book late into the night, tapping away on Adrian's old typewriter – a Remington portable with its annoying red sticker bearing the maxim 'To save time is to lengthen life' – anxious to complete it before the Spanish civil war became history. She was sure the rebels would win – it was only a matter of when – not that she would ever have admitted so much even to Edward or Adrian. Rereading her *New Gazette* articles gave her the opportunity of re-evaluating her experiences. Her first reports were alive with indignation, confident of the justice of the cause she had espoused. Her naivety made her blush. As the weeks became months, she detected a shrillness in her writing which reflected her growing panic. Why would the democracies not help Spain in its agony? Why were the politicians so venal, the peasant soldiers so badly armed and – more agonizingly – the rebels so convinced right was on their side and justified the most terrible acts of cruelty? And what justified the Communist Party's vicious war against those who had once been its allies and who still considered themselves part of the Popular Front against Fascism – the anarchists, the syndicalists, the separatists and, most bitter enemy of all, the Trotskyists?

She had been given two hundred pounds advance on royalties by Victor Gollancz, the left-wing publisher and founder of the Left Book Club. It was the most she had ever earned and, for that reason alone, she was determined to do her best but it was even more important to her to make sense of her activities in Spain, culminating in the shocking defeat at Toledo which, as Edward had guessed, had shaken her to the roots. She had to believe that she had not been mistaken – that the cause to which she had attached herself so uncritically was worth her allegiance.

When at last she went to bed, she looked at her face in the mirror as she removed the traces of lipstick and rouge she allowed herself – in part to avoid her friends remarking on how pale and drawn she was. She saw a white, round face with a stubborn chin and burning, black eyes which seemed to accuse her. She wondered if courage was self-renewing or whether it ran out like petrol in a car. She felt her store of courage was diminishing and it was odd that being near Edward seemed to help. She didn't believe women needed men to complete them, as she had been taught. She liked men, she liked sex, but she had convinced herself she did not need a man in her life. And yet . . . she was beginning to wonder if she did not, in fact, need Edward. She had been profoundly shocked to hear of his night with Dannie and she didn't quite know why. Was it simple jealousy? Or was it that she felt he needed a 'good woman' to save him from such squalid affairs?

She fell asleep wondering and arose the next morning unrefreshed, her doubts unresolved. After a hasty breakfast, she went into the *New Gazette* to catch up on the news from Spain and to see if there was anything for her to do. Lord Weaver was out of the office until four when he had an appointment to talk to Daphne Hepple-Keen about backing her charitable work for children orphaned by the war. Verity put her head round the door of the editor's office but Godber refused to acknowledge her greeting, to the ill-concealed glee of the staff who were within earshot. He had taken to pretending she did not exist. He had heard on the grapevine that she was once again going over his head to the paper's proprietor to win his backing for some wild scheme, and he was seriously considering resigning if this proved to be the case. The editor wasn't alone in his jealousy of Verity. Men who had worked at the paper for decades resented a woman – not a proper journalist in the eyes of many of them – getting bylines and pretending she was a war correspondent, a job totally unsuited to her age and sex. They made jokes about 'sleeping one's way to the top' and asked themselves if their years of apprenticeship on local newspapers and then on Fleet Street counted for nothing.

Verity knew all this without having to be told and, since there was nothing she could do about it, ignored it. Mentally shugging her shoulders, she decided to go down to the archive and see what she could find about Lewis Van Buren, the man who Molly said had introduced her to the Prince of Wales.

There was nothing at all about Van Buren but there was something about Hepple-Keen. The *New Gazette*'s archivist, an elderly man by the name of Purser, directed her to several volumes of the paper covering the 1920s and, though the references to him were maddeningly few and almost always coupled with other more newsworthy names, Verity began to feel she was on to something. It appeared that Hepple-Keen, before he became an MP, had been some sort of government agent in Ireland. He was mentioned in a surprisingly critical account – given the newspaper proprietor's close relationship with the government – of the activities of the Black and Tans who had murdered two of Michael Collins's men in November 1920 and again, in February 1921, when fifteen army cadets had been murdered by the IRA. Precisely what official position he held which brought him to the scene of both crimes was not made clear, but Verity concluded that, though he wore no uniform and was certainly not a member of the RUC, he was a policeman of some kind and a senior one at that.

Even more interesting was an account of the arrest the following June of a girl called Eileen O'Sullivan who had been in her bath when her Dublin flat had been raided by the British police. The unnamed *New Gazette* reporter had obviously been amused at her predicament and there was mention of Hepple-Keen 'escorting her, semi-naked' into a police van for interrogation. 'Gallant British officers had protected her modesty', according to the report but secret files belonging to the IRA leader, Michael Collins, had been discovered under her bed. Out of interest, Verity looked up Eileen O'Sullivan's name in the index and discovered she had 'died in gaol' before she could be brought to trial. It made her boil to think of this Irish girl dying for her cause – a cause she, Verity, shared: an end to imperialism.

She had been so deep in her reading that she had forgotten to keep an eye on the time and it was three thirty when she at last looked at the clock on the wall and realized Lady Hepple-Keen was due in the building in half an hour. Oddly enough, her instinctive dislike of Geoffrey Hepple-Keen – the heavy-handed, brutal policeman the files revealed – made her even more enthusiastic about helping Daphne. At the least, it would annoy him to see his wife become a public figure, applauded for her charitable works. At the best, it might provoke him to do something stupid. Evidence or no evidence, Verity had selected Geoffrey Hepple-Keen as the villain of the piece and the cold-hearted killer. She would ask her friend at Party headquarters if she knew anything more about him.

Just before she left the archive, she thought she might as well see if there were any references to the other guests at Haling. Unsurprisingly, there were many to Lord Benyon and a few to Larry Harbin, who was described as having 'the ear' of President Roosevelt, a phrase that always amused her. She turned rather wearily to Leo Scannon. His public career was covered in considerable detail and his social life was also chronicled with numbing flattery. Verity looked up ten or twelve references during the previous decade but came to the conclusion that, if she wanted 'dirt' on the man, she would not find it in the nauseatingly respectful columns of the *New Gazette*. However, as she was thinking she really must go up to reception to meet Joe's visitor, she saw that immediately before Leo Scannon's name in the index was that of Arthur Frank Scannon. This turned out to be Leo's father. Twenty minutes later, with a grim face, she thanked Mr Purser for his help and hurried up to the entrance hall to discover that Lady Hepple-Keen had already arrived and had been taken up to see Lord Weaver. She went over to the lift and, as she was whisked upwards, went over in her mind what she had just been reading. By the time she reached the top floor where Miss Barnstable shepherded her into the great man's office, she was certain she had found a motive for murder.

On Edward's return to Albany after lunch at his club, he was met by a more than usually lugubrious Fenton.

'Chief Inspector Pride is here to see you, my lord.'

'Pride? Good heavens! What does he want? Has he been here long?'

'Some half an hour, my lord.'

Edward blanched and contemplated turning tail. He really didn't want to meet his old enemy at this particular moment but he realized Pride must have heard his voice as he entered his rooms so, taking a deep breath, he pushed open the drawing-room door.

'Chief Inspector,' he said, holding out his hand and forcing his face into what he hoped was an insouciant smile. 'How very nice to see you again. I do apologize for having inadvertently kept you waiting but I did not know you were intending to call on me.'

Chief Inspector Pride did not smile but he did, rather grudgingly, take his hand. 'That's all right, my lord. It was just on an off chance. You know Sergeant Willis?'

'Yes of course, how are you?'

'Well, thank you, my lord.'

The Sergeant was a pock-faced man with a pleasant smile and good-natured eyes. He had been helpful to Edward when he had been investigating the death of his old school friend, Stephen Thayer, and Edward had wondered then, and wondered again now, how the Sergeant put up with working for Pride.

'Please, do sit down,' Edward said. 'Fenton, have you offered the Chief Inspector something to drink?'

'Nothing, thank you, my lord,' Pride broke in. He was looking uneasy and, at the same time, pleased with himself. He did not like Edward; he did not like being on his territory – he would have been more comfortable if this interview had been at the Yard – but he was cautious enough to know that, if he was too minatory now, he might regret it later. He thought he had this complacent, arrogant drone where he wanted him. He had been over the evidence so thoroughly and so often but he had enough respect for Edward and, it had to be said, for his 'connections', to be wary of making a mistake.

'So what can I do for you, Chief Inspector?' Edward said at last, since Pride seemed so reluctant to state the reason for his presence.

'My lord,' Pride began with a heave of his shoulders, 'I have reason to believe you have something to tell me about the deaths of Mrs Raymond Harkness and Mr Leo Scannon.'

'Indeed? You mean beyond the statement I made to Inspector Lampfrey?'

'Yes, sir. I have your statement and also those of the other guests staying at Haling Castle at the time of Mrs Harkness's death. I have also read the Inspector's report following the examination of the room in which the lady died and there are certain things which . . . shall we say, "don't add up".'

'Fire away, Chief Inspector. If I can help in any way . . . '

'You were the last person to see Mrs Harkness alive?'

'Yes, except for the murderer, of course. No, wait. I believe that Miss Dannhorn went into Mrs Harkness's room during the night but we don't know if she was still alive at that point. Or perhaps you do know, Chief Inspector?'

Pride chose to ignore the question. 'You had been asked *to recover some letters belonging to a certain personage* . . . '

'To Mrs Simpson . . . yes.' Edward was not prepared to let Pride get away with 'certain personage'. If the Chief

Inspector wanted to accuse him of anything, he wanted him to know that he would not be protecting anyone's reputation as he sought to defend himself.

'And you were selected for this by the lady in question because you were an intimate friend of the deceased?'

'I had been a friend of Mrs Harkness in Kenya, Chief Inspector, but I had not seen her since she had returned to England.'

The Chief Inspector changed tack. 'According to Inspector Lampfrey's report, you failed to say that you had ... ah, spent much of the night with one of the ladies staying in the house.'

'That is correct. I did not mention it until I heard from the Inspector that the lady had no objection to her name being mentioned.'

'That was Miss Dannhorn?'

'Indeed.'

'Did you know at the time, Lord Edward, that the lady was hand in glove with a known foreign agent and was herself determined to gain possession of these letters?'

'I wasn't aware of it, no, but after the event I did begin to suspect. In fact, I asked Miss Dannhorn if she had gone into Mrs Harkness's room during the night and taken the letters. She denied it.'

'I see. And you did not believe her?'

'No, but there was nothing I could do.'

The Chief Inspector consulted his notes. 'Mrs Harkness died from taking an overdose of veronal mixed in brandy from her flask. Your fingerprints and Mrs Harkness's were the only ones on the flask. Your fingerprints were also on both handles of the door which connected your room with hers. Can you explain why, subsequently, you had to wait for Mr Pickering, the butler, to bring a master key so you could enter Mrs Harkness's room from the passage? That was when you found her dead.'

'Yes, but you see I didn't notice the door between our rooms was open until after I found Mrs Harkness dead. My man, Fenton, had told me the night before that the door was locked. Since it was hidden by a screen, I did not know it had been opened – presumably sometime during the night.'

'By whom, if not by you?' the policeman said menacingly.

'By Miss Dannhorn, I imagine. Have you asked her?'

'She is no longer in the country. I am told she is in Germany.'

Edward was taken aback.

'You didn't know, my lord?'

'No, I did not. Why should I have known?'

'It is my belief, my lord,' the Chief Inspector said ponderously, 'that you and she were in league to obtain the letters stolen from Mrs Simpson, not to return them to her but to spirit them out of the country to an interested foreign party.'

'But that's preposterous! Why should I have done that – for money?'

The scorn in Edward's voice was wasted on Pride. 'I was hoping you could give me the answer to that, my lord. Inspector Lampfrey says you admitted to him that you had in your possession the deceased's handbag in which the letters were probably kept by the lady – I understand she told you she always kept them on her.'

'But the bag was empty.'

'Of course it was empty. You had passed on the letters to Miss Dannhorn.'

'But Lampfrey opened the bag, using force to break the lock.'

'Very ingenious, my lord,' the policeman said, unmoved.

'I had no motive for doing what you are accusing me of.'

'Mrs Harkness was pregnant either by you or by . . . someone else. Perhaps she was blackmailing you – saying she would tell the world you were the father of her child.'

'I told you, Chief Inspector, I had not seen Mrs Harkness since she returned to England until we met at Haling. Even if I had been . . . . as you put it "the father of her child", it might have embarrassed me but I wouldn't have killed her.'

Edward was sweating now. He looked at the Chief Inspector with disgust. 'So, are you going to arrest me?'

The Chief Inspector looked at him for a moment with satisfaction, and Edward realized how much he was enjoying seeing him squirm. A calmness overcame him and he understood that the man was trying to rattle him – to make him say something incriminating. There was plenty of circumstantial evidence to involve him in Molly's death but not quite enough to make Pride certain he could get a conviction.

'No, sir, we are still in the process of investigating Mrs Harkness's death and Mr Scannon's – a man you had no reason to love, I understand.'

'Oh, don't be absurd, Chief Inspector. Are you going to accuse me of murdering Mr Scannon?'

'I can assure you that there is nothing absurd about our investigations and you would be mistaken if you believed you were above the law just because you have friends in high places.'

Edward, with a great effort, kept his temper in check. 'Mr Scannon was an old friend of my family. I had absolutely nothing to do with his murder and I very much regret his death.' He knew he was being disingenuous and he feared his protestation sounded feeble, but he had to say something. 'If you are not arresting me, Chief Inspector, and if you have no more questions for me, I must ask you to leave.'

'I have no more questions for the present but I would be grateful if you would keep me apprised of your whereabouts until this investigation is complete.'

'You think I might skip the country, do you?'

'It is one of the difficulties of this investigation that several of Mr Scannon's house guests – Mr Harbin and Miss Dannhorn – are no longer in the country. I am sure you can understand, my lord, why I am anxious that no further . . . witnesses . . . leave England. Good day to you.'

With that parting shot, Pride left and Edward was in no way mollified by an apologetic glance from Sergeant Willis behind his superior's back.

'Fenton,' he yelled, when he heard the door of his chambers close, 'a whisky and soda as soon as you like and if you leave out the soda that'll be all right by me.'

In Lord Weaver's magnificent office with its huge plate-glass windows and seated in a deep leather chair in front of his oversized desk, Daphne Hepple-Keen resembled nothing so much as the proverbial country mouse. Her coat was a little shabby, her shoes too heavy and her hat distinctly un-chic, but when Verity shook her hand she was startled by the firmness of her grasp and a light in her eyes which indicated she had steeled herself for battle. Even though she was used to Lord Weaver, Verity was still a little in awe of the bear-like man with his wrinkled face and bushy eyebrows. After all, this was a man who could bring down governments and make or break reputations while Lady Hepple-Keen, at dinner at Haling, had hardly spoken except to talk about her children and had been terrified by the rat on the billiard table. Verity was quite unprepared for what followed.

Weaver had beckoned Verity to enter his presence with his normal if rather contemptuous, 'Come!' Then he said irritably, 'Where have you been? Miss Barnstable has been looking all over for you.'

'Sorry,' she said meekly, slipping into the chair drawn up beside Lady Hepple-Keen. 'I got rather absorbed in some research.'

'Well, never mind that now.' He got up from his chair and began to pace about. Verity recognized the signs. Her employer was in a thoroughly bad mood and was looking for someone on whom to vent his bad temper. He was quite clearly irritated that he had been persuaded by Verity to meet this insignificant woman and was not going to any trouble to disguise it. Grudgingly, he said, 'How's Geoffrey?'

'I'm not here to talk about my husband,' Lady Hepple-Keen said briskly. 'I'm here because Miss Browne tells me you might be prepared to put your weight behind the Red Cross's operation to save orphans of the war in Spain.'

Verity's ears pricked. Perhaps Daphne Hepple-Keen was not going to be squashed as easily as one might have imagined.

'I don't know about that,' Weaver interrupted her, waving his cigar in the air for punctuation. 'As you may be aware, the *New Gazette* has supported HMS *London* in her efforts to rescue refugees off the Spanish coast. She's due back in London next week or the week after.'

'I'm delighted to hear it,' Daphne Hepple-Keen said, 'but that's by the by. I want you to send me out with a group of volunteer nurses to inspect the orphanages of Madrid and other cities – find out what supplies are needed and then initiate a fund to which the public can subscribe to support our efforts. I understand from Miss Browne that the condition of some of these orphanages is appalling. Some have no medical supplies, very little food and . . . '

Verity broke in: 'You see, Joe, whatever medical supplies there are have to go to the soldiers at the front. The civilians are suffering worse than the troops and Madrid is in danger of being starved into surrender.'

Weaver looked at the two women sitting in front of him on the edge of uncomfortably large chairs and seemed to be weighing them up.

'It would be a great gesture, Joe,' Verity began, but stopped when he waved his cigar at her.

'It must be more than a gesture,' Daphne Hepple-Keen said.

'Would we be restricting ourselves to aiding children on the Republican side?' Weaver asked her.

'Certainly not. This effort would be made under the aegis of the Red Cross and they insist on making no distinction between warring parties. Our priority is helping the children regardless of the political views of their parents.'

'The danger is that neither side would co-operate with you,' Weaver said mildly. 'However,' he added quickly, seeing Daphne's face tighten, 'you are quite right in what you say.' He took another few paces and dragged on his cigar. 'Hmm, I am inclined to support you, Lady Hepple-Keen – Daphne. What does your husband think about all this?'

'Whatever do you mean, Lord Weaver? He knows nothing about it. What has it to do with him?'

Verity hid a grin behind her hand. This was getting better all the time.

'I only meant . . . but are you sure you are up to it? No offence, but the work would be tiring, the demands on you unimaginable. Are you really prepared to – if I may put it bluntly – do the work?'

'I am,' Lady Hepple-Keen said resolutely.

'Well, then,' said Weaver, smiling, 'I too will put my shoulder to the wheel. But first there are things to discuss, practical things.' He spoke into his intercom. 'Miss Barnstable, ask Mr Godber to come for a moment, will you? If he has time,' he added insincerely.

Three-quarters of an hour later, Verity escorted a triumphant Daphne Hepple-Keen off the premises. Just before she left the building, she leant towards Verity and grasped her hand. 'Thank you, my dear, thank you. We have done a good thing today. There is so much evil in the world and what we can do seems so . . . insignificant but we must do it. I could not sleep thinking that my children might one day need the help of strangers.'

'Will your husband be pleased?' Verity asked disingenuously, curious to know what the relationship between them was. She fancied Hepple-Keen might not like being upstaged by his wife whom he patronized and bullied.

'As I said to Lord Weaver, I haven't told him yet what I am planning to do. If he doesn't like it . . . well, he must live with it. You see, my dear, when you are married to that nice Lord Edward Corinth, you will find that men – even men like him – are the most dreadful liars and cheats – at least mine is. Do you know, I discovered he had been . . . intimate with that poor dead woman? I don't mind for myself, of course, but . . . for the children . . . But why am I telling you all this?' She giggled nervously. 'I think talking to Lord Weaver like that has made me a little . . . drunk.'

Verity, who had hardly recovered from being told she was to marry Edward, said faintly, 'Your husband was intimate with Mrs Harkness?'

'That's right, my dear,' she said brightly, 'but I was going to say that when you are married, you have to put up with a lot of things you never imagined you would have to . . . '

She trailed off. Then she added, still clutching Verity's hand: 'But we are stronger than them in the end, aren't we? Much stronger. Goodbye now. I will let you know the date of our first meeting.'

'Oh but . . . ' Verity was not sure she had agreed to be part of the crusade, but Daphne Hepple-Keen had apparently decided for her.

12

Edward was sorely tempted – and sorely was the word that seemed to him most appropriate – not to go with Verity to Eton to hear her lecture to young men who would be more than likely to jeer, hiss and otherwise pour indignities on her head. Wasn't it enough that he should have been almost crippled by honest working men in the East End of London? On the other hand – dash it! – he had promised and, as a gentleman, he could not go back on his word.

In the event, the day proved uncomfortable in a very different way from how he had imagined. He picked Verity up in the Lagonda just after three o'clock – the lecture was to start at six after which they were to have dinner with Frank's housemaster, Mr Chandler – and on the way he told her of his visit from Chief Inspector Pride.

'That man's a menace to decent law-abiding people,' Verity exclaimed, forgetting for a moment that she was an enemy of the state and would, in other circumstances, have been insulted to be described as law-abiding. 'Can't we do something, get him defrocked or whatever it is they do to bad cops? Cut his buttons off?'

'Mmm, I doubt it,' Edward answered her seriously. 'We'd have to prove him incompetent or negligent and even then I expect the Yard protects its own.'

'Edward!' Verity said, shocked. 'You're beginning to sound like me. I hope I haven't soiled your innocent faith in authority.'

'Don't flatter yourself, V. It was not you but the man himself who did that. You know, I desperately want to go to Haling and interview Pickering and, if possible, Miss Conway – find out how the land lies. She *must* know something. Hey! What is it? You look as if you've just been stung by a wasp.'

'That's what I've been trying to tell you, only you've been going on and on about Pride and I haven't been able to get a word in edgeways. That was what I found out from my assiduous research in the bowels of the *New Gazette*. Ruth Conway had a motive and a half for killing Scannon. His father made a fortune from matches.'

'We know that.'

'Yes, but what you don't know is that Scannon senior was prosecuted for letting three of his employees get phossy jaw and one of those was a Miss Emily Conway. Now, maybe she's no relation of Ruth's, but I don't think it likely. It's too much of a coincidence.'

'V, that's brilliant! I knew I couldn't do without you! We have to talk to her. It must be the key to the whole business. I wonder if Pride has tumbled to the connection? But there was something else you said you'd discovered?'

'Yep, there sure is, pardner.' Verity loved Gene Autry westerns and was too inclined to try out her American accent. 'It's about your pal Hepple-Keen. I had a most interesting afternoon with Daphne Hepple-Keen and she told me he was sleeping with Molly.' The Lagonda swerved violently. 'Whoa there, Captain Campbell. Remember, *Bluebird* burst a tyre at three hundred miles an hour.'

'Sorry, V, but that's sensational. I mean, is she sure? She's not just being hysterical?'

'She's sure all right and she's no fool. She told me wives have to get used to husbands lying and cheating. Do you think she's right?' Verity opened her eyes wide in mock innocence, but Edward was thinking of what she had told him.

'I've made an appointment to see my Foreign Office friend, Basil Thoroughgood, when we get back from grilling Miss Conway.'

'What's he got to do with Hepple-Keen?'

'Nothing, but he's going to introduce me to a man who does know about him – at least, I hope so.'

'Gosh, secret service stuff?'

'I don't know – maybe. Perhaps I'll be able to tell you more when I've talked to him.'

'Perhaps? You mean you might not?'

'Well, I might be sworn to secrecy,' Edward said reasonably. 'And damn it, you are a Communist and a journalist – a lethal combination, I would have thought, to any self-respecting secret service bod.'

'Huh!' Verity exclaimed. 'In that case, I resign. I've got a book to write, remember? I'm only doing this because you came to me on bended knee. Ungrateful hound! What happened to all that Watson and Holmes stuff?'

'No, I say, V. Of course I'll tell you, if I can. Don't be an ass. I told you, I need you. I can't do this sleuthing without you.'

He slowed the Lagonda as they turned into Eton and crossed the bridge.

Verity was touched by Edward's evident sincerity but she hesitated. What *was* she doing getting mixed up in all this? She really did need to get on with the book. She glanced at his profile. He really *was* good-looking, she thought inconsequentially. 'It's not really much to do with me, but . . . ' she added hastily, seeing his face cloud over, 'I suppose, as you said, I might get a good story out of it.'

'Hmff. Don't sound so enthusiastic,' he said, ignoring a pedestrian crossing guarded, unsuccessfully in this instance, by Belisha beacons and almost destroying a man with a dog.

'No, I am enthusiastic, honest injun,' Verity protested. 'Anything to avoid work. Anyway, musketeers and all that. You helped me in Spain. I'll be your sidekick now. What is it – "one for all and all for one"?'

'*Contra mundum*?'

'If you say so,' – none of the schools she had attended having gone in for teaching Latin – 'but we can't just barge in on Haling. Pride would have our guts for garters.'

'I know, so I've been thinking about employing a sub-terfuge.'

'I didn't know one actually *employed* subterfuges, but say on.'

'Why don't we go to Mersham, borrow a couple of bikes and ride over to Haling? It's not that far.'

'Then what?'

'Then we call in for a glass of ginger beer or – better still – you have a puncture.'

'Why me? I suppose you think girls get punctures and men don't?'

'Well, I seem to remember half killing myself mending punctures on your Morgan.'

'Oh well, let it be a puncture then. You think you know what questions to ask?'

'Not really, but I've got a few ideas. Ah, here we are. Look, there's Frank.'

They had arrived at the Burning Bush, an oddly shaped cast-iron lantern outside the school hall, where Edward had agreed to meet his nephew.

Frank was with a good-looking young man in a tattered black gown, too old to be an Etonian so, Edward deduced, a junior 'beak'. Frank kissed Verity and shook his uncle's hand before introducing them to the master. His name was John Devon and he taught Frank history and English. When he told Verity how much he admired her articles in the *New Gazette*, she flashed him a brilliant smile which made Edward blink. He checked himself. It was really too absurd to be jealous of a man who had known Verity less than a minute, but he couldn't prevent himself taking an instant dislike to him.

Frank hurried them off to New Schools where the lecture was to take place and, as they walked, he said to Devon,

'Verity's writing a book on Spain for the Left Book Club. Isn't that what you said, Uncle Ned?'

'How very interesting, Miss Browne,' said the master, beaming. 'You'll sell at least one copy to me and I shall have to ask you to sign it.'

'Please,' said Verity, a little faintly, 'call me Verity. I've never liked Miss Browne somehow. It makes me feel like a stenographer.'

'If you'll call me John.' Edward decided he loathed him above all men, even including Chief Inspector Pride.

The meeting was called to order and Verity spoke lucidly and passionately about the war in Spain which she called 'the first battle in the war against Fascism'. Edward was impressed but he was unable to concentrate fully because he was watching his nephew and John Devon. There was the odd glance of complicity between them and it crossed his mind that there might be something sexual. He thrust the idea from him but it remained in the back of his mind to irritate and alarm him.

The boys were courteous and two or three of them were knowledgeable and committed anti-Fascists. Frank had recently joined the Young Communists and Edward knew from Connie that the Duke blamed Verity for his son's politics. It was true that she had encouraged his left-wing views and, on a visit to Eton the year before, had light-heartedly suggested he might like to join the Party, but his burning fervour for the cause was all his own.

They had dinner with Mr Chandler and Devon was also a guest. Edward was unable to ask the housemaster about him but he made a mental note to write to Chandler, if only to ease his fears of the man's influence over his nephew. He did, however, when Frank and Verity were deep in conversation with Devon, ask him about *Beyond Bounds*.

'I was worried, but now I think it was nothing but the usual youthful need to rebel,' the master said comfortably. 'Of course, it wasn't possible to let him write articles demanding Eton's abolition on the grounds it encouraged

211

class war, but it was harmless enough. Frank wants a cause and he thinks he's found it. That's all.'

Before Edward could pursue the subject, he was swept up by Verity and Frank in a debate on the rights and wrongs of capital punishment. Edward was well aware there was that in his nephew which struck a spark in Verity he could never strike. It wasn't anything to do with love though there was, he thought, an erotic element there – and that was natural given they were two handsome young people with a shared enthusiasm. However, in the end, it wasn't about sex. It was that Frank's certainty, his passionate commitment to Communism, bolstered Verity's own commitment and that was particularly welcome at moments like this, when she had been badly shaken by events in Spain. Her belief that there was only one right way of viewing the world, and that was through red spectacles, was sometimes difficult to maintain in the face of Edward's gentle scepticism. He had been aware that, since her return from Spain, she had been far less certain of the rightness of the cause and Frank was giving her an injection of adrenalin which was restoring her belief in herself.

Edward assumed it was all for the best but, secretly, he had been hoping that Verity would begin to see Communism more – well, he would say realistically. In his view, the slogans, the glib generalizations, the parroted opinions of Comrade Stalin were symptoms of the Party's disregard for individual liberty and frightening contempt for old-fashioned democracy. He sighed and reached for a cigarette but, intercepting a glance of disapproval from Devon, remembered he was not supposed to smoke in boys' houses.

It was fortunate that the Duke was away in London – or rather Edward had gone to some trouble to ascertain that his brother *would* be away – when he and Verity drove down to Mersham Castle on Friday, with a view to borrow-

212

ing bikes and dropping in on Haling. In the Lagonda Verity had said, 'You're sure he won't be there? I promise you, the Duke frightens me more than Franco.'

'But not Connie?'

'Oh no, she's a dear but she can make me feel a little guilty, even when I don't know what I might have done wrong.'

Edward chuckled. 'She's a good woman – too good for the likes of us. By the way, talking of Franco, try and make her understand that Frank is just a normal boy kicking against the sticks. She's got it into her head that he's really serious about this Communism thing.'

Verity looked at him doubtfully but, for once, he had his eyes on the road and did not notice. She was going to offer a word of warning but he was already talking about something else.

'Going back to what you were telling me about Daphne Hepple-Keen, V, I really can't believe it. I mean, Molly told me quite without my prompting that she was "fancy-free". And even if she were lying for some reason, I would never have put money on Hepple-Keen being the one. Carstairs, possibly, but H-K! I doubt it.'

'Well, I heard he was a bit of a womanizer. On the other hand, Daphne did sound a bit hysterical. It's possible she's one of those women who *imagine* their husbands have lovers.'

As they came to a halt in a shower of gravel in front of Mersham Castle, Verity felt a slight sinking in her stomach. She hoped it was all going to be all right but, just at that moment, she had a premonition that some unimagined disaster was about to strike them. She made an effort to throw off her fears which she knew were completely illogical and the warmth of Connie's welcome quickly put her at her ease. She remembered how well she always slept at Mersham.

The next morning, Edward took a reluctant Verity on a tour of the Mersham stables. She thought he was going to present her with an aged bicycle, awkward to ride and unsuited to a girl with not very long legs. She was therefore thrilled when Edward produced not a bicycle but a motor bicycle.

'Gerald's a friend of Jack Sangster. Know who I mean? He gave him two of these little beauties but my dear brother couldn't ride a motor bike to save his life. Look! This one's pristine, not a speck on it.'

'It's beautiful,' Verity said, stroking the shiny leather seat and running her hand down the handlebars and on to the gleaming metal headlight. 'So, who is this Mr Sangster, anyway? Father Christmas?'

'He's the owner of Triumph and this is his latest master-piece – the 500cc Speed Twin. Like her? Air-cooled 4-valve OHV pushrod parallel twin. 600rpm and a top speed of . . . Sangster says ninety, if you can believe it.'

'Golly, yes I can. It puts the heap of scrap I had to ride in Spain in its place.'

'Well, I thought I'd take you to Haling on it.' He patted the machine proprietorially. 'Connie says it's all right to borrow it.'

Verity raised her head from her examination of the glittering beauty. 'You thought what?'

'I said I thought I'd take you to Haling on this. What's wrong? Don't you like it?'

'I love it but, if you think I'm riding pillion with you, you're mistaken. I think you said there are two machines. I'll ride this one and you can ride the other. That is unless you want to sit behind me.'

'Oh, I say, V! Gerald wouldn't like it, don't y'know. He'd say it ain't done, dash it.'

Five minutes later, Edward was filling the tanks of both machines, grumbling to himself as he did so.

'Oh, do stop moaning,' Verity said crossly. 'I can't think what you're on about. You know, I'm planning to have flying lessons. Now that will be interesting.'

Edward looked up aghast. The idea of Verity piloting an aeroplane filled him with what he had heard described as a 'nameless dread'.

As they were ready to depart, Verity suddenly took off her goggles and said, 'I know! I'm going to take your photograph. You said I should bring my Kodak.'

'That was to take photos of the evidence,' Edward said weakly.

'Bah! What evidence? No, I'm going to take your photograph, so look happy about it.' She went to the back of her motor cycle and took the camera out of the saddlebag.

At that moment Fenton appeared carrying a parcel of sandwiches and a flask of ginger beer. Seeing what Verity was doing, he stepped forward. 'Excuse me, miss. Might I . . . ?'

'Thank you, Fenton.'

'Oh no, please Verity! I was just thinking how boring I look.'

'What do you mean, "boring"? You look rather dashing in your leathers. Those boots are very Cecil B. de Mille. You remind me of Mussolini. Doesn't he you, Fenton?'

'Possibly Colonel Lindbergh, miss?'

She examined Edward judiciously. 'Mmm, I'd say Musso. I mean, look at that jawline . . . '

'Verity, stop taking the mickey.'

'And both of you together?' Fenton said, having snapped Edward and then Verity leaning nonchalantly against her machine.

'Why not?' she agreed and, before Edward could demur, went round and stood with her arms about him as he sat astride his bicycle. Edward started to say something but she stopped him. 'Do shut up and don't smile. I always think photographs of people smiling make them look idiotic . . . There, that'll make your grandchildren laugh.'

'If I have any! That reminds me: you said you'd show me that photograph of you in Spain, that one your friend took. You were on your motor bike, weren't you?'

'That? Oh, I'll look it out for you. I've probably lost it. When you haven't got a home you tend to lose things.'

He looked at her meditatively. 'Well, why don't we . . . ?'

'Thanks for the sandwiches, Fenton,' she broke in. 'Sleuthing can be hungry work. Why did you tell me to bring the Kodak, anyway?' she said, turning back to Edward.

'Well, I wanted us to look like tourists and, you never know, we might find something worth photographing at Haling.'

'Footprints, murder weapons – that sort of thing?'

'Hardly. Scannon's been dead a few days now and the police will have found anything of interest. Pride is thorough – one must give him that.'

'He just doesn't know how to use the evidence he finds.'

'Apart from wanting to question Miss Conway, I want to have another look at Molly's room inside and out.'

'The Virginia creeper?'

'Yes. Perhaps I've been wrong in assuming Molly was killed by one of the house guests. And I want to ask Pickering to recall in detail what happened that night and see if he will talk about his master's death. It must have been a great shock for him.'

'You are sure he's still there? I mean, they haven't closed up the house?'

'Not yet. You don't think I would have planned this little expedition without having checked, do you? I got Connie to telephone on the excuse of asking about the funeral. She and Gerald saw quite a lot of Scannon at one time. Anyway, for the moment at least, the house is still occupied by Ruth Conway and, I suppose, Mrs Scannon. Miss Conway told Connie that none of the servants have been turned off.'

'There weren't very many in the first place.'

'That's right. Scannon was tight with his money, no question. The house needs a lot doing to it but, much as he loved the place, he wouldn't spend the money. Even Connie remembers hearing that he was letting the house fall into disrepair and we noticed it ourselves.'

'So who's the lucky person who gets their hands on the house?'

'That's one of the things I want to find out – *cui bono*?'

'Um, Cui . . . ?'

'Who benefits. Scannon was rich and I have no idea who his heirs might be.'

For the first time since she had come back from Spain, Verity was totally, mindlessly happy. Between her legs the powerful motor bicycle seemed alive, begging her to open the throttle and take it beyond the limits of earthbound machines. She accelerated past Edward, ignoring his shouts of protest and alarm, her long scarf streaming out behind her like a pennant. Crouching low over the handlebars, she watched out of the corner of her eye as the needle on the speedometer flickered around the forty mark and then, in a burst of reckless energy, spun past fifty towards sixty. The lanes were narrow and the surface uneven but she felt as though the machine was part of her, as much in her contol as her arms and legs. The wind pulled her face into a grin and suddenly she found herself laughing and then screaming in joy and defiance. She was young, she was alive, she was capable of anything. But then the thought came unbidden into her mind – why not die like this? Why not hurl herself into that ancient oak beside the road as one of her heroes, Lawrence of Arabia, had died a couple of years before? And then she caught herself. It was madness. All her doubts and frustrations were making her mad. She must stop, she must think, she must decide – it was not her way to abdicate her responsibilities, her duty. With a wrench, she slowed her motor bike and then halted altogether. In a moment of disgust with herself, she thrust it from her into the ditch, removed her goggles and stood akimbo waiting for Edward.

At that moment a large car – a Wolseley, she thought – passed her going fast in the opposite direction and taking up most of the road. In a moment of frightening calm she recognized that had something – some premonition – not made her stop her wild career she would almost certainly have smashed into the car and been killed. What had made

217

her pull back? What power had checked her? She could not answer. She did not believe in the supernatural but instinctively she knew that she had been spared because she still had work to do. She hugged her secret to herself in fierce embrace. Then she suddenly thought of Edward again. Where was he? What was taking him so long? Had *he* met the car at speed, perhaps while trying to catch up with her? An icy hand seemed to grip her heart. She would never forgive herself if she had been responsible for the death of the one man she . . . . Just as she was putting her thoughts into words, Edward came steaming into view. He stopped beside her, took off his goggles and opened his mouth to speak.

'Don't say anything!' she commanded him. She put her arms around his neck and kissed him with a passion she could not begin to understand. Then, when she took her mouth from his, still clasping him in her arms, she stared at him, searching his face for some answer to the questions she had been asking herself, unaware of the tears which made channels in the dust that caked her cheeks.

'Hey, Verity, what's all this about?' Edward said gently. 'Let me put the bike down. It's not very comfortable kissing you at this angle.'

'Damn you, I thought you were dead,' she said, releasing him.

'Dead? Oh, you mean that car. It was rather hogging the road but there was plenty of room. I was worried about you though. You were going like the clappers. I say, V, I forgot to ask, do you have a licence?'

'A licence?'

'A driving licence – you oughtn't to be driving if you haven't got one, you know.'

'I drove all round Spain on a bike.'

'That doesn't matter,' he said sententiously. 'It's my fault. I shouldn't have let you. Anyway, girls go on the pillion.'

'Oh for God's sake, Edward, do shut up. You're making me sorry I kissed you. You deserve to be squashed like a hedgehog . . . ' She saw his face fall. 'Well, I suppose I don't mean that but you can be so annoying! Where are we anyway?'

'Haling's just round the corner. I wouldn't be surprised if that car came from there. Anyway, it's time you had your puncture.'

'Why should it be me? I suppose you think it's not masculine to have a puncture or something.'

'Do shut up, Verity. We've gone through all that. It's what we agreed, remember?'

While he was talking he took a screwdriver, which he had had the foresight to bring with him, and went over to Verity's bike lying in the ditch and pierced the front tyre with it. He watched with satisfaction the rubber tube exhale and then returned to his machine and started it. 'Hop on my bike, won't you, while I push yours.'

Submissively, she did as he asked and rode slowly round the corner with Edward in pursuit, huffing and puffing, as he pushed the heavy machine, its front tyre flapping ridiculously.

'I'm most awfully sorry, Pickering, but we've had a bit of an accident.' Edward indicated the machine he had been pushing which he had leant against a wall. 'Miss Browne's machine had a flat – lucky she didn't fall off and hurt herself. I suddenly saw where we were – I mean, just here at Haling – so I wondered . . . we wondered whether it would be asking too much if you could supply us with a bucket of water. Look, see, I've got a repair kit in my saddlebag but . . . '

There was just a moment when he thought Pickering was going to be difficult but the moment passed and the butler said, smoothly enough, 'Of course, my lord. Perhaps you would care to follow me. I will let Miss Conway know you are here.'

'Oh, I wouldn't want to bother her . . . '

A figure appeared in the hall carrying flowers.

'Lord Edward! Is that really you?'

'Yes it is, Miss Conway. Sorry to come barging in like this. What lovely roses!'

'Yes, the very last. Williams grows them under glass. Mr Scannon so loved having them in the house. But did I hear you saying you had an accident?'

'Not an accident, just a puncture. I was telling Pickering, we were passing the end of the drive when Verity . . . . by the way, you remember Miss Browne, don't you? . . . her bike . . . her motor bike, don't y'know,' he burbled on, 'it developed a flat tyre . . . '

'Miss Browne,' she said, shaking Verity's hand, 'I don't think we did meet when you were here, did we? Mrs Scannon was very ill that night and I wasn't able to leave her. But don't tell me you have been on a motor bicycle? How could you let her, Lord Edward?'

Edward considered asking how he could have stopped her.

'Williams!' she called to the gardener who was passing with a spade in one hand and a bucket in the other which he now courteously put down on hearing the summons. 'Would you be kind enough to mend this puncture for Lord Edward?'

'Oh no, please. I'm sure he has a great deal to do . . . ' Edward protested.

'It won't take very long, will it, Williams?' Miss Conway said, ignoring Edward.

Verity smiled at the gardener and that decided the matter. Williams blushed deeply and made a gesture which might have been half-way to touching his forelock. 'No time at all, miss!' he mumbled in a broad Wiltshire accent.

'Come and have some tea. Take off your things . . . ' Miss Conway gestured at their dirty boots and jackets. 'Pickering, can you bring us some tea?'

'Yes, miss.'

Edward was struck by the alteration in her manner. The shy, monosyllabic woman tied to Scannon's bedridden mother was now very much the lady of the manor – confident, at ease ordering the servants around and obviously happy to play hostess to the unexpected visitors. The mystery was soon explained. As they sipped their tea, Edward and Verity expressed their condolences over Scannon's death and Edward asked after the old woman.

'Oh,' said Miss Conway breezily, 'Mrs Scannon's in hospital. I just wasn't able to cope with her any more – now I've got so much more to do, you understand.'

Edward did not understand. 'So much more to do? You mean the funeral?'

'That and running the estate. I'm afraid Mr Scannon let the house deteriorate. The first thing I did was get on to the builders. The roof needs to be replaced, for one thing.'

'That will be very expensive.'

'Yes, Lord Edward, but money's not a problem.' She smiled smugly.

'How do you mean?'

'Well, Mr Scannon was always pretending he was on the breadline but actually he had pots of money.'

'And, if I might ask,' Edward ventured, 'who inherits it?'

'I do, of course! He had no other relatives apart from his mother and he left everything to me. That was so good of him, wasn't it?'

Verity and Edward could hardly hide their amazement. Edward managed to say, 'That's splendid, Miss Conway. But I had no idea you were a relative.'

'No one knew. It was the old story . . . well, I don't mind telling you. The fact of the matter is my mother worked in the accounts department at old Mr Scannon's match factory. You know he made his money from Starburst matches?' Edward nodded. 'He fell in love with her and I was the result.'

So baldly did she tell her story that it left Edward at a loss for words. It was Verity who ventured, 'Mr Scannon was married when he fell in love with your mother?'

'Oh yes.'

'And you were accepted into the family?' Edward asked.

'Not at first. Mr Scannon bought my mother a house in Cheam. He paid for my education and gave my mother an allowance. He was generous in the way such men are generous. As long as my mother . . . played the game, as it were, she was well cared for.'

'But your mother's not still alive?'

'No. By some unlucky accident, she contracted a disease called phossy jaw.'

'How terrible,' Edward said, not wishing to tell her he knew already. 'But I thought only those poor girls who were actually working with the phosphorus were in danger of being contaminated.'

'That is so but, before my mother was promoted to the accounts department, she had worked on the factory floor. To tell the truth, though I never discussed it with her, I think she had an affair with the chief accountant and he must have . . . you know, fixed things.'

Edward had a vision of a pretty girl handed from man to man as casually as a packet of cigarettes. He could imagine how powerless such girls were to withstand the attentions of men who literally had the power of life and death over them. Even a minor functionary, such as the head of the accounts department, was in a position to remove a girl from the hard and dangerous work on the factory floor and, if she resisted his advances, she would be thrown on the scrap heap with every possibility of having to prostitute herself to put food in her belly. Mr Scannon, as the factory owner, had all the power over his employees of some Eastern potentate.

'So your mother got ill when you were . . . ?'

'About twelve. I was brought to Haling as a servant to Mrs Scannon and my mother was taken off to some sort of a hospital. I never saw her again.'

'How terrible!' Verity exclaimed. 'The way those men treated women like your mother was abominable.' She looked at Edward accusingly.

'I don't suppose Mr Scannon saw it that way,' Miss Conway said, mildly. 'He probably thought he was saving me from the gutter – which he was.'

'But you were his daughter!' Verity said. 'And you never saw your mother again – not even when she was dying?'

'It is the most terrible disease, you know. It eats away at your bones, Miss Browne. I read up about it. I think he

222

thought he was saving me from the horror of seeing my mother . . . deformed.'

'But does Mrs Scannon know you are her husband's daughter?' Edward asked.

'We have never talked about it. She must have done, I suppose.'

'You never talked about it – not in all those years you've been with her?'

'Never!'

Verity was aghast. To think of the little girl torn from her mother and placed in a strange house as a servant with no one to love her or care for her . . . it did not bear thinking about. She surely deserved recompense.

Ruth Conway, seeing their faces and misinterpreting their expressions, said, 'You mustn't think ill of my mother.'

'Please, Miss Conway, don't think for one moment that we were thinking badly of your mother. I was only feeling ashamed for my sex,' Edward said.

Miss Conway looked at him in surprise. 'I don't see why you should be. It's nothing to do with you, Lord Edward. I mean, it's not your fault. It's the way of the world.'

'A world we must change,' Verity said indignantly.

Ruth shot her a look of amused contempt. 'You think it can be changed – the way men behave to women?'

'I certainly do,' Verity said stoutly.

Edward said, hurriedly, 'But Leo obviously made up for what his father . . . '

'We grew up here together. He liked me, yes.'

Edward wondered if there had been any childhood romance and, as if she had read his thoughts, she continued, 'I think you know, Lord Edward, that Leo did not like girls very much but he was good to me.'

'And you must have talked to him about . . . about your situation?'

'About money, you mean?'

'Well, yes, that, but I've got no right . . . '

'Don't be embarrassed. I'm not. Anyway, the police have already asked me and I told them. When his father died,

Leo told me he was going to leave me some money. He said there ought to have been some compensation for my mother getting ill but, what with the war and everything, nothing had actually happened although his father always intended to do something for me. I don't know if that was just Leo being kind. I rather doubt the old man had given it a thought, but perhaps I'm doing him an injustice.'

'And ... forgive me, I'm being impertinent ...'

'Did he say he would leave me all this ...? Is that what you were going to ask?' Miss Conway said, waving her hand to indicate the house. 'No, he didn't.'

'But he welcomed you as a member of the family?'

'That's an odd way of putting it, but I suppose that was what it amounted to. He was very proud of his father and yet ... taking my mother as his mistress ... I think he was a bit ashamed of that.'

'He didn't hold it against you?'

'No, why should he?'

'Some men might,' Verity broke in. 'When you're in the wrong or ashamed of something you tend to lash out at the victim rather than the ... you know. At least, that's what I've found.'

Ruth Conway and Edward looked at her curiously, wondering what had prompted her to speak with such feeling.

'No, he was very good to me. He asked me to stay and continue to look after his mother but he said that if I wanted to leave, he would add to the money his father had left, so I could buy somewhere to live.'

'But you didn't?'

'No, I had no reason to leave. Haling's my home but I never thought ... that one day it might be mine.'

There was a moment's silence and then she continued, 'Now tell me, Lord Edward, why did you really come here? The puncture was just an excuse, wasn't it?'

Edward looked at her, his mouth agape. 'Was it so obvious?' he said with a wry smile.

'I'm afraid it was,' she replied. 'I guessed something was up when your sister-in-law telephoned and started

224

asking questions about the funeral and who was here in the house.'

'The truth is,' Verity broke in, 'we want to find out who really killed Mrs Harkness. Molly was a friend of Edward's and we don't have a lot of faith in the police.'

'Why not? Chief Inspector Pride seems good at his job.'

'The Chief Inspector is very thorough but we have had dealings with him before,' Edward said. 'You may remember reading in the newspapers that one of the guests at a dinner party my brother gave at Mersham last year was murdered, and we don't think he did much to find out who did it. He was more concerned to push the whole thing under the carpet.'

'I see. And you think you can do better?'

'Probably not, but I feel I owe it to Molly to try. You see, I had been invited to Haling to get from her, with the minimum of fuss, some letters she had stolen from . . . a certain personage . . . '

'Mrs Simpson? Leo told me all about it.'

'Oh, he did, did he,' Edward said, annoyed that Scannon had been indiscreet. 'Well, I failed and poor Molly was murdered. You can understand that I feel in some way responsible.'

'Molly was a particular friend of Edward's – in Kenya,' Verity added mischievously.

'I *see*,' Miss Conway repeated. 'Well, what can I do to help? Shall we ask Pickering what he remembers?'

'Yes, if that's possible. I'm sorry to be a nuisance.'

'You're not a nuisance, Lord Edward. To tell you the truth, I *have* been a bit bored. Mrs Scannon not being in the house any longer, my whole daily ritual has disappeared.'

'But you must know a lot of people round here.'

'Not really. Leo knew everyone, of course, but I kept in the background. They didn't come to see me.'

'But we almost ran into a car on the way here – a Wolseley, I think.'

'Oh, that was Colonel Philips, the Chief Constable. Do you know him? He has been very helpful. I think he thinks

Chief Inspector Pride has been bullying me.' She giggled nervously. 'I think he thinks I killed Leo. As if I ever would!'

'When is the funeral? Connie said you didn't know exactly.'

'Next week if the coroner allows. It's his having been poisoned, you know, that's the problem. He can't be buried before everything has been examined. After the funeral, I might go abroad. See something of the world. You know, I have never been out of the country! I'd like to see Venice before I die.'

'And what about Mrs Scannon?' Edward, without meaning to, sounded as though he disapproved of Miss Conway taking so much pleasure in being rich.

'She is virtually comatose, I'm afraid. The doctors say she may die at any moment.' She had the grace to look a little guilty. 'I have done everything I can for her. She doesn't need me now. There's a family tomb in the village churchyard. Leo's father liked owning property,' she said with a trace of rancour. 'I loved them both, you know,' she added after a pause, as though she wanted to make them understand that she wasn't without feeling. 'Even the old woman – though she never loved me. Even when I was a child, she never kissed me or hugged me. I suppose I was a living reminder of her husband's infidelity.'

Edward was moved to ask, 'Tell me to shut up if I'm speaking out of turn but, to me, Leo was a cold fish. Could you really love him? You were grateful to him for having been your protector – I understand that – but for years you were treated like a servant . . . I can't work it out. On the one hand, he was your benefactor but, after what happened to your mother, it would have been quite natural for you to have resented being nurse to Mrs Scannon.'

'It's difficult to explain. In books love and hate seem black and white. Either you feel one thing or the other. In real life – in mine anyway – it was different. I certainly didn't love Leo as a woman. I mean, I wasn't *in love* with him and he certainly didn't love me in that way – or at least I never felt that he did. I suppose I always knew he wasn't interested in girls. I knew instinctively that he didn't love anyone except his mother so it was a sort of compliment being entrusted with her, but we came to feel . . . I don't know . . . an affection for one another. Partly habit but . . . we understood each other – I suppose that was it.'

'Presumably, it was Leo who told you about your mother, how she died . . . ?'

'Yes, I only knew she had disappeared from my life and, as you do as a child, you grieve but you accept. I had just one photograph of her which I used to keep under my pillow until it became really creased and battered. Then I put it in my Bible. One day – it must have been when I was fourteen, yes, it was my birthday – Leo came to my room to give me my present. He happened to open the Bible and saw the photograph. He asked who it was – because, of course, he had never seen my mother and, when I told him, he told me everything he knew about how she died.'

'But not about who your father was? Old Mr Scannon was still alive then?' Edward asked.

'No, but I think, looking back on it, I did know somehow.'

'Did you not want to talk to the old man about it . . . about your mother?'

'My first impulse was to ask him about it, but I didn't.'

'You were frightened of him?' Verity guessed.

'I was frightened of him, yes, but it wasn't quite that. It was just that I decided that I didn't want to know. I didn't want to have that conversation with Mr Scannon. I was embarrassed. I don't expect you to understand.'

'I think I do,' Edward said. 'I felt the same when I was told my brother, Frank, had been killed in the first week after the expeditionary force landed in France. They told me he died heroically – which indeed he had – and I was satisfied. I didn't want to know the details. I wanted him to be a hero figure not a real person.'

Miss Conway looked at him gratefully. 'You *do* understand then,' was all she said.

After a moment, Verity pushed on. 'So you have no idea who killed Mrs Harkness?'

'I thought it was probably you, Lord Edward', she said simply. 'I didn't know then that you had come to retrieve the letters. I thought Leo was doing that. But I knew you had come for some reason – not just social, I mean. And you seemed determined enough. But, of course,' she added quickly, 'as soon as I got to know you a little, I changed my mind.'

'I'm glad to hear it!' Edward said, rather unnerved to find that someone other than Pride had put him down as a cold-blooded murderer. 'You didn't suspect Leo? As you say, you knew he was trying to get Molly to give up something he wanted?'

'I certainly think he *could* have murdered. You're right, he was rather a cold person, but he seemed to me genuinely shocked after Mrs Harkness was found dead. Didn't you think so, Lord Edward?'

'I did but it was odd – Mr Harbin noticed it – he was still in the clothes he had been wearing at dinner when he came to see why we were trying to break into Molly's room. He'd taken off his coat and put on a dressing gown but he definitely hadn't got into pyjamas.'

'I didn't know that but I still think he didn't kill her. Why should he? He was a respected MP with a busy life. I can't believe he would have risked all that to help Mrs Simpson.'

'I agree, but someone did it,' Edward said, almost irritably. 'Maybe there was some other motive – after all, he was murdered himself. Someone wanted him out of the way.'

'Inspector Lampfrey told Edward that Mr Scannon's diary had disappeared,' Verity said. 'The most likely thing seems to be that Mr Scannon had seen, or at least knew, who had killed Molly and that person was afraid of being blackmailed. You've no idea where the diary might be?'

'No. The police have searched everywhere – even my rooms – and I know they have been looking in London as well.'

Edward, rather daringly, said, 'May I be very impertinent, Miss Conway, and ask if Leo ever brought any of his . . . his friends here? I don't mean his ordinary friends, I mean . . . '

'Did he ever bring his boys here, that's what you mean?'

'Yes.'

'No, he never did. You see, he would never have brought them to the house his mother lived in.'

At that moment, Pickering came in to say the puncture had been mended and Miss Conway asked if he would mind answering a few questions Lord Edward wanted to put to him about the night Mrs Harkness died.

'A terrible business,' the butler said, shaking his head mournfully. 'To think there should have been two murders in the house and the master himself . . . '

'Please, do sit down,' Miss Conway said, seeing the man was actually shaking with emotion.

'No, miss. I have never sat down in the drawing-room in my life and the master would not like it if I did now.'

'Were you very fond of your master?' Edward asked sympathetically.

'He was a great man, your lordship. The famous men he knew! Why, I have welcomed three Prime Ministers to Haling,' he said with evident pride. 'I felt sure there would never be another war knowing that my master and his colleagues were looking after things.'

This striking tribute to Scannon amazed Edward and Verity had to check herself from expostulating.

'It's a sad business,' Edward said. 'Tell me, Pickering, did you notice – when Mr Scannon came to help us open Mrs Harkness's bedroom door . . . '

'When we found the poor lady dead, my lord?'

'Yes. Did you notice that he had not undressed? He was wearing his evening clothes under his dressing gown.'

'Yes, my lord, I did notice.'

'Can you think why that was? Did Mr Scannon sleep badly?'

'Yes, my lord. The master often stayed up half the night reading in his study or working. I did see him quite late that night with Mr Carstairs. As I prepared for bed, I happened to look out of my window and I saw the two gentlemen in the garden.'

'What time was this?'

'About midnight, my lord, or perhaps a bit later. By the time we had cleared dinner, it was after eleven and the master was kind enough to tell me not to wait up until he and the other gentlemen had gone to bed, which is what I would have expected to do.'

'I see. So it was unusual for you to go to bed before all the guests had gone to their bedrooms?'

'Yes, my lord, but the master was always most considerate.'

'Did you tell the police that you saw Mr Scannon in the garden with Mr Carstairs on the night Mrs Harkness was killed?'

'No, my lord,' said the butler, looking troubled. 'Should I have done? They did not ask me.'

'No, I expect Mr Carstairs had already told them,' Edward said soothingly. 'I meant to ask you whether your master key, which opened the bedroom doors, could have been borrowed or stolen?'

'That was what the police asked me.'

'And you said . . . ?'

'I said the key was hanging on a hook in the pantry so it was possible a visitor – someone who knew the house – would know where to find it.'

'And had it been borrowed?'

'It was there when I was called to help you and the other gentleman get into Mrs Harkness's room.'

'But . . .'

'There was no reason to keep the key locked away,' Pickering said defensively. 'There was only one key to the safe and Mr Scannon kept that on his key-ring. The key to the bedrooms wasn't . . . special.'

'No, of course not,' Edward said reassuringly. 'Mr Scannon kept the key to the tantalus himself?'

'Yes, my lord. I had no key to that or to the cellar. Mr Scannon was very particular about his wines and spirits.'

'And where were those keys kept?'

'The key to the tantalus Mr Scannon also kept on his key-ring. The cellar key was too big so he kept it in the safe.'

'A careful man, Mr Scannon,' Edward said, hoping to get a reaction from the butler but in this he was disappointed. The man was not prepared to volunteer opinions about his late employer, at least not in present company.

Miss Conway said, 'The police have taken away the tantalus but I can assure you, Lord Edward, that Leo alone opened and closed it, as Pickering says.'

'Forgive my ignorance,' Verity said, 'but what actually is a tantalus?'

'Correct me if I'm wrong, Pickering, but it's usually three or four decanters on a wooden tray. At each end of the tray there are panels that support a hinged bar which fits over the decanters and prevents them being unstoppered. Is that right?'

'Yes, my lord. Mr Scannon's had a silver bar holding three decanters in place.'

'And the bar could be locked?' Verity asked.

'Of course. That was the point of it,' Edward said sharply, and Verity felt snubbed. He turned to the butler. 'You have been most kind, Pickering. It must have been a terrible shock for you.'

'It was, my lord, and with the master's mother so ill . . . '

'She does not know about her son . . . being murdered?' Verity asked.

'No,' Miss Conway replied. 'I wouldn't tell her if she *were* conscious but she has not . . . '

Edward risked one last question – the obvious one. 'Did Mr Scannon have any enemies you knew of? Forgive me, Pickering, but a man in the public eye often makes enemies without meaning to.'

'Oh yes, my lord, the master had many enemies,' the butler said, surprisingly. 'He made a point of security. He was always afraid of someone breaking into the house.'

'But the creeper up the walls . . . ' Edward said. 'Wasn't he aware it provided an easy way for burglars to get into the house?'

'Yes, my lord, he had just given orders for it to be cut down.'

'Yes,' Miss Conway said, 'but I have decided not to go ahead. It seems it's so deeply embedded in the mortar that there is a good chance of the house falling down if it's torn off the walls.'

'I see. Well, thank you again, Pickering. I do hope our questions haven't upset you.'

'Not at all, my lord,' the butler said, bowing gravely.

It was time to leave and, as they got up to go, Verity said brightly, 'Miss Conway, would it be all right for me to take a photograph of the room I slept in – the room where Mrs Harkness died? I don't suppose it will come out but it could be useful.'

Ruth Conway looked doubtful. 'I suppose so, but I can't see why you want to. Pickering, take Miss Browne and . . . '

'Oh, don't worry, Pickering. I can find my own way. I'm sure you're very busy.'

'While you are doing that, I'll go and find Williams in the garden and thank him for repairing the tyre,' Edward said.

Miss Conway seemed at a loss to know whether to accompany Verity or Edward but, in the end, she went out into the garden. Edward had hoped to have had a chance of wandering round on his own. He particularly wanted to inspect the wall outside Molly's room but that was now impossible. He consoled himself with the knowledge that Verity was sure to take the opportunity of examining it from above, not that it was at all likely there was anything significant to see. Both Lampfrey and Pride had searched the Virginia creeper and found nothing. It was more important to talk to Williams. There were two or three questions he wanted to ask, preferably in the absence of Ruth Conway, but she seemed unwilling to let him out of her sight.

They tracked the gardener down to a greenhouse and Edward made a speech of thanks and pressed two half-crowns on him.

'It's only temporary, my lord, but it'll get the lady home,' the gardener warned him. 'It must go to the garage to be done proper like.'

Edward had the feeling that Williams was disappointed Verity was not there to thank him in person. 'Of course, I'm most grateful.' He gently pulled a bunch of grapes towards him and sniffed appreciatively. 'These are magnificent, better than the vine at Mersham.'

'Please, do take a bunch,' Miss Conway said and Williams obligingly took out his pruning knife and cut two large bunches. Edward nibbled a grape and found it sweet.

'What do you do with all this wonderful produce?' he inquired. He had passed through an acre of vegetable garden and an orchard, the trees showing signs of having been carefully tended.

'We sell some in the village shop and give away the rest. There's a hospital in Salisbury which likes to have fresh fruit and vegetables,' Ruth Conway answered.

'And do you not have any help, Williams? It must be a lot of work.'

Miss Conway answered for him. 'It is. There's a boy from the village who comes when we need him. Actually, I have decided to offer him full-time work as your assistant, Williams. Would you like that?'

'Very much, miss,' the gardener said, looking quite cheerful. 'Thank you, miss.'

'Oh, Williams,' Edward said as unthreateningly as he could manage, 'have you any idea who took the rat poison from your shed? I gather you didn't keep it locked so it could have been anyone.'

'That's right, my lord,' the gardener said, grudgingly. 'As I told the police, anyone could have got at it.'

'But who knew you had it? Did Mr Scannon know?'

'Yes, sir. The rats had got into the house and he told me to deal with them.'

'When was that? Was it the weekend Mrs Harkness died? We all saw a rat on the billiard table. Gave us quite a shock, I don't mind telling you.'

'Yes, my lord. That were it. He called me in – on the Monday it was – and told me to buy some poison and get rid of them. Mr Pickering was there when he told me.'

'Was anyone else there?'

'Mr Carstairs and Mr Keen – I think that's the gentle-man's name – the Parliament man.'

'Sir Geoffrey Hepple-Keen?'

'Yes, sir. That'll be him.'

'And you killed the rats?'

'I killed two, both males.'

'And you destroyed the corpses, I suppose?'

The gardener looked uneasy. 'Speak up, man,' Edward said testily. 'Did you or didn't you?'

'I dunno, sir, to tell you the honest truth. I put them on the compost heap and then I forgot about them. I has plenty to do in this garden without bothering my head about dead rats.'

'But you remembered about them eventually?'

'Yes, my lord. I did. I was afraid my dog might have got chewing on them. He's a devil for rats.'

'And had he?'

'No, my lord. That's what was queer. When I got to thinking I should burn the vamints, they was gone.'

'Gone? What do you mean?'

'They was gone, sir. Someone, or some animal, had taken them.'

'When was this?'

'On the Thursday. That was when I remembered them.'

'And you never saw them again?'

The gardener looked worried. 'I saw one of them again, sir. On the Monday. Mr Pickering gave it me. He said it had been found in one of the ladies' beds. I don't know how it got there, my lord. I reckon it may have been a practical joke, like . . . by one of the gentlemen.'

They mounted their motor bikes and rode off, with a final wave to Ruth Conway who suddenly looked rather forlorn standing alone outside the front door. Just before they left, Edward asked her what had happened to Mrs Scannon's

Pekinese, expecting her to say it had accompanied the old woman to hospital.

'Horrible little dog,' she said viciously. 'I had it put down. I had been wanting to do it for ages.'

Verity had been anxious to leave Haling as quickly as possible and put several miles between it and the object she was hugging to her chest – nothing less than Scannon's missing diary. She was on tenterhooks to examine it properly. She would show Edward her sleuthing was not to be sneezed at.

As he bucketed over the pot-holed lanes, Edward went over in his mind what he knew about the circumstances of the two murders at Haling. He was beginning to get the feeling that he ought to know who had killed Molly but there were still a number of things which puzzled him. He had a feeling that her murder had been the result of panic. Why would one *choose* such a time and place to commit murder? Surely, it would have been easier to break into her flat in Trevor Square and kill her as she slept. After all, Molly had said her flat had been burgled and there was no reason to disbelieve her. He made a mental note to ask Lampfrey if he had investigated who occupied the other flats in the house, but he knew he must have done and he would have heard if any of Molly's neighbours had been suspicious characters.

At Haling, the home of an influential Conservative MP, Molly's death was bound to attract more attention than if it had occurred in London and the list of suspects was far fewer which should, in theory, have made the killer easier to identify. Or had the murderer wished to confuse the issue by indicating that, because Molly met her death at Haling, it necessarily had to do with the theft of Mrs Simpson's letters? Perhaps the motive for murder was quite different. Leo Scannon's murder, on the other hand, was planned coldly and deliberately and had been carried out by someone who knew his victim's habits and had almost certainly stayed in the house as a guest. The murderer, Edward was convinced, had at some time or other seen Scannon open the tantalus and pour himself and his guests whisky. He – or she – knew that Scannon was the sort of employer who did not trust his staff not to drink his spirits. The murderer was sure that, at least during the week, the only person who would drink from Scannon's tantalus was the man himself.

When they had gone half the distance back to Mersham, Verity waved Edward down. She could wait no longer to show him her trophy. As they got off their motor cycles, Edward told her about Williams and the lost rat – the rat which had turned up in her bed. Verity spluttered, with laughter and a touch of indignation. She had been the victim of a practical joke and she normally hated practical jokes; they were usually cruel and seldom funny but she couldn't be too angry. She had knowingly entered among her enemies and had probably got off lightly enough in the circumstances.

'So what have you got there?' Edward inquired, as she removed her leather jacket and extracted the exercise book from beneath her jersey.

'Tra-la! Be a good boy and beg!'

'For goodness sake, V, give it here. Is it what I think it is?'

'It is indeed,' she said, holding it just out of his reach. 'But, before you can examine it, you must grovel and and tell me all sorts of flattering but completely true things about how clever I am.'

Edward threw himself at her and promptly fell over her bike which she had propped against a hedge. Laughing, she led him puckishly through a gate and into a field. Edward, complaining loudly and rubbing his shins, followed her.

'Don't damage it,' she warned, suddenly serious, as Edward once again made a grab at her. 'Here it is.'

He opened the book, his hands fumbling the pages in his excitement. He had guessed what it was Verity had found but had no idea how she had discovered it. As he began to read he said, 'You are quite certainly a genius, my companion in crime. Hey, but what's this?' He looked in consterna-

236

tion at the black streak his fingers had left on the white page. 'Is this stuff soot? Where did you find it . . . up a chimney?'

'You've got it in one, and you can't go up chimneys without getting sooty. While you were talking to the gardener, I had a quick look at the bedrooms. Molly's, which was also mine, your old room, and the one the other side, Mr Harbin's, and . . . '

'And . . . ?'

'And I found nothing. I took a few photographs but I don't expect they will come out. The light wasn't good enough. Then I asked Pickering if I could look in Mr Scannon's bedroom. He was dubious but I put on all my charm and, at last, he said he supposed there was no reason why I shouldn't. Again, I found nothing but, just as I was about to leave, I remembered what you had told me about the ledge in the fireplace in your room and I wondered if *all* the fireplaces had them. And – open sesame – there it was.'

'Did Pickering see you?'

'No. Fortunately, he had left me alone for a minute so he saw nothing.'

'But I don't understand,' Edward said, rubbing his forehead, 'Why didn't the police find this? Pride is very thorough, whatever else one might say about him.'

'The reason's obvious, dummy. It was only lodged there after the police had completed their search.'

'Yes, or maybe they just *did* miss it. Was it hidden? I mean, would anyone looking up the chimney have seen it?'

'No,' Verity said consideringly. 'Not unless they ran their hand along the ledge as I did, I suppose.'

'Perhaps the murderer, after poisoning the whisky downstairs, decided to search Leo's bedroom. He found what he was looking for and then was disturbed. He heard footsteps, let's say, and stuffed the diary, which was too bulky to conceal easily, in the chimney, planning to come back for it later. By the way, how did you smuggle it out?'

'Why do you think my blouse is ruined, fathead? I slipped it under my jersey.' She lifted up her jersey and he saw her white shirt was covered in soot.

'Golly! Well done, Watson. Very well done. Your sacrifice shall not be in vain.'

Verity considered complaining at being cast as Watson but then couldn't be bothered.

'Hey, let me look at that blouse,' Edward said and, not waiting to be told he should keep his distance, he took her in his arms and kissed her.

A whole range of emotions overwhelmed Verity. She had kissed him, of course, but that had been the result of some kind of fit – a madness – the nature of which she could now hardly remember. Now he was kissing her, as though he had a right to kiss her. She struggled, cross at being taken for granted, but she was feeling weary after so much excitement and drained of her usual combativeness. Really, it was rather nice being kissed. She relaxed a little. She felt all at once a deep sense of relief – almost of healing – as though her will had been overcome by a stronger. She began to enjoy herself. If she had a criticism of Edward, it was that, by comparison with her ex-lover, the American novelist Ben Belasco, he was too much the gentleman. He let good manners get in the way of action. Good manners were fine in their way – rather restful after Belasco, who had the manners of a pig – but, in the end, a girl wanted a little of the Tarzan.

Just as she was wondering when she would need to stop kissing him and draw breath, out of the corner of her eye she saw, trotting purposefully towards them, a black bull, the size of a small house. It was like some Donald McGill postcard, as she said afterwards. She tried to remove her lips from Edward's to warn him but he, interpreting her squirming as encouragement, held her ever more tightly. At last she managed to twist him round so that he, too, could see the interloper now clearly determined that there was to be no spooning in his field without he was doing it himself.

Releasing her in his arms with a cry of alarm, Edward looked for the gate, saw it a hundred yards away and shouted, 'Run!'

As he helped Verity over the gate, she tore her stockings and swore. And Edward, as he scrambled over after her, managed to fall in a patch of stinging nettles and he too swore vigorously. These cries of pain and frustration seemed to irritate the bull, which peered over the gate at them with small, angry eyes.

'Look,' Verity said, gasping, 'he only wanted to play. Didn't you, diddums?' She poked the bull on the nose which, he indicated by rolling his eyes, was an impertinence. She turned to her companion and a huge grin covered her face. 'Oh, Edward, I wish you could see yourself!'

'What about you!' he rejoined.

Verity was now laughing so hard she could hardly stand. That made Edward start and, had anyone come down the lane, they might have been taken for dangerous lunatics. Dirty, dishevelled, their clothes torn, their faces red and Verity's make-up streaked across her face so she looked more like a Red Indian in the Gene Autry films she liked so much than a nice middle-class girl who had just been kissed. It was a good five minutes before they recovered themselves and Edward could ask, 'You've got the diary?'

'No, haven't you got it?'

'You're joking, V. Please say you're joking.'

'I'm not joking. You must have dropped it.'

Edward went over to the gate and stared. The bull stared back. Yes, there was the diary. He could see it, about fifty yards behind the bull, its white pages waving in the wind.

'So, what do we do now?' Verity asked, trustingly.

'There's only one thing for it,' Edward said grimly. 'I'll have to get over the gate and distract the bull, while you go and pick up the diary.'

'Gosh, you do remind me of Ben. He took me to a bull-fight once and the bull escaped and he left me to fend for myself while he chased it.'

'Shut up, V. I really don't want to talk about your lovers at this particular moment – or, for that matter, at all.'

'Oh?' she said, bridling. 'And I don't want to hear about yours.'

They stared at each other, Verity with her hands on her hips, ready for a fight.

Then Edward, taking in her appearance, burst out laughing again. 'I've always wondered about that expression "pulled through a hedge backwards" but now I see what it means.'

Verity, also seeing the funny side, tried to scrape down her hair. 'Well, get on with it then. And I hope the bull catches you.'

Ten minutes later, puffing and panting, Edward was safely back. 'I haven't run like that since I won the hundred yards my last year at Cambridge,' he said, rather pleased with himself. 'That bull was quite outclassed and he knew it.'

'Huh!' said Verity, unimpressed. 'Stop congratulating yourself and come and look at this.'

Companionably, they pored over the diary.

'Here, let me see,' he said, shuffling through the pages. 'The important thing is: did Scannon put the name of his murderer in his diary? No, damn it, that would have been too easy.'

Two pages had been torn out just where the writing ended.

Verity took the diary and started reading: '"As soon as I entered the room, I saw it. I put it in my pocket and I don't think anyone . . . " The last words he wrote killed him,' she said grimly.

'Damn and blast!'

'Yes, but look. There are indentations on the pages immediately after the tear. Do you think your friend, Professor what's-his-name, might be able to make out something? What we can't see with the naked eye, perhaps he . . . '

'Brilliant, Verity. You're a genius! That's it! If anyone can read it, Davidson can. May I kiss you again?'

She looked at him critically. 'If you must,' she said at last. He did so and then kissed her again and this time she made no objection.

13

Monday afternoon he dropped Verity in the King's Road and went on to Albany. After refuelling on a mutton chop washed down with a glass of champagne, he went in search of Carstairs but before he did so he telephoned Dr Davidson at Hendon's Forensic Laboratory and made an appointment to see him on the following day. Davidson had been understandably chary about meeting him when he heard what he was being asked to do, but Edward was quietly insistent.

'It's highly irregular, Lord Edward. I really think you should pass on the diary to the police.'

'I will . . . I will, James, I promise you, but just indulge me this once. I give you my word I'll not bring your name into it.'

'Well, I expect you'll get me into trouble whatever you say but, for Gerald's sake, I'll see you.'

Davidson was an old school friend of the Duke's and, it was rumoured, had proposed marriage to Connie the same day she accepted Gerald. The rejected lover, gentleman that he was, had never reproached either Connie or his more fortunate friend but had remained a bachelor and devoted his life to developing scientific methods to defeat crime. It had been an uphill struggle. The powers-that-be were suspicious of science and profoundly ignorant of its potential but he had been fortunate enough to gain the support of Lord Trenchard, Commissioner of Police from 1931 to 1935.

Hardly had Edward put down the receiver when Charlotte telephoned to say that Lord and Lady Benyon were coming to tea. They had something they wanted to say to him and would he please present himself at 4 p.m. precisely for Lapsang Souchong, crumpets and information.

Carstairs, prone in a low, battered, leather armchair, gazed hungrily at the fire in the grate. Edward had tracked down his quarry to a seedy club catering for colonial officials on leave, situated in Northumberland Avenue, close to Trafalgar Square.

'I suppose my blood's thinned,' he complained, 'but England seems damn cold after Africa – cold and damp. Was it always this beastly in autumn, Corinth? I seem to remember leaves turning gold in sunshine but it must just have been "home thoughts from abroad".'

'And now you're "the hunter home from the hill"?'

'What? Ah yes, Stevenson. I don't go in much for poetry and that sort of thing but Stevenson – he rings a few bells – and W.E Henley. But I hear he's out of fashion nowadays. "Play up, play up and play the game!" Lot of tosh, ain't it, old sport?'

'Newbolt.'

'Eh?'

'Sir Henry Newbolt, not Henley.' Edward looked at Carstairs with something bordering on contempt. He exhibited the faded charm of the defeated or was that just spite, he wondered. His great mane of white hair, which was impressive enough at Haling, now looked unwashed, greasy and – he must have been imagining it – tinged with green. 'A mangy lion' was the expression which came into his mind and he had to settle himself before he could pursue the conversation.

'Forgive me for trailin' you to this cosy dug-out but at Haling – don't y'know – we never had time for much of a chat.'

'A chat? About what?' Carstairs said, stretching himself lazily and reaching for his whisky. Then, realizing he could hardly not offer his inquisitor a drink in his own club, he said, 'Whisky?'

'Thankee, yes.'

Carstairs clicked his fingers at a passing waiter and ordered whisky for Edward and another for himself. 'Look here, old sport,' he said, raising himself slightly out of his chair, 'what's all this about? You don't like me and, God knows, I could never stand you.'

This bluntness, oddly enough, seemed to make things easier for Edward. He could toss away his pose as the rather dim man-about-town and come to the point. However, he spoke mildly enough.

'Not true, old man. I don't dislike you. In fact, I thought you the finest white hunter I ever came across – a first-class shot and all that. I didn't altogether share your views on – what shall we say – weakening the weaker sex. I suppose that's why you're over here – woman trouble?'

'Damn you, Corinth. I always considered you a most awful ass and, if you think you can patronize me because I'm on my uppers . . . well don't, that's all.'

It was typical of Carstairs that he began with a roar and ended with a bleat.

'Cut it out, old boy. I ain't come to patronize you but to get information about our mutual friend, Molly Harkness.'

'Ah, there we are!' exclaimed Carstairs. 'I heard Molly and you had a fling after that bad business with her husband shooting himself. Damn fine filly, I always thought, but not quite my type.'

Edward restrained himself from punching the man in the teeth and said lightly, 'I never touched her, scout's honour.' He made the sign.

Carstairs looked at him incredulously. 'Why then, you're a bigger fool than I took you for. Dannie said you were a disappointment that night Molly died – couldn't think till now what on earth she meant.'

243

Edward was quite aware that Carstairs was trying to make him lose his temper so he would storm off and he would be rid of his inquisitor and the knowledge made him icy calm. 'And without wishing to speak ill of a lady, Dannie's had some experience.'

'That's rather a cad's remark,' Carstairs remarked piously, 'and you an Eton man. I went to some tinpot place in the colony so you wouldn't expect me to talk about a lady in that way.'

'But is she a lady?' Edward continued. 'She as much as admitted she used me to get into Molly's room to steal some letters she wanted, but I expect she told you about that.'

'Yes, it made us both laugh – the way you fell for that. Nothing to do with me, old chap,' he said, raising his hands above his head in mock surrender.

'Did she tell you why she did it – take the letters, I mean?'

'Money – what other reason is there ever? She was pretty short. That old swine, Lord Weaver, had discovered she was two-timing him . . . you knew she was his mistress?' Edward nodded. 'Well, when he found she had been using the apartment he had put her in to entertain other men, he threw her out . . . '

'Of the apartment?'

'And his life. He said he had been meaning to do it for some time because his wife – Blanche, isn't that her name? – had found out somehow and it was making her unhappy.'

'Do we know who she was – as you put it – two-timing him with? Not you?'

'Not me. I didn't get to know her till that weekend at Haling. We just clicked. Don't know why.'

Edward suspected he was lying. When the two of them had returned from their ride the morning Molly had been found dead, he had sensed they shared the intimacy of lovers.

'So who? Who was Dannie sleeping with?'

'Don't think I can tell you, old sport. One shouldn't bandy a woman's name about, eh?'

Edward considered throttling him but said, 'I think it was that German – Major Stille? Ever come across him?'

'Mum's the word, old sport,' said Carstairs, putting a finger to his lips.

Edward changed tack. 'So, if you're not here to escape woman trouble in the colony, why are you here?' He tried to sound like a man joshing another in hearty admiration but failed dismally.

'Damn it, Corinth, I'm here on official business.' Carstairs sounded genuinely upset and Edward guessed he must have something to hide. 'Lord Erroll asked me to come, if you must know, but it's frightfully hush-hush. I daren't breathe a word.'

'Old Joss sent you?' Erroll was a friend of Edward's and a leading figure in Kenya. He had heard his friend had been vocal in his support of Mosley's Fascist party and had made an attempt to start his own branch of the movement in the colony but it had petered out. Edward had been grateful he had left Kenya when he had. Otherwise he might have been in the awkward position of having to tell his friend what an ass he was making of himself.

'Yes,' Carstairs said, almost eagerly. 'I shouldn't tell you this, old sport, but Joss is worried about Tanganyika. He doesn't want to see it go back to the Germans.' Tanganyika had been a German colony before the war. 'He thinks – and I have direct evidence he's right – that the Nazis have several of their people in place to seize the whole colony, including Kenya, if war comes.'

He looked earnestly at Edward who had to agree that what he was being told sounded more than plausible – in fact was was highly likely.

'Erroll wants the British government to support his plan for a union with Tanganyika.'

'So he's no longer a Fascist?'

'Joss? No, he's a great patriot. He was only a Fascist when he thought it was patriotic – a belief in King and

Empire – that sort of thing. He hates the Huns – and the Eyeties for that matter. He thinks we should have weighed in and stopped Musso in Abyssinia. Too late now.'

Edward certainly agreed with this. It was the first great failure of the League of Nations not to protest when the Italians attacked the Ethiopians.

'The Eyeties have been arming the natives, you know. Giving guns to the Mandera and Moyale tribes . . . a bad business.'

'But, Carstairs, with all due respect, why didn't Joss send someone a bit more . . . heavyweight? No offence.'

'He's planning to come himself early next year but he wanted someone who wouldn't attract too much attention to sound out a few friends here. He don't want to come and find himself cold-shouldered.'

'And that was why you were at Haling?'

'Yes. Leo Scannon had been supporting Joss and is – I mean was – putting together a posse of Conservative MPs to put pressure on the government to take him seriously.'

'I see. So Scannon's death is a setback?'

'Certainly is, old sport. Deep gloom. I can hardly go back and tell Joss it's all over. He'd kill me. Anyway, I had a spot of trouble with . . . oh, no names, no pack drill. Anyway, they just about threw me out of Muthaiga Club. I can't go back without something like good news, you understand.'

'That was what you were discussing with Scannon in the garden the night Molly was murdered?'

Carstairs looked surprised. 'Suppose it was – who wants to know?'

'Just curious, that's all.'

Edward suddenly felt rather sorry for the man. Cold, short of money and unable to go home – he was a pathetic figure. 'Look,' he said impulsively, 'I know a few people at the Foreign Office who may be ready to listen to what you have to say, and have you talked to Lord Weaver? The *New Gazette* is pro-Empire and this could be a cause he'd back you up on.'

'Weaver wouldn't see me. That was what I was trying to get Dannie to do – get me an interview with the old boy.

When she told me on our ride – you remember, the morning you found Molly dead – that she had been cast off by him, I was pretty upset. I say though, do you really think you could get me in to see Weaver? I'd be eternally in your debt.'

Carstairs was sitting upright now, his eyes shining.

'I do, but you've got to tell me all you know about Molly's murder – and Scannon's.'

'Of course, old sport, ask away. I say, I'm sorry I said those things about you just now. I was depressed. Didn't mean any of it. Oh, and tell that girl of yours – Verity Browne – tell her I regret putting that rat in her bed. Silly joke, eh? Sorry and all that. Stupid thing to do.'

'Never mind that. I thought it was just the sort of mean trick you would play – you or Leo. Now listen, just tell me the truth.'

'About what?'

'When you got back from your ride with Dannie, I got the feeling you already knew Molly was dead. Am I right?'

'Yes, Dannie told me.'

'Did she kill Molly?'

'She said she hadn't. She had been in her room – looking for something. Do I gather some rather hot letters had gone missing? Anyway, she went into the room but she said Molly was already dead.' Seeing Edward's face, he repeated with rather less confidence, 'That's what she said, old sport.'

Edward had had only the briefest of chats with Benyon at Haling. He had been distracted first by Dannie and then occupied with Molly Harkness's murder. He felt he had made rather a fool of himself in front of a man he liked and respected, and was looking forward to effacing the impression he had given of a lovesick schoolboy. When he arrived at the Hassels', he found Verity already deep in conversation with Lady Benyon.

Despite her loathing for the regime which had destroyed the Russia she had known as a child and which had forced her to take refuge in England, she had taken an instinctive liking to Verity at Haling. She found her views on Russia and Communism distasteful and impossibly naive, but this had not prevented her from seeing her essential goodness. How could she comprehend the terror that Stalin was now inflicting on her beloved country? She excused Verity her blind admiration of Stalin, realizing that if so-called wise men like George Bernard Shaw and H.G.Wells could visit Moscow and come back spouting praise for 'a just society', and claiming to have seen the 'future in action', then how could young people like Verity be expected to know any better? However, she sensed that this intelligent young woman had begun to question her beliefs and she took the opportunity of taking her to one side while Edward and Adrian talked to her husband.

'My dear,' she said, 'forgive an old woman, but you look unhappy. Tell me I'm an interfering old busybody but I sense that you saw things in Spain which have made you angry and unhappy.'

'You're not old, Lady Benyon,' she said, drawing up a chair beside her. 'You think Communism is evil, don't you?'

'I think the ideals of Communism are good,' she replied softly, so as not to be overheard by the men, 'but I am sure they are being used by powerful and unscrupulous men for their own purposes. God knows, the Russia in which I was born was in need of reform. The Okhrana, the secret police, could imprison and torture at will. There was terrible poverty and the violence was endemic. I mean, endemic in society. Husbands beat their wives and children and left them to starve while they drank away what little they earned. I'm talking about the peasants ... but,' she said, seeing Verity open her mouth to protest, 'the aristocrats were no better. My uncle was a drunkard and a lecher. He fumbled me in my own bed when I was just twelve and seemed to think I should like it. It was a corrupt society but is the cure not worse than the disease? I think it is.'

'It's true, it all seems pretty hopeless,' said Verity soberly. 'I had thought, as Communists, we could turn back the tide of Fascism but I don't believe that now. Although I would never say it in public, nor even in private to anyone but you, I don't believe the Republic can win the war in Spain. Evil will triumph.'

'But that's not why you are so sad?'

'No, not just that. In Spain, I've . . . I've seen what you describe.'

'Idealism perverted by ruthless men?'

'Yes,' she said shortly. 'My friend, Mr Griffiths-Jones . . . he says the ends justify the means and I tried to believe him. But you're right, I have seen such terrible things in Spain . . . ' She was suddenly unable to continue.

Inna Benyon put out a hand and laid it on Verity's shoulder. 'My dear, you are in mourning. The sadness you feel is grief – grief for the death of your hopes and expectations. The pain will always be with you, like the pain of an old battle wound, but your grief is also . . . what shall I say? . . . the education of your soul. You must not despair. You can look at the world – all the horror and the despair – and see not the end of hope but the real meaning of our struggle here on earth.'

Verity looked into the woman's lined but still beautiful face and thought, I don't understand what she means but she's right about grief. I do feel as if I am in mourning, though I hardly know why. She said out loud, 'Mr Gollancz wants me to turn the articles I wrote for the *New Gazette* into a book, but there's something which always seems to stop me. I have tried looking at them again but, you know, I can hardly read them.'

'How exciting to be asked to write a book. It could be just the opportunity you have been waiting for to get your thoughts in order.'

'But the articles don't seem to belong to me any more. It's as if they were written by someone else.'

'I know what you mean, my dear. You have outgrown them. You know so much more now than you did when you first went to Spain. If I might suggest, you shouldn't even try to read them. You must start afresh. Begin with Toledo – tell us what it was like to be there and then go back and explain why it happened.'

'But the Party won't like that. They want me to write about the victories, not the defeats.'

When she looked at her again, Verity saw that Lady Benyon had said whatever she had wanted to say and her eyes were beginning to stray towards her husband. Before she brought their conversation to an end, she said, gently but firmly, 'You must do what you feel is right, my dear, but you have to be honest. If you are not honest, you will never be able to live with yourself.'

Lord Benyon came over to his wife, whispered in her ear, nodded and said, 'You must forgive us, dear Charlotte, but Inna has not been feeling very well of late and I must take her home. It has been such a pleasure meeting you again, Lord Edward, and you, too, Miss Browne. Please remember me to your father. He is a man of principle in an unprincipled world.'

When the Benyons had left, Charlotte said, 'So, what do you think of that?'

'Think of what?' Verity inquired, feeling that she had missed something.

'Of course, V, you were closeted with Inna, weren't you? Edward, you tell her what Lord Benyon told us.'

'He said that Daphne Hepple-Keen had lost one of her gloves – a white glove – and that Leo Scannon had found it. Leo could never resist passing on gossip and he had told Benyon what he had seen. He also said that he had it on good authority that Sir Geoffrey had been a policeman – a particular type of policeman. He had been in Ireland but something had gone wrong – Benyon didn't quite know what – and he had left the police and attached himself to Oswald Mosley. He thought it was highly likely *he* had stolen Mrs Simpson's letters.'

Dr Davidson raised his head from the diary and gestured to Edward to look through the glass. The powerful instrument made legible several lines on the seemingly blank sheet of paper.

'Whoever tore out those two pages would have been well advised to remove two or three more. It's quite clear – see?'

Edward read as easily as if the words were in ink rather than mere impressions from the pressure of a pen on the previous page: 'Daphne told me she had no idea how her glove had found its way into Molly's bedroom but, when I pressed her, she said her husband had borrowed them because he had been searching the room. I didn't quite believe what she told me and said I would talk to Geoffrey. She begged me not to and said he would kill her but . . . '

'And there's nothing else?'

'You mean, did Scannon turn over the page? He may have done but it's impossible to "read" anything. My own feeling is he broke off there and never completed the sentence. By the way, have you read the rest of the diary? It's explosive stuff.'

'Indeed! But, as far as I can see, not relevant to Molly's death – or his own.'

'He's poisonous about the Prime Minister and he has some spiteful things to say about your friend Lord Weaver.'

'I know,' Edward said, grimly. 'I'm rather glad he never got to write about me. I fear he would have had some fairly choice words of abuse about my part in all this.'

'You'll take this straight to the police, Corinth?' Davidson said anxiously.

'I will, I promise, and I won't say a word about you having looked at it for me. Really, I am most awfully grateful.'

'Oh, by the way, have you noticed the smell on the diary? There's the soot, of course, which is explained by where you say it was found, but I'm rather puzzled; there's another scent – to put it crudely, one would think it had been dropped in a cowpat!'

'But why did Scannon stop when he did?' Verity said, when Edward came round to report on what he had learned from the diary.

'He was obviously interrupted and never went back to it. Diarists don't always write everything up at the end of each day. Some wait until the end of a week or even longer.'

'So you want me to come with you to see Inspector Lampfrey?'

'You don't have to but . . .'

'You go. I really must write this book. There was something Lady Benyon said which has helped. She said not to try and rejig my articles for the paper but to write from scratch. Start with Toledo and . . . well, anyway, I think I know how to do it.'

'Oh well,' said Edward, slightly put out, 'you must get on with the book, I see that. Shall I ring you when I've seen Lampfrey?'

'Of course! Edward, you do understand don't you? This is really important to me.'

Edward melted. 'I understand. You get on with it and I'll telephone you tomorrow.'

Verity got up and kissed him on the lips. 'Dearest Edward, I'm such a bitch and you're so patient with me. I do care about all this, you know. I just need to do this damn book.'

Edward, feeling the warmth of her lips on his, wanted to pursue his advantage but something warned him it might spoil things. She gave him what she could and, if he asked for more now, like Oliver Twist, it might end in tears. He contented himself with what he hoped was a manly nod of his head and made a dignified exit. But his heart was racing. He promised himself that, when it was all over, he would damn well ask her to marry him.

Inspector Lampfrey was not in the police station when he bowled up in the Lagonda and, to his acute discomfort, he was ushered into the presence of Chief Inspector Pride who greeted him with a smile Robespierre might have envied.

'Lord Edward, you again! Have you come to give yourself up?' Only the teeth snapping shut, as sharp as a guillotine, indicated that the Chief Inspector was being humorous.

'No, indeed, but I do have some information for you.'

'If it's concerning Mr Scannon's murder, you are too late. I am happy to tell you that we have completed our investigations and made an arrest.'

'Good lord! I hadn't heard.'

'No, the arrest was only made this morning.'

'Many congratulations, Chief Inspector,' Edward said insincerely. 'Am I permitted to know whom you have arrested?'

The policeman stroked his chin and then, unable to resist celebrating his triumph, said, 'I don't see why I should not tell you. The press will be told later this afternoon and it will be in tomorrow's papers. We have arrested Miss Ruth Conway for the murders of both Mrs Harkness and Mr Scannon.'

Edward drew a breath. 'I hope that was wise, Chief Inspector.'

Pride looked at him with loathing and restrained himself with an effort. 'In what way might it have been unwise, Lord Edward? You may be unaware that Miss Conway stood to inherit the bulk of Mr Scannon's estate and that she had reason to resent his treatment of her over many years. She was his half-sister – the daughter of old Mr Scannon's mistress.'

'I know, but what possible motive had she for killing Mrs Harkness?'

'I am not yet certain, but I believe she feared Mrs Harkness might marry Mr Scannon and do her out of her inheritance.'

'You must be aware Scannon wasn't the kind of man who was interested in a woman . . . sexually?'

'Maybe, but perhaps Miss Conway did not know that.'

'But that's quite absurd, Chief Inspector. The reason why I came here . . . '

'Is to sneer at the efforts of the police,' Pride hissed, unable to hide his fury any longer.

'Not at all,' Edward said calmly. 'I have the greatest respect for the police and I apologize for saying the arrest of Miss Conway was absurd. She certainly had a motive for killing Mr Scannon and the opportunity. She was best placed to put rat poison in the whisky but I am convinced she did not do it.'

'And what reason have you, Lord Edward, for saying so? Or is it just "a hunch"?'

'Not at all. When we dropped in on Haling the other day, Miss Conway was kind enough to let us look round the house and talk to Mr Pickering and the gardener – both of whom had access to the poison.'

'You said "we"?'

'My friend, Miss Browne, was with me and it was she who . . .'

The Chief Inspector went red in the face and then white. For a moment Edward wondered if he was going to have a seizure. He had wanted to keep Verity's name out of the conversation because he was aware that, if Pride disliked anyone more than him, it was her. They had crossed swords the previous year when Pride had all but accused her of being an enemy of the state.

'Miss Browne? I thought she was in Spain. What was she doing at Haling, might I ask? Though now I think of it, she invited herself to Haling with you previously. There was some story of her taking a rat to bed?'

'The rat was put in her bed by some joker and she did not invite herself to Haling. She was invited by Mr Scannon. His friend, Miss Dannhorn, wished to meet her.'

Edward immediately regretted bringing up Dannie's name when he saw a leer cross the policeman's face.

'Now, there is something you can put me right about, Lord Edward. I see from your statement – your second statement – ' he said, meaningfully, 'that Miss Dannhorn is your mistress. Inspector Lampfrey informs me that Mrs Harkness was also your mistress and Miss Browne . . .'

Edward stood up, rattling his chair so that it almost fell backwards. 'Chief Inspector, if you are determined to insult me, I shall leave and you will hear from my solicitor. You know perfectly well that Miss Browne is a friend and Mrs Harkness was never my mistress. As for Miss Dannhorn, as

I admitted to Inspector Lampfrey, I did return from my talk with Mrs Harkness to find her in my bed – not, I would emphasize, at my invitation. To my great regret, instead of turning her out of my room, I allowed her to stay. I ought to have guessed she was just using me to obtain access to Mrs Harkness's room – but this is all in my statements.'

Pride realized he had gone too far but he had at least achieved what he had set out to do – namely to disturb that infuriatingly smug look on the man's face.

'I apologize, Lord Edward,' he said stiffly, 'I had no wish to insult you. I was merely trying to make sense of your relationship with . . . the ladies in this case.'

'But Miss Browne is not, as you put it, a lady in the case.'

'But you have just told me that you and she went to Haling recently and looked round the house.'

'We were riding past the house . . . '

'Riding? On horseback?'

'On motor bicycles. Miss Browne had a puncture and so we called in.' Edward was aware how thin it sounded and he wished now he had taken more trouble with his excuse.

'I see. You were riding a motor bicycle past the house,' the policeman said with studied irony, 'and you had a puncture. What a coincidence. So what did you discover that the police search had missed?'

'This,' Edward said, passing Leo Scannon's diary across the desk. 'Two pages have been torn out, no doubt because the murderer was mentioned, but it would be possible, I believe, to read something from the impressions left on the blank sheet following the torn pages.'

He saw no reason why he should divulge that he had already been to Hendon and had the blank page 'read'.

'Where did you find this?' Pride said roughly, opening the book.

'Miss Browne found it on a ledge inside the fireplace in Mr Scannon's bedroom.'

'Why did she look there?'

'There is a similar ledge in the fireplace of the room I was in. If you read my statement, it was there that I foolishly hid the bag I took from Mrs Harkness's room before handing it over to Inspector Lampfrey.'

'I see. So you have had this . . . what, three days? Why did you not pass it to the police immediately?'

'I am giving it to you now,' Edward said shortly.

'I could have you arrested for impeding my investigation.'

'I think that would be rather ungrateful, don't you, Chief Inspector? I would hate Miss Browne to tell the *New Gazette* how she found what you had overlooked. It might bring down criticism on the police and that's the last thing we want, isn't it?'

'My men made a very thorough search. Perhaps the diary wasn't there then? Perhaps you put it there?'

'Please, Chief Inspector,' said Edward wearily. 'My aim is the same as yours: to put the murderer, or murderers, behind bars. I find it quite extraordinary that you won't recognize that simple fact. Good day, Chief Inspector. You know where to find me if you want me.'

Edward was not pleased to find, when he left the police station, a constable marking the Lagonda's tyres with chalk. 'I say, officer, hang on a moment! I've just been with Chief Inspector Pride. Surely I can park here on official business?'

'No, my lord,' the constable said, showing he knew perfectly well to whom the car belonged, 'there's no parkin' under any circumstances in front of the station.'

At that moment, Lampfrey drew up in a police car and wound down his window. 'What's the problem, constable? Oh, Lord Edward, I didn't see it was you. Not been breaking the speed limit, have we?' he said, grinning.

'No, damn it, I've just been handing over an important piece of evidence to Inspector Pride and I come out to find I'm being booked for parking in the wrong place. I sometimes wonder if England's turning into a police state.'

'That's all right, constable,' the Inspector said, indicating with his thumb that the latter's presence was no longer required. 'The constable was quite in order,' he said, to mollify the red-faced officer who appeared ready to argue the toss with his superior, 'but on this occasion we'll let you off with a warning.'

When the zealous officer had made himself scarce, Lampfrey said, 'What's this important new evidence?'

'I came to give it to you but you were off sleuthing so I was shown straight in to see Pride. I gave him a diary Miss Browne and I discovered when we dropped in on Haling the other day. Seems the police search wasn't as thorough as it ought to have been.'

'A diary? Mr Scannon's missing diary!' Lampfrey exclaimed. 'What did it have to say about . . . ?'

'The vital pages had been torn out but, between ourselves – and I didn't tell Pride this – I showed it to Davidson at Hendon and he made out quite a lot from the impression on the blank page after the ones that had been ripped out. Here, take this. It's a copy of what Davidson read. Oh, don't say where you got it. Davidson examined the diary as a favour to me – strictly off the record, don't y'know. Don't want to get the old lad into any sort of trouble. Telephone me when you've digested it and let me know what you think. By the way, Pride says he's arrested Miss Conway.'

'That's right,' Lampfrey said, pocketing the paper, 'she had the opportunity to kill Scannon and the motive. You know she's inherited everything?'

'I do, but that doesn't make her a murderer. A little bit too obvious, I'd say. She's not a fool and, if she had wanted to kill her half-brother, she'd do it much more subtly. Well, I've got to get going. Mustn't park in a restricted area.' As Edward got into the Lagonda, he had a thought. 'I say, Lampfrey. Miss Conway's in "durance vile" at Devizes, I suppose?' Devizes was the assize town.

'Yes.'

'I'm glad about that. At least she's out of harm's way. You see, Miss Conway knows who murdered Leo Scannon and I think the murderer knows she knows – and that's dangerous. But she should be safe enough in prison. Cheerio, Inspector.'

Edward put the Lagonda into gear and sped off, covering the police Wolseley with dust.

'I haven't got time!' Verity wailed. 'I've just got to finish this . . . ' She gestured at a pile of foolscap and then banged the typewriter, which rang its bell in protest.

She was talking to herself – reluctant to respond to the demands of whoever-it-was banging on the front door. Tactfully, Charlotte and Adrian had gone about their business and left the house to her. And it was working. She had thrown her articles for the *New Gazette* into a pile in the corner of the room. She would take Lady Benyon's advice and start from scratch. The first paragraph had been a problem – she had recast it several times. The first page had taken almost an hour, and the first chapter all morning, but suddenly it was beginning to flow. Her sub-conscious had deigned to release her memories of what she had seen in Spain – memories shackled by a growing cynicsm, almost despair. She wanted to write both a call to arms and a serious evaluation of the situation in all its horrible reality, and there were moments when she thought 'never the twain would meet'.

But she had cracked it. It was flowing and now there was this knocking on the door. She ignored it for several minutes. Surely, whoever-it-was would take the hint and leave her alone. But no – this was someone who knew she was there and was determined to talk to her. Wearily, she got up from her chair, her back aching and her wrists stiff, and went downstairs.

'Verity, Miss Browne, it's me – Dannie. I must talk to you. It's important.'

Verity looked at Dannie uncomprehendingly. It had not crossed her mind to wonder who was at the door. Her one aim was to get rid of him, or her, as rapidly as possible. That it might be Dannie . . . wasn't she supposed to be in Germany with her lover, the sinister Major Stille?

'I thought you were in Germany . . . ' she managed, before Dannie swept past her and up the stairs. She made straight for the window and looked out over the street.

'Sorry, I don't want to be melodramatic but I think I was being followed.'

'Followed? I don't understand. Followed by whom? Anyway, why are you here?'

'Is this where you work?' Dannie said, ignoring the question.

There was something almost wistful in the way she spoke, fingering the page in the typewriter. 'To save time is to lengthen life.' She read the aphorism affixed to the machine. It seemed to amuse her.

'Leave it alone,' Verity said, suddenly angry. This was the woman who had seduced her . . . her friend and used him as one would a chisel to break open a lock. She hated her; she hated her politics; she hated her friends and, most of all, she hated her beauty. Because she was very beautiful.

'Sorry, I didn't mean to upset you,' Dannie said humbly. 'I came to give you these.' She pulled out a small package from inside her coat and tossed it on the table.

'What is it?'

'Look for yourself. They're the letters Molly Harkness stole from Mrs Simpson and I took from her room at Haling.'

'I don't want them! Give them to Edward or to your "employer".'

'My employer? You mean . . . ?'

'I don't know who I mean, but presumably you do. Lord Weaver or Major Stille? You tell me.'

'I thought it might do you some good if you gave them to Joe. He's not my employer though I was his whore. That was fun. He may look like a stewed prune but he's by far the best lover I've ever had – better than . . . . He talked himself into my bed. You've no idea how dull most men are . . . or perhaps you have. Joe was never dull. Wicked, yes, but never dull.'

'But he threw you out in the end. You were two-timing him.'

'That's not quite true. I found out . . . from Blanche, as it happens, that he wasn't faithful to me. That sounds rather absurd, doesn't it? Expecting a man to be faithful to his mistress, but he was – so Blanche told me – sleeping with

Molly Harkness. Maybe it wasn't true. Perhaps Blanche was trying to rile me, but I believed her at the time.'

'When did she tell you this?'

'Blanche? Oh, the night Mrs Simpson came to dinner to meet Edward. I decided I was going to get the letters off Molly and take them somewhere where they would cause as much trouble as possible. I wanted to get back at Joe . . . at the whole pack of them.'

'You decided to give them to Stille?'

'Yes, but he told me to return them to Mrs Simpson.'

'Why?'

'Because Germany wants the King to stay king. He loves Germany and does whatever the Führer wants him to do.'

'So Stille told you to hand them back?'

'Yes, but I was damned if I was going to. I had gone to a lot of trouble – sorry about that, but you know what I mean – to get those letters and it had all been wasted.'

'It doesn't sound as though it was too difficult.' The sarcasm in Verity's voice was cutting.

'Not that part, I agree. He's very good-looking, isn't he? But rather a prig, don't you think?'

Verity gritted her teeth. 'So you thought you'd give the letters to me?'

'That's right. I thought the Communist Party might like to use them.'

'Very kind, but what if I don't want them . . . if I just burn them?'

Dannie shrugged her shoulders. 'Do what you like. I don't care.'

'And what will you do now?'

'I'm not sure. Go to Germany. There are people there who'll look after me. I have a friend in the Luftwaffe. He's even better looking than Edward.'

Again Verity managed to rein in her anger. 'And did you kill Mrs Harkness?' she asked as casually as she could manage.

'No, she was dead when I went into her room. I saw that at once. That was odd: I thought I was too late. I thought the murderer would have taken the letters but they were there, under her pillow, so she must have been killed for some other reason.'

Verity was shocked. Dannie had coldly searched under the dead woman's pillow for the loot she wanted, her only thought that someone else might have been there before her.

'The only reason you slept with Edward was to get into Mrs Harkness's room without being seen?'

'No, that wasn't it. I didn't need to make that detour. I thought it would be fun – that's all.'

'And was it?' Verity inquired acidly.

'Yes and no.'

'What does that mean?'

'Oh, well, as you can imagine, I had other things on my mind. I had to get into the next room without waking Edward or Molly, of course, though Edward had told me she had taken a sleeping draught. It was a bit distracting.'

Verity found Dannie's egotism horrifying. 'You said you found her dead when you went in?'

'I don't know how it happened. I didn't do it and I didn't hear anyone but, of course, I might not have done. I . . . I had my hands full. However, I have an idea I know who did do it.'

'Who?'

'You work it out.'

'Did you have the key to the connecting door?'

'Yes, I borrowed it from the pantry. I knew where Pickering kept the keys. I returned it before I went back to my room.'

'And you left through the door into the corridor?'

'Yes. It would have been too much of a risk coming back through Edward's room. He might have woken. Anyway, there was no need. I wanted to get back to my room as quickly as I could.'

'With the letters.'

'Yes, with the letters.'

'Why did you lock the door to Molly's room?' it occurred to Verity to ask.

'I thought it would confuse things. I thought the police would think the murderer climbed up the creeper from the terrace, killed Molly, took the letters and left the same way. I don't know what I thought, really. Just that it would confuse things – which it did.'

'Surely you must have known the police would think you killed Mrs Harkness? After all, they were pretty certain you had taken the letters.'

'I didn't care. Life's so boring. I'd had enough of it here. England's finished. You know that, don't you? Germany's the future. I have to admit I hadn't wanted to leave so . . . immediately. It was the fault of that awful policeman – Chief Inspector Pride. I thought he was going to arrest me and I lost my nerve. My friend gave me a lift in his aeroplane . . . to Germany.'

'But you came back.'

'Yes, when I heard they had arrested that housekeeper woman . . . what's her name?'

'Ruth Conway.'

'Yes. Such a dull, plain thing. I had to laugh because, of course, I knew she hadn't done it. She hadn't murdered anyone, though in her place I would have killed Leo years ago.'

'So who did kill Mrs Harkness, if you didn't?'

'I told you, work it out for yourself. It might have been Leo. He wanted those letters badly. Perhaps his nerve failed and he couldn't bring himelf to look for them properly after he had drugged her. Or maybe it was that horrible man Hepple-Keen. The one who bullies his wife. I think Molly was his mistress too, but . . . I don't know why he would have killed her.'

'What about Boy Carstairs?'

'He's a darling. I let him make love to me because he wanted to so badly. He said he'd take me back to Kenya and we would take the place over . . . but, in the end, I thought no. He's always going to lose, isn't he? But he does look rather wonderful and he rides like a dream.' She looked wistful again and, for a moment, Verity almost felt sorry for her. 'I must go now. I've got a plane to catch. Have fun with the letters. Oh, and tell Edward I found him . . .

no, on second thoughts, just give him my love. And tell him: sorry.'

When Dannie had gone, Verity sat at her desk with her face in her hands. A shadow had passed over her and left her numbed. She could not think what to do with Mrs Simpson's letters. She did not want to read them. She didn't even want to see them, so she pushed them under a pile of *New Gazette*s on the floor. She tried to get back to her work but the inspiration had deserted her. She could not write anything.

She sat there, unmoving, for ten minutes, gazing at the blank sheet of paper in her typewriter, unable to think straight. Her trance was broken by the shrill call of the telephone in the hall. As if in obedience to a higher power, she trotted meekly down the stairs and lifted the receiver.

14

'He's a sort of policeman,' his Foreign Office friend, Basil Thoroughgood had said. 'Hush-hush and all that . . . he'll brief you on Hepple-Keen. Actually seemed quite keen to meet you. Goes by the name of . . . ' There was a crackle on the line and Edward was unable to catch the man's name. 'He'll be at Albany tomorrow about four. Oh, and don't be fooled. He may not look anything much, but he's top of his particular tree in his particularly dangerous part of the jungle.'

It wasn't *about* four but on the dot of four when the little man knocked on the door of Edward's set of rooms. And he was a little man. Hardly five feet, very straight of back, with a small moustache and spectacles. When he took off his hat, Edward saw he was almost bald. There was a deep scar just above his right eye. To the casual observer, he looked inoffensive enough – unmemorable to the point of invisibility – but, when you looked into his brown eyes, formidable.

After Fenton had relieved his visitor of his hat and coat, he brought in tea and muffins. Edward offered his guest a cigarette but he refused, taking out his own packet. He tapped it apologetically. 'Egyptian – a low taste, but there you are.' He smiled. It was a tight though not unattractive smile but it never reached his eyes.

'I'm so sorry but, when Thoroughgood telephoned, the line was bad and I didn't catch your name.'

'Major Ferguson.' His voice was hoarse, as though he didn't have much use for it. 'Our friend said you wanted to know about Geoffrey Hepple-Keen.'

'That's right. I don't know whether you can answer this but does Hepple-Keen work for you, or someone like you?'

'He's an MP, isn't he? Why should he be working for me?'

'He was in Ireland during the worst of the troubles and he was a policeman then.'

Ferguson looked at him, the scar above his eye twitching but probably, Edward thought, not from nerves. He didn't look the nervous type.

'What makes you think that?'

Knowing it must come, Edward had considered how he would answer that question. Since he had no wish to involve Verity in any of this – as a Communist Party member, she would never be a secret policeman's favourite person – he had decided to say he had been delving in the archives of the *New Gazette*. But, before he could say anything, Ferguson asked, 'Did your friend, Miss Browne, find some references to him being in Ireland when she was looking through the files?'

'What?' Edward said, nonplussed. Was Verity so dangerous a character that her every move was being watched?

'Not magic,' Ferguson said, with a grin which made him suddenly likeable. 'Mr Purser, the *Gazette*'s archivist, keeps an eye on things at the paper for us – but that's confidential. I must have your word you won't pass it on to Miss Browne or anyone else.'

'But that's outrageous! We *do* live in a police state. I thought it was a Communist Party exaggeration, but it's true.'

'There is a very thin line between the personal liberties we all value and the security of the state, Lord Edward. Certain European countries have an advantage over us because their police can act with total freedom in suppressing dissent and enforcing adherence to the party line. That is not the British way, and never shall be, but we do have to make some compromises if we are to defend the very freedoms we both value against less scrupulous regimes.'

'Yes but . . . '

'I wouldn't have come to see you, Lord Edward if I had not been perfectly certain of your patriotism and your discretion. I am not unaware of how you conducted yourself in Spain a few months back. In short, I am prepared to help you but first I must hear from your own lips why you need this information. You suspect Sir Geoffrey Hepple-Keen of murder? Is that it?'

'I do, but if you tell me he was working for you and if, as I take it, you represent the . . . '

'What I represent is not important,' Ferguson interjected.

'But if Hepple-Keen was working for the government, then that would explain some of his actions which, on the face of it, are suspicious.'

Ferguson did not answer immediately. Then he said, 'I can't tell you much, I'm afraid. He was working for the government in Ulster a few years back but he went a little too far . . . off the rails, so to speak . . . so we parted company but . . . '

'But . . . ?'

'But it is possible he was acting on behalf of some important people when he was at Haling. He is – or rather was – a close friend of Leo Scannon, as you know, and the latter was a close friend of the King. That's all I can say.'

'But he wasn't working for you?'

'It's a difficult one to answer honestly, Lord Edward. As you can imagine, we rely on information from a variety of sources – many of them suspect or unreliable. We have to touch pitch, so to speak. Sir Geoffrey is an influential Member of Parliament and, now and again, he hears things and some of those things he feels able to pass on to us.'

'But some he does not?'

'That's correct. For example he is, as you know, a close associate of Sir Oswald Mosley. For some time he passed us information about that gentleman's activities which was . . . useful in keeping tabs on him.'

'But no longer?'

'No longer.'

266

'Have you asked him why he has given up talking to you?'

'We have considered doing so but, in the end, we thought it better to watch and wait. We attribute his silence to his being involved with a particular lady.'

Edward's head, which had begun to ache, cleared. 'His affair with Mrs Harkness?'

'That is correct.'

'Have you any objection to my going on digging, then?'

'None, so long as you are aware that you are walking on shifting sands. I came to warn you that both you and Miss Browne may be in danger and that, even if you do discover who killed Mrs Harkness, you may never see the killer brought to justice.'

'You mean Hepple-Keen has powerful friends?'

'I can say no more, Lord Edward. I have probably said more than I should have already.'

'I am grateful, Major Ferguson. Is there any way I can get in touch with you if I have any information I think would be of interest?'

'Leave a message for me with the porter at your club. I will get it within the hour.'

Edward was impressed and rather alarmed. 'I had hoped that at least one's club was safe from surveillance, but I see I'm wrong.'

'Our safety, at this perilous moment in our history, Lord Edward,' the little man said gravely, 'rests on the thinnest of ice and we can only negotiate it with the sort of faith which enabled Our Lord to walk on the waters of Galilee.'

Verity had always dreaded that the moment might come when her loyalty to the Party was at odds with her loyalty to her country or, worse still, to her friends. That moment had arrived. The Party ought to receive these letters belonging to Mrs Simpson – there could be no doubt about it. In the *Daily Worker*, Verity would write a hard-hitting article on the King as a lackey of the Nazis, of his tawdry affair with Mrs Simpson and the rottenness of British society. She could write such an article in an hour and it would burn with moral fervour and righteous indignation. By selective quotation from the letters, she could probably bring down Baldwin's government and she might shatter the confidence felt by most ordinary citizens in their leaders and in their king. It was heady stuff and would make her the most celebrated journalist of the day.

On the other hand, what did she owe to her employer at the *New Gazette*, Joe Weaver, and to her country? Most of all, what did she owe Edward Corinth? He had once asked her what she would do if her loyalty to the Party conflicted with the interests of the country and she had not been able to answer. On another occasion, he had asked if she would suppress stories about the Communist Party which might injure its reputation. She had to confess that she probably would and they had gone on to discuss if means were ever justified by the ends to which they were directed. Now she was faced with just the moral quandary she most dreaded.

Her torment was relieved momentarily by the telephone ringing in the hall. Wearily she clambered down the stairs and lifted the receiver. It was Tommie Fox, in a high state of excitement.

'Verity, is that you? Have you forgotten?' His voice sounded more like a parrot's squawk than a human's and in the background she could hear people singing and whistles being blown and the occasional shout of command. 'The Jarrow Marchers – they're only a few miles away. It's a most wonderful thing! I joined the march yesterday. So many people are coming to walk with us. The crowds are bigger than anything I've ever seen. You must come . . . come now. I have to go. I'm in a pub and there's a queue of people wanting to use the phone.' He told her where to find him.

Tommie's call galvanized her. She had, shamefully, almost forgotten about the march and yet this was a cause close to her heart. It was a visible reminder to the soft, complacent southerners of what the north was suffering – and she had to be there for the final march on London.

She took a tram and then a bus, sitting on the top deck so she could smoke. Tommie had told her that the pub from which he was speaking, and around which they were resting, was only three or four hours' march from Marble Arch. He said they had left St Albans the day before and would stay just outside London so that they could march into the city without displaying the signs of exhaustion they normally felt at the end of a day's walking.

She got off the bus well short of her target, partly because the crowds had reduced its progress to a walking pace and partly because she was embarrassed to hop off a bus near men with blistered feet and boots destroyed by walking.

There was a palpable air of excitement around her as she weaved her way towards the centre of the crowd. A field kitchen had been set up and women were serving stew, tinned fruit and hot tea. It was cold but the rain had eased and many people were stretched out on mackintoshes on whatever patches of grass they could find, trying to sleep or at least rest their aching legs.

At last she spotted Tommie's substantial figure behind a tea urn. 'May I help?' she said shyly.

'Verity! I knew you'd come. Of course, take over from me. There's some fellows over there with the most terrible blisters which need bathing. Yesterday I literally had to cut off one chap's socks. They had embedded themselves in his feet. Do you know what a boot-repairer said to me? He said, "It seems sort of queer doing your own job just because you want to do it and for something you want to help, instead of doing it because you'd starve if you didn't. I wonder if that's how the chaps in Russia feel about it, now they're running their own show?" If you don't mind cramped conditions you can stay with us tonight,' Tommie continued. 'The daughter of a parishioner of mine lives close by and is going to let us doss down on her floor.'

Verity reminded him, testily enough, that she was a war correspondent, not a debutante, but in truth she felt ashamed. She ought to have walked the whole way with these men rather than joining them at the end for cakes and ale.

That evening, tired but much happier, she joined Tommie with a clear conscience at a meeting addressed by Ellen Wilkinson, the indomitable MP for Jarrow, who was very much the spirit of the march. It was her fiery speeches which had kept up the men's spirits in the terrible twenty-mile stretch between Bedford and Luton when the wind had driven the rain into the marchers' teeth all day and chilled them to the bone.Tonight, however, there was a feeling not of triumph but achievement. Lugging their huge oak box containing the petition they were to present to Parliament, many people had said they would never get so far.

Before Ellen Wilkinson went off to spend the night at the home of the secretary of the local Labour Party, Tommie introduced her to Verity. The MP said how much it meant to the marchers to have sympathetic journalists along with them reporting the march fairly. 'Whatever their proprietors think,' she added meaningfully, and Verity again felt ashamed. 'You've only just joined us, Tommie tells me?'

'I'm afraid so.'

'But you're here now. That's what counts,' Ellen said, smiling at her confusion, and Verity wanted to kiss her.

'Where's everyone sleeping tonight?' she asked.

'We sleep in schools and drill halls, casual wards – wherever they let us. Then we get up at six thirty and parade at eight forty-five, all packed up and ready to go. You've got somewhere to sleep?'

'Yes, thank you. Tommie has a friend who lives near here and we're going to sleep on her floor.'

'Good! I'll see you in the morning. I think you'll find tomorrow interesting.'

'She's the most wonderful woman,' Tommie said reverently after she had departed. '"Indomitable" hardly does justice to her fortitude. Nothing seems to depress her – not rain or wind or the indifference of Parliament. You know Baldwin has let it be known he won't see us when we present the petition to Parliament? And she certainly isn't depressed by the attitude of the newspaper proprietors either.'

'I gather the bishops haven't been exactly supportive,' Verity said tartly.

'No,' he sighed. 'The Bishop of Durham called us revolutionaries and he made Bishop Gordon – Jarrow's bishop – apologize for blessing the marchers when they set off. I sometimes think they would ask Jesus to recant if he was foolish enough to come back to earth. They don't seem to understand,' he said unhappily, 'that poverty is not an accident, a temporary difficulty, but the permanent state in which most people live.'

'That's what I'm always telling you – it's the basis of the class struggle. Men are regarded as mere instruments of production and their labour a commodity to be bought and sold. That's why the Communist Party is the only realistic alternative to capitalism.

'Businessmen can destroy a town overnight and take no responsibility for the social consequences of their decisions. It's iniquitous!'

Tommie laughed. 'You may be right but I still distrust your people.'

'How can you? I was doing some research in the files: Palmer's Shipyard in Jarrow employed ten thousand men at the end of the war. Almost twenty years later, a letter addressed to Palmer's Shipyard, Ellison Street, Jarrow was returned marked "Not known. Gone away."'

In the morning, feeling tired and dirty, Verity splashed her face under the kitchen tap and joined Tommie for the march. Every bone in her body ached – the floor had been particularly hard – and it was good to be out in the fresh air. As they approached the assembly point, they heard a strange groaning sound.

'What on earth is that?' Verity inquired.

'The mouth-organ band. The journalists with us, knowing that many of the men play the mouth-organ, got up a subscription to buy some. You can't have a march without a band.'

After a brief but highly effective call to arms from Ellen Wilkinson, the marchers set off – excited, but also full of trepidation. Many of the men Verity spoke to had never been out of Jarrow before and, to them, London was as foreign as Vienna or Berlin. They had no idea how they would be welcomed. The collective memory of the working class included being charged by mounted police, cut at with sabres, chained to railings and beaten. Although they had faith in their MP that nothing like that would happen today, they were still frightened – determined but frightened.

It didn't rain, for which Verity was profoundly thankful, and she felt she was in her rightful place, middle class though she was, and a woman at that – surrounded by gaunt, hollow-eyed men in cloth caps and threadbare coats, their boots often tied up with string or gaping at the toe. When she remarked on the state of their clothes, Tommie said that many towns had been generous with their support and the men were actually in better health than when they had started out. 'People have been so kind,' he went on. 'In the last month, they have had better food than they are used to but, most important of all, Ellen has given them a sense of purpose. If you've been without a job for as long as these men have, your sense of worth has taken a fearful battering.'

As the marchers neared Hyde Park more and more people joined them so that those who had started out from Jarrow twenty-seven days earlier were far outnumbered and only recognizable by their dress and the way they stared about them at London's great buildings and wide thoroughfares. At Marble Arch, they were greeted by the Mayor of Jarrow and Verity was moved to see that he was weeping as he embraced Ellen Wilkinson. The Mayor announced that the marchers were to be given lunch at the London County Council Training Centre in Stepney, after which they would march through Mayfair to Hyde Park for the great final rally.

Verity decided she had time to go to the *New Gazette* and write a piece about the march. She assumed the editor had other journalists covering it but she wanted to do something personal – a ringing denunciation of the government which had left towns like Jarrow to rot, out of sight and unimagined by the comfortable clubmen dozing in their leather chairs and the smug politicians in Westminster. As she made her way across Hyde Park, she suddenly felt a touch on her shoulder. She turned to find Major Stille at her elbow. For a moment, thinking of the article she was going to write and how she would hold up Ellen Wilkinson as the kind of MP she could honour, she did not recognize him.

'Have you decided yet?' The German spoke perfect English.

'What? Decided what?'

Verity had no desire to speak to this man whom she hated and despised and who she knew hated her. She recalled the dinner party in the German Embassy. He had been fooled then, not knowing she was a member of the Communist Party, and he had not liked being made to look foolish. He had taken his revenge in a particularly spiteful way by killing the little dog she doted on. It was clear he had by no means finished with her.

'Decided if you're going to use the letters Dannie brought you.'

'How did you . . . ?' she began, unwisely, before checking herself. She knew that the first rule of engagement was never to admit anything.

'Dannie is a naughty girl.' He wagged his finger at her in mock exasperation. 'Germany has no wish to see the letters used to embarrass the King, but we have need of them. When I catch up with her – and I will catch up with her – she will be . . . reprimanded. Now, if you would be kind enough to return them to me . . . '

Verity shivered and felt momentarily sorry for Dannie. Here was a man as deadly as sin and to cross him was to make a terrible enemy.

'I don't know what you mean,' she said. 'I have nothing to say to you, Major Stille. If you harass me, I shall call rape and have the police arrest you.'

Stille laughed, almost heartily. Looking around her for assistance, Verity saw that they were quite alone. Hyde Park, which had seemed so crowded a moment ago, was now deserted.

'What letters?' she said again. 'I don't know what you're talking about.'

It occurred to her – rather late – that Stille might not be sure Dannie *had* passed the letters to her and, whatever she decided to do with them, she certainly was not going to give them up to him.

'Well, have it your own way – isn't that what you English say? – but it's a pity you don't trust me.'

'Trust you! When you have haunted me, disrupting my lectures and pretending to be what you're not. In Spain, we know all about spies and traitors.'

'Ah, Spain. I wish I had been at Toledo. I have a friend there who says it was most amusing. I probably should not tell you this but Toledo was only the beginning. *Kindergarten*! We shall test our weapons on the peasants and make the necessary improvements before we use them in earnest.'

Verity, who had been walking fast to get away from the man, turned suddenly to face him. 'We shall win, I promise you, Major Stille. Perhaps not this year, but in the end. Your world ends in the dustbin of history – what do you call it? – *Der Mülleimer*, the rubbish dump . . . '

For a moment she thought he might attack her but a group of young people from the march came into view and he obviously thought better of prolonging the conversation.

'I give you till tonight to return the letters to the German Embassy. Otherwise . . . '

Verity gave a shout. She had noticed that Tommie Fox was among the group strolling towards her. 'Tommie, am I glad to see you . . . '

She looked round, but Stille had vanished as silently as he had arrived. She shivered.

'What is it, V?' Tommie said, concerned. 'You look as if you've seen a ghost. Who was that man you were talking to? Was he worrying you?'

'Oh, no,' she said, pulling herself together, 'but it is good to see you. Walk with me to the bus stop, will you? I'm just going to the *Gazette* to write a piece on the march. You can tell me what to say.'

She put her arm through his and together, surrounded by his friends who chattered amongst themselves like excited children, they strolled across the park. Verity held on to Tommie so tightly he was almost driven to protest, but then he saw she needed him and he liked to be needed.

At the *New Gazette*, she ran into the newspaper's proprietor who was about to be wafted up in his elevator to his eyrie.

'Verity!' Weaver called. 'That little woman – Daphne Hepple-Keen – is quite something. I admit it, I was mistaken. I thought she was a milk-and-water sort of woman. *Kinder, kirche, küche* – you know what I mean?' He took the cigar out of his mouth. 'She's really got things moving. Don't know how she's done it but both sides have agreed to let us organize a mercy mission to rescue the abandoned children of the war. She got Ribbentrop, no less, to talk Franco's people into giving her neutral Red Cross status, and the government is eating out of her hand. I've told Godber to make a big thing of it. Anway, where have you been?'

'The Jarrow marchers have reached London. I'm just going to write it up. There's going to be a big rally in Hyde Park this afternoon. Will you make it front page?'

Weaver looked doubtful. 'That's not for me to say. It's up to Godber.'

'Come off it, Joe. It's your decison.'

'I don't know. There's not much to say – page two, perhaps.'

'Page two! But Joe, these men have achieved a most extraordinary thing. They've brought the situation in the north to the attention of the south and the support they have had . . . it's very moving. The stories they have to tell . . . '

'We'll see. If there's a riot in Hyde Park, perhaps.'

'So what will you lead with?'

'HMS *London*'s back from her mercy mission to Spain packed with refugees. Oh, and Queen Mary has a slight cold . . . '

'Bah!' Verity exclaimed.

'And Edgar Wallace's books have been banned in Germany because they say he's a Jew, but his daughter says he's not a Jew . . . '

'Please, Joe, spare me the rest. I thought this was a newspaper not *Tatler*!'

'Well, if you don't like it, Verity . . . Godber's always begging me to fire you. And where's the book? If you want it serialized, I'll need it yesterday. I told Gollancz he might as well give it up if it isn't published soon. The King – I'm seeing him tomorrow at Fort Belvedere . . . it's all coming to a head.'

'Come on, Joe, be fair. I haven't had time . . . Anyway, you just said that I've given you a great campaign, courtesy of Daphne Hepple-Keen.'

'Was it you introduced me to Daphne?' he said, waving his cigar in the air. 'My memory isn't what it used to be.'

'Joe!' Verity exclaimed but, before she could say anything more, the lift gates clanged shut and she found herself watching Lord Weaver's feet disappear into the ether, leaving only the aroma of a half-smoked Havana cigar to proclaim that he had been there at all.

She sat in front of her typewriter and tried to think. She needed to write this article and it had to be so powerful that Joe wouldn't be able to 'spike' it. She had to write her book – she *had* to . . . . And then there were the letters. What should she do with them? Give them to Edward to return to Mrs Simpson, or should she give them to the Party after all? That was what she *ought* to do. As a Party member, it was her duty and if anyone found out she had not done so . . . well, she might have to fall on her sword. In any case, she believed – she truly believed – that the monarchy ought to be shown up as the rotten heart of a corrupt capitalist system which these letters demonstrated it was.

She hardly bothered to consider Major Stille's demands. Then she gasped as a thought struck her. Where were the letters? It was madness but she really couldn't remember what she had done with them. Had she left them on her desk or had she tossed them in a corner? The latter, she thought. But shouldn't she go back and retrieve them? Put them somewhere safe? Yes, but first she had to write this article.

15

Edward had telephoned Lampfrey and the Inspector had obligingly agreed to acompany him to Devizes to, as he put it, 'have a chat with Ruth Conway'.

'You'll have me carpeted,' Lampfrey said with gloomy relish.

'Don't worry, it'll be worth it. I think she'll have something to say which will make the trip worthwhile.'

Edward's confidence was not misplaced. Ruth Conway had got things to tell them – things she ought to have told Chief Inspector Pride, but had not.

'He was such a bully and so sure of himself,' she said angrily. 'He didn't give me time to tell him what I knew. I *thought* he believed I had killed Leo but I imagined he was clever enough to work out who had really done it. It never occurred to me that he'd have me arrested.'

'I'm sorry about that,' said Lampfrey, but Edward had the feeling he wasn't that sorry.

It turned out she had actually seen Hepple-Keen on Wednesday lunch-time, the day after Leo had left Haling to go to London. It was Pickering's day off, and she was alone in the house reading a novel in the drawing-room, when he had appeared at the front door quite without warning. She had been surprised to see him, of course, but it was lonely in that big house by herself and Hepple-Keen was, she thought, an attractive man. She had offered him refreshment, but he had explained he was in a hurry. He thought he might have left some papers behind in his room.

Miss Conway had seen it as the thinnest of pretexts for being admitted to the house but she had managed to persuade herself that he had come to see her. He had made a pretty speech – perfunctory enough, Edward imagined, reading between the lines, but sufficient to convince this plain, lonely woman that he had an interest in her. He had made her promise not to mention his visit to anyone and she hadn't.

She again made clear her dislike of Chief Inspector Pride. Lampfrey felt that, if he had interviewed her, he might have got her to tell him about Hepple-Keen's visit.

'The Chief Inspector shouted at me and I got flustered,' she said defensively. 'He's a rude, bad-mannered man. Geoffrey's a gentleman. He said he would come and see me again, but he hasn't yet,' she added mournfully.

It was hardly surprising as she was in prison, Edward thought grimly. He imagined Hepple-Keen's satisfaction when he heard she had been arrested. Even if she had confessed to the police that he had been to Haling that Wednesday, he could have denied it, said she was infatuated with him and, when he had told her he wasn't interested in her, had tried to throw suspicion on him by saying *he* had killed Scannon in a feeble attempt to save herself.

'But surely, Miss Conway, when Mr Scannon was poisoned you must have suspected something?' Lampfrey said disbelievingly.

'I did but . . . I had promised and . . . well, to tell the truth, I was frightened what Geoffrey might do. I mean, he trusted me but if I had betrayed him . . . '

Edward thought she had every right to be frightened. Hepple-Keen was not a man to cross. He must have thought he had her under his thumb but, the moment she gave any hint of causing trouble, he would have acted – and acted ruthlessly. This was a murderer who wouldn't have thought twice about killing again to save his neck.

'That was what I suspected,' Edward said, 'and why I was glad when I heard you were in prison. I feared that, once he had thought about it, he would have seen that to be safe he would have to kill you too. The problem was he had to get Leo's diary and poison the whisky. Perhaps he hoped you would drink from the decanter as well.'

'I don't drink spirits,' she said virtuously. 'Anyway, he wouldn't have hurt me . . . I think . . . '

'But how did he know about the diary?' Lampfrey inquired. 'He could hardly have known Scannon had named him as Mrs Harkness's murderer.'

'He might have guessed it,' Edward said. 'It was well known among his friends that Leo kept a highly indiscreet diary. He used to boast about it. In any case, my bet is that Leo was blackmailing him and had actually *told* him he had put it all down in the diary.'

'Blackmailing him?' Miss Conway said. 'About what?'

'I don't know,' Edward confessed, 'but it must be something political. Perhaps Hepple-Keen had got too close to Mosley, or perhaps Leo wanted him to get closer – to do something for the BUF he didn't want to do. There must have been something which would have damaged his political career if it became known. You're going to have to ask him that, Lampfrey.'

'But why poison his whisky? He'd got the diary so why kill Leo?' Miss Conway asked.

'Because Leo had some evidence against him. Reading the diary, he realised Leo knew too much to be allowed to live. He had to be silenced.'

'All right,' Lampfrey conceded, 'let's accept that for the moment. But how could he poison the whisky? It was in the tantalus and that was locked.'

'I think he said his goodbyes to you, Miss Conway,' Edward said, 'and then went to the gardener's shed, took some of the rat poison, re-entered the house and did the dirty work on the tantalus. You see, he had been in the secret police and I'm sure opening a simple lock like the one on the tantalus would have been child's play.'

'But that suggests killing Scannon was unpremeditated,' Lampfrey said slowly. 'Otherwise he would have come prepared with poison.'

'I would guess he read the diary and then decided he could not afford to let Leo live. And don't forget the episode of Miss Browne and the rat in her bed. He knew where the rat poison was kept without having to bring it with him. I imagine he wouldn't have had any trouble re-entering the house without being seen, Miss Conway? He would have needed at least ten minutes to tamper with the whisky – probably nearer twenty.'

She considered for a moment. 'No, it was the middle of the day. The front door is not locked until nightfall and there were windows open. I had told him when I opened the front door that it was Pickering's day off and I was by myself. I went to lie down on my bed after I had said good-bye to him. I had rather a headache. In fact, I think I told him so.'

Lampfrey grimaced. 'This is all speculation. Sir Geoffrey's visit to you, Miss Conway, may have been completely innocent. Still, when we go back to the station, I will have to persuade Chief Inspector Pride to tackle him. It may not be so easy. I wish you had told us before about his visit to Haling . . . I know, I know, the Chief Inspector can be difficult to interrupt. The trouble is, once he's made up his mind – and I should tell you, he *has* made up his mind – he doesn't like changing it.'

'But you believe me?' she asked anxiously. 'I can see now I've been a fool. I don't know why I should think anyone would be interested in me.'

'We believe you,' Edward said, taking her hand. 'And you mustn't think no one will be interested in you, but you are right to . . . to think carefully where men are concerned. You're a rich woman now and you will find some men are interested in that, even if they pretend not to be. Promise me . . . promise me you will be careful.'

'I promise,' she said, but Edward was by no means easy in his mind.

When they left Devizes prison, Lampfrey said to Edward, 'Don't expect any thanks for setting the cat among the pigeons like this. I'm going to get hell.'

'Better it comes out now than in a court of law with the wrong person in the dock, eh, Inspector?' he retorted, unhelpfully.

That evening, as he had promised, Edward gave Verity, Charlotte, Adrian, Tommie Fox and Ellen Wilkinson dinner at the Café Royal to celebrate the end of the Jarrow March. But it was a gloomy party which foregathered in the Grill Room to quaff champagne cocktails and toy with Omelette Arnold Bennett, *Crêpe de Volaille Royale* and *Escalope de Veau Maison*.

Verity had tried to duck out of it altogether, but Edward had pressed her. 'I want to tell you how I got on with Ruth Conway. I think I've cracked it and, anyway, we promised to celebrate the success of the march.'

'Oh, I don't know, Edward, I've got so much to do . . . '

'On the bloody book?'

'Yes, on the bloody book,' she said irritably. 'Also, I'm not sure Ellen feels the march was such a success.'

'I don't understand. Surely it's been a triumph? The petition has been handed in to Parliament.'

'Yes, but now it's such an anticlimax. Don't you see, London just absorbs events, even ones as big as the Jarrow March. It's like a sponge. London, by which I mean society, just ignores it and nothing changes. Weaver won't even put it on the front page.'

'Oh well, I still say we should celebrate. We owe it to Ellen. We can't let her feel no one cares. And I chose the Café Royal with care for this occasion. It's full of journalists and other riff-raff.'

'Thank you very much. All right then, I'll be there. Now, clear off. I've got to work even if you don't.'

Edward was hurt by Verity's lack of interest in what he had found out from Ruth Conway and now, seeing the gloomy faces of his guests reflected in the ornate gilt-framed mirrors, he felt cheated of something – he didn't quite know what.

'So there it is – I'm certain Hepple-Keen is our murderer,' he concluded, having told them of his visit to Devizes.

His words were greeted with silence. He hadn't expected to be mobbed, but a word of praise might have been welcome. At last, Verity said grudgingly, 'It sounds very speculative to me.'

'Pride will get the truth out of Hepple-Keen once he sees it's all up.'

'But is it?' she persisted. 'I think a practised politician could make mincemeat of it all.' Edward started to speak but she stopped him with a wave of her glass. 'No. I'm sorry, Edward, but it doesn't sound right to me. And, in any case, what am I going to say to Daphne tomorrow? Daphne's his wife,' she explained to Ellen, 'and she's doing wonders for the abandoned children of the civil war. We've got a committee meeting tomorrow. What do I tell her? Lord Edward Corinth thinks your husband's a murderer, but don't let it prevent you carrying on the good work?'

'Lampfrey was convinced,' Edward said defensively.

'Well, I'm not,' she said, and lapsed into a sullen silence.

Ellen, seeing that the dinner was turning into a disaster and liking the young man with the aquiline nose and firm jaw too much to let it become one, decided she had better change the subject. She started talking about Jarrow. Among friends she could allow herself to be bitter, however. 'It's odd how traditions linger . . . how social strata run true to type. I was really hurt when the Bishop of Durham called us a revolutionary mob, but I shouldn't have been surprised. In 1810 his predecessor lent his stables as a concentration camp and had striking miners chained to the mangers. When the class struggle comes to the surface, "progress" is seen to be a very thin veneer.'

Verity said hesitantly, 'I agree with that. What I saw at Toledo convinced me that civilization is nothing but an illusion we find it useful to believe in. Let me tell you what it was like in the end when the Moors and the Legion raised the siege. I have just been trying to write about it for my book, so it's in my mind.'

'It pains you to talk about it?' Tommie said gently.

'It pains me here,' she touched her heart, 'but it would pain me more to pretend to forget.'

'What is the Legion?' Charlotte ventured.

'It's almost the same as the French Foreign Legion but worse – much worse. It was founded in the 1920s by a general called José Millán Astray. He would greet each new recruit with the words "You were dead when you arrived here. You have arisen from the dead and you must pay for your new life with your death. *Viva Muertre!*" Gibberish, maybe, but it makes me shiver. Along with the Moors, they are the most ferocious fighters in the war. They don't know the meaning of the word "mercy".'

She stopped and her face went quite white. Edward risked saying, 'Can you tell us what happened, V?'

His honest, familiar voice steadied her a little and she managed a wan smile. 'It was in those last few days of September – not so long ago, but it seems an age. We did not know that the Moors had broken the Republican lines at Maqueda, twenty-four miles to the north-west of Toledo. Our leaders thought they had all the time in the world to destroy the Alcázar and the few army officers who still held in it. Our people placed a huge mine under the gate in the north-east corner of the fortress. When it exploded, we would overwhelm the defenders. It was inevitable and the world's press would be there to witness it. Then, at dawn on the twenty-fifth, three Nationalist bombers came over the city and bombed our positions. The next day, about two o'clock, one of our guns brought down one of their planes. The pilot bailed out and came down alive. It was the most awful thing I have ever witnessed. I tried to do something to stop it but I was pulled away or I, too, might have been murdered. The women of the town attacked him with razors and cut off his genitals and then trampled him to death. I heard him shout "Oh! Mamá!" before he died.

'I don't understand why but our generals still did not explode the mine. They waited and waited until it was too late. I think now they may have been in the enemy's pay but I don't know. All I do know is, that when at last it did explode – sending up a huge plume of smoke and dust – as they advanced our men came face to face with the enemy. The Moors in their white turbans and the Legion had come on us quite unexpectedly. I remember the sound of them – they did not shriek or scream but barked like dogs. Then we were all running. At the Alcántara Bridge, we were gunned down and the Tagus turned red with the blood of men falling from the bridge. By nightfall – and it was a perfect night, with a beautiful moon and crystalline sky – all resistance had come to an end and the Moors set about killing. I don't know how many they killed – civilians as well as militia, they said there was no difference – but some say a thousand. Fires were burning everywhere and the smell of burning flesh nauseated me. I was beyond fear, beyond exhaustion. I just wanted to die.'

'But you didn't. You escaped,' Ellen said. 'How did you manage it?'

'Chivalry, I suppose,' said Verity, with a rattling laugh. 'Chivalry from the people I have just told you did not know the meaning of the word. I had crawled round the side of the Alcázar and suddenly found myself with a group of soldiers from the Legion. They asked who I was and I said I was a woman – I can tell you, by then it wasn't too obvious – and an English newspaper correspondent. I showed them the baby and that seemed to confuse them, but they knew enough to take me to their officer – a boy in his teens.'

'A baby? What baby was this?' Ellen asked in amazement.

'Oh yes, didn't I say? Crawling through the rubble, I found this baby underneath a dead woman – the child's mother, I suppose. As soon as I touched it, it began to cry so I knew it was alive. I didn't know what to do. You'll understand the state of mind I was in when I tell you I seriously considered leaving it where it was.'

'But you didn't,' Ellen said gently.

'No, I took it with me – like an inconvenient parcel. I dropped it once when I tripped, but it seemed determined not to die.'

'This officer you stumbled upon – what did he do when he saw you and the baby?' Tommie asked, his eyes intent on Verity.

'He was supervising a group of our men . . . prisoners. To my horror, as I watched, he had them lined up against a wall and calmly ordered his men to shoot them, one by one. He smiled as he did so and watched me, as if to see how I would react. I don't know – I tried to shield my eyes behind my hands but they wouldn't let me. When the last man was dead, he pointed his pistol at me and I was certain it was my last moment on earth. Then, he lowered it and bowed to me, in mockery perhaps, because you can imagine the state I was in. I was filthy dirty, my clothes were torn and I was weeping. And I was still holding the baby – well, as I say, you can imagine. Anyway, this boy passed me over to a priest – there were many priests attached to the Legion – and he took me to General Franco who arrived at Toledo the next day.'

'And he released you?' Edward said.

'Yes, without even having me interrogated,' she said bitterly. 'I was handed over to some American journalists. I suppose he had no wish to be seen to be "uncivilized".'

'Gosh!' Adrian exclaimed, inadequately. 'It must have been terrible.'

'It changed me,' she said simply. 'You'll say I'm melodramatic but, once you've looked death in the face, it does change you.'

There was a moment's silence as they each thought about this. Then Charlotte said, hesitatingly, in case she was treading on dangerous ground, 'And the baby? What happened to the baby?'

'I took it to Madrid – to an orphanage,' she said, shortly.

It was as though she was waiting for someone to say she ought to have brought it back to England with her and adopted it, but if anyone was thinking it, no one dared say it.

'I think the worst thing was that, before we left, the American journalists took me on a tour of the ruins. I had been fed and bathed and thought I was more or less all right – but then we came to the swimming pool. Yes, the Alcázar actually had a swimming pool but it was empty of course. Or rather it wasn't empty; it was full of dead bodies. The stench was unbearable because the sun was very hot. One of the Americans asked the soldier in charge why he did not cremate the bodies. The officer was shocked: "Señor," he said, "we are Catholics!"'

Verity was now shaking with dry sobs and it was obvious to all of them that she was in a bad way. Edward still dared to think it had been good that she should have told her tale. It might help her come to terms with what she had experienced. Ellen Wilkinson said her goodbyes and kissed Verity. Tommie also made his farewells so it was left to Edward and the Hassels to take her home. When they arrived in the King's Road, they found a police car outside the front door.

'Oh my God! What now?' Charlotte exclaimed.

Adrian and Edward got out of the cab and went over to talk to the policeman standing outside the door. Adrian returned to inform them they had been burgled. 'Someone actually saw the burglars drive off in a black car.'

'But what have we got worth stealing?' Charlotte said, puzzled. 'I would like to believe there are some discerning art thieves in London, but I rather doubt it.'

Then Verity spoke in a small, low voice from the back of the cab: 'I know what they were looking for.'

16

Major Stille's men had caused havoc. It was perfectly evident that this was no ordinary burglary but rather an act of deliberate vandalism. Many of Adrian's paintings had been ripped or defaced but, what was much worse, Charlotte's photographs of her parents, and one of her aged six with a favourite dog, had been torn from their frames, crumpled and ripped.

'It's vicious!' she said angrily. 'Vicious and hateful. How could people behave this way?'

'Only too easily, I'm afraid, Charley,' Edward said, taking her in his arms to comfort her. 'This is the modern age, God help us.'

'And it's all my fault!' Verity exclaimed. 'You see, Dannie came to see me – when was it? yesterday – and she gave me the bloody letters.'

'Mrs Simpson's letters!'

'Are there any others?' she inquired, ironically.

'So she *had* stolen them! Damn it, I was sure she had! But I don't see: why did she give them to *you*?'

'She's broken with Weaver so she wouldn't give them to him. She's broken with Stille who seems to want them badly enough to have paid her to get them for him. So she thought she'd give them to me. She wants me to cause trouble by giving them to the Party.'

Edward was icy. 'And have you?'

'No. If you must know, I forgot all about them. I chucked them in a corner somewhere.'

'You forgot all about them! For God's sake, woman, which corner?'

'Don't talk to me like that, Edward. I've had just about enough tonight with your ridiculous, horrible party and now this. I'm so sorry Adrian, Charlotte, I'm just so sorry . . . I'm not fit for decent people to live with.'

Verity collapsed into a chair and burst into tears. Adrian sat beside her on the floor and held her hand. Charlotte stroked her head and said, 'You're exhausted, that's all. We love you, Verity. This isn't your fault. It's what we have to fight.'

'But where are they – the letters?' Edward said desperately.

'Damn the letters,' Adrian said, 'What we care about is Verity.'

'They're in a corner in my bedroom, I think,' she said, sniffing. 'I threw them under some copies of the *Gazette*.'

Without another word, Edward strode out of the room and up the stairs. Verity's room was a complete shambles with furniture and bedding everywhere. A wardrobe had been overturned and a table cut across with what might have been an axe. In one corner, under a chair, he saw a pile of newspapers. He moved the chair with some difficulty and knelt to go through them. He was breathing fast and he noticed, quite coldly, that his hands were shaking. At first, he thought there was nothing there except back issues of the *New Gazette*, but then he saw them – a small bundle wedged under a three-month-old paper. There were seven altogether. He could hardly believe he had them in his hands at last. They had caused him such trouble and here they were. He walked downstairs to find Verity where he had left her.

'I've found them. I'll take them back to Mrs Simpson as soon as possible.'

'Hold on a minute,' Adrian said angrily. 'What does Verity say? They were given to her.'

'Dannie had no right to give them to her,' Edward said.

'Oh, let him have them,' Verity said wearily. 'I'm sick to death of the whole thing.'

'Thank you!'

'And that goes for you too, Edward.'

The next morning Verity insisted on getting up and going into the *New Gazette* despite Charlotte's instant diagnosis that she looked like death not even warmed up. There were black circles under her eyes and her skin had that grey, waxy look which made her avert her eyes when she glanced in the mirror. Perversely, she chose to wear no make-up except for a scarlet slash on her lips.

When she got to the office, there was a message that she was to go straight up to the top floor. Miss Barnstable just had time to tut-tut and say she looked as though she needed a bath before showing her into the great man's presence.

Even Weaver noticed that she wasn't looking her usual self.

'You look a bit rough, Verity,' he said peering at her. 'Been burning the candle at both ends?'

Since he never commented on a woman's appearance except, perfunctorily, immediately prior to suggesting bed, Verity knew – if she hadn't known already – that she really must look bad. Characteristically, it made her stick out her chin and tough it out. She thought she might as well go for the shock attack.

'Dannie came round the other day to give me those letters of Mrs Simpson.'

'Oh? And what did you do with them?' he asked with studied indifference.

'She wanted me to give them to the *Daily Worker*. I can't think why, but she seemed not to want to give them to you.'

'And did you . . . give them to your Commie friends?'

'No. I gave them to Edward. Dannie said she was your mistress but had now transferred her affections to a German air ace.'

'I shouldn't believe everything that lady tells you,' Weaver said coldly.

Verity knew he was close to lashing her with the full force of his rage. These rages were rare, and she had never experienced one, but those who had spoke of them with awe. She could not, however, prevent herself making one more stab at her employer in an effort to pierce his armour of arrogance.

'Did you require her to seduce Edward or was that – what shall I call it? – one of the "perks" of the job?'

There was a pause but the expression which passed over Lord Weaver's face was not quite what she had anticipated. If it was not shame, it was something close to it.

'What Miss Dannhorn does in her spare time is nothing to do with me,' he said, with an effort. 'Now, we must prepare ourselves for Lady Hepple-Keen's arrival. I'm going to have to ask her to step down from chairing this charity for the Spanish children. It won't do to have the wife of an MP accused of murder taking a leading part. I thought I might let you explain it to her. I shall leave you alone with her in this office for ten minutes. That ought to be ample.'

He was clearly taking pleasure in making Verity do his dirty work for him. There would be no question of 'standing by' the Hepple-Keens. They were now just an embarrassment.

'How do you know Hepple-Keen is suspected of murder?'

'Edward was good enough to ring me earlier this morning. He thought I should know. He wanted to save me embarrassment, I think.'

Verity fumed inwardly. Why had Edward not told her what he intended to do? She ought to have given Mrs Simpson's letters to the *Daily Worker*. She couldn't think why she hadn't.

'And if Daphne refuses?' she said.

'Then, of course, we disband the charity.'

'I see. And aren't you interested to know what's happened to Mrs Simpson's letters?'

'Edward told me that too. He has an appointment with the King at the Fort today. I must say, Verity, I don't understand why I had to hear this from Edward and not from you – my employee.'

This fairly took the wind out of Verity's sails and made her feel a fool. 'I would have . . . ' she began. Damn Edward. It was not something she was going to forgive easily.

'In any case,' Weaver went on, 'it's of little account now. You may as well know, the King has decided to abdicate.'

'Oh, I see,' she said weakly.

'All the world will know tomorrow but, if word leaks out before then and it is traced back to this office, you understand you will never work for this newspaper again.'

There was something so vitriolic in the deadly calm with which he made this threat that Verity could scarcely believe this was the same man she had so recently been licensed to tease and whom she had treated almost as a father. She was about to protest when something stopped her. She had the imagination to see that Weaver himself had been humiliated by Dannie – the story of her defection would be round London society in no time – and also by the King, who had obviously refused his guidance and acted with his usual disregard for the feelings of his friends.

'Of course. I won't breathe a word of it – not even to Edward.'

'He knows,' Weaver said grimly.

'Your Majesty.' Edward made a small bow. Mrs Simpson smiled at him with the faint, distracted air of someone quite out of their depth. The King seemed to be smaller and less physically prepossessing than when he had last seen him but, as Edward realized, it was hardly surprising given the strain he must have been under. All at once he wanted nothing more than to be out of their presence. He was, as Molly had once labelled him, simply a messenger boy. There must be not the slightest hint that he was expecting praise for his efforts, let alone reward. He turned to Mrs Simpson.

'You asked me to recover certain letters which the late Mrs Harkness took from you when you were staying with the Brownlows. Here they are.'

He handed them over and she took them so limply he thought she might drop them.

'That's so good of you, Lord Edward. I like to keep everything from David safe.'

She smiled at the King and he smiled back – a smile of total trust, almost of complicity. They were like two naughty schoolchildren playing at being kings and queens. There was something so unconvincing about their behaviour that Edward was tempted to laugh. The situation was all the more comic because, although the couple acted as if they were sitting on thrones, they were actually in armchairs in the rather poky little drawing-room which the King found so much more comforting than the great drawing-rooms of Windsor Castle and Buckingham Palace. The stags' heads on the walls, the photographs, the rather ghastly pictures, the overstuffed sofas – it was a parody of a drawing-room, reminding Edward of the 'set' from a West End comedy.

There was no further attempt at conversation. Edward clearly wasn't going to be asked how he came by the letters. He had a sudden desire to puncture this dream of royalty, if only for an instant.

'Oh, I almost forgot, sir. I found these in Mrs Harkness's flat.' He thrust the little packet of love letters at the King. For an instant, he thought he was going to refuse to take it. Then, gingerly, he put out his hand and, without once looking Edward in the eye, took the packet. Without glancing at it, he put it on the table beside him. He said nothing at all.

Five minutes later, Edward was back in the Lagonda. As he switched on the engine, he whistled and then said aloud, 'That man's no good. Hollow man, hollow crown.'

It was December 2nd 1936. The next day the newspapers broke their silence and the British people read that, unknown to them, their King had fallen in love with an American divorcee and intended to marry her.

'I'm so sorry.' Stumbling, awkward, Verity had told Daphne Hepple-Keen that she was no longer allowed to help the Spanish children because her husband was suspected of murder.

'But it's so unfair,' she said at last.

'I know it is,' Verity agreed.

'No, I mean it's so unfair because he didn't do the murder. Well, of course, he had to kill that horrible man Scannon because he was blackmailing us, but it was I who killed Mrs Harkness. She was an evil woman.'

'What are you saying, Daphne?' Verity said, horrified. 'You didn't kill Molly.'

'Oh yes, I did,' she said firmly. 'You see, Geoffrey was sent to warn her not to make a nuisance of herself – teach her a lesson – but, somehow, she got round him. I don't expect it was difficult,' she added bitterly. 'They became lovers. Geoffrey has had many lovers and I don't mind that much so long as he remains faithful to the family.'

Verity found she could understand what she meant. It was what she herself had felt when she had learnt that Edward had slept with Dannie. It was nothing to do with the rules of being married or not married. Hepple-Keen had sinned against the very core of their relationship: the family.

Daphne was speaking again and Verity made herself pay attention. 'Then it turns out she's pregnant and she says it's Geoffrey's baby and she wants to marry him. Well, of course, I couldn't allow that, could I?'

'You couldn't allow her to have your husband's child?'

'No. Anything but that.'

'Do you know when they became lovers? I mean, it could have been someone else's child. She was . . . seeing someone else, you know.'

'Oh no. I always know when Geoffrey has a new woman. Anyway, she told me. It was in the summer . . . he had first met her in June. She told me they had sometimes made love outside. She said he liked it being dangerous.'

Verity wondered if Hepple-Keen had guessed how dangerous it was going to be for him. 'So you went to her room that night you were at Haling . . . ?'

'Yes. It was very late but Geoffrey hadn't come to bed. I thought he might be with her. But when I listened at her door, I realized it wasn't my husband but Lord Edward. I had to wait until he had left her. It was a long time. I don't know what it is about that woman but she attracted men like moths to a flame.'

'Lord Edward wasn't . . . that way . . . I mean he was just *talking* to Molly.'

'That's what he told you, was it, dear? Never mind.'

For a moment she sounded almost motherly. Then her face crumpled, as if she suddenly realized what she had done. 'I only meant to talk to her but she laughed at me. She said Geoffrey was bored with me. She said I was . . . ' She hesitated, as if trying to recall Molly's exact words. '. . . a frumpish old boot that no man would ever want to make love to again. I called her a whore and then I went.'

'So you didn't . . . ?'

'Oh yes, I did,' she said again, and for a second Verity was reminded of some nightmare pantomime dame. 'I knew she was waiting for my husband and I couldn't allow her to see him and persuade him to do something stupid. I went back to my room to collect my evening gloves and then I waited in the corridor until I heard her go to the lavatory. While she was out of her room, I let myself in. I had noticed the bottle beside her bed. I use veronal myself so I knew what I was doing. I poured it all into the flask on her bedside table. Then I went back to my room but Geoffrey still wasn't there, so I got into bed and went to sleep.' She sounded satisfied – almost proud of her competence. 'I thought no one had seen me but it turned out Mr Scannon had. He was so sly, that man. He told me later he hardly ever went to sleep before three in the morning and I don't think he went to bed at all that night.'

'But he didn't know what you had done?'

'No, but in the morning, when Lord Edward found her dead, he discovered one of my gloves on a table and guessed immediately. You see, I had worn gloves because I know all about fingerprints. I read quite a lot of detective stories. I get them from Boots,' she added brightly. 'But the doorknob was stiff to turn so I took off one of my gloves when I left the room and I must have left it behind.'

'Yes, I remember, it was stiff.' Verity had a vivid recollection of trying to open the door with one hand, while holding the rat in the other, when she had occupied Molly's room. 'And Leo Scannon tried to blackmail you?'

'He tried to blackmail Geoffrey. He told him what I had done – not that I cared. He said he would tell the police I was a murderer.'

'What did he say . . . your husband . . . when you admitted what you had done?'

'He said he loved me. He said she wasn't carrying his child and that she was a whore and a liar but, of course, I didn't believe him.'

'Perhaps it was true. Perhaps he does love you in his way.'

'Oh no. He has never loved me. I asked him why he had married me, and he couldn't answer.'

'So Scannon wanted something from your husband, not you?'

'Yes. He said Geoffrey's career would be ruined if his wife was arrested for murder, and he was right. I knew that.'

'But what did he want from your husband in return for his silence?'

'I don't know – something about Sir Oswald Mosley. Mr Scannon was a great friend of his and Geoffrey used to be as well. When Geoffrey decided he had gone too far and he wanted to leave the BUF, Mosley didn't like it. He was too useful.'

'But Scannon and your husband were Conservative MPs.'

'They thought it was safer to remain in the Party but actually they were working for Mosley. They thought the

Führer was wonderful – a god. They thought England should be on Germany's side in the struggle. That's what they called it: "the struggle". I never quite understood who they were struggling against. The Jews, I suppose.'

'But listen, I think you're wrong. I think your husband did kill Mr Scannon to protect you.'

'To protect me! Why on earth do you think he would do that?' Daphne Hepple-Keen looked at Verity incredulously. 'He hates me and I hate him.' She spoke with such utter certainty that Verity found herself shivering. She knew for certain she was in the presence of a madwoman. 'You're looking ill,' Daphne said, as though noticing Verity properly for the first time. 'You must look after yourself. No one else will, you know. Not even that man you love.'

Verity blushed. 'I don't . . . ' she began, but Daphne was talking again. She was like a drunkard who had been off the bottle for some time and was now indulging in a binge – a binge of talk.

'The only thing I care about is the children. We all know they are going to have a horrible time of it when they are grown up, particularly the girls, so we must do everything we can for them. I'm sorry I won't be able to help any longer with the children in Spain. You must promise me not to give it up. It is your duty.'

Not ten minutes but a full half-hour had passed since Lord Weaver had vacated his office to enable Verity to tell Daphne it was all over as far as the charity was concerned. Now he wanted to get back behind his desk and was curious to know what was taking Verity so long. He had imagined that Lady Hepple-Keen would come storming out in floods of tears after ten minutes, but that had not happened.

'Ah,' he said awkwardly as he opened the door, 'Verity has probably told you about the charity. I'm so sorry about it but . . . '

'Oh yes, that's all right, but you must continue with it, Lord Weaver.'

'I will,' he said, delighted to see that she was taking it so calmly.

'I won't have the time,' she went on blithely. 'I'll be in prison.'

'Whatever do you mean, Daphne?' he asked.

'I've just been telling Miss Browne how I murdered Mrs Harkness. It's such a relief to tell someone. Will you be good enough to call the police? I think I ought to tell them now, don't you? But, please, be quick, I want to get back to the children.'

17

They were having breakfast at Mersham – Connie, Edward and Verity. It was a peaceful sight. The newspapers were strewn over the table – a sloppiness the Duke could never abide so it was fortunate that he was in London attending the House of Lords. The munching on bacon and eggs (Edward), kippers (Verity) and porridge (Connie) was only interrupted by occasional cries of amazement.

'It says in the *News Chronicle* that Wallis's flat in Cumberland Terrace has been stoned,' Verity said, 'and the crowd chanted, "Hands off our King – abdication means revolution."'

'That's too absurd!' the Duchess expostulated.

'Oh, I don't know,' Verity said, careful not to catch Edward's eye. 'Oh look! This is even better: Mosley and his mob paraded through Westminster shouting "Stand by the King" and "How would you like a cabinet of old busybodies to pick your girl for you?"' She raised her head considerably. 'That must be wrong. How could you chant such a long sentence? It doesn't have any rhythm.'

'Oh, well, you would know,' Edward said, unwisely, and Verity threatened to throw a slice of buttered toast at him.

'Well, I don't care to read any more. I think it is all too horrible,' the Duchess said, folding up her copy of *The Times*. 'I don't blame Mrs Simpson – I feel sorry for her –

but I do blame the King. He's endangered the monarchy. He'll never be forgiven for it.'

'He's a bad lot,' Edward agreed. 'He treated me as if he'd accidentally come face to face with the bootboy.'

'Tut tut!' Verity mocked. She was looking a different person from the thin, almost haggard girl Connie had collected from the Hassels' three days earlier. When, in a terse telephone call from Edward, she had heard the state Verity was in – totally exhausted and unable to do anything but rail against Edward and Lord Weaver in particular and the male species in general – the Duchess had swept up to London in the Rolls. Disregarding her protestations that she couldn't come because she had a book to write, Connie had in all but name kidnapped her.

'Now listen to me, Verity,' Connie had said sounding almost fierce. 'You are dog-tired. You've not been eating. There are circles under your eyes which tell me you haven't been sleeping either. Mr and Mrs Hassel are at their wits' end to know what to do. If you want to avoid a total breakdown, you must come back with me to Mersham and rest for at least a week.'

'But,' Verity began feebly, 'the Duke . . .'

'The Duke's not a monster, you know, and anyway, with all this about the King, he's staying in London until it's all over.'

Edward hadn't been able to get away from town immediately. He had things to tie up with Chief Inspector Pride and Lord Weaver. In any case, Connie said it was better if she had Verity to herself for a few days 'before you come down and confuse the poor child'.

Pride had been surprisingly polite when Weaver had summoned him to his office to hear Lady Hepple-Keen's confession. He had shot a look at Verity, which might have made her blanch had she not been too busy comforting Daphne to notice. Daphne was by now sobbing and asking how her children would manage if she went to prison.

Fortunately, it had not occurred to her that she was in danger of being hanged. It was clear, even to Pride, that she was not entirely in her right mind and a doctor was called.

Verity asked if there was anyone she would like to be with her, praying that she would not ask for her husband who was in prison charged with one murder which – if Daphne was to be believed – he had not committed and one which he had. Verity's prayer was answered. Daphne had a sister who, when she rang her and explained that Daphne had admitted to murder and needed succour, proved admirably calm and competent. She came round in a taxi and took her home to be with her children. Pride had hesitated before permitting this. He was aware that he ought to take her into custody but even he quailed at having a hysterical woman in his keep and, as there was no likelihood that she was going to abscond, he released her into her sister's care. She was to be delivered to Scotland Yard the next morning, accompanied by her lawyer.

Verity had been deeply shocked by Daphne's confession and subsequent arrest. When everyone had departed – Daphne touchingly unwilling to let go of her – she had to take refuge with Miss Barnstable on whose substantial bosom she had wept and been comforted. It was not the behaviour of a hardened war correspondent and she was ashamed of her weakness. She was not much cheered, when she returned to Weaver's office, to be congratulated.

'What a coup!' he enthused. 'To have had a murderer confess in our office . . . in *my* office, and not any old murderer but the wife of an MP who is also accused of murder. An old-fashioned scoop if ever there was one! I can just see the headline . . . No, I can't . . . Miss Barnstable, get me Mr Godber right away, will you . . . '

The *New Gazette* had its scoop and Verity was hailed as its originator, much to Godber's fury. The press interest was intense but to her relief, short-lived. When news of the King's decision to abdicate came through, the whole of Fleet Street cleared its pages to concentrate on what all the papers recognized as an historic event. Nothing would ever be the same again, was the general feeling. The unthinkable had happened and now anything became possible.

On his way down to Mersham two days later, Edward called in at Marlborough police station. Lampfrey suggested going to the pub as it was almost lunch-time and neither of them had eaten. Each with a pint in his hand and a white-foam moustache, they found a corner where they could not be overheard. Lampfrey found it hard to know what to talk about first – the arrest of the Hepple-Keens or the King's abdication. Edward settled the matter by giving him a brief account of his audience with the King and how disgusted he had been.

'The man's as weak as water with a strain of obstinacy like a spoilt child's. He never said a word about Molly – well, I suppose I knew he wouldn't do that – but, I don't know, he wasn't even ashamed of himself, and the lady wasn't much better.'

When they had finished discussing the abdication, the policeman said, 'I still don't quite understand what happened to Mrs Harkness or rather, *why* it happened. I can see that Lady Hepple-Keen – poor woman – hated and feared her husband. I could understand her killing *him* but why kill Mrs Harkness?'

'You have to understand the strength of a mother's love,' Edward said in his lecturing voice. 'She hated her husband as a man but he fulfilled a vital function for her. He completed the family. He was a father and, for her, that was a crucial role which no one else could take on. Her children were the only thing she cared about – she was a sheep except where they were concerned, and then she was a tiger. Verity noticed it at dinner at Haling – so did I,' he added modestly. 'She could not bear the idea of children being ill treated. That was why she felt so strongly about the refugee children in Spain.'

'That was genuine?'

'Oh yes, I'm convinced of it. She cared all right. She cared most, of course, about her own brood. They had to be protected at all costs. When she went to speak to Mrs Harkness that night, it was to beg her to leave her husband alone. Somehow, she had discovered she had become his mistress. I don't suppose he made much effort to conceal it. He was cruel to her in that sort of way, I believe. However, she had no thought of killing her until Mrs Harkness was stupid and cruel enough to tell her she was pregnant with Geoffrey Hepple-Keen's child. That was the breaking point and it really sent her mad. She went out of the room in a state of total despair. If her husband wanted to divorce her she wouldn't know how to go on. She wasn't one of those modern women you read about who would have said "good riddance" and gone on to live the life she wanted. She needed her husband – however inadequate he was – and she was prepared to kill to keep him. She went back to her room briefly and then returned, hoping to gain entry to Mrs Harkness's bedroom. She paced about in the corridor until she heard her go to the bathroom and then, seizing the moment, slipped into her room, poured the veronal into the flask and left. It shows she wasn't thinking straight, taking the empty veronal bottle with her. However, Molly can't have noticed. Maybe she had already taken Maalox. She must have taken a swig from her flask – probably more than a swig – and then sunk into her last sleep.'

'But the door was locked in the morning and we couldn't find the key.'

'Miss Dannhorn went into Mrs Harkness's room through the door which connected with my bedroom but she left through the other door – the one leading on to the corridor. She locked it and took the key.'

'But why, for goodness' sake?'

'Out of devilry . . . to confuse the issue? I never got the chance of asking her. She must have been shocked to find Mrs Harkness dead, but she's a cool customer. She made her search, found the letters under the pillow and then decided to mystify the whole thing by locking the door – thereby hinting that the murder and the theft of the letters

303

must have been carried out by the same person, who had got in through the window using the creeper as a ladder.'

'But the white glove Scannon found . . . that was Lady Hepple-Keen's, not Miss Dannhorn's?'

'Yes, the doorknob was stiff – I noticed that myself when Verity had the room. It took her ages to open the door after she found the rat in her bed. So Lady Hepple-Keen took off one glove to open it. She had the veronal bottle in her hand. She wasn't thinking straight. She would have done better to have left the veronal bottle behind and kept her gloves on. But there we are. It shows the murder was unpremeditated and the result of panic. All the evidence confirms that and I'm hoping it will weigh with the judge.'

Lampfrey looked dubious. 'I don't know about that. The fact that she went back to her room to fetch her gloves, with the express intention of not leaving fingerprints, suggests premeditation to me.'

'Not in my view – for what it's worth. She was mad when she killed Mrs Harkness. Her reason for killing was not that of a sane person. I don't dispute that she did it as surely as if she had cut her throat. Even though she didn't administer the poison herself, leaving that lethal brew by her bed in a flask she could see she had been drinking from . . . I suppose I should have realized who had committed the murder earlier, but I couldn't see the motive. There were motives for almost anyone else to have killed Mrs Harkness except her.'

'And of course we were confused by the open window and the creeper – which anyone might have climbed up.'

'Except they didn't. I must say I thought it was unlikely,' Edward added comfortably.

'Do you think Sir Geoffrey did go to Mrs Harkness's room? I mean, did they have a tryst?'

'I don't know. I don't think she would have been surprised if he had.'

'To plead with her not to give him up?'

'Maybe. My belief is she had not yet given him his quittance and that she intended to tell him the affair was at an end that weekend . . . that evening, perhaps. If he did go to her room, he would have found her dead. Chief Inspector Pride will get that out of him.'

'And when Scannon was killed . . . ?'

'Well, like you, I thought it must have been either Hepple-Keen or Carstairs. I never thought Miss Conway had done it – she's been released now?'

'Oh yes.'

'Good! When I talked to Carstairs, I saw it certainly wasn't him. He was too transparent. He is what my brother would call a cad and a bounder, but he isn't a killer – except of animals, of course. He was – and is – a great hunter but quite out of place in London. I gather he's on his way back to the colony?'

'Yes. Apparently, rather to everyone's surprise, he did quite well here – met a lot of important people. Was that anything to do with you, my lord?'

'I gave him a couple of introductions,' Edward said modestly. 'Anyway, if Hepple-Keen killed Scannon it had to be because he was being blackmailed, but there I came unstuck. It was Verity who spotted that I had gone off the rails and my theory didn't ring true. When we had dinner at the Café Royal to celebrate the success of the Jarrow march I was miffed when she called my summary of the case mere speculation – and yet . . . '

'So Miss Browne "cracked the case"? Smart lady,' the Inspector said admiringly.

'She did, as you say, "crack the case" but in the process, I think, cracked my chances – if you follow me, Lampfrey.'

'Oh, I don't know about that, my lord. Of course, it's not my place to say so but you two belong together. I may be just a country copper but even I can see that.'

'Get away with you,' Edward said, nudging him just as he was lifting his pint to his lips. 'I was never fooled by you, Lampfrey. You're as shrewd a copper as ever I've met.'

'Good of you to say so, my lord, I'm sure. Since we have finished our beer and finished complimenting each other, if you'll take my advice – as a friend, mind you, not as a policeman – you'd best be getting on over to Mersham.'

Without further ado, the two men got up from their bench, shook hands and parted – Edward in the pursuit of love and Lampfrey, with a shrug of distaste, to meet the Chief Constable who he knew would be full of praise for the way Chief Inspector Pride had 'nailed' two celebrated murderers. Lampfrey would listen patiently and say nothing.

After breakfast, Edward took Verity for a walk in the garden. It was cold and Connie said they should only be ten minutes if they did not want to catch pneumonia. When they reached the bottom of the lawn and looked over the ha-ha at the fields beyond, Verity said, 'It's so peaceful here, I have even begun to sleep at nights. It was so kind of Connie to bring me to Mersham. I'm going to start work on my book again this afternoon. I spoke to Mr Gollancz on the telephone yesterday and, despite the King's abdication, he still seems to want it. He said the readership for my book is not interested in royalty and I think he may be right.'

'Verity,' Edward said in a rush, 'I wanted to apologize to you for my behaviour over the last few weeks. I have tried to bully you and I was pompous and I got so worked up about those damn letters and, in the end, they really didn't matter. I thought I knew what I was doing and who had murdered Molly, but it was you whose instinct was right. You sorted it all out.'

'Oh, Edward – that was just being in the right place at the right time.'

'Like any good journalist.'

'Maybe. There's one thing, though – just something trivial. You said Molly told you she was fancy-free. Why did she say that if she was Hepple-Keen's mistress?'

'I was discussing that with Lampfrey. I think she had chosen that evening at Haling to give Hepple-Keen the boot. That was what was so ironic. If only Molly had told Daphne she was finished with her husband! You see, Molly had convinced herself the King was going to summon her back. Madness, of course, but despite what she said to

306

Daphne, she believed the baby she was carrying was the King's – and it probably was. Her logic was that, if she were to get the King back and make him acknowledge the baby as his, she had to be purer than pure. She had to be able to say she had no lovers – no one else could possibly be the father – so she wanted nothing more to do with Geoffrey. She saw him as an obstacle to regaining royal favour. She even thought she was being followed by people who would report on her behaviour, and it could well have been true. Major Ferguson's people keep the King's friends under close scrutiny for security reasons. Mrs Simpson's relationship with Ribbentrop is enough to make the government uneasy, to say the least of it.

'As I say, it was all madness – a pipe dream. Molly would never have been allowed anywhere near the King again whether she was bearing his child or not; whether she was, or was not, sleeping with the whole of Knightsbridge. In fact, her life was in danger once it became known she was claiming to be pregnant with the King's child. The government could never have allowed the scandal. It might have meant him having to abdicate but, as it happened, it was all beside the point. Molly died at Daphne's hand and the King abdicated anyway.'

'So, if Molly had told Daphne she had given up her husband and the child she was carrying was not his but the King's, she would have lived?'

'Yes, but who knows for how long. She had a talent for making enemies.'

'But Edward, how do you know for sure the baby was the King's?'

'I can't be absolutely sure but Molly certainly was. You know those letters from the King I found in her flat?'

'Yes. You said they were love letters.'

'They were. But they included one from Molly – a copy of one she had sent the King telling him she was pregnant. That was why she never heard from him again – why he would not speak to her when she rang, why he never said goodbye.'

'And the jewelled swastika you found under the bed?'

'I still don't know if it was given her by the King or Hepple-Keen. Ribbentrop apparently dishes out such gewgaws to his favourites, so the King might have had one to give his mistress, but Mosley also has rubbish like that to hand out and H-K might have got one from him.'

'One last thing, Edward. Do you think Daphne was right?'

'Right?'

'When she refused to accept that her husband might have murdered Leo Scannon in order to save her from the gallows, not just because he feared for his reputation?'

'Who knows!' Edward said, taking out his cigarette box and offering it to Verity, 'Who knows. Their marriage, like all marriages, is a mystery that outsiders can never decrypt.'

As Edward escorted Verity back to the house he felt his heart beating rapidly. For a moment he did not understand why, but then he knew his body was telling him that this was the moment when he ought to take her in his arms and ask her to marry him. It probably wasn't fair to ask her in her weakened state but, to hell with that; he would ask her anyway and, if she refused him, there was an end of it.

He tossed away his half-smoked cigarette and turned to Verity. Just as he was about to speak, he heard Connie calling. There was an anxiety in her voice which immediately made him conscious that she had had bad news.

'Ned! Ned! I have just had a telephone call from Eton – from Frank's housemaster, Mr Chandler. He says Frank has run away with a junior master, a man called Devon.'

'Run away?' Edward said, coming up to his sister-in-law and putting his arm around her. 'Where has he run to?' As he said the words, the answer burst upon him. 'To Spain? Has he run off to Spain?'

'Yes, I'm afraid so, Ned. He left a note. He's gone to join the International Brigade. Oh Ned, I'm so frightened. If Frank were hurt or even . . . even killed, Gerald would never . . . we would never get over it.' Her voice faltered and she grabbed Edward to stop herself falling.

A cool, clear voice broke in upon their embrace. 'Connie, I am so, so sorry. This is all my fault. I must start out immediately. I know Spain – I can find him. I know I can.'

Edward looked at her. 'And I shall go with you, V. Connie, this isn't Verity's fault. Frank has made up his own mind and you must try not to worry. We'll bring him back. I promise you, we'll bring him back to you.'

The three of them gazed at one another in dismay, full of fear for the future.

'Yes, bring him back to me, Ned,' Connie said in a dark, urgent voice he had never heard before. 'Bring him back.'

It was brought home to him once again that no love could ever be stronger than a mother's love for her child.